BL**A**CK
BALLED

ANDREA SMITH   EVA LENOIR

Sandra,

So glad
you enjoyed our guys!

Andrea Smith

Black Balled

Andrea Smith – Eva LeNoir

Copyright © 2015

All rights reserved.

This book is intended for mature audiences only.

ISBN-13: 978-0-9861385-4-6 (E-Book)

ISBN-13 978-0-9861385-5-3 (Paperback)

Cover Design: Damion Damiani, Fuzion Multimedia
Editing: Trina Losoya
Formatting: Erik Gevers

Contents

Acknowledgments

Eva LeNoir

First and foremost, I want to thank Andrea Smith for taking a chance on me, trusting me and embarking on this adventure with me. 84 plus thousand words later, here we are preparing a release. I will never forget!

My life-saver Lisa Sleiman who gives me honest and intelligent advice, guiding me when I couldn't make a decision to save my damn life. Your worth is immeasurable.

Oh, our Beta readers: Lisa, Amber, L.e. and Janett...I'm not quite sure what we would have done without you. Seriously, your input was invaluable! Thank you a million times!

Trina Losoya, my most treasured editor. Thank you for a wonderful job, I cannot imagine my edits being done by anyone else!

Damion, my brother and my favorite artist. I love your work, I love your book-covers and yeah, yeah...I love you or whatever.

Erik Gevers...I'm not sure we have enough words in the English language to express how much we appreciate your work. Thank you so much for all of your formatting/last minute editing/advice/ego boosts. You are amazing!

To Shannon and Ipek...without you, I don't think this book would have been possible. I love you girls, hard core!

Now, this book has nothing to do with my #UCC girls but I cannot forget their help, enthusiasm and the fact that every single day, they make me smile. You are gold. You are my naughty light in a dark vanilla tunnel! Jade's book is next, I promise!!

Now, I cannot write my acknowledgements without mentioning my husband and children. They are my pillars in life although my biggest distraction in writing. I love you from here to the moon and back...non-stop. Thank you for your patience, your love and most of all...your unrelenting encouragements. And nope...you still can't read my books. Go to bed.

To my mother who is probably thinking..."Since when does my daughter write M/M and why have I not heard about this." Well...Mom...

Surprise! Love you!

And saving the best for last: I have often times heard the phrase that we authors write for ourselves. Well, I'm pretty sure that's bullshit because without our readers and reviewers, our words would mean very little. Thank you all for trusting us and taking a chance on Black Balled. Please take some time out to leave us a review...your words mean just as much to us.

I'm off to write!

Acknowledgments

Andrea Smith

I want to thank Co-Author Eva LeNoir, who is so much fun to work with and so pure of heart that she renews my faith in humanity. Eva makes up for all the mean girl shit that goes down in this business for sure.

Thank you Catherine Wright, Janett Gomez, Ashley Blaschak, Amber Gladson, Christy Wilson, Kimberly Parker Addison, Clare Flack, Erica Bryan, Ashley Gibbons, Candi Gabbart, Stacie Stark Morton, Tiffany Woy, Patricia Maia, Kim Sowards, DawnMarie Carpintero, Carly Milam, Princess Christina and the rest of the street team who always have my back, and work hard to promote my books, while also helping me dodge bullets! I love each and every one of you!

To each and every reviewer and blogger out there, please know that Black Balled, despite those who would say otherwise, is nothing if not a tribute to the hard work, dedication, and often thankless work you do for the Indie author community. The dynamics between authors and critics is a lively one, and though they may find themselves at odds occasionally, they both deserve mutual respect for the professionals they strive to be.

Thank you for all that you do!

.

Dedication

Eva LeNoir

Ce livre est dédié aux journalistes et dessinateurs de Charlie Hebdo et leurs familles. Merci pour votre bataille quotidienne pour l'on puisse tous s'exprimer librement. Le journal avait demandé a ce que nous nous abonnons en guise de dons pour que Charlie continue à vivre et publier. C'est ce que nous comptons faire avec une partie de nos gains.

This book is dedicated to the journalists and artists of Charlie Hebdo as well as their families. Thank you for your daily battles so that we may all express ourselves freely. The newspaper asked that we subscribe to their journal instead of sending donations. That is what we are planning on doing with parts of our proceeds.

Je Suis Charlie.

Nous Sommes Charlie.

Dedication

Andrea Smith

This book is dedicated to the First Amendment of the U.S. Constitution. *Circa. December 15, 1791.*

"I believe in freedom of speech, but I believe we should also have the right to comment on freedom of speech."

>   -   *Stockwell Day*

"I live in America. I have the right to write whatever I want. And it's equaled by a right just as powerful: the right not to read it."

>   -   *Brad Thor*

"We should silence anyone who opposes the right to freedom of expression."

>   -   *Boyle Roche*

"Confidence is knowing who you are and not changing it because someone else's version of your reality is not *their* reality."

>   -   Shannon L. Aldor

"I hope you love Black Balled--but if you don't? I respect your right to say so!"

>   *- Andrea Smith*

Prologue

Online Newspaper: Bluffington Gazette

Babu's Book Talk

March 13, 2013
Title: Quincy's Soul
Genre: Crime/Suspense
Author: L. Blackburn
Publisher: Self-Published
Status: Book 1 in the "Soul Searching Series"
Babu's Grade: DNF

The Gospel According to Babu:

For those of you who follow my weekly column, and at last count my editor said it was somewhere just shy of four hundred thousand, you know that I am brutally honest, in particular, where self-published (or as they prefer to be called "Indie") authors are concerned.

Let me digress for a moment to educate those not familiar with the "Indie-Author" label. It means *independent* as in *independent of a publisher.* And there's a reason for that. If their manuscripts had potential, then they would've been picked up by a legitimate publisher, right?

Of course I'm right. Babu is always right!

Now that's not to say that many good works of fiction have not been born of an Indie Author, but as my most ardent followers will attest, that is simply a fluke.

1

An accident of nature.

Now, back to "Quincy's Soul." The fact that I couldn't bring myself to finish this--and I use this word loosely--*work* of fiction was no accident. Let me put this into perspective so that anyone considering one-clicking this bitch might give it a second thought.

Given the choice between having a root canal with no anesthesia and finishing Quincy's Soul?

I choose the root canal.

Given the choice between burning my corneas and finishing Quincy's Soul?

Bye-bye corneas.

Given the choice between having my dick sucked by a cannibal chick wearing braces?

Well, I think you get the picture by now and it certainly isn't a pretty one, is it?

Now on to the specifics of this book.

L. Blackburn's synopsis of Quincy's Soul held some minimal intrigue with the promise of hard core criminals who take the hero hostage and for weeks, torture and play mind-fuck games with him in order to break him to get some secret code that holds the key to our national security.

The promise of torture is real; unfortunately, it's the reader who is tortured.

And the mind-fuck?

You guessed it. L. Blackburn's overdone plot will definitely fuck with your mind. It's white bread trite and sophomoric in places. And that brings me to my next point.

"What does the "L" in L. Blackburn stand for? I'm hoping like hell it stands for "Latisha" or "Lydia." While this book tried (and failed miserably) to have a fast-paced, testosterone-induced rush of action to put the readers on the edge of their seats, the whole time I was reading the first twelve chapters, that old song played in my head.

What song you ask?

That old Aerosmith tune kept playing over and over again in my head, "Dude Looks Like a Lady." Only exchange

"Looks" with "Writes," and there you have it.

So, L. Blackburn, if you are a lady, then please, for the sake of not alienating the handful of readers you may have garnered, stick to writing what you know. How about cute little chick-lit stories—first deflowerings or romantic triangles? I daresay even tales of yeast infections or ingrown pubic hairs would be less painful than the drivel you attempted in Quincy's Soul.

And if you are a dude, L. Blackburn?

Well, then my best advice to you is come out of the closet; stop hiding behind your lacey doilies and be the woman your writing says you can be!

Put on your big girl stilettos and see what happens!

That's it for this week's review! As always, you are free to voice your comments, criticisms and opinions right here, and don't forget to visit my Greatreads page if you're a member of my following and we can always chat there. I *welcome* your feedback and opinions, but remember, I reserve the right to tell you if you're full of shit or to fuck off, and if necessary, block your ass, but that's the beauty of Babu's Book Talk!

Speak Your Mind

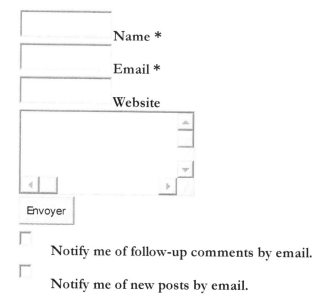

Name *

Email *

Website

Envoyer

Notify me of follow-up comments by email.

Notify me of new posts by email.

I have a few minutes until the flood of "beeps" will start hitting, signaling me that my followers are loyally sending me condolences and best wishes for a better next read. I won't lie, the stroking feels fabulous.

I get up and grab a beer from the fridge and a bag of pretzels to enjoy when the first responders start weighing in on my column.

Beep!

Let the stroking begin.

Hitting a key on my laptop, my column comes up. I scroll down to the comment responses as a cluster of more 'beeps' sound one right after another.

Hot damn!

Krissie wrote: Gosh, I'm sorry you couldn't finish it, but still I appreciate that you shared your honest review with us!

Babu wrote: Aww thanks, hun. **hugs**

Lil Likes Books wrote: Condolences you had to suffer through this. Sending hugs.

Babu wrote: Thanks Lil. In everyone's life, a little rain must fall. ☹

Book Bitch wrote: Well that sucks! Guess I should pass on this one. Thanks for saving me from it! **kisses**

Babu wrote: That's why I'm here, BB. To save all of you the unnecessary pain and distress. Muah!

Loves Lizzies wrote: How miserable for you, love. I will send positive vibes that your next book will be enjoyable!

Babu wrote: Thanks, Lizzie! I'm trying to let the alcohol wash away the bad taste I was left with on this one!

Cindy Lou wrote: Well, I guess all we can do is thank you for your honest and objective review. You take a lot of pain for the sake of your followers, so just need to say that we appreciate your saving US from the PAIN. You are a valuable asset to the literary world. Don't ever leave us!

Babu wrote: That's why I'm paid the big bucks, Cindy Lou!

Lefty wrote: You know your review tickled my funny bone big time! I love your way with words! I did have this on my TBR list, but I'm dumping it. Thanks for making my reading decisions----squeeeee!

Babu wrote: Nothing says 'thank you' quite like $$$

Ruby Red wrote: Okay, well here's the thing, you didn't finish the book so why would you leave a review? How can you leave a review for a book if you didn't finish it? That kind of blows my mind. Now, I finished this book and disagree about the plot being overdone. Maybe if you had just hung in there, you would have seen what a compelling story it turned out to be. It's such a shame when critics don't understand a book and why things happen in it because they didn't take the time to read it through the ending. But it's your loss I guess.

Fuck! Looks like I have a dissenter in the ranks. Get ready to blow this bitch into oblivion.

Foot soldiers--man your stations!

Babu wrote: Are you kidding me??

Lefty wrote: Ruby Red it sounds like you're questioning Babu's intelligence and disputing his opinion?? How fucking dare you! Without Babu, we wouldn't know what the hell to read! Why don't you take your sorry, trolling ass and crawl on back to the bridge you live under!

LeLeaveMe-Aloney wrote: Babu, please ignore the likes of Ruby Red. She obviously doesn't understand the magnitude of service you provide to all of us. How in the hell would we know what to read and what not to read if not for you? The fact that you have over 400,000 followers speaks volumes about the value of your opinion--of our opinions when it's all said and done! Keep on keepin on, dude!

Cindy Lou wrote: Block Ruby Red, Babu! You don't need trolls like that coming onto this site and voicing their opinion of your review! It's blasphemy pure and simple!

And *that* ladies and gentlemen is how it is done.

Chapter 1

ℒ L. Blackburn

Babu? What the fuck kind of name is that? It's like a bad porn name he chose after watching Aladdin one too many times. "Abu and Babu sitting in a tree..." There is a plethora of smart-ass responses I want to throw at him for that less than stellar...No. Scratch that, it's pathetic.

The sorry excuse for a review posted this morning on the web's biggest book critique site just obliterated my latest novel. I poured my blood into that manuscript, searching my inner tortured soul to describe the scenes of the captives begging for their lives. It was all supposed to be a metaphor depicting the lives of Indie authors who live at the mercy of their characters and overbearing imaginations.

Motherfucker.

Now, the four hundred thousand plus members of Babu the-monkey-fucker's column will be shelving my greatest novel, all because the man seemingly does not get laid on a regular basis.

Or maybe at all.

I try to picture the guy in my mind, giving him scraggly grey hair, round glasses adorning beady brown eyes and thin lips turned down into a grimace.

The Scrooge of the Indie World.

The Charlie of the Literary Factory.

The Pain in my Fucking Ass and not in a good way.

Staring at my computer, I am about two mouse clicks away from giving him a piece of my mind when I'm saved by the bell. My cell is ringing atop my kitchen counter, buzzing away and doing its own little dance informing me that someone is trying to reach me. I should answer. I really should face my agent, whose name is flashing on the screen. There is no need for this conversation, because I already know what he's going to say: 'Ignore him, Larson. He's an asshole, man. Quincy's Soul is a fucking masterpiece.'

Luckily, my agent Brent is a die-hard fan so he easily strokes my ego the way the blonde-guy from last night stroked my dick for hours. Sighing, I pick up the cell just before it goes to voicemail answering in my typical one word greeting, "Blackburn."

"Larson. Shit, man, did you see the review?"

Little naive Brent. Did he actually think it wouldn't be my first destination before even pouring myself a cup of coffee? What the fuck planet has he been living on?

"The hell do you think, B.? Of course I saw it, and I'm telling you right now..."

I'm ready to go off on my only friend if it ensures that I keep my sanity in check.

"Do. Not. Respond. Larson, I swear to fucking God, if you leave a comment, your career is over. Done. Don't be stupid, man. For once in your life just listen to me and not your hot-tempered need to confront every asshole who thinks he's the best thing since Hemingway went to rehab."

Jesus, someone needs to remind Brent that Hemingway wrote shit when he was sober so his little rant means nothing. Plus, I'm pretty sure that genius never went to rehab.

"Brent, he called me a pussy. No, worse, he called me a fucking woman! We'll see if he's so cocky when I stick all nine inches of my dick down his throat and pump my load all over his face."

Crude? Yeah, a little bit.

Yet, interestingly enough, my words are closer to a children's tale than his pretentious reviews. It's not even fit to be used as toilet paper. Too harsh for my pretty ass.

"Who cares, man? And please, I'm begging you, do not throw visuals of your cock in some dude's mouth at me. It makes me ...uncomfortable."

Now, Brent is just trying to make me laugh...poor sap.

"Shut the fuck up, B. You love my visuals, said so on my manuscript."

I hear him chuckle, which calms my nerves for an iota of a moment, but his next words bring my focus back to the review. "Look, all I'm saying is that he didn't even finish the book. Readers will take into consideration that it wasn't read from cover to cover. Plus, your fans love you. Don't let him get to you. Ignore him and this will blow over by tomorrow."

He's right. Of course, he's right and I should undoubtedly take his advice, close the tab on Babu's Book Talk and start writing the follow-up to Quincy's Soul...Harsh Reality. I know all of this, I really do. But fuck it, I just can't. It's one thing to attack my work, my genius, some have called it. But my personal life? Oh hell, no. That will not fly with me.

"I gotta go."

I hear Brent yelling at me, begging me not to respond but it all goes silent as I press the red button to end the call.

Alright, Babu. Game on.

> L. Blackburn wrote: Thank you, Babu, for that life-altering review of my work. No, I do not use the word lightly because, unlike you, I actually "worked" to finish my novel. Your review, however, is subpar seeing as you could not even be bothered to read the entire book. Since I'm a generous guy, I have decided to answer all of your inquiries about my gender, my shoes and...was that my dick size you were interested in knowing? Well, just in case, it is eight inches at rest and ten while getting sucked. For convenience sake, I usually tell people the average of nine. Happy? Oh, right...my shoes. I don't wear stilettos but if you're into that kind of cross-dressing I do know a good place you can go that's very discreet (I'll send you a private email if you're afraid of getting caught wearing a lace thong). As far as my name is concerned? Fuck you. You don't deserve to have it unless you're curious about how it would sound pouring from your lips just before you come all over yourself. Get a real job.

I read my trash answer twice before I press the send button and basically say farewell to my career. Funny, there is that Hemingway reference again except I'm sober *and* suicidal, apparently.

Chapter 2

I power off my e-reader and toss it over on the sofa, pressing my fingers to my eyes and rubbing the tiredness out of them.

What the fuck did I just read?

Why does it even matter? It all pays the same which is in the high six figures. My following grows every quarter by seven to twelve percent, which has my editor Clark jizzing himself. The advertising revenue alone generated by my column more than pays both his salary and mine.

Put out one review a week and then spend the rest of those days answering the peeps who leave comments, opinions and wisecracks on the website and on Greatreads. And the dissenters? *Hah!* As if I would ever let *them* have the last word, stupid fucks.

The Indie book reviews always garner a shitload of activity in my reviews' comments. You see, the problem with Indies is that they have thin skin, because if they didn't, they'd submit their masterpieces to one of the Big Five and take their just desserts. Most of the time that would be a boilerplate fuck-off notice on formal letterhead, if they get a response at all.

Now some of them, at least, have managed to latch on to an agent, but that is no guarantee of literary success. An agent is just another leech who sucks a percentage of royalties out of the pot, and usually that is on foreign rights to self-published books. The agents then pick and choose which future manuscripts they might try to shop to the big publishing houses right here in New York.

So, yeah, I am well aware of the publishing circle-jerk that exists, but hell if that hasn't all changed with the influx of self-published Indies. Like anything else, it's just another way for any idiot to get their fifteen fucking minutes of fame.

Am I right?

Fuck yeah. I'm *always* right.

My attention is drawn to the light scratching on the door of my loft. It's after five in the afternoon.

Muffy's here.

Fucking pussy at my door.

I open it, and the long-haired, gray angora feline sashays into my apartment like she owns it.

"Meoww," she whines, looking up at me.

"Purr for me first, baby," I reply heading towards my kitchen where I know she'll follow. This is a daily routine for us.

Mrs. Ida Whatley's prized kitty loves the caviar I feed her daily. I don't dare tell the old lady that I do, otherwise, she'll expect me to cat-sit for her when she makes her semi-annual journey to Palm Beach to visit her sister.

No fucking way am I up for that shit!

I place two spoonfuls of the fresh caviar into Muffy's bowl by the stove. She has her purr going on high volume. I place the bowl on the floor next to my feet and watch as she quickly runs to it and begins devouring the Beluga.

"Only the best for you my lovely pussy," I say, feeling myself smile. "If only other female species were so quickly satisfied by so little," I say to no one.

That reminds me.

I grab my cell from the granite countertop and press Linc's number.

"My man," he answers with his usual ghetto panache.

"Yeah, Linc. I'm in the mood for some company tonight. About seven?"

"Who's your poison, Boss?"

"I think I'm in the mood for an 'L,'" I reply, watching as Muffy cleans the last of the Beluga from her bowl and licks her whiskers.

"Done, Boss. Loretta will be at your place promptly at seven. Any special requirements for her wardrobe or accessories?"

"No. Not tonight. Just make sure her swallow reflex is up for the game."

Muffy is finished and contentedly grooming herself like the pristine cat that she is. Just then, I hear Ida calling for her in the hallway.

"Time to go," I say.

As I open my front door, I catch Ida ready to knock. "Oh hello, Mr. B," she says, smiling her wrinkled smile. She's eighty-three but that has not diminished the sparkle she still has in her blue eyes.

I'm not a social person. That much you need to know. But I have somehow managed to allow Ida Whatley into my inner circle, which is made up of just two.

Me and her.

"Hello Mrs. Whatley," I greet. "Muffy came over for her daily visit."

"I just don't know what it is with my cat," she replies, bending down to scoop Muffy up into her arms. "She never takes to anyone the way she's taken to you. That means you're a good person, did you know that?"

"I didn't, but I'll take Muffy's word on it," I reply, giving her a wink.

"Oh, Mr. B," she says, flashing me a shy grin, "I don't know why some fancy woman hasn't already staked her claim on you! I mean, I know you *date,* but how do you expect to keep a girlfriend when you don't take them out?"

I shrug and give her a look of confusion. "I don't know, Ida. I guess I just can't find one that likes to stay in with me."

She shakes her head, tossing out a couple of tisks. "Such a shame," she replies. "Such a shame."

"But hey, I've got a date tonight so we'll see."

"Fingers crossed, Mr. B.," she says, walking down the hallway towards her apartment. "By the way, loved your review of Quincy's Soul. Made mincemeat out of that Indie, didn't you?"

She is still cackling in amusement as she closes the door of her apartment.

Yeah, Ida Whatley knows that I'm Babu, and she doesn't hold that against me. In fact, she's quite entertained by my reviews and recommendations. I have to admit I'm intrigued that a woman her age embraces the Internet the way she does. My own mother, who is way younger, is still intimidated by the information highway.

Go figure.

Back in my apartment I hear the familiar sound from my laptop indicating that "I've got mail!"

I walk over to the desk and flip it open. I scroll downward to the comments and there it is:

Reply from L. Blackburn.

Hell hath no fury like an Indie scorned.

I have to admit, his response gives me a couple of *LOL* moments.

What a douche bag.

But this is what it's all about.

Draw the Indie tools out into the open; expose them for the amateur wannabes that they are. Call them out on their unprofessionalism in responding to literary criticism. Tell them not to quit their day jobs.

Finish the book?

Is the dudette serious?

Did the he-she not read just how painful those twelve chapters were for me in my DNF review?

Hah!

This is going to be a fun-filled week.

Cha-Ching!

Chapter 3

Forty-two.

That would be the number of times I have checked the blog for a message from His Almighty Highness of Literary Criticism. The man is known for his cut-throat responses, his overwhelming need to have the last word, his Indie blood sucking desires.

I may be going insane, at least just a little, because I am now obsessed with his inevitable riposte. Running my hands through my already disheveled hair, I make my way to the kitchen counter where my newly-brewed coffee awaits me. With both hands gripping the counter, I let my head fall forward and take deep, measured breaths.

I need to let this go. Bastard has no idea what it's like to spend days upon days sorting through the innumerable voices that scream for my attention. The man simply reads to his heart's content and then whips up a mediocre literary review before he calls it a day. He's lethal, he's brutal and he has no empathy for the absolute gut-wringing trials and tribulations that we all face while chasing our dreams.

Ding.

Fuck.

"Don't look. Don't look. Don't fucking look, Larson. Listen to the voice of reason. Brent was right, just ignore the bastard," I whisper, trying to convince myself. Taking in a deep breath, I raise my head to the ceiling and slowly open my eyes that now stare straight at the perfectly white plaster above. *Breathe.*

I reach for the coffee pot, forgoing the espresso machine for the larger, less caffeinated concoction and pour myself a life-sustaining amount of brew in my Quincy swag mug. I can do this. I can be the adult here.

Ding.

No, he did not leave two messages, did he?

Shit. .

Ding. Yep, that's it. My career is over.

Ding.

Putting two sugars in my cup, I slowly twirl the contents and inhale the sweet aroma of my most compelling addiction. Well, besides sex. If it weren't dangerous to do so, I'd fuck and drink coffee at the same damn time, but I digress.

Ding.

Dammit.

Once I'm satisfied that the sugar has effectively sweetened my java, I take out the spoon and place it methodically into my mouth, licking up the enticing droplets.

Ding.

Jesus fuck. I'm going to kill someone.

Slightly turning my head to glance at the computer, I see a long list of messages that fill the screen. This is it; my demise. A fucking critic has destroyed my five-year career for what? A thrill? A self-empowering moment? A blood-sport?

Correction...I killed my dream all by myself as soon as I decided it was okay to write a message to the douche bag like the fifteen-year-old idiot that I apparently am.

Ding.

Don't people have fucking jobs instead of wasting their time on the Internet?

Lowering my mug to the marble counter, I fasten the strings of my pinstriped pajamas and make my way to the bathroom. I should shower, maybe even shave. I look in the mirror and run a palm over the two day growth along my jaw line.

Writing is time consuming but I love every second of it. Editing is hell on earth especially when Madeline, the editor in question, is no holds barred. The woman is an expert on grammar and syntax, not to mention a maniac when it comes to using synonyms.

These last four weeks of editing and formatting have taken about five years off my life. My eyes have lost their usual piercing green, leaving them dull with fatigue. The dark brown hair that was always well groomed is now a mess with silver making an unwanted appearance along the sides. My naturally tan skin has a pasty hue that tells me it's time to get the fuck out and make nice with the sun.

That's what I'll do. Go out, go running, and get laid. In that order, with just a little shower thrown in for good measure. I think

I'll keep the two day beard, men love to feel my whiskers scraping alongside their thighs before I suck off their cocks like the master I am.

Already, I feel better knowing I have a plan that doesn't involve writing, editing or dealing with ass munchers who know nothing about the sacrifices of an Indie author.

Fuck you, Babu, and your magic carpet ride.

Pushing down my pajamas, I reach for my running shorts and a half decent tee shirt before making my way back to the kitchen to finish off my coffee. I can do this. I can ignore the dinging, beeping and all around annoying symphony of sounds that surround my virtual world.

Ding.

Assholes.

"Just one look," I tell myself before taking the three steps to my open laptop. "Do not freak out, Larson. Keep your fucking cool."

Unfortunately, my cool left the building the minute I gave in to temptation and verbally reamed the critic's ass.

Chapter 4

Loretta is on her knees in front of me. Linc did me justice with sending the "L" that I ordered. Of course, I've been Linc's steady customer for more than four years now. And he's been paid very well for providing the services I require, when I require them. He ensures that his ladies accommodate whatever my mood requires, including any of my idiosyncrasies, regardless of their nature.

He understands my requirements, and he never questions them. He knows that it's always at my place. I never go out. I don't go to fancy hotels or penthouse apartments. His ladies are A-list—beautiful, clean, disease-free and always discrete. They come to me. I don't go to them.

Ever.

Loretta is looking up at me now. She's already blown me once just to take the edge off, per my instructions as soon as I allowed her through the door.

"How was that, gorgeous?" she asks, her voice practically a soft croon. She is quite beautiful. Straight, long dark hair; chocolate brown eyes with a hint of Asian ancestry evident. She's slender, but big breasted--no doubt possessing the best fake tits money can implant.

"That was just fine, Loretta," I respond.

"What shall I call you?"

"Sir," I reply. "You will call me Sir."

"Very good. What is it you would like me to do for you now, Sir?"

I reach down and grab my new digital camera from the polished oak table next to my desk and position it on the tripod next to the sofa. I preset the timer, and get the wide-angled focus set.

"I want you to get my cock hard again, using only those full, pouty lips of yours. I want you to moan and call me "Sir" while you do it, and tell me how fucking big and hard my dick is, and how much you want to suck my cum from it. Do you understand?"

She nods calmly.

"Good. Because I'm going to video record the whole thing. You have nothing to worry about. This is for my own private and personal use. When I come, I want you to take as much as possible into your mouth. Do. Not. Swallow. When I finish, I will hand you this book," I instruct, nodding to the paperback gifted copy of "Quincy's Soul" that was sent to my editor in exchange for an *honest* review. I've already placed it on the table. "I want you to let my cum spill out all over the front cover. Any questions?"

She looks at me for a moment, and then replies, "No questions. I understand."

"Good," I reply, giving her a smile. "Let's begin."

I lean over once more, and push the "record" button on my camera, making sure it is angled to only catch from my waist down.

Loretta begins her slow, sensual tonguing of my shaft, and immediately I feel myself rising to the occasion. All eight-plus inches. Her tongue is working its swirling magic, and her moans are worthy of an academy award. Her hands play no part in getting my dick hard, which is exactly as I had instructed.

Within several minutes, she's deep throating me like a pro, even allowing the head of my cock to hit her gag reflex several times, which adds to the confirmation that I am well-hung.

Because I am.

Her soft, sexy voice croons aloud, marveling at my thick, long cock, assuring me just how much she loves it. She tells me it's the biggest cock she's ever sucked.

Our session continues, and I feel my balls tighten up as I prepare to unload my jet stream into her sexy, waiting mouth. Her moans get louder, her head bobs faster as I fuck her mouth with the full intensity of my need to show L. Blackburn just how it's done.

I rock back a bit on my heels just a bit as I feel my cock throb several times and then I still as the spasms of warm cum are released into her mouth.

As I finish, I reach down and hand her the book, and then I slowly back out of her mouth. I grab the camera from the tripod and focus it downward as she takes the book, raising it just enough for the title to show, and allows her mouthful of warm jism to dribble down the front cover at a slant, spilling over the title and running down to the bottom edge where the name 'L. Blackburn' is printed in fancy gothic font.

Perfection.

I turn off the camera, setting it back down on the table. "Very good, Loretta," I praise. "You were perfection. I'll let Linc know just how pleased I was tonight with your performance."

Later, after Loretta has gone for the evening and I've had my supper of grilled salmon and a tossed green salad, I shower and then sit down to check my column for comments.

More than a dozen others have been posted since L. Blackburn left his earlier. Most of them are berating the author for his "bullying" tactics against a literary critic, especially one of my caliber, one of my followers wrote.

Here's a sampling, and I have to say, my followers absolutely reinforce on a weekly basis that, yes, I am a *God* when it comes to book critiquing:

> Cindy Lou wrote: L. Blackburn are you not aware of proper protocol here? Let me educate you, Babu has an opinion of a book. His opinion is right. Your book is wrong. So stop being an ass and attacking the critic!

> Xenia wrote: Show some class L. Blackburn or your name will be submitted as a Badly Behaving Author and then a flock of carpet bombers and sock puppets will attack you and you'll be fucking sorry!!

> Shelby-Doo wrote: Uh, L. Blackburn--I'm not certain but I'm pretty sure that authors aren't allowed to comment here. Don't you have some Author Bitch Group you can post in and not bully this critic? Shame on you!

Yes. Shame on you, L. Blackburn.

Five more of them simply thank me for my review and mention they will definitely not be one-clicking this bitch. They console me for the pain I have endured and send their best wishes that my next read is a pleasant one.

Hah!

Only one commenter advises L. Blackburn to ignore the criticism and continue to live his dream.

Seriously?

Probably the mofo's mother, or some trolling fan-poodle!

I type a short and crass response to L. Blackburn's diatribe: *Maybe if you suck J. Grisham's dick he'll give you a pointer or two.*

I pull up my sock puppet's email address and copy and paste L. Blackburn's email address into the 'To' field. I attach the video of Loretta blowing my dick, complete with my cum spilling out of her mouth and running down the front cover of his loser book to the email.

There.

When I click "Send," I feel the smile spread across my lips. This fucking feels nearly as good as the orgasm I had earlier.

I grab my e-reader and head off to my bedroom to finish another WTF Indie book.

Chapter 5

Earlier, I decided I would go running to empty out the incessant conversations that reside permanently inside my head. I needed this time to concentrate only on my breathing and the monotonous sounds of my footsteps. I was ready, I was willing and above all, I was desperate to go. That, however, was hours ago. That was before I gave in to temptation and looked at the laptop that sat on the table, taunting me.

Mistake number two of my shitty day.

Among the litany of accusations throughout the messages on the blog, the one that had my blood pumping was the "bullying." What the motherfucking fuck? How *am I* the aggressor? How am I the one doing the victimizing? All I want to do is write, try as best I can to silence the voices that wake me in the middle of the night forcing me to settle for a maximum of four hours sleep.

I should not have commented on that review. Idiot. Brent is going to have my ass for this, and he'll be in the right.

In the middle of my self-inflicted flagellation the pop-up signaling an incoming email takes my attention away from my internal rant. Switching tabs to my perpetually open email account, I frown at the sight before me.

I don't recognize the address, am even surprised it didn't go directly to the spam folder. I have two accounts, one personal for my agent, my family and my extra-curricular activities and the other for the fans, blogs and other authors. The latter associated to all the social media that take up more time than I care to count.

Promotional work is going to be the death of me. The countless inbox messages propositioning me for sexual activities. Men, women...some I have no fucking clue what gender they are judging by the irrational names of their profiles. Facebook, Twitter, Instagram...I have them all, including Tsu, which claims it will be the new platform of social media.

Whatever.

I rarely run those things. My personal assistant, Lisa, has the details to my accounts and, more often than not, she is the one keeping up with that shit. Except during promotional time. It's a vortex. Once you enter the world of "buy my book," you get lost in a black hole of smiles, chats, negotiations and giveaways.

Strategizing is the name of the game where the number of players is growing every day. Ever since publishing went viral with the self-made authors birthing books like rabbits, the market has been saturated. At least that is what most critics think. It's bullshit, if you ask me. Readers will always buy good books, no matter how many of us are selling.

The key is to put it out there and advertise the fuck out of it. I know I'm good, and it sure as hell doesn't take a genius to realize that! However, I suck at social skills, which is what has put me in this exasperating predicament. I have to deal with self-proclaimed judges of literary creations, like that banana-eating piece of shit Babu. Again, what's with the name? Seriously?

Shaking my head to clear my mind from the dark desires to shred the man from gut to neck, I click on the email and again...I frown. Or maybe I scowl because I have just realized who sent this little love note sprinkled in arsenic.

Staring at the one-word message with a video attachment, I consider the option of discarding it, clicking the trash button and ignoring the offending message all together. The problem is that I'm a curious asshole and this type of carrot has always clouded my better judgment.

"What are you sending me, you prick?" I ask out loud. There is no doubt in my mind that he is trying to trick me, trying desperately to poke me with the proverbial stick; one I'd like to shove up his ass.

Taking a deep breath once my distorted mind has made yet another crappy decision, I open the attachment. I regret that move the instant I see a pretty brunette on her knees blowing the pants off some guy. It does not take a genius to realize who the recipient must be. Babu is getting his dick blown and has apparently decided to share this pleasurable moment with me.

Oh, joy.

Turning up the sound because, yeah, I'm a glutton for punishment, I put the video on full-screen and watch, in rapture, as the woman's lips slide up and down a pretty decent-sized cock. Her rhythm, though, is off and from where I'm sitting I'm pretty confident her suction is too timid.

We men prefer a nice tight grip from root to tip with a little swirl of the tongue around the underside before releasing the head and licking up our pre-cum.

It is what it is, but women are too soft, too gentle, and too damn sweet. I know this since I haven't sworn off women as of yet. There is something about them that still keeps my interest. Their silky skin is quite the turn on, their mewling noises still get my dick hard and yeah, I like to sink into a nice tight pussy once in a while.

The problem is that I like to fuck hard, and men satisfy that need for me much better. Ideally, I prefer a nice threesome with another guy and fit chick. Best memories of my life involve a fuckfest where everything and *anything* goes.

Again, I digress.

While my thoughts are collecting those vivid memories, I zone back into the video and realize Babu is about to blow except he's grabbing for something.

A tissue, maybe?

What a joker. If I *were* him, I'd come all over her face and then make her...

What the *fuck?*

Is that *my* book? I frown because, really, what is there to say when some dude who is about to explode after getting a decent blowjob, grabs for your book and...*Motherfucker!*

I watch, my anger boiling to the point of no return, as he comes in the woman's mouth and brings my book up to her lips where she in turn lets his spunk run all over my cover. I would have thrown the computer across the living room had I not been a tiny bit turned on by his audacity.

Babu wants to play?

Well, asshole, *game on.*

Clicking the reply icon, I proceed to give him a detailed explanation of everything that went wrong with that visual, including the woman's blowjob techniques. The nice guy in me even gives him some tips on how she could have made the climax more interesting. Or maybe, he could have just blown his load directly on the cover. For obvious reasons, I omit the possibility of being a tad turned on by the visual in my mind.

Before I send the message, I take a little selfie of my best asset and make sure to add a catchphrase to the picture:

"Eight inches and soft, yet it would still make you feel much more pleasure than her mouth ever could."

I press "send" before I grab my running shoes, my iPod and a bottle of water. Five minutes later I'm out the door and pounding away the memories of my nemesis' hard, pistoning cock with every step on the hard black asphalt.

It's dark out, but I don't care that I've wasted the day away licking my wounds. I'm rejuvenated now, and hopefully, there's still time to hook-up before the night is over. I will only be thinking of one dick—the one I will be using to fuck my future lover.

Where is the mind bleach when you need it?

Chapter 6

It's Tuesday afternoon.

I fucking *hate* Tuesday afternoons.

It's the one day each week that I'm forced to leave my loft and go out into a world that I've tried to avoid for the last two years. Everything in my life comes to me. My groceries are delivered, loft is cleaned weekly by a service, and dirty laundry is picked up, and then brought back clean and pressed. Everything I need, from appliances to my wardrobe, is ordered online and delivered to my door. Linc keeps me hooked up with "dates," and I work from home.

So, the only time I actually *have* to go out is to keep my weekly appointment with my shrink, Dr. Bencdict, who refuses to make house calls.

Son of a bitch.

My cab is waiting for me as I walk out into the March sunshine. It's only a twenty minute drive to lower Manhattan, where Benedict's office is located.

For twenty minutes, I feel my jaw clench as the cabbie weaves in and out of downtown traffic; my thoughts are scrambling with every blast of a car horn or screech of tires on the pavement. The echoes of sirens in the distance remind me of just how exposed I am when I'm not tucked away in the safe sanctuary of my loft.

It hasn't always been like this. There was a time when the crowded sidewalks, traffic jammed streets, plethora of noise and smells of the city made me feel alive. I actually embraced the lifestyle I'd come to know and to be a part of. The chaos of New York City kept me on top of my game, invigorated me in every sense of the word. I relished my work, and as my column gained notoriety in the business, I was deluged with review requests.

And then things changed.

The cabbie's voice breaks through my recollections. "Hey, mister? We're here."

I pay him, quickly exiting the cab and heading through the glass doors that a doorman has politely opened for me.

I can do this.

One, two . . . buckle my shoe.

The elevator doors open, and I suck in a deep breath as I step inside.

Three, four . . . shut the door.

I would consider taking the stairs if the fucking shrink wasn't located on the fifteenth floor. At least it's not overly crowded this afternoon. I may just survive the journey without hyperventilating today.

Five, six . . . need a nirvana fix.

Bell dings. Door opens. I step out and exhale slowly.

Seven, eight . . . damn right I'm straight.

My mind wanders. L. Blackburn is one conflicted mofo. What was up with that asinine reply he gave to my sock puppet e-mail to which I've ignored up to now?

But I have a plan.

"Well, I see you've survived yet another elevator ride," Dr. Benedict says as I step into the inner office of his shrink sanctum.

Asshat.

"Yes, it was a breeze," I reply, mentally flipping him off. "I think these three hundred dollars an hour sessions are finally starting to pay off."

"Why don't you let me be the judge of that? Now, tell me how this past week has gone? Any local excursions?"

"No time. Busy with reading and reviewing."

"I see," he replies, scribbling on his notepad. "Read anything good lately?" He chuckles at his own lame brand of humor.

"Actually, the book I'm reading for this week's review is quite good," I reply, studying my nails and making a mental note it's time to call Brittany over for a haircut and manicure. "Last week's book sucked donkey dicks. The he-she who wrote it is stalking me."

"You don't sound alarmed about that," he acknowledges, quirking a questioning brow.

I smirk. "Well, maybe that's because he provides no real threat. He's simply a cyber-bully."

"I see. And he hasn't actually threatened you . . . like *before?*"

I frown at his casual reference to the maniacal author who had physically stalked me two years prior and followed through with her cyber threats. "Well, if you call emailing me a picture of his flaccid dick a threat..."

"What?"

"Yeah," I chuckle, sitting up straighter. "Dude's a fucking queer who can't write for shit. Didn't like my DNF'ing his piece of dung novel."

"Mr. Babilonia, have you considered toning down your reviews?"

"Please, call me Babu, and why would I want to do that?"

"Well," he says, and then pauses, "it's just that I follow your column, and you can be fairly brutal in a *non-constructive* way."

"Listen," I reply, my voice getting just a bit louder, "I'm not playing shrink to a bunch of wannabe authors. I tell it like it is. If they can't handle the truth, then fuck 'em all. I'm not there to correct their lack of talent, Doc. They either have it or they don't. If they don't, it's best they realize that now and find another hobby or a different career."

"But you must realize with the following you have, what you publish online can make or break an author, right?"

"It's called power, Doc. I have it because I've earned it. Those who follow me know that I'm honest—they might not agree with the brutality of my honesty, but they respect the fact that it's my right to voice it."

"With one major exception. Delores Friedman."

"Fuck you!"

"I've made you angry."

"No fucking shit!"

"It's why you're here, and at some point, you have to recognize the power she still has over you."

"The cunt is in prison. She has no fucking power over me."

"Really?"

"The fucking bitch stuck a knife between my ribs in a crowded elevator. I clocked her out. She went to jail. End of story."

"You've left the part out where you annihilated her New York Times Best-Selling series, calling it rubbish that any sixth grader could have written."

"It was the truth. Hey, just because her shit hit NYT doesn't make it a classic. It just meant she sold a shitload of copies. I recall that I pointed that out to her. I even gave her kudos for her obvious marketing and promotional talents."

"I believe you referred to those talents as 'those for which any snake oil salesman would have admired her?'"

"Tomayto, tomahto."

Doc Benedict shakes his head. "My only concern is that you may find yourself at the receiving end of another . . . *weapon.*"

"Trust me, Doc, I'm not about to let that happen. And I won't for a second consider backing down—or *toning* down what I do. That means I let that psychotic bitch win. I'm healed. All that's left is a tiny scar on my left side."

"I have to disagree, Babu. Your non-physical scars run much deeper than that. Until you start forcing yourself to join the living again, and that means going about your life the way you did prior to the attack, then I'm afraid Delores Friedman has won."

Back at my loft, I finish my review for this week's column.

Babu's Book Talk

March 20, 2013
Title: Dire Straits
Genre: Crime/Suspense
Author: Eliza St. Clair
Publisher: Harper-Rollins
Status: Debut Novel
Babu's Grade: 5-Stars

After coming off the disaster of "Quincy's Soul" last week, "Dire Straits" was a blessed reprieve. L. Blackburn could take notice of this properly written debut novel in the crime-suspense genre. St. Clair's characters were well-developed and realistic. No whining in this book or overdone self-pity to the extent readers vomit in their mouths as I did with "Quincy's Soul."

St. Clair keeps the plot flowing with just the right amount of twists and turns, so that the reader is not only engrossed, but thoroughly invested in the outcome of the story. Flashes of the past are sprinkled throughout the book, which brings the reader to the cusp of indecision as far as ascertaining "whodunit." I won't spoil the surprise, but I can assure you that this is one book you'll find spunk-free.

Great job, Eliza St. Clair! I look forward to reading and reviewing your next installment in the series!

Side Note: I appreciate the support of my followers last week relative to the "critic bashing" I received from the thin-skinned L. Blackburn, who evidently felt the need to not only lash out at me with insults, but go on to host his own 'whine-a-thon' in the comments section of my column. Hopefully, L. Blackburn has finished licking his wounds, and has now moved on to showing his love to his pocket pussy.

That's it for this week's review! As always, you are free to voice your comments, criticisms and opinions. And I'm free to tell you if you're full of shit or to fuck off. That's the beauty of Babu's Book Talk!

Chapter 7

"What in the living hell, were you thinking?"

I have been waiting for this since last weekend. It did not take Brent very long before contacting me, threatening my balls for my hasty reply to *Babu* and, FYI, I still hate that name.

I knew it was a mistake as soon as I pressed the send button, but am I ready to admit to that? No. Not because I was right in defending my honor. Not because that wannabe critic was wrong. Not even because I'm a masochist hiding in the well-elaborated clothing of a sadist. Okay, that's a bit of a hyperbole but fuck it, I like exaggerating. No, I refuse to admit it was an error on my part because I am, and always will be, one stubborn motherfucker.

In any case, it's a done deal so there is no reason to dwell on the events as they are up there on the wide world of the web and there is absolutely nothing I can do about it.

"I was thinking that I at least deserved to voice my own opinion." I'm sitting in the center of my soft leather couch, my legs spread, and my arms laying across the back in a seemingly relaxed posture. I'm anything but. Brent knows this, he knows *me*.

Towering over me, he has a look of pure disappointment with a tinge of anger displayed over his quite handsome face. This man, who I have known for nearly three years, is the closest thing I have to a best friend. I am no idiot, by any standard of the word, but I know he sees me more as a client than he does as a friend, which is why I pay him a considerable percentage of my sales. He gets the job done, sending out my manuscripts to various, ridiculously popular review sites, bloggers and even some of the Big Five Houses. To Brent's utter frustration, I have never accepted the deals from those places.

Yeah, I know. I'm a narcissistic asshole who thinks he is better than them. That's because I *am.* No matter what *Babu* says, my books are tight. The characters *are* believable, the plotlines are perfectly designed, and the endings are always a surprise. I mean, come on, I've read my stories. Hell, I've *written* them and sometimes, even I'm astonished by what I've accomplished. So yeah, I'm not giving three-quarters of my sales to publishing houses that pocket my earnings like they actually did something to earn them. Sure, they have editors on staff. They have marketing departments that help get an author's name out there and an entire building with minions running around making sure their slaves push out book after mind-numbing book. I will not be a part of that.

"Since when have you become a pain-slut, Larson?"

Funny, I was just thinking the same thing. Maybe I should start writing erotica, that shit is getting some serious attention out there.

With a smirk adorning my lips, I arch an eyebrow and just stare at my agent/publicist. "Why? You want to try your new whip out on me, Brent? I thought you batted for the other team."

So I'm an asshole. Sue me.

Brent just shakes his head with his hands firmly planted on his hips as his eyes briefly close, probably trying to rein in his rising anger.

"Man, you are self-destructing. Do you know how many letters I have received in just the last few days? Not emails, fucking handwritten letters?"

Interesting.

"You mean people actually use paper and pens these days?" Of course, I would focus on that little detail. I mean, come on, the fact these people have taken the time to lay out a piece of paper, search out a pen and sit themselves at a table to write my agent says something very clear to me.

Passion.

"Jesus, man. You really are an egocentric prick, aren't you?"

"Is that a rhetorical question?" Because, really? Do I seriously need to answer that?

"Have you met me? I know what I'm worth, Brent, or I wouldn't be here today selling a fuck load of books." Okay, so that would be another hyperbole since I have only sold about two hundred thousand since I began writing.

Brent sighs before he flops down onto the couch next me, rubbing his eyes with his palms. "Yeah, handwritten and as much as I hate to admit this, your book has actually been selling like crazy since your little ping-pong bitchfest with that critic."

My head snaps to the side, my back ramrod straight as I stare at my very well paid friend. "You're shitting me."

I do not even recognize my voice, it sounds almost in awe. Of myself? Not really. I'm in shock. Since the email fiasco where I sent a picture of my well-endowed cock to my enemy, I haven't so much as looked at the Internet.

"Nope. Sales have been skyrocketing. I guess it's true what they say...negative exposure is still exposure. Most are just curious bystanders but yeah, you're number thirty-two on USA Today and eighteen on NYT."

Now my mouth is gaping, my eyes feel like they are about to pop out of my head. Brent sighs and shakes his head.

"I guess congratulations are in order?"

"Do I have a chance to stay on there?" I ask, springing to my feet, heading straight to my laptop that has been sitting on my kitchen table, lonely, for the last few days.

This entire "thing" with *Babu* has completely wreaked havoc on my writing, instilling a temporary writer's block. Or maybe I am just tired. That would seem more plausible as there is no way I am ready, now or ever, to admit that cocksucker has any influence on my art.

"Probably," he answers on another sigh. Brent is trying to make me feel like a petulant child, but he's shit out of luck because I feel almost high on my adrenalin boost.

"Okay, so what's our strategy? When's the closest author signing?"

I need to get out there, shake hands, kiss blushing women's cheeks and spread the charm I know I possess.

"There is one more thing, Larson." Brent's tone makes my shackles rise, my body freeze. Well-trained instincts are telling me this is not good. For fuck's sake, could I not get at least a five minute break, here?

"Don't." That's my answer to his pussy-footing around. Something has happened, and I have only heard this tone with him over one particular subject.

"You need to be aware, man. Shit could go down if you don't nip this in the bud."

This?

I know what *this* is, but I choose to ignore my presentiment.

"No, I don't. I just want to focus on my sales and get back to writing."

Brent understands this; he knows that I live for my books. "Seriously, you need to hear me out, Larson. This could be big; we have to talk about it."

My laptop is firing up as I take out two mugs and serve us both a healthy dose of coffee.

Black. Well, not entirely, since mine is spiked with Jack Daniels. I save the Scottish shit for when I drink it straight.

Walking over to Brent, I hand him his cup and bore my gaze into his dark brown eyes. Again, I notice he is a handsome man. Not a gay bone in his body and completely in love with his wife of six years now. He and Marlene have a little girl, Sue Ann...Suzanne...Suryana? Fuck, I should know this.

"You only use that defeated tone when there is one bitch of a problem on the table. Is it too much to ask that I bask in the beauty of this moment? NYT, Brent. I have sold books, I have been number one on Amazon and B&N. Hell, I've hit the middle on USA Today before, but never...NYT. Please, man. Just give me a few minutes, at least, before my whole world comes crashing down."

Notice my signature charm working its magic? Ignore my exaggerated tone, like that of a battered child begging for the beatings to stop. Jesus, since when am I such a fucking drama queen? Oh, yeah. Since always.

"Okay, Larson. Fine. You really laid it on thick right then, yeah? Been practicing your puppy eyes in the bathroom mirror again?"

I laugh, hard, because shit...I kind of have.

Visibly relaxing, we both take a sip of our coffees and make our way to the laptop where I proceed to search out the listings. And sure as shit, I'm in on both USA Today and NYT for this week.

Fuck you, all you non-believers.

Fuck you, *Babu.*

After playing around with scheduling, strategy and some parts of the storyline for my next book, Brent leaves. I'm still feeling high from the power trip, but as I make my way back to the kitchen, I notice a neatly folded piece of paper sitting on my marble counter. It's out of place, and I know for damn sure it's not mine.

I just stand there, staring at it for minutes before giving myself a mental pep talk because deep inside I know what it is. Brent left it there; I have no doubt about it.

Downing the last drops of my coffee, I place the empty cup right next to the letter and take in a deep breath. If I look at it, my day will definitely be shot to shit. If I ignore it, my future will be annihilated.

A fortifying breath later, I pick up the offending sheet of paper and hold it between my index finger and thumb as though it were dipped in dog shit. "Come on, you pussy, just fucking read it."

And there it is...

My own personal nightmare has come back to haunt me.

Chapter 8

I can hear Muffy's meowing as I'm getting off the freight elevator on the second floor. She gets quite miffed on Tuesdays when my appointment conflicts with her caviar fix.

"Pussy needs to be patient," I remark as I insert each of the three keys into their respective locks.

Once inside, she makes a beeline for the kitchen as I leaf through my collection of mail.

Junk

Junk

Bills

Letter? Hmm. From MacMullins Publishing.

I toss it on the table for the moment. Number two of the Big Five will just have to hold on until I get pussy satisfied.

Once Muffy is face deep in her bowl of Beluga, I open the letter from MacMullins.

Dear Babu,

Your managing editor was kind enough to provide me with your mailing address.

Fuck Clark - I'll definitely ream him a new one for that!

I'm an avid follower of your weekly review column, and must say how impressed I've been with your recent reviews. There is a matter of importance that I'd like to discuss with you at your convenience. I would like to offer you a proposal. Perhaps we can meet for a drink? I've enclosed my business card, Please feel free to reach me anytime on the cell number listed. I look forward to discussing this opportunity with you soon.

Very truly yours,

Noelle B. Crawford

V.P. Product Development

What the hell? Can this chick be any more cryptic? My curiosity is piqued just enough to pick up my cell and dial Noelle B. Crawford's personal number.

A feminine voice answers; it's almost a throaty whisper. "Hello?"

"Is this Noelle?"

"It is."

"Babu here. You've got my attention."

"Hey, thanks for calling me. Sorry I couldn't provide more details in my letter, but this is of a sensitive nature. Can we meet for a drink this evening?"

"No paper trails, eh?"

"Something like that."

"I don't go out much, Ms. Crawford. Is there any reason why this can't be discussed over the phone?"

Pause.

"It really is a somewhat private matter. I can tell you this much, it involves L. Blackburn, and his latest book, Quincy's Soul. Your review has served to launch this book right up to number twelve on the New York Times Best-Seller's list. Our publishing company is poised to offer him a contract, complete with movie rights."

"And this affects me how?"

She pauses and her silence is speaking volumes. This chick has a back story involving the douche bag, and by God, I'm not above wanting to hear every lurid detail of it.

"I have something to show you...something that shows that L. Blackburn plagiarized portions of that book, with a book that was previously self-published by... another author."

"Ms. Crawford--"

"Noelle, please call me Noelle."

And something about the pleading in her voice melts me just a bit. "How can I help, Noelle?"

"I need to show you what I have. I need for you to review the previously published book. You can blast it to hell and back, but I need for you to expose the fact that Blackburn's novel is a thinly veiled plagiarized version of this one."

"Why would your publishing firm want to sign him knowing this?"

"They don't know it."

I'm starting to feel as though I'm pulling teeth here. "Why don't you enlighten them?"

She sighs audibly. "Because I'm the one that wrote the original book. It didn't sell well, and obviously, I didn't advertise the fact that I'd written it for that reason. If I brought this up now, it would be considered a conflict—not to mention, difficult to prove. This industry is as cut-throat as any...maybe more so. I would be regarded as a non-team player."

I could easily understand her angst under the circumstances she'd just described. I've been around the publishing world long enough to see just how dynamic it is.

"Are you amenable to meeting with me at my loft? We can have a drink here and discuss how to proceed."

"Oh, absolutely," she says, her voice laced with hope. "I'll bring everything I have to substantiate the validity of my claim. But confidentiality is paramount, you understand?"

"That works both ways, Noelle."

We agree to meet around sevenish.

This may prove quite entertaining. I hope L. Blackburn isn't getting too comfortable with his fifteen minutes of fame. Something tells me that it's going to be short lived.

Chapter 9

"Ellie, answer your fucking phone! I swear to fucking god, I will hunt you down and ruin you!"

That is message number six and still no sign of life from my ex-wife. I must have read her letter a hundred times, trying desperately to understand why she is attacking me again.

That's right, *again*.

Apparently, women do not take too kindly to their husbands being honest with them, laying it all on the line from the get-go.

Life as a bisexual is not an easy plight. Straight people think we are simply sex addicts, not caring where or with whom we get off. Gays think we are just experimenting and haven't yet decided our orientation. Me? I think I just like both.

Simple as that.

Why does everything need to have a well thought out explanation? Is it not possible that some situations have none?

I like pussy. I love the taste of it against my tongue as I lick the succulence dripping down the slit. I love watching a woman orgasm, her spasms as her clit gets thoroughly lavished. I crave their mewling every time I bite down on that hard little nub, sending them off into another stratosphere. I also love fucking their tight little asses while another man pounds them relentlessly. Their soft skin, their glowing beauty that has inspired millions of paintings, songs and of course, novels. And wars. Let's not forget the number of deadly battles that have been started over singular pussy.

But *men?*

Damn. I can be myself with them; rough, demanding and my usual assholiness. I do not need to worry about hurting their feelings because sex is just that...sex. It's about the pleasure, the instant gratification from spilling my spunk down a male throat. Their firm lips sucking me off like their lives depend on it. Knowing exactly what they are feeling while I'm buried deep inside them. It's a power trip, it's carnal and it's un-fucking-believable.

So, when it was clear that Ellie only enjoyed missionary with a lot of declarations of love and very little dirty talk or ass play, I woke up and smelled the burnt coffee.

With the phone still in my hand, I am staring off into space, my eyes fixed on some far off spot on the kitchen wall. The letter accused me of fraud. Apparently, my latest sales and ranking should be a testament that her alimony is lacking...in zeros.

Let's face it, I just learned this morning that I am slowly making the Best Seller's list on NYT; the cash is not exactly flowing in real time.

The shrill ringing of my cell startles me, almost making me drop it right onto the hardwood flooring. "Blackburn." I know who it is.

"Hello, Larson. Long time, no talk." Her voice is like honey, dripping with deceit.

"Took you long enough." My voice is spitting with disdain.

"Well, I just needed to make sure I had your attention. Besides, I'm a busy woman, love, you know this. I cannot simply drop all of my appointments at your convenience."

What a crock of shit.

"Don't bullshit me, Ellie. You and I both know it's just a game to satisfy your morbid need for revenge. Let's cut to the chase, shall we?"

The faster I get this over with, the faster I'm back to my writing.

"How about we meet? I can take a quick flight up to Boston and we could have dinner say..."

I can hear her flipping through pages, like her schedule is overflowing with meetings. It may be, but this is too important for her money hungry appetite. Plus, I know for a fact she has a digital agenda. She is trying to play on my lack of patience and dammit, it's working. I am about two seconds away from climbing into the phone, pinning her against the wall and demanding that she lay her cards out on the table.

Except Ellie doesn't play fair.

There is always a trick up her sleeve and I have no doubt that the same applies here. Thank fuck that in our five years together, we never envisioned having children. The therapist bills alone would have drowned us in debt.

"Hell no, Ellie. I am not meeting up with you. Not now, not ever.

Do you remember the last time we had dinner together?"

And I use *dinner* lightly.

We met, she tried to feel me up before our drinks were even served and then she proclaimed her undying devotion to me. I don't need a pet, I need a partner with whom I can share my days, my successes and my failures. Cue in The Sound of Music, right there. Now, if that person can also satisfy my sexual hunger then I say it's a win/win. The cherry on top? She was engaged to be married at the time. It was her last ditch effort to see if we could reconcile before she tied the knot.

Needless to say, the poor chump saw her true colors before he declared his everlasting vows. I'm pretty sure my little phone call informing him of his fiancée's whereabouts may have had a hand in his decision making.

Strike two for Ellie.

At some point, I tune her out as she begins to talk about how good we could be together. With her working at MacMullins, we would be the unstoppable power couple. Never once, in all of our time apart, has she ever mentioned love. Devotion, yes. Respect for my work, numerous times. The fact that I make her hot and bothered, her words not mine, *definitely.*

Love? Not once since marriage.

While we dated, we had exchanged our feelings, declared our vows and though sincere at the time, we were young and struggling so everything seemed beautiful and unbreakable. At thirty-one, that beauty is fragile and love holds deeper consequences.

"Look," I start, cutting her off mid-sentence, "I'm not meeting with you, Ellie. I'm sorry for how things worked out but you knew from the start that I had certain needs. We tried, we failed. End of story."

Silence.

I try again. "You need to find someone who desires only you." I'm making an effort here, my charming personality making an appearance. "Any man would be lucky enough to have someone as smart and ambitious as you. Let us go, Ellie. It's time."

Sniffling. Are you fucking *kidding* me?

My ex-wife did not even shed a single tear when I packed my bags and walked away from our sterile relationship but now she's crying? Or faking it.

"Ellie. You forget that I know you. I know what you are capable of doing to get what you want. I do not believe for one second that you are crying, right now. "

And that's when bitchy Ellie joins the conversation.

"Fuck you, Larson. I will make you pay for this. We could have worked things out. But no! You just couldn't ignore the calling of your fuck buddies, could you?"

There she is.

"I never cheated on you." Now, we're just rehashing old conversations.

"I don't know that!"

"You do. I have never lied to you, that's just not who I am. Besides, the last time we had this conversation, you accused me of being heartless by telling you the truth. Make up your damn mind, Ellie."

"I'm not done, Larson. I promise, this is not the last you'll be hearing from me." With that she hangs up. And here I thought she was after my money. Albeit virtual for the moment.

With a heavy sigh, I make my way to the cupboards and pull out a whiskey glass along with the bottle of Jameson that I keep especially for occasions such as these.

When I'm done numbing out the torturous conversation I have just lived through, I will book my flights for New York, New Orleans and Las Vegas. It's time to show my face, kiss some ass and sell my books.

Chapter 10

Babu's Book Talk

March 27, 2013
Title: Sympathy for the Devil
Genre: Crime/Suspense
Author: Alexis Duvall
Publisher: Self-Published
Status: Title Retired
Babu's Grade: DP

Readers,

As you can see, I've added a new grade level to the normal star-count and DNF rating system that I've used for the past seven years. I sincerely hope that it's a rating label I don't have to use often, because what it stands for is "Despicably Plagiarized." And even that may not truly and adequately represent my total abhorrence of what this book represents.

Oh, I'm not talking about the content of this short-lived novel self-published four years ago, although it *does* suck donkey dicks. No, what I'm talking about is the recent rise to the top of L. Blackburn's novel, entitled "Quincy's Soul," which, as you know, is also a book that sucks donkey dicks.

What is interesting in this particular situation is that L. Blackburn took advantage of the original author's retirement of SFTD. The *he-she* changed a few words, character's names and rewrote some paragraphs here and there, gave it a new title, and self-published it garnering kudos from all of the no-taste readers who continue to 1-click this plagiarized bitch!

You ask how I know all of this?

I will tell you how. The original author of SFTD approached me and asked for my help in outing this criminal. You see, the bastard has intimidated her, threatened her, and has her living in fear for trying to right this wrong.

And despite this particular author's propensity for bullying women *and literary critics,* this critic won't shrink from his despicable, and quite frankly, illegal activities. I have been presented with valid and objective evidence that the SFTD manuscript existed long before Quincy's Soul ever raised its ugly head.

So readers, there you have it. I base my career and my reputation on the facts provided to me by the original author. I can't provide you with the particulars of her association with L. Blackburn for confidentiality purposes, but I can say that it is enough to satisfy any questions or concerns that I may have that her allegations are valid.

All she asks for is justice. Not the type she would likely get after protracted litigation. She hasn't the financial resources to pursue that, but maybe there's a different kind of justice that *is* possible by appealing to the conscience of every reader out there.

I'm not on a mission to start a campaign against L. Blackburn. I don't believe in bullying or mob tactics like that. That's his game. All I *can* say is that for this critic, L. Blackburn and any of his subsequent works are *black-balled* from this column. It will be as if he *does not exist.* I'm returning my gifted copy to his agent, with a stringent request that nothing further be forwarded to me on L. Blackburn's behalf.

Here's hoping next week's review promises to be something worthy of a star.

To L. Blackburn?

Karma's a bitch.

Chapter 11

As authors, we have no concept of weekdays or weekends. Every day is writing day. For me, being single and somewhat anti-social, I find myself losing track of the hours and sometimes even the weeks when that horrid deadline closes in on me.

Deciding to get some fresh air, a healthy way of clearing my head all the while thinking of my next book, I make my way downtown on foot. It only takes a good twenty-minute walk before I'm engulfed in the daily humdrum activities of my fellow Bostonians. By the look of the hordes on the sidewalks, I would have to guess it is a weekday since most are either dressed in business suits while others are sporting designer backpacks as they head to or from classes.

Boston...home to Harvard where our nation's future adults are being sculpted into moguls ready to take on the world. Ready to bite, suck and swallow all of the little people just for their own personal gain.

Am I bitter? Nope.

I may very well be among the one percent of this country if my books keep selling. Again, not conceited, just a realist. With my hands buried inside my jeans pockets and my leather jacket keeping me warm, I walk at a leisurely pace never failing to observe the masses.

Couples are kissing at the bus stop before going their separate ways. A child is discreetly crying while his mother tries to soothe him, for what I have no idea. Across the street, a store owner and his client are talking and laughing right outside the shop's entrance. The news stand is overflowing with customers waiting to grab their favorite papers.

Walking past, I see the New York Times and grin. I'm egocentric enough to buy it just so I can see my name among the Big Five represented authors. Yeah, they have it made when they rise to the top because their publishers buy their books on release day then sell them back out. It's a dirty business and I want no part of it.

While waiting in line, I vaguely hear the disapproving conversation between the clerk and the client. On any other day, I would ignore the gossips and their trivial two-cent contribution to society but today I'm in a giving mood. So, I give them my attention.

"Such a shame to have to revert to such shenanigans," the woman says as she shakes her head, putting her change back in her wallet. "I'm ashamed to say that I actually bought his book."

My ears perk up because who doesn't love to hear his competition get shat on?

"Don't I know it, Mrs. Rivers. You even told me how much you enjoyed it. I almost bought it yesterday but then I read the article and decided I wanted no part in it." The vendor looks at me, apologizing with his eyes for what I am assuming is my wait. I don't mind though, this conversation is fascinating.

"Plagiarizing! I'm just flabbergasted! How could any author worthy of the name stoop down to such behavior?"

Oh shit. This *is* getting good. Maybe I'll be able to get the scoop on this idiot in the New York Times, as well.

As the conversation dies out, the woman turns, looks up at me and smiles before walking away. With a grin, I nod to the man and ask for the sought out paper.

Before I leave, I pause and cock my head to the side. "What author were you just talking about?" I really hope I don't have his book, although who has time to read these days?

"Oh, haven't you heard?"

Obviously not, man, or I wouldn't be asking. Of course, I don't say this since I'm actually trying to be a nice guy today. I'm in a good mood, I feel high on life and ready to write my little heart out.

"Sure haven't." Now, I just sound like Beaver Cleaver or some shit.

As he hands me the NYT, the vendor shakes his head right before he ruins my entire life.

"It was that new guy, some hot up-and-coming author, you know...L. Blackburn. Seems he plagiarized from another book that was taken down from the shelves. Something about a symphony and the devil. I can't remember the name."

While these words have no importance to his daily life, they have just sliced me into a million pieces. They have locked onto my heart and ripped it straight out of my chest before stomping on it with supernatural force. They have destroyed my life as I know it.

"Sympathy for the Devil," I whisper as I stare blankly at him.

"Yeah, yeah, that's the one. Shame, really, seemed that Quincy book was pretty good."

I tune him out after that because...what the fuck?

"Hey, mista, you doin' okay?" Another man's voice calls out to me but it sounds like it's in a tunnel, pulling further and further away from me. Or am I the one running? What the hell just happened to my life? No one knows about SFTD. No one. Just me.

Suddenly, the noises of the city, the men yelling at me to slow down and the sirens of the nearby ambulances come crashing into me as I stop abruptly in the middle of the street. Realization is like a meteor that is honed in specifically on my head from a faraway galaxy. Like fate. Like Karma. Like a fucking death sentence.

No.

No, no, no.

That fucking bitch.

Noelle Fucking Crawford.

The entire trip back to my brownstone is a complete blur. Intellectually, I know there were sidewalks, roads to cross, people I must have passed but it is all just a blank canvas of nothingness. I find myself walking numbly up the seven steps that lead to my front door, keys in hand, ready to hole myself up in my quiet little haven.

How did I not see this coming? I am a planner, an organizer. For as long as I can remember, I have always seen beyond the present, been able to anticipate the course of my life. This is why my career is...no, was...on the path to success, because I had planned it that way. I had seen it. I had craved it so thoroughly that the reality was an end to the countless means I put forth. I am a fucking planner.

So, how did I not include this possibility into the obstacles I would eventually have to hurdle?

"Sympathy for the Devil" was mine. Noelle knew nothing of this story, I was too afraid to let anyone see it. At the time, her opinion meant something to me; we were a team after all. As an aspiring editor, her attention to detail would have been a saving grace for the story but my ego was still in its early stages of growth. The mere thought of having Noelle criticizing or god forbid, laughing, at my work was unfathomable.

At one point, she had shared my dreams of publishing, voicing her desire to write a novel that had been trotting in her head—some sort of fiction inspired by her life events. That, right there, was a sure sign of failure as her life held nothing but good memories. The most drama she could conjure was when her father refused to buy her a pony. Understandable since they lived on the twenty-third floor of a New York high-rise. Needless to say, her work was shit, the plotline completely lacking of any purpose and her writing sterile of any personal style. No humor, no angst, no depth whatsoever.

I had tried to be gentle when giving her feedback, I really did. Yet, she refused to speak to me for a week. That damn manuscript even ended up at her parents' house where, of course, her father bathed her in compliments, expressing his pride for such a talented daughter.

What the fuck did he know?

Apart from reading the Wall Street Journal, I doubted Mr. Carlton H. Crawford II had ever picked up a work of fiction that was not forced upon him.

Like myself, Noelle had a Master's in English Lit and was on her way to getting a Doctorate. Eventually, excitement made way to boredom and Noelle finally directed her attention to more realistic endeavors, editing. It never once occurred to her to work her way up the ladder, starting at a small firm and making a name for herself in this cut-throat business.

Of course not.

Only five firms were on her radar, that's right. The Big Five. I am man enough to admit that her sleeping her way up to the top did cross my mind a time or ten. The problem with Noelle was not her intelligence; it was her lack of loyalty, her disrespect for hard work.

During one of our late night, drunken, discussions, she had admitted to playing one house against the other. Now, I know I'm full of myself but Noelle? She is worse, she is the reason women have a bad reputation in the workplace. She is the reason women are paid less in the business. That woman is the reason the French invented the expression "promotion canapé." Rising in status while on her back on any given office sofa was not beyond her capabilities.

Of course, I have no proof of this because she has never admitted to cheating on me during our marital excursion. She did, however, threaten to cut off my balls when she heard a voicemail from a female friend informing me of a couple of websites that were quite helpful for self-publishing. The woman was twice my age, a loving wife to her husband of thirty years and a mother to four children. Obviously, I'm not the only one with a flair for drama.

The first time I hinted at having a more experimental sex life, she laughed it off. The next day, I had a piece of paper with the name of a shrink written in bold type letters. So, the fact that I wanted to fuck her in the ass was now a pretense for getting mental help. Imagine her reaction when I reiterated my bisexual tendencies. Noelle's acting skills are famous throughout the circles of the New York socialites, often ignored, seldom acknowledged. As though I had never breached the subject, she began to hyperventilate, crying herself into a frenzy...screaming betrayal.

Right.

Never mind that she knew of my sexual orientation from our first date. Naively, I thought I could ignore that part of me because I loved her so much. At that time, she was fun, she had dreams, and she worshipped me. The latter is probably what blinded me to the harsh reality of her dual personalities.

Note to self: Listen to your mother more often. Good old mom had called her out from day one. Told me to run far and run fast but what did I do? I fucking married that psycho.

"I've been looking for you for two fucking days, Larson! Where have you been? Why haven't you been answering your phone?" Still standing in front of my door, my key extended ready to slide in the hole, I shake my head, humorlessly chuckling. That key inching into the keyhole is like a metaphor of my life right now. I'm getting fucked.

Hard.

Repeatedly.

Painfully.

Simultaneously turning my head and wrist, I open the door as my eyes meet Brent's, three steps down from me. When our gazes lock, I see understanding cross my agent's face. I know him; he wants to be the first one to tell me about this shit storm. This man who has been dodging my impulsive fuck-ups from day one is now feeling guilty because he's too late. Great, now *I* feel bad for *him*.

"I turned off my phone so I could write in peace." My voice is flat. My high from this morning has dropped to all-time low, like the deadly effects of uppers and downers at a rave party.

"Fuck."

Yeah, that sums it all up, Brent. Thanks buddy.

"Please tell me this is bullshit. For the love of god, tell me you did NOT plagiarize."

At that very moment, I can feel my stare harden, my nostrils flaring with the indignity of his accusation. My brain is very well aware of the fact that Brent needs to cut his losses, just in case I am the scumbag author everyone is assuming I am. I know this. Still,

I'm pissed. We've been friends for a long fucking time and he needs to ask me this? Okay, so, *I've* considered *him* my friend. I have no idea what label he would tag onto our relationship.

Pushing the front door open, I step inside, ignoring his question. I can't deal with this right now. There are things I need to get done, people I need to contact, lawsuits I need to get rolling. If that cunt thinks I'm just going to lie back and let her stick a king-sized dildo up my ass with "Plagiarizer" written all over it, she has another thing coming. No pun intended.

"Fuck you, Brent. Fuck you for asking." At least I found the strength to actually answer his inquiry.

Behind me, I hear my agent release a sigh of relief before the door slams shut and hurricane Brent gets a move on. "You need to tell me everything. I need to know who the fuck tipped off that Babu guy..."

The hell?

My head swings back so fast I actually feel dizzy for a few seconds. "What did you just say?" My words are barely whispered yet they cut through the air between us like Wusthof knives. Brent's brown orbs go wide just as realization hits him.

"You don't know, do you?" What's with the rhetorical questions today?

"Obviously, not. Care to enlighten me?" I'm lethal right now. I'm sure that if I dug deep enough, I could commit the irreparable.

"Babu ran the article in his column. He outed you. Said he had a source, but that he refused to give "her" up because of past threats you sent her." Brent shrugs, which is understandable. In his shoes, I would be skeptical as hell given the lies that have been spewed with these recent events.

"Noelle." At this point, my agent, my friend, should understand what I'm dealing with here. To my relief, he does, if the accelerated pulse on the side of his neck is any indication.

"How?"

Great question, Sherlock.

"I have no fucking clue. Sympathy for the Devil was the predecessor to Quincy's Soul. The early version I worked on when we first married. I mean I rewrote quite a bit of it to make it palatable, but it was never her fucking manuscript. I'm not sure how she even got access to the early version. I had it on a flash drive, maybe even on my hard drive but I never...never, showed her that manuscript. In fact, to my knowledge, she didn't even know the fucking thing existed."

Brent is nodding, seemingly putting a plan into place. This is why he and I get along so well. He's a planner. We are organizing soul mates. I really should write romance, I've got the verbal diarrhea smelling like red roses going perfectly.

"Call your lawyer, it's game on."

Halle-fucking-lujah.

Chapter 12

Jesus H. Christ, the beeps of responses coming from my laptop on my latest column kept me up all fucking night. I've never had this much response to a column. My editor, Joel, is jizzing himself over it. He loves the publicity, and more than that, he loves that I've outed a plagiarist to boot.

I grab my mug of black coffee, still wearing my pajama pants and my tattered but still comfortable "Motley Crew" tee, sit down in front of my computer, and lift the lid.

The comments are rolling down for more than five pages.

Here is a taste of them:

Snappy-doo wrote: What a wonderful service you have done in calling out L. Blackburn on his theft of another author's work! He is definitely blacklisted from my TBR list! BTW - I returned my e-book! I suggest everyone else that opposes theft do the same!

Stilts wrote: I'm horrified at finding out what this author did! I've returned my e-book for refund.

Sunny wrote: No more 1-clicking from that bitch!

Bubba wrote: I hope L Blackburn goes to prison and gets butt-fucked by his bitch named Bubba!

Ginger wrote: You da man!! Way to out the thieving asshat! I'm so glad you black-balled the mofo!

Mummy's Naughty Book Club wrote: My whole book club returned our e-copies of that stolen book! We've black-balled Blackburn as well!

So that's pretty much the common theme of responses to my column. My cell rings. It's Joel.

"Yeah, Joel?"

"Man, your column has gone fucking viral, Troy."

"It's *Babu*," I correct him firmly.

"What the fuck ever, I'm in my office, the door is shut. Don't worry your paranoid ass about it. My point is, you're the man of the hour right now, so enjoy it. But be prepared for some backlash. You and I both know what a loose cannon Blackburn can be when someone ruffles his girly feathers," he says, chuckling at his own comment.

"We'll deal with that when and if," I reply, rolling my eyes and sipping my coffee. "In the meantime, I've got company so is there anything else?"

"Ah….one of Linc's girls?" he asks.

His fucking nosiness is getting on my last nerve. What the fuck business is it of his, anyway?

"Later Joel," I reply, ending the call.

I take a piss; brush my teeth and gargle, and then head back to my bedroom where Noelle's sweet pussy is waiting. I did the practically non-existent thing and let her spend the night once we got our initial fuck out of the way the evening before.

Fuck if she couldn't give good head.

That reminds me.

I grab my cell and download the video I'd taken last night when her pouty lips were wrapped around the base of my cock, her tongue swirling over and over the head of it, moaning her pleasure and begging me to fuck her raw with it.

Perfecto.

She hasn't gone into any details of how she knows or had come to know L. Blackburn, mainly because I don't want to know. I simply don't give a shit. She brought me dated proof, and that's all I need. She has the ISBN Number showing the date issued, and it being issued under her legal name, with the pen name of Alexis Purdy. She pulled up her account on her laptop and verified the manuscript that had been uploaded under that ISBN number and title.

And right now? I'm loving the fact that I'm rocking the dickhead's world. I have no interest in anything long term—or even short term—with her, but hey, I'm a man. If the chick enjoys blowing me, then who am I to turn it down?

Back to current business. I pull up my sock puppet email account and find the one the asshat L. Blackburn had sent critiquing the blowjob that Loretta had given me.

HIT: Reply.

TYPE: *How's this? Better?*

CLICK: Attach.

HIGHLIGHT: Video XXX.

HIT: Send.

ME: *Lol, butt-wipe!*

Now I can head back to my bedroom where Noelle waits patiently to service my cock once again. I don't think I'll be getting bored with her talents anytime soon though. That might be a problem.

Chapter 13

Three hours. That is how long I have waited, desperately trying to fend off the gnawing need to check the column where all of this bullshit began.

I tried writing. Then failed.

I did laundry. The brand new red boxers did a number on my white tee shirts. I scrubbed the kitchen sink. It was already clean but screw it, I needed the distraction.

Now, with nothing left for me to do but stare at my beckoning laptop, I open the lid and start it back up. Earlier, Brent had left with specific instruction to not, under any circumstances, go after Babu. I agreed, at the time.

The problem with making promises you can't keep is that more often than not, they come back to bite you in the ass. Mind you, I'm not opposed to a good ass-bite but I do need some pleasure with the hint of pain. This situation feels more like a Rottweiler has latched on to my cheek and is threatening to make hamburger meat out of it.

In principle, I don't lie. But I knew as the words slipped out from between my lips, that there was no way in hell I could stay away from that article.

No. Fucking. Way.

So, here I am, typing in the name of the newspaper that hosts my nemesis once a week. Apparently, this same paper is jacking off to the fact they are destroying a legitimate author's career over a bullshit lie.

Classy.

Staring at the article Babu wrote, I can feel my temperature rising, the throbbing of my heartbeat accelerating with every new jab he takes at me and my integrity.

I'm sure he lives in New York. His writing style, the way he holds himself higher than anyone else has Manhattanite written all over it. I bet he's a secret kitten killer. The cocksucker probably sells babies as a side job.

As I'm mentally berating the man, a little email window pops up letting me know I have a new message.

Great, just what I need.

Probably another ex-fan ranting about how ashamed I should be with myself. I almost answered last time. I almost told her that my dick size alone was enough to make me proud. I refrained, of course, because I'm not that much of an idiot.

Clicking on the email tab, I groan when I see who has reached out to me. I stare at the link, contemplating my next move. Suddenly, The Clash comes to mind and I find myself mumbling, "Should I click or should I spam?" Deep down, I know what I have to do. But do I do it?

Of course not.

Like the masochist I apparently have become, I open the email and, again, groan when I notice the brand spanking new video that is appropriately advertised as XXX. Maybe this time his blowjob will be more enticing.

It feels like an eternity before the video uploads and the image starts moving. The man, I'm guessing is Babu, stands beside the bed while a woman, kneeling on the mattress, is whole-heartedly licking and sucking on his impressive cock.

The camera is filming a side view, their profiles facing me. The man's face is off screen and the woman's face is sheltered by her long black hair draping down along her cheek and neck. The sounds of slurping and moaning have my own dick twitching, not because she's turning me on but for a completely different reason.

I want to be the one on my knees, drawing my mouth so far down his cock that he can feel the back of my throat closing in around his tip. Waiting for the need to bite it off, I'm surprised when that image does not flare in my mind's eye. Instead, my dick goes instantly hard as steel, painfully so, and I'm suddenly glad to be wearing pajamas instead of jeans.

The woman sounds like a two-bit porn star, exaggerating her cries of pleasure. Hell, he's not even flicking her clit. In fact, he's being a selfish prick, fucking her face as he fists around a handful of hair at the nape of her neck.

Averting my eyes from the sexual scene, I rake them up the side of his toned body. Jesus, does he have to have a killer body? Of course, he does. Sex is my kryptonite, and right now all I really want to do is shove my Superman dick inside his ass.

My attention returns to the woman who is desperately trying to make Babu come. Cocking my head to one side, I wonder if all women use the same sucking techniques because I feel like I've been blown that way a million times.

Shaking off the bad memories, I palm my cock through the cotton material of my pants and squeeze to calm it down a notch or two. The video abruptly ends with no cumshot.

Fucking amateurs.

I'm done playing. Shit just got real. Like, Jerry-fucking-Springer real.

Subject: C-

I seriously do not know where you get your cocksuckers but I'm willing to give them some pointers. By the way, you'll never make it as a porn producer if you forget the cumshots. Facials are always a good way to go.

All joking aside, I will destroy you for what you have done. You have no fucking clue what you are talking about. Before you continue on your vigilante crusade consider the fact that your source is a fucking lying bitch.

That being said...before I drag you to the ground, I plan on showing you what a real blowjob looks and feels like. You know what they say..."Once you go Blackburn..."

I am so screwed. I didn't even hesitate when I pressed "send".

Searching out the tab for the column, I painstakingly read through the messages and stop at one written by "Bubba."

No fucking way.

L. Blackburn wrote: You should be so lucky, man.

After that, I decide I've had enough of this crap and slam the lid down, effectively cutting off the world and relishing the feeling of my much needed solitude.

Believe it or not, I'm the victim here. I have done absolutely nothing wrong.

I'm tired.

I'm also horny.

As if my life isn't already a bad sitcom, I hear the very distinct sound of my mother's ringtone. She insisted I use Madonna's "Like a

Virgin" song specifically for her, saying that any artist who openly sang about the Lord's mother should be respected. I really did not have the heart to argue with her. Now, every time I hear her calling, I think of my sister Kennedy who had started giggling and pretending to be deep in prayer. That's when I added "Like a Prayer" as Kennedy's ringtone. Unfortunately, it's been a long time since that particular song has echoed from my phone.

"Hey Ma, how are you?" One of two things could happen here. Either she is bored and wants to tell me about her nurse Rose and all the trouble her children cause around the neighborhood or...

"Larson Maverick Blackburn, what the heck did you do?" Or...she is keeping up with my shitty life.

"I miss you too, Ma. How's Rose doing?" Yes, I'm trying to distract her. No, it's not working.

"Don't you try and change the subject, young man. Tell me, did your father and I teach you how to steal?" Oh sweet Jesus.

"Ma, seriously..."

"Answer the question, Larson. Did we?"

"No, Ma. You most certainly did not." I feel like I'm ten and just got caught stealing the warm cookies from the cooling rack before Kennedy got a chance to do it.

"That's right, son. If your daddy were here, God bless his soul, he would kick your behind so raw it would look like one of those monkeys. I don't know what they're called...something about..." See, I get that whole digression thing from her.

"A baboon, Ma." Not distracting, just trying to speed things along.

"That's it. A baboon. If I could, Larson, I would do it for him. Did you go to confession?" And here we go again.

"Ma. We're not Catholic."

"Nonsense, your father was half Irish so you can still go to church and get your conscience all cleared up." Oh yeah. I'm sure that would go over real well. A bisexual atheist seeking forgiveness for a crime he did not commit. See?

Bad. Sitcom.

"Mother, I swear to you, I did not plagiarize. Come on! You know me better than that, right?" I mean, she did give birth to me after all so she should know me best. I mean shit...if my own mother doesn't believe me, I'm fucked.

"Well, I don't know...I never thought you would be capable of cutting off the hair from your sister's Barbie and yet...you got caught with the scissors in your hand." Holy shit, I was like eight years old.

"Uhm...Ma? Darn it, I have to go...the uhm...buzzer from

the...uhm...thing is... Oh, a tunnel...can't hear you ...bzzzzz...sshhhhh....love you...." And like the coward I am, I hang up on my own mother.

New time low? Check.

Chapter 14

"Mr. B? Are you in there Mr. B?" Ida Whatley's shrill voice breaks the spell. I've been reading the smart-ass email reply that L. Blackburn sent and frankly, my sock puppet is not fucking amused!

"Yes, Mrs. Whatley, I'm here," I call out, going to the door and flipping the locks to open it. "What can I do for you?"

"Well," she says, putting her hand on her hip, "I wanted to let you know that your new girlfriend is just lovely." She's beaming—like a mother who's proud of the girl her son brought home to meet mother.

"Say again?"

"Oh...I'm sorry," she giggles, "Noelle, right?"

"Not following, Ida," I reply tersely.

"The lovely girl with the long dark hair that stayed over the other night? Such a pretty thing, she is. Well, I saw her yesterday morning when she was leaving. I was downstairs getting my mail and newspaper. She introduced herself to me as your girlfriend...and well, I'm just so tickled you've finally found a keeper."

I clear my throat loudly. "Uh...well she's not actually a girlfriend," I explain. "More like an associate...yeah, she's an associate."

"Oh," she says with a sigh, obviously disappointed, "Well, she sure has a thing for you. Mr. B, that was clearly evident. Me and my big mouth—well, no worries. I hope you let her down gently. Have a nice day."

"Yeah...uh...you do the same."

I close my door, and my hand furiously rubs the back of my neck in irritation.

The fuck?

I rack my brain replaying our night spent together.

Nada.

There was nothing I did or said that would have given Noelle the impression that we would ever be a *couple.* In fact, I didn't intend to call her again.

I shrug.

Problem solved.

My cell rings and I'm relieved to see it's only Joel.

No stalker...yet.

"What?"

"Jeez, who pissed in your Wheaties this morning?"

"I'm just in the middle of something, Joel. What do you need?"

"Hey, I've got some good news for you. You've been invited to attend the upcoming Gotham Greatness Author Ball the first weekend in April. The invitation came with VIP tickets from Noelle at MacMullins Publishing. Looks like you're A-listed, baby."

"Why would I want to attend a signing? I prefer—no I *insist* in remaining incognito from the author community, you know that."

"That's the beauty of this, dude. The theme is masquerade. It's like the ultimate way for you to meet authors you've made, and authors you've slayed. I suggest you go in a suit of armor," he says, chuckling.

"Very fucking funny."

"Seriously dude, it's not up for negotiation. Clark wants you there. It's a great opportunity for you to eavesdrop on some of these prima donnas without them knowing who you are. Can you imagine the juicy tidbits you'll have for the next few columns? I mean it's fucking brilliant, no?"

"I don't like to be forced into shit like this, Joel. What the fuck? Is Clark trying to turn my column into some freaking Jerry Springer show?"

I can tell I've pushed a button with Joel. "I think you've done a good job of that already," he snaps, "Besides, it's good therapy for you. You need to start getting out more. Clark's a patient man, but shit, it's been *two* years, you know?"

"I'm aware of how long it's been. I'll think about it, Joel. You tell Clark that I'll *think* about it."

End. Fucking. Call.

I sit at my laptop and Google 'Gotham Greatness' quickly scanning the attending author's banner at the top.

Fuck!

There it is.

L. Blackburn.

Well, well—maybe it will be worth the stress and string of the panic attacks I'm sure to endure in an effort to attend this little soiree after all. My favorite black-balled queen will be attending.

I laugh out loud picturing him parading as some drag queen or maybe a crack whore.

Game on.

Chapter 15

There are two. Large and imposing. I'm standing over them, watching warily as though they are going to jump up and bite me. In normal circumstances, I would be quite the sucker for a good nip and lick but this is very far removed from normal.

Uncomfortable.

Dubious.

Hell, I'll even own up to nervous.

These are the feelings that torment me at the moment. The black cloud of insecurity is slowly wrapping itself around me like an ominous blanket ready to choke me. My heartbeat is accelerating at the mere thought of using them. Damp palms are now rubbing against my jean-clad thighs, trying desperately to relieve the awkward sensation that this is completely wrong.

Staring at their immobile position, my mind is already racing through the multitude of acceptable reasons of why I should not use them.

Too soon.

Too dangerous.

Too fucking embarrassing.

Brent, my long-time agent and friend, is pushing me to do it. "Just rip off the Band-Aid," he said.

At the time, I had had a snide remark to accompany his worthless humor, but I made an effort and shut my mouth. I know, I should be rewarded for my show in restraint, especially since I am clearly being pushed to the limits of my goodness. Next time, I'm lashing out.

All of my internal bickering will not solve my problem. I have my tickets to the New York signing...plus one.

But that is the least of my worries, because not only must I show my face in public and risk a front and center lynching, but I apparently need to do this all in the presence of a date. I asked Brent to do his fucking job and attend the event with me, but judging from the repulsion written across his features, he would have preferred an enema. Difficult to argue with that.

No, the problem is not having to go, it is having to share space with an acquaintance witnessing the end of L. Blackburn. Luckily for me, this farce is being disguised as a Masquerade Event...pun firmly intended. Of course, this would not stop the readers from knowing who is who, but at least it offers a moment of respite between each wave of fans.

If there are any left, that is.

Running my fingers through my hair, I blink and resume my stare down at the offending tickets marring the top of my kitchen table. I hate New York just as much as I love it. At any other time in my life, I would have welcomed this trip for a multitude of reasons. Unfortunately, this little voyage would merely go down as the "Breaking Bad" of literature.

"Time to face the music, Larson. Even if it is Chopin's Funeral March," I mumble to myself as I pull out my phone and scroll through my contacts. Who would be the unknowing victim of an open bar lashing?

Leslie. Too clingy. I cannot take the risk of her thinking this little escapade is anything but a date with no strings.

Jessica. Too blonde and busty. The unwanted attention she would garner is not on my priority list.

Melbourne. Who the fuck names their kid after a city? No, if only on principle.

Jasmine. Oh fuck no. That would make me Aladdin, which immediately has me thinking of that fucking monkey, Abu. And whenever that stupid critter infiltrates my mind, the image of a balding, crooked-nosed, fat-ass enters my mind's eye. My greatest wish, right now, is for my description to fit to the tee. One thing is for sure, I do not need some kind of physical attraction deterring me from my goal. If I see him? I will punch his lights out for a day or ten.

Babu. Will he be there? Will he be laughing at his accomplishments? Maybe he will even toast a general round for my imminent demise. My brain analyzes the various scenarios where he and I would be found in the same room, breathing the same air, hearing the same sounds.

At the signing table.

At the bar.

At the dinner buffet.

In the elevator, each destined to our own rooms.

To my utter disgust, the image of his long, thick cock fills my inner conscience making my dick instantly hard.

Fucking traitor.

Without realizing it, my finger scrolls down to a familiar, welcomed name.

Lloyd Ledbetter.

Despite the lack of sexy in his name, the man is utter perfection, unequaled in his submission.

Tonight, he will soothe me. Relieve me of this permanent stress infecting my body and soul, rendering me incapable of writing a single word on either paper or screen. I need the release to bring me back to life, the only one that holds any importance to me: Writing.

As I press the green button on my phone, I suck in my breath hoping there are no complications, no denials.

"Well, well, Sir. I have been waiting for your call for the last two days."

The smooth timber of Lloyd's voice bathes me in quiet comfort knowing I can soon be buried so deeply inside him that all of my troubles will dissipate. He is my destination when shit gets out of control. Life would have been so much easier had I fallen deeply in love with him, but apparently that condition is foreign to me.

According to my ex-wife, I am incapable of showing emotion let alone the complicated, multi-faceted one that is love.

Of course, she is wrong. I show quite a few different feelings while deep in the throes of passion. Sometimes I even thank god for the gift of orgasms, which is quite a feat seeing as He and I are not on speaking terms, anymore.

"Did you, now? And why is that?" I know the answer. Lloyd is an avid reader and quite the boisterous fan when it comes to me. This whole disaster has probably been pissing him off almost as much as it has driven me to drink.

Almost.

"Please, Sir. You do not need to hide behind your mask with me. I'll be over in an hour."

Blinking, I realize the man has just hung up on me, probably eager to clean himself up and get his gorgeous ass over to my house.

Suddenly, I wonder what Babu's ass would look like. How it would feel trapped between my two large hands squeezing each cheek like a gift of nature. I imagine sliding my tongue along the crack, tasting his essence, inhaling his scent and emptying my sack on the canvas of his skin like fucking Dalì on crack.

Shit, I need to stop the madness.

Taking a deep, fortifying breath, I run my hands through my hair before grabbing the tickets and trapping them inside the desk drawer. Lloyd cannot see them. He cannot imagine himself as my date in any public event. Not because I am in the closet, I most certainly am not. But simply because the man is just waiting for me to collar him, something that will never happen.

One, I'm not a Master, no matter how many times he calls me "Sir" and kneels at my feet like a good little pup. My temper is too out of control for that shit.

Secondly, being married cured me of any need to be in a long-lasting relationship especially with someone as invested as Lloyd would, no doubt, become. No. Thank. You.

This is the reason the "No Call" rule was instated, to avoid being hounded anytime he feels the need to lay across my chest and have me pet him like the subservient he thinks he is. I am not into that type of play. I like rough sex. Hard, potent thrusting where my balls slap so hard against skin that the neighbors can feel the beat of the rhythm. I like to talk dirty, filthy even. My mouth just acts of its own accord with every pump of my hips nearing the final note of my fucking. Beyond that, I'm just not available.

Making my way to the kitchen, I take out a bottle of Merlot from the wine bar and uncork it, allowing it to breathe while I shower and shave. Although, Lloyd is quite the fan of my five o'clock shadow, especially the burning sensation it causes.

I open the refrigerator to check for finger foods and am happy to find some grapes, leftover chicken and celery. It will have to do for tonight.

I love my home; it is exactly how I pictured my living quarters when I was younger. Not flashy, yet far from small. Again, I am an organized creature. Everything has its place and, order is my friend.

Some of the walls have apparent bricks, giving the house an old feel all the while being completely renovated. The hall that separates the living room and the bedrooms is sprinkled with picture frames of my parents and sister, Kennedy. I smile as I walk by, feeling a little pang in my chest as I quickly count the months since last I saw them.

When my father passed away, last year, our world came crashing down. My already weak hold on reality was obliterated, and I found myself completely immersed in my fiction. Heart disease, the doctors informed us. Difficult to comprehend such a diagnosis, when my father always had a healthy diet with regular exercise. After some research, it was evident that the illness simply runs in the family.

Needless to say, I am equally at risk.

My sister Kennedy stayed with our mother for a couple of months until the weight of his disappearance was too overwhelming. We have not heard from her since.

Ten months, she has been gone. Ten months in which my guilt has gnawed at me from the inside out. Ten months that my mother has been dying a slow, painful death borne from sorrow.

When the investigator we hired told us he had zero clues, we lost hope. Kennedy and I are only eleven months apart. I know she is still alive, I can feel it. I just wish she could feel the pain from our loss. If something does not change soon, I fear our mother will wither away.

I should call Mom.

I will call her.

I cannot lose her, as well.

Rubbing my hands down my face to dispel the somber thoughts, I make my way to the bathroom and quickly undress as I let the water heat the large Italian-style shower. I love it here. The terracotta tiles add to the charm of the house and I cannot help but feel safe, content, and almost happy.

My watch tells me I have about twenty minutes before Lloyd arrives, so I make quick of washing, shaving and rinsing myself. I needed to freshen up but I know damn well I'll be taking another shower all too soon. Whether I'll be alone, that is, altogether, a different story.

Without bothering to check myself in the wide mirror above the sink, I merely wrap myself in a white towel and shake the excess water out of my hair. There is no need to dress up, no need to make myself presentable. This is, in no way, a date. At least not in the traditional sense.

Tonight is about fucking. Tasting. Forgetting about my career that is slowly spiraling down the drain like the soapy water of my recent shower. Tonight is about shutting off my brain, halting all thoughts of my enemy and his unnatural need to ruin me. And his cock. I seriously need to stop thinking about sucking his cock and showing him a proper blowjob.

Fuck.

Sliding on a pair of black sweatpants, I loosely tie the string around my waist and slip on a grey V-neck tee shirt. My hair has been growing out; the brown strands, made darker from the water, are falling haphazardly around my face but I know for a fact it will turn Lloyd's dick to granite the minute he sees me.

It's not conceit, it's the truth.

And I am all about the fucking truth...unlike some wannabe critics out there. That singular thought has me heading straight to my laptop. I have exactly ten minutes before my lover knocks on my door. I have a message to send, a final white flag to raise.

Pulling up my email, I create a new message and start typing

Mr. Babu,

I wonder how many times since my last message, you have thought about my cock. Have you imagined what it would feel like to have it buried deep in your mouth? Have you wondered how salty my cum is? If it's hot as it slides down your throat? What about your tight little virgin ass, Mr. Babu? Has it clenched at the thought of being breached?

Tell me, Mr. Babu...How hard is your dick right now?

How badly do you want me to fuck you?

Retract, apologize publicly and I promise you...I'll make all your fantasies come true.

LB

The doorbell rings, it's game time. I press send as a smirk adorns my lips. Yes, I'm feeling pretty self-satisfied right now. That being said, my enemy could very well ruin my life with that singular email. For some reason, I have a feeling he won't because deep down, a man who is this obsessed with another, has dark secrets and I am dying to uncover every single one.

"Lloyd," I say in my low, lustful voice.

"Sir." My cock goes rigid in a second.

"Come in, get naked and spread your legs." I'm not fucking around tonight.

"Yes, Sir." His words are submissive but his attitude is far from it. He wants to steer this game but he is afraid I'll call it all off. He should be. If I'm not in control of my fucking, I'll escort him straight to the exit.

"Good." I watch him as he makes quick work of his slacks, sliding them down his toned legs before kicking them off to the side. I fight the urge to pick them up and fold them carefully over the back of the kitchen chair. I'm that much of a freak.

I haven't moved an inch, watching him as he sheds all proof that he was ever dressed. His golden hair is styled back, longer on top and shorter on the sides. The small growth of his beard tells me he wants to play, suck on my dick for a couple of hours, rubbing himself across my inner thighs.

My eyes drift to his pouty mouth, lips made for blowing cocks. He is perfection and yet...I feel nothing more than lust, a hard-driven desire to be joined carnally, physically, but never emotionally. Maybe I am sick, but I won't be analyzing it tonight.

"On your knees, Lloyd. Wrap your lips around my dick and suck it like you own it."

My lover's eyes light up with need, a deep driven lust that makes his entire face glow with delight.

"Your eyes on me."

He loves *this* shit. My commands, my filthy mouth...his submission.

Lloyd slides his palms up the outside of my thighs, his eyes fixed on mine, his breath heavier as his mouth draws closer to my erect cock. I move my hands so he can untie my draw string and pull down my sweats, and he is greeted by bare skin since I opted for going commando. Lloyd moans, his shudder visible to the naked eye.

Hell yeah, this is going to be good.

With the first lick of his hot tongue, I groan at the much needed sensation. Never have I met a man as capable as Lloyd, when it comes to oral. Mad skills is an understatement so, right now, I'm going to enjoy every second and will avoid all thoughts of a certain asswipe who is trying to ruin my life.

As my mind is wandering to places it should not go, I suddenly feel wet heat surrounding my dick, the head lightly bumping against a soft surface. *Holy shit,* Lloyd is swallowing my head, his gag reflex practically nonexistent. Unfreakingbelievable.

Grunting as my lover hollows out his cheeks, making my entire body shiver with unbridled hunger, I latch on to his head and curl my fingers around the silky strands. This man takes impeccable care of himself. Always perfectly groomed with a handsome smile on his face, he makes both sexes melt into a puddle.

Outwardly, he is a confident, demanding man. However, his deep azure eyes grow molten at the mere thought of being dominated. Lloyd is searching for his happily ever after, which involves a leather collar with a lock and key. It's just not who I am. I can do it for play, but I won't do it as a lifestyle. Not only do I lack the time to care for another, but the responsibility is too heavy a burden to bear.

"Suck harder, Lloyd. Don't fuck around, or you'll be heading out the door so fast it'll make your head spin." Now I'm helping him, thrusting my hips forward as my grip in his hair grows tighter. Every time his nose hits my neatly trimmed pubic hairs, I feel his throat contracting and I almost lose my load.

It feels good. So fucking good.

"Yeah, baby, just like that," I encourage him as his sucking grows more and more avid.

"Don't stop. Fuck, yeah. You like my dick in your mouth, don't you?" Lloyd's grip on my thighs is nearly painful but it helps me keep my control. No need in coming down his throat so soon. Besides, I would rather make my mark on his ass.

As his hand snakes up between my legs, he begins to roll my balls between his fingers. I love this. The sensation is exquisite, the high all-consuming...the need to come almost unbearable.

"Stop." My command is clear, no questions asked.

Lloyd knows the rules. His head stops bobbing, and his hand immediately drops from my sack as he leans back on his heels.

What should I do...?

Couch? It could be nice but my leather is soft and buttery, I would hate to ruin it.

Kitchen counter? Fuck that, I would end up spending an hour cleaning it afterwards. Not my idea of relaxing after a good fuck.

The bed it is.

"Bed. You know the drill." It takes him no more than twenty seconds to jump to his feet and make a hasty retreat down the hall and inside the second door on the right. My bedroom.

I grab a couple of condoms from my desk drawer and slowly make my way to my room. I can already picture Lloyd; I know exactly how he is presenting himself to me.

As expected, my lover is spread out on my dark blue sheets, his arms around his knees, his legs drawn up to his chest, his asshole winking at me from across the room.

"You are quite the sight for sore eyes, Lloyd. Do you want me to fuck you good?"

It's always safe to ask such questions; surprises in the middle of sex are disastrous for the ego.

"Yes, Sir. Please..."

Passing by my dresser, I open the top drawer and slowly take out the lube. I do this for show, Lloyd loves the anticipation. He loves watching me prepare for the finale. On my way, I had pulled my sweats back up. Now, I'm shedding them altogether. Grabbing the back of my tee shirt, I shrug it off and methodically place it on the chair next to the window, along with my sweats.

My cock is slapping my stomach with every one of my steps. I reach Lloyd swiftly, who is beautifully spread out like a Thanksgiving meal ready to be devoured. Out of nowhere, the image of a stranger I have yet to meet makes an unwanted appearance in my head. The man is taking over Lloyd's features, making me frown at the mirage.

"Everything okay, Sir?"

"Yeah, don't move."

Dropping a big dollop of lube onto my palm, I rub nice and hard from tip to root, moaning at the sensitivity around the bulbous head of my cock.

Next, I lavish Lloyd with a generous amount of lube around his asshole before dipping first one finger, then another. I'm pumping in and out, trying to hit the spot that will make him come like a thirteen–year-old who recently discovered porn.

Quickly, I find it and just as I expected, his eyes roll in the back of his head. His mouth opens, forming a perfect "O" as his breath seeks out the much needed oxygen. I'm a good lover. I like to please my partners, so I do what any man loves to experience.

I bend down, running my tongue along the pulsing vein that runs along Lloyd's decent-sized shaft. When I reach the tip, I simultaneously push my fingers deeper and rub hastily along that magical spot that makes grown men cry. Lloyd curses as my mouth engulfs his trembling member, his load ready to erupt like Mount St. Helen's. I withdraw my mouth, replacing it with my palm, and begin jacking him off to the beat of a perfect hand job.

The gorgeous man occupying my bed is still holding his legs up, but his hips are thrusting in midair, seeking out his orgasm. The first spurts are almost violent, spraying across his abdomen like a painting. I keep pumping his slick cock as he empties himself of all his semen. Beautiful.

"My turn."

Lloyd is no virgin. He doesn't need it slow, and he most certainly does not want it sweet. Fast and dirty is exactly how I had planned for this night to go. The little tin foil packet sits precariously between my fore and middle fingers before I carefully sheath my dick. The lube is conveniently placed right next to me so I use a little to make my entrance more about pleasure and less about pain.

In one smooth move, my hardness slides inside his warm hole, and my entire body relaxes as my balls meet the tender skin below his anus.

Heaven.

Could almost make me a believer.

My hands latch on to his upper thighs and my body goes into auto-pilot, my carnal needs speaking for themselves. I ram Lloyd's ass, my sack slapping harshly against his skin. My breathing becomes shallower as I fight the impending orgasm that is threatening to erupt.

"Fuck yeah; your ass is so damn tight. Don't fucking move, Lloyd."

We both grunt on my final thrust. I'm rendered immobile while my cum shoots violently inside the condom. I can feel the heat of it surrounding my shaft. So much for making him my cum-canvas.

My fingers dig into Lloyd's flesh as a testament of my satisfying orgasm. Closing my eyes, I picture falling stars, roaming comets and a big ass dick buried in some strange woman's mouth.

Motherfucker.

I am supposed to be forgetting, not fantasizing.

Chapter 16

Yeah, despite my better fucking judgment, and the realization that I really need to distance myself from a chick like Noelle, I capitulated and answered her thinly veiled bootie call this evening.

I mean what the fuck?

It's just sex.

And pretty damn good sex at that.

She stopped over. We ordered Chinese that was delivered. Drank some good Chardonnay and then ended up in the sack. Fucking like a couple of sex-crazed inmates on ecstasy.

And that's where I am now. Fully awake as she sleeps comfortably underneath my sheets.

Sleep won't come to me and I know why. I'm not comfortable with this. I don't like for women to stay over, and I generally have no reluctance in letting them know just that, but shit. She's not one of Linc's girls that I order in advance, setting the guidelines and parameters of our date.

I consider waking her up. Telling her that it's time she grabs her jeans and sweater, slips on her leather boots and matching jacket, and hits the bricks.

I don't do that because she knows who I am. Well, not *really* who I am, but she knows that I'm Babu the God of Literary Reviews for the Bluffington Gazette, clearly one of the most powerful and cut to the chase critics in the business, notorious for telling it like it is, and sending the Indies crawling back under the rocks from which they surfaced.

There's a lot she doesn't know about me—that most people don't know about me. Well, except for Joel, and he's got no reason to breach confidentiality.

I get up from the bed, grab my discarded boxers from the floor and pull them up over my nakedness. Slipping from my room, I close the door softly behind me so the light from my office won't wake her up. I don't need the irritation of having to explain what I'm doing up at two a.m. to someone who shouldn't be here anyway.

I switch the light on over my desk, and open the bottom drawer of my tall metal filing cabinet, pulling out the box that contains the four hundred plus crisp white typewritten pages of my manuscript.

As I lift the lid of the cardboard box, my eyes are greeted once again with the stack of envelopes all containing the boilerplate 'fuck-off' letters from the various publishing houses.

I'm not sure why I've kept them. They are nothing more than sore reminders that the one dream I poured my heart into for two years will never come to fruition. After six years, the stark disappointment and pain of rejection has yet to totally subside. It's still a dull ache, an effervescent reminder that I'm not all I want to be. That my life has not gone as planned.

I pull the stack of envelopes out, laying them aside while my hand captures the rubber banded manuscript, lifting it out carefully. One of these days, I know the pages will have yellowed. I only hope by that time, I'm fucking over it.

My eyes caress the title page. The ornate font, beckons me to leaf through my work and for the hundredth time, give it a fresh look and consider the possibility that despite the rejections, those publishing trolls were clueless as to the unique plot and powerful twists contained in these pages. The heart and soul that became part of this story, and the reckoning of my past, piecing it together so that some sense could be made of it.

Bridge to Lonely.

How prophetic the title is to what my life has become since finishing this literary masterpiece six years ago. So much has changed since then, but none of it in the way that I would've chosen, or the way that I had planned.

I scoffed at Joel's suggestion four years ago when I started Babu's column to self-publish my book. I had known Joel from way before then. He served as a beta reader for BTL.

Self-publish? Hell to the no.

If the publishers didn't want it, then it's because my treasure is simply their trash. I must have been delusional in thinking it was something unique—some non-cookie cutter masterpiece that the reading world awaited.

I press the pages back into the cardboard box. I toss the rejection letters back on top, thinking that one day soon, I need to part with it. Why keep it here as a perpetual reminder of my failure?

As I lean forward to place the now closed box back into its dark crypt, I spot the manila envelope that the box has been sitting atop. The red splotches of blood, my own DNA, have turned to a rusty brown now.

Delores Friedman.

My hand instinctively brushes against the small puckered scar on my left ribcage as I recall how the psychotic bitch accosted me in the crowded elevator that day more than two years ago while I was in Toronto for a literary convention for bloggers and critics.

She stalked me prior to that, mostly cyber as far as I know, but I had never taken her threats seriously. I mean why would I? She was simply someone who couldn't take constructive criticism. It certainly hadn't affected her books from hitting a list or two, had it? 'There's no accounting for taste,' I had commented on one of her many web posts showing a screenshot of her latest book title on the NYT Best Seller's List, pointing out to her that The Jerry Springer Show had the largest daytime audience of any show running for six years in a row, but did that make it any less rank--beep-beep?

It was after that, she posted I was a dead man walking. How original, I had replied.

But on that day, she had meant to drive home that promise with this manila envelope shielding the knife she plunged into my ribs. Before I knew what the fuck was going down, I'd managed to knock her back, her head hitting the wall of the elevator and her limp body sliding unceremoniously down to the floor with her legs spread apart in the most unladylike fashion, what with her being in hose and heels.

It was only later, after I had been treated at the hospital that the authorities handed me the manila envelope found at the scene. My name had been neatly typed on the front. My blood was splattered across the center of it.

I opened it, pulling out a neatly typed copy of the review I had posted in my column of her latest book nearly six months prior. The one that had apparently pushed her over the edge.

I pull the papers out now. I haven't read it since the night of my attack. Maybe I should revisit this review and try to see just what was so fucking brutal in the content to cause her to fucking wig out that way.

To my ardent followers, I must ask your indulgence in advance.
This critique isn't going to be pretty, but it's going to be
accurate. And should I rant? Well, please understand what

perpetrated it.

Under the genre of contemporary romance, "Sins, Lies and Deceit," reads like a low-budget, Triple X porn film. The heroine is a clap-trap of throbbing desire who can't seem to get enough of scumbag dudes who fuck her simultaneously, painfully and endlessly. One must wonder if her sphincter muscle has been irreparably compromised. (Only her underwear and proctologist know for sure).

Let's talk about the M/C's. Wow, there were so many contradictions in the way they acted and/or reacted, that I couldn't connect with any of them! I hated them. I wanted them dead. I was appalled by the lack of character development and the messy, over-the-top sex scenes. At one point, I was tempted to cue in the striptease music and enter the territory of vomitus maximus. The book reeked like month old, unrefrigerated Limburger cheese. In other words, it stunk! It was an offensive stench at that. I found the dialog extremely stilted and shallow. The author succeeded in totally desecrating the English language. The only emotions this book prompted in me were anger and irritation that I wasted my time on this pile of dung.

Considering how many five-star ratings this book has received, I can only fathom those readers were under the influence of something, and I'm pretty damn sure whatever it was is illegal. I'm seriously blown away by the high praise this author has received on the whole Vulva Monologue Series! Seriously? Are we reading the same shit, Ladies? These are marketed as standalone books, and since this is Book 3, one would think this author's writing skills would have become well-honed over time. That is simply not the case with this sub-par work of fiction. On the bright side, this author delivered what her admiring fan-girls convinced themselves they wanted. Kudos on pre-release marketing. A snake oil salesman could not have done better.

Bottom line, "Sins, Lies and Deceit," is pure literary trash. It isn't romance, not by a long shot, and it failed miserably to do anything other than repulse me! I pride myself on having better taste in literature than these obvious sixth graders posing as adults buying trash like this and promoting it as being something worthy of purchasing. Once again, the Indie Author community has managed to pull the wool over the ever vigilant sheep that follow. My parting words for the Friedman sheep,

"Baa--baaa…"

I sit back and shove the papers back inside the blood-splattered envelope.

Was that really so bad?

I decide that I will gladly sport this scar for the remainder of my life knowing that it just might have been worth it since Delores Friedman is locked up and thankfully will no longer be permitted to self-publish her insidious porn from prison.

To the readers of America, you are welcome!

Right before I switch off the desk lamp, I check my emails for the hell of it. Two from Joel, pitching that fucking Gotham event, one from Clark, pitching it a bit more forcefully.

What the fuck ever.

I check my sock puppet account for shits and giggles.

L. Blackburn's latest email awaits my eyes.

Do I even want to open it? Maybe I should simply trash it and let the idiot think that he's had the last word. But I'm a slave to curiosity and as this idiot's audacity seems to know no bounds, what the hell?

I click on it, speed reading down the body of his message, and with each word, phrase and sentence, I feel my blood start to boil.

L. Blackburn goes too far!

His cock? Deep throating me? Print a retraction and make my fantasies come true?

I glance at the date and see that he sent this a day ago. He's only guessing I'm behind the sock puppet email address. He knows nothing for sure because I've never confirmed it one way or the other.

I grab my digital camera and perch it atop the tripod, angling it just so, and set the delay for the flash. Quickly I drop my boxers, stepping out of them. I turn my back to the camera, bend over at the waist, and my hands reach back to separate my ass cheeks to allow full view of my virgin bung hole.

3-2-1

Flash!

I grab the camera, upload the picture and off it goes to L. Blackburn for his viewing pleasure.

Dream on, asshat.

Dream fucking on!

I return to my main email account, and quickly pull up Clark's email for a reply, making sure I add Joel to the distribution.

Re: Gotham City Event

I'll go on the conditions that my appearance there is not shown on the roster and that it is entirely off the record with the event sponsors and coordinators, with the exception of Noelle of course.

-Babu

Chapter 17

Nothing compares to the sweet melody of fingers clicking on the keyboard. Letters forming into words. Words morphing into sentences. Sentences creating entire worlds. This is my reality; the creation of fiction. It's my drug, my ultimate high...my sanity.

How do you put any monetary worth on this type of satisfaction? How can any one person judge your imagination as being too lipid or too sappy? Too unworthy? Of whom, I ask?

Who are any of these critics to judge the value of my mind's creation? These things, to me, are immeasurable and yet they are being sized up on millions of blogs and columns every single day. I usually ignore the criticism. Sometimes, I actually take to heart the constructive reviews but that is so rare, I'm almost wondering if I'm not making this shit up as I go along.

I know my talent. I don't need validation from others. So what made me go utterly ballistic over Babu's review? The gratuitous cruelty with which he affirmed his opinion. Am I saying he doesn't have the right to hate my work? The thought never occurred to me. Seriously, it didn't. Who the fuck in their right minds would not like my work? Okay, that sounded a little bit pompous and arrogant but then the truth often does, right?

My guess is that dear Mr. Babu has probably been trying to conceive a book for a quarter of his lifetime and still hasn't seen it on any vending site. This type of outward lashing is often the direct result of self-loathing.

The fuck do I know? That's my shrink talking.

Apparently, after my father's death and my sister's disappearance, I was a bit...rash. My guilt was the responsible party in those days.

Now, I'm a born-again asshole, which in psych terms is a whole different ball game. Whatever, it all adds up to the same shit. You hate others because on some level you hate yourself.

Kumba-fucking-ya.

My mind is spilling directly onto the keys, emptying my current stress load onto the white pages of book two in Quincy's struggles. He is alone. Finding redemption for the innocent lives he had to take in order to save the one soul he cared for above all else.

Himself.

Not because of his narcissistic view, but simply because his sister depends on his strength to get her through her current hardships. Sound familiar? Good. That's because it is. Minus the array of dead bodies loitering in the corners of the novel. Let's face it, I'm not a killer. I just write about them.

Most of the time, my actions have nothing to do with my own goals and everything to do with finding my sister. She used to love my stories, craved them. My only tie to her is my writing so that is the hope that keeps me sane. Maybe, somewhere out there, Kennedy is reading and realizing how badly I need her back in our lives.

At one p.m. I hear my stomach calling me out on my lack of nourishment. After last night's sexapades, I should have filled up with a good, healthy breakfast—an abundance of proteins and liquids. However, I was overly busy convincing Lloyd that he needed to leave before he got down on one knee and set a date. Been there, paid for that mistake in the grand total of fifty thousand.

Ultimately, I'm writing to pay off my ex-wife's mental breakdown. She should be paying me for being honest, but that is an entirely different story.

Besides writing, I need to find my cajones and decide on a costume as well as a date for the Masquerade signing in New York. Jesus, could they possibly get any more cliché?

I suddenly stop typing, and stare into space, weighing the possibility of my internal accusations. Picking up my phone, I quickly dial Brent waiting for him to pick-up and reassure me.

"I'm not working right now, Larson. It's my lunch break and I'm spending it with my beautiful wife."

Oh, please, gag me before I say something inappropriate.

"Planning to fuck her on the restaurant table? I could be there in ten minutes to watch."

Too late.

"Larson." Interesting, Brent's voice took on a type of venomous tone able to even scare me. This, right here, was my definition of love.

Or a really good fuck.

"Sorry," I mumble although my regret is nowhere to be found. "I just have a quick question. You didn't, by any chance, get mixed up in the signings and book us on a Romance Novels' event, did you? Because, I gotta tell you...Masquerade sounds awfully chick-lit to me."

Nothing against the Fifty Shades types, but a room full of horny women when you look like me? No, thank you.

"Give me some credit, Larson. I'd hate for you to be in the New York Times headlines for causing a riot."

Somehow, I'm guessing his take on it has nothing to do with me being mauled and everything to do with my uncontrollable temper.

Whatever. Same shit, different version.

I hang up and suddenly find my inner silence where words come to me effortlessly. In this place, there are no ex-wives, no present lovers and no future reviewer killings. Here, only my story exists...my sanity surviving for just a little while longer.

Chapter 18

It's been nearly five minutes since any words have been exchanged between Dr. Benedict and me. I'm passing the time by Zen gardening, totally absorbed with the patterns I've been raking in the sand around the rocks in the doc's tabletop version. It's supposed to clear my mind of the chaos of everyday life, and it occurs to me that spending thirty bucks for one of these just might be a more cost-efficient means of doing just that. Plus I wouldn't have to leave my apartment on Tuesday afternoons.

Yeah, I know. That defeats the purpose of these visits. I get that, but what the hell? How long is he going to drag this shit out?

"What are you contemplating, Mr. Babilonia?" he asks, finally breaking our self-imposed silence.

Why the fuck can't he call me Babu?

"Call me Babu, please? I was just thinking it might be a helluva lot cheaper for me to buy one of these contraptions instead of spending three hundred a week coming here," I reply honestly.

He gives a soft laugh. "The minutes pass one way or another; I suggest you make this visit worth the expense."

I look over at him. "Alright. How's this? I'm committed to attending some fucking costume gala ball, which will require me to spend the night at the St. Regis Hotel in midtown, and then attend an awards breakfast the following morning. I'm fucking freaked about the thought of it."

Dr. Benedict leans forward a bit in his high-backed leather chair and studies me for a moment. "I think it's a big step in the right direction, Babu. Clearly, I'm pleased that you're taking it. I think our sessions have helped significantly."

"Hold off on the back patting for a moment. This whole thing wasn't my idea. It's sort of a condition of my continued employment if you catch my drift."

"I see. Well no matter. It's still a hurdle that I have every reason to think you'll cross unscathed."

"And what makes you so fucking sure?" I'm not paying this dickhead to be my own personal cheerleader. I mean, seriously?

He's unaffected by my harsh tone, probably because he's been at the receiving end of it for a couple of years now. "Look, I think you're ready. It's like anything else; you're simply allowing the fear of it to exaggerate the stark reality of the situation. You mentioned previously that you had been a fairly social person prior to your attack. Is that a fair statement?"

"Well, it's not like I was ever the life of the party, Doc, but yeah, I did travel in a somewhat tight knit social circle. I did have occasional dates with *women*," I reply succinctly, "Attended the occasional dinner party."

He removes his glasses, pulling a linen handkerchief from his pocket, and gently wipes the lenses clean before putting them back on. "It's interesting that these last few sessions we've had together seem to generate a bit of hostility you seem to have bottled up. Is there anything new with the author you claim to be cyber stalking you?"

There it is. I knew the fucker would manage to mention L. Blackburn. He's done it in every fucking session we've had since the first one where I mentioned in passing the asshole's aberrant behavior.

"No, Doc, nothing new. He continues to send an occasional suggestive email to my anonymous account like I'm interested in switching sides," I snap. "I'm not sure if I'm more offended by his vulgar and *graphic* suggestions, or the fact that he's obviously labeled me as 'queer-bait' in his depraved mind."

"Hmm," he replies, leaning back and tapping his ballpoint pen against the top of his polished mahogany desk. "Strange that he is continuing with these unsolicited advances you're ignoring. Makes me question what his motivation is if not some reward or satisfaction."

I squirm a bit in my seat, and the body language doesn't go unnoticed by Dr. Benedict. "Well, I've not exactly ignored his emails. I mean, fuck, he's provoking me for Chrissake."

"I see. So how have you responded to this...person?"

"Various ways, Doc."

"Can you elaborate just a bit?"

I sigh, and run a hand through my hair. "The last one he sent was extremely vile. He suggested I wanted to deep throat his cock, and there was some mention of my 'tight little virgin ass,' and what he might want to do to it. He went too far."

"Did you respond?"

"Well, hell yeah," I respond. "What the fuck?"

"How?"

And now I have to own up to my own over-the-top response to L. Blackburn's lewd and lascivious suggestions. "I sent him a digital picture of my virgin bung hole," I snap. "He's probably jacking off to it as we speak."

A slight smile crosses Dr. B's lips as he shakes his head at my reply. "Babu, I need to ask you something here, and please don't respond with your typical knee-jerk reaction when I do."

I nod.

"Have you considered the possibility that you're homophobic?"

"Homophobic? As in I don't like queers?"

"No. In that you have a phobia...an innate fear of homosexuality."

"Why in the hell would I *fear* something like that? I don't fear it, Doc. I simply find it disgusting."

"And yet," he continues, "You seem to be drawn into this homosexual seduction or choreographed fantasy that this individual has created for you—maybe even *with* you?"

"At three hundred bucks an hour, can you fucking cut to the chase here, Doc? I'm simply fucking with the son of a bitch! And let's lose the fucking word *seduction*, thank you very much."

"What I'm saying is that homophobia is classically an internal response to one's questioning of his own sexuality. The fear of admission for whatever reason."

I stand up, grabbing my jacket from the back of the chair.

"You're fucking fired."

Later, after I'm finally within the safe and secure confines of my apartment, I allow Muffy to rub against my jean clad legs, her feline way of showing gratitude for the caviar for which she's acquired a taste by now.

"You won't have to wait on your Tuesday fix anymore, Muff," I say to her softly. "I won't be seeing that quack again. Fucking idiot. You know better than anyone just how much I like pussy, don't you?"

I realize that I could be labeled as certifiable by anyone observing me in my one-sided conversation with a cat. And worse than that, for expecting said cat to affirm my sexual orientation as being totally hetero.

Jesus H. Christ.

My cell rings.

It's Joel.

"Yeah, Joel," I answer.

"How did your appointment go today with the shrink?"

Now why is he asking me this of all days? It's not typical. It's none of his fucking business. "Why do you ask?"

"Just figured you probably filled him in on your upcoming trek out into the world for a full twenty-four hours. Did he prescribe stronger meds?"

"As a matter of fact, I did. He's pleased, really pleased. In fact, his work with me is finished."

"Now that's some awesome news, dude. Glad to hear it. Glad you're finally back. Hey, the real reason for my call is to find out what your costume selection is for the ball. It has to be literary in either author or character, time period is open."

"Yeah, I've decided I'm going as Cyrano de Bergerac. So, I'll need a wig, moustache goatee, sideburns and the sixteenth century garb of course."

Joel chuckles good-naturedly. "You'll have to let me know how many people call you out as fucking Pinocchio," he says, "Don't forget the long nose."

"How could I?" I reply with a smirk, "It's symbolic of my dick after all."

And as Joel laughs at my last comment, something inside of me knows that I hadn't said it entirely in jest.

Chapter 19

I knew it!"

Once I get over the initial shock of having, quite frankly, an enticingly tight ass winking at me through the virtual mail, I jump from my seated position as though the Giants had just won the Super Bowl.

Brent, who is studiously working through some of the lawyer's jargon, gasps and then glares at me. I would not be surprised if he hasn't grown a few grey hairs during the night. I admit, my reaction is dramatic but the victory tastes so fucking sweet, it must be overtly celebrated. I've got him. He wants to make my life a living hell? Well, two can play that game and, frankly, I'm one hell of a competitive asshole.

"What the hell, Larson?" Brent shakes his head as though my victory dance is ridiculous. It may very well be, but I just don't give a shit. Between my office chair and my desk, I'm grinding my hips and circling my arms overhead as though that touchdown were mine.

"I. AM. THE. MAN!" Now I'm singing, and Brent has a look of fear splayed across his face.

"Oh, lighten up, Brent. This is cause for a celebration! Where is the Champagne?" I make my way to the kitchen almost skipping to the beat of my own drum. When I first decided to write, I refused to hole myself up in the guest bedroom where my office was intended to be. I hated being completely secluded. That was when "Operation Living-Office" came about. Brent and I spent the entire day setting up the living-slash-dining-slash-office room. My loyal agent thought it was a crappy idea, argued that I would eventually need a secure space to keep my manuscripts safe from curious, prying eyes. I

95

simply told him to fuck off. End of discussion, and I got my new and improved office. He really is a good friend even though he would rather be with his wife than with me. I wonder if that is grounds for disowning a one-way friendship?

Opening the refrigerator door, I look down at the contents and frown when I notice my lack of Champagne.

"Beer it is, my friend."

I grab two bottles and return to my desk before flopping down in my office chair and sighing like the weight of the world has just evaporated from my shoulders.

Brent takes my offered beer and is about to set it on the dining room table when I tsk loud enough to make him pause.

"Coaster. You know the rules, Brent. Please don't activate my OCD in a negative manner."

Jesus, that just sounded like my mother. Shouldn't I sound more like my dad?

"Has anyone ever told you that you're a pain in the ass, Larson?"

Well, I'm not sure I can actually count that high without a calculator.

"I'm pretty sure you still hold the record for it. That being said, all of the other times it was moaned with satisfaction so I never took it as an insult." My voice is level because, come on—what's so fucking hard about setting a glass or bottle on a coaster instead of the polished cherry wood table top?

"My point is that you need to lighten up. I hear ulcers are painful." My quickly becoming ex-friend informs me.

"Well, then, they'll match your pain in the ass. Then we'll really be BFFs." I wink as I take a swig of my beer, careful not to laugh and spit my drink across my desk. Brent just rolls his eyes and goes back to the lawyer's jargon.

Silly, wabbit, you shouldn't try to have the last word with the master of one-liners. Win number two in the span of ten minutes. I'm feeling pretty good about myself.

"So, what was all that about, anyway?" Right. The email.

"Just a bet I was having...I win." I'm one smug motherfucker, right now.

"Congratulations," he adds absentmindedly.

"Indeed, my friend. If I play my cards right, I could win big time."

I wonder how the literary world is going to react to having Babu's asshole winking at the World Wide Web? Guess we'll have to wait and find out, won't we?

"By the way, Larson, have you decided what costume you're wearing for the Gotham Book Signing? I took a look online for some

of the popular ones, but I don't think Christian Grey is your style."
He's chuckling like an eighty year old grandma who just discovered
her first vibrator.

"Funny," I deadpan.

"Or, there's always Edward Cullen...I think my baby girl has
sparkles in her bedroom if you need any." His whole body is shaking
from silently laughing at his lame ass jokes.

"Are you done?" I don't even bother looking up at him. I'm still
fascinated by the beautiful image on my laptop. What I wouldn't
give to pop that dark cherry.

"SpongeBob is quite popular, too."

Has he been smoking weed or something?

"Maybe I'll just go as a dildo since everyone thinks I'm such a
dick, anyway."

Although, I would stop at the color purple. Fuck that.

"Or a pimp...it would be credible with your attitude," he offers.

Now he's got my attention.

"A pimp...," I mumble, because that could be bold and humorous
all the while giving every last one of them a big middle finger salute
for burning me at the cross before I even got a chance to defend
myself.

"Larson." Brent's voice has a paternal warning to it, like he knows
exactly what's going through my head. "I was joking. Do not pull a
publicity stunt that could have you thrown out of the signing."

Is that fear I smell?

"Well, it can be done tastefully. Maybe an eighteenth century
pimp. Gallant and deadly."

"I don't think they had pimps back then. They had whorehouses
run by women."

He does have a point.

"Marquis de Sade. That's who I'll be. Maybe I'll just walk around
with my dick sticking out to drive the point home." I'm kidding of
course, it would cause a riot and my cock can't take that much action
in one night. I am human, after all.

"Classy and sexy. I like it." Brent stands up and gathers his files
before turning to me. "Get back to writing; we need book two in
editing in two months. You're behind schedule and that's just going
to fuck with your OCD. Remember?" Placing one of the files on top
of my keyboard, he stresses, "Sign those papers so we can file
charges for defamation. Then we'll see what other actions we can
take."

"Aye Aye, Captain." I give a salute without getting up from my
chair and watch him head straight for the front door. Before he turns

the knob, he looks over his shoulder at me and grins.

"You really want to be my BFF, Larson?"

Oh shit. Are we having a moment, here? "Aren't you already?"

I shrug because...well, that's what men do in these sentimental moments sponsored by Tampax.

Brent follows suit and shrugs as well. "Yeah, I guess."

The Larson/Brent Bromance moment was brought to you by Trojan...for his pleasure, too.

Chapter 20

Saturday, April 25, 2015
St. Regis Hotel, NYC
Suite 1102

I glance at my watch for the umpteenth time, the knot in my stomach seeming to enlarge each time I do. With every ticking minute, the time for me to leave the luxurious confines of my suite to mingle with the masses draws closer.

I can do this.

I will do this!

It's five-fifteen. The signing event ended fifteen minutes ago. Happy hour is at seven. I'm starting mine now.

I swallow one of my prescription Xanax tabs with water, and the bright red warning label catches my eye.

Do not drink alcohol while taking Xanax. This medication can increase the effects of alcohol.

Let's fucking hope so.

Noelle, dressed as Marie Antoinette, knocks on the door of my suite at ten after seven.

"Are you ready?" I hear her ask from the other side.

"I can't get this fucking nose right," I reply, totally exasperated after trying for the third time and failing miserably at getting it properly attached.

"Let me in, Babu, I'll give you a hand."

I open the door and she steps over the threshold. As she does, the multiple layers of crinoline and petticoats, along with whatever else is under that huge satin and lace hoop skirt making crackling sounds. I watch as the silvery white cascades of ringlet curls from the wig she's wearing bounce up and down like springs as she glides into my suite.

"Well, what do you think?" she asks, turning to present herself and dipping into a shallow curtsy.

"I'm not sure," I reply, with a slight smirk, "You may be mistaken for Medusa with that wig."

"Hah," she scoffs, coming over to where I'm now standing by the mirror with the uncooperative nose. "No more than you'll be mistaken for Pinocchio by some Philistine I'm sure."

Fuck if she isn't taking her costumed role seriously.

She takes the long, flesh-colored silicone nose from my hand and carefully places it over my own, making sure my nostrils aren't covered. "Where's the adhesive?" she asks.

"That tube on the table," I reply pointing to the left.

"Spirit gum adhesive," she reads from the label. "Let's do this."

Once she has the nose secure, she opens the make-up kit that accompanied it and uses the color wheel to blend the skin tone to match my own. Five minutes later, it's a wrap.

"Voilà!" she exclaims, trying to toss a French accent into it.

Geez!

"Not bad," I say looking at my reflection in the mirror. "Appropriately foppish don't you think?"

"Yeah, it's awesome so get your wig on and let's hit it, Babu. We're missing some prime drinking time and gossip as we speak."

I give her a frown, my fake eyebrows moving with it. "Cyrano," I abruptly correct her, "I'm going totally incognito, remember our agreement, Marie? Call me Cyrano."

"Oui, Monsieur Cyrano, je vous demande pardon."

Fuck. Where's a guillotine when you need one?

Once my wig is in place, I pour another shot of Jameson and toss it down quickly. My second in less than thirty minutes. Fuck I hope it starts to make me relax, or I'll be forced to pop another Xanax.

"Let's do this," I say as I grab the fencing sword that is part of my costume. And mentally, I repeat it three more times.

"I'm stoked," Marie Antoinette says with a girlish giggle. "This is going to be one helluva party."

I lack her enthusiasm, but then again, it might be fun. Especially if I can determine which costumed author might be L. Blackburn. I don't mention that to Noelle, because she has no clue as to the depth of my disdain for the imbecile.

I smirk quietly as I imagine what type of costume L. Blackburn might wear.

Tarzan maybe?

After all, Tarzan of the Apes was a novel written in the early twentieth century by Edgar Rice Burroughs. It might be the perfect costume for someone like L. Blackburn, with his propensity for exposing his junk.

Of course, Peter Pan would be an obvious choice, but then again, L. Blackburn was still pretty much entrenched on Mt. Denial.

We're at the bank of elevators now, and a crowd of people has gathered waiting for one of them to open.

"I'm taking the stairs," I announce to Noelle, as I turn to leave the group.

"Are you crazy?" she asks, her ringlets bouncing as she gapes at me.

"It's good exercise for me since I missed my workout today. Catch you downstairs."

I leave no room for argument as I take off and head back down the carpeted hallway. My eyes search and find the red illuminated exit signs that ultimately lead to the stairwells on each floor.

Once I'm through the door to the stairwell, my breathing once again normalizes. My legs, that had started to turn to jelly, firm back up as I begin my trek down the concrete steps.

Fucking elevators.

Once I reach the mezzanine where the ballroom is located, Marie Antoinette is quickly at my side.

"I swear, Cyrano," she gushes, having imbibed a glass of wine by the sound of it, "you can be quite the enigma, can't you?"

"Enigma is good," I reply, turning my nose up at her. "I need a shot."

"The bar is over there. Will you grab me another Chardonnay, s'il vous plaît?"

Christ. This is getting old already.

"Sure if you promise to sip this one slowly."

She giggles as I walk away towards the bar. There are various clusters of costumed authors standing around. My ears are on high alert, hoping to pick up fragments of conversations that will enable me to identify some of them.

"Did you see how fucking pissed he was this afternoon?" a female dressed as Scarlet O'Hara from 'Gone with the Wind'," asks a male who is obviously dressed as her paramour, Rhett Butler.

"Well shit," he replies, "I mean what the fuck was the dude thinking? No one respects a thief, and plagiarism is theft plain and simple. I can't believe he had the cojones to even show up at this event."

Another woman, dressed as Cleopatra, quickly comes up and joins the conversation. "At least your table wasn't next to his," she complains, "My God, his vulgarity was off the charts by four o'clock, and we still had an hour to go! I don't think he sold more than two books all day. He was on a rant about someone having to pay for this 'motherfucking shit'—his words, not mine."

The others laugh at this. They have to be talking about L. Blackburn. The line at the bar is moving, but I continue to strain to hear more of their conversation.

"Oh, and get this," Cleopatra continues, "He said we could all get fucked. He has no intention of showing up for the costume ball this evening. As if his absence will spoil the whole event for the rest of us."

"Seriously?" Scarlett asks, "Dude needs a wake-up call, I mean shit, he ain't all that anyway."

Rhett pipes in, "He's been officially blackballed by Babu. I think that pretty much seals the deal for him."

"What can I get you?"

My attention reverts back to the task at hand. "Glass of Chardonnay and a Jameson on the rocks, please."

My thoughts drift to what I've just overheard.

So, L. Blackburn is content to lick his wounds, and hide out in his room like the wussy he is. I laugh to myself, picturing the queen probably sprawled out on his king sized bed at this moment, sipping a frilly umbrella drink that room service has delivered. I predict that the highlight of his day will be when he finishes his Pink Squirrel and then proceeds to choke his chicken, blaming the world for this patch of bad luck.

"Here you go," the bartender says, placing the drinks in front of me. I stick a wad of bills in his tip glass.

"Thank you," he says, giving me a smile.

"No, thank you," I reply, picking up the glasses.

As I turn, I see Marie Antoinette waving me over to where she's found seats for us at a table near the front stage. I nod, giving her a wide smile.

Cheers, L. Blackburn.

Chapter 21

Today, I ruined my career. I mean, it was already on the verge of extinction but I managed to throw it off the cliff towards which it was whole-heartedly heading. I'm done.

Yesterday's news.

Sitting, or rather slumping, in the comfortable hotel sofa chair that faces the spectacular view of New York City, I feel only the need to lick my wounds. Quite literally since I cut my finger on a stack of papers that we all commonly call books. How fucking ironic is that? I'm bleeding from my own unsold books.

It's like fate just took my beloved novel and bitch slapped me across the face...twice. For good measure. This is where I'm supposed to learn from my mistakes. The thing is, this shit was not my error to own. It is a fabricated lie that is drowning me in...what the hell is it that I'm drinking, anyway?

I look down at the amber liquid and bring the glass up to my nose. Oh yeah, Jameson. I love that name. Maybe, I'll name my future son, Jameson. "Jameson, bring me my Jameson."

Fuck, I'm pathetic. Where was I in my quest for self-loathing?

Right. I'm drowning.

Of course, maybe L. Blackburn is drowning but what about Larson Black? I could forget about this series and start something new. I can do whatever the fuck I want, right? Maybe go by the name of Lars Black. Lars Burn? Lars B. Black. The possibilities are endless.

Hell, I could even pose as a woman and give a grand middle finger at the entire literary community and its ranks of snobbish assholes.

It could be the Jameson, or it could be that the fight has not left me yet, because I decide that I am not done. I will not drop to my knees and suck Big Five cocks. I won't even suck big wannabe critic cock. That, however, is a lie. I would deep-throat his member and make him beg for the rest.

With every thought that crosses my mind, I feel myself getting more and more psyched up. I can do this. I can go down there, incognito, and charm my way around the hotel. Being an asshole was not to my benefit but getting laid will help with my sour mood.

Standing abruptly and bracing myself against the sudden spin of the room, I smirk once my head brings everything back into clear view. Facing me is Manhattan, in all its glory.

The lights, the activity, the money.

This city can make you, break you or fuck you in the ass. How you survive any of those possibilities is up to you. I choose to fuck it right back using a dildo for double penetration.

A devilish grin makes its appearance across my lips, the reflection of it staring me in the face from the immaculately cleaned bay windows.

I am Larson Blackburn.

I have survived the loss of my father.

I am surviving the disappearance of my sister.

I will survive the imminent emotional destruction of my mother.

But if I don't face the assholes that be, I will not survive the disintegration of my career. So I fight. I fight and I win.

Fuck you, New York. The Marquis de Sade will once again teach you all about being sodomized and enjoying the hell out of it.

It takes me an hour to put on the costume, make-up included. Yes, I said make-up. Men in the eighteenth and nineteenth centuries wore fucking powder and shit. I am nothing if not true to character.

In that time, I succeeded in lowering my blood-alcohol level to a reasonable degree. This means I am quite sober, and that does not bode well with me.

I do not want to be drunk, but I do want a pleasing little buzz keeping my mood in check. With the pasty tint to my normally tan face and the kohl around my green eyes, I am practically unrecognizable. Add the pompous wig to the entire ensemble and voilà! I am the Marquis, and I am ready to conquer this motherfucker.

The faint buzzing of a phone garners my attention but fuck if I know where I put that thing. Last time I saw it was at the signing but the incessant pings from the text messages Lloyd was sending me had me burying it somewhere in a box stacked with my novels.

That man is going to be the death of my sanity if he keeps stalking me like a crazed New Jersey housewife. That thought has me ignoring my phone and heading out the door with my access badge and my newly found good mood.

Tonight I am opting for pussy. I need a soft body to slide up and down my cock, make me feel cherished and loved all while I fuck her with reckless abandon. This contrast is why I cannot give up women. I may prefer men, but women? They are my safe place whenever I feel attacked by the wolves. Maybe it's the innate sense of maternal duty that makes them instantly attuned to our physical and emotional needs. How could I possibly ignore that? I cannot, so I won't.

Sliding my aluminum fleuret into its leather holster, as though fencing were of second nature, I pull my shoulders back and raise my chin. It's party time, baby, and the Marquis is ready to play. Sade was known for carrying both a sword and a cane but I just can't be bothered to deal with too many props.

All I need is my wallet and my key card. The rest stays in my room where it is safe. My prowl face is on, and as I make my way down the hall of my floor where bodies are all heading in the direction of the elevators, I catch the lingering looks of eager women.

Some are dressed as elegant nobility, others as famous authors while a few have chosen the representation of carnal women from the nineteenth century. Those are my favorites, which is fitting since I am incarnating the Marquis de Sade.

In the lobby, after a long, body-filled ride in the elevator, I take a moment to absorb the crowded comings and goings of guests all around. Anonymity is my friend tonight.

Out of the corner of my eye, I notice a couple getting a bit frisky at one end of the bar. The woman, Marie Antoinette from what I can decipher from my position, has her hands travelling all over what must be Cyrano de Bergerac if the size of his nose is any indication. I chuckle to myself, wondering if the size of his nose is any indication to the length of his cock. I have pondered that question on many occasions and no, one does not equate the other, unfortunately.

Slowly slaloming the laughing, drinking and ass kissing crowd, I perch myself on a stool on the other end from the groping couple. I cannot hear the conversation but my overly active imagination is already creating their dialogue from their body language alone.

Marie A. is willing and ready to spread her legs, but Cyrano is more annoyed than turned on. His eyes are darting from one person to the other, his minutely trembling fingers circling his glass in an attempt to calm his nerves, maybe?

In my mind their conversation is going something like this:

"Take me back to the room, Cyrano."

"Get a grip, woman, you're making a spectacle of yourself."

"Fuck me, Cyrano."

"Is this seat, taken?" Well, well, that is definitely not a voice borne from my inner musings. I turn to my left just as the bartender makes his way to my end of the bar.

"It is now, ma belle." My French will be coming in handy, tonight. I turn my attention to the barman in front of me and order a Jameson as well as a flute of champagne for the lovely lady dressed as someone I cannot distinguish.

"Who do I have the honor of meeting?" The shit is just spewing from my lips. This classically beautiful woman is not dressed in elegant clothing but rather is wearing trousers and a man's coat.

"Je m'appelle George Sand, enchantée, Monseigneur le Marquis."

George Sand, of course. How the fuck did I miss that?

"Enchanté, Mademoiselle Sand."

Tonight, I'm taking her to my bed because any woman who dresses up as George Sand is worth my attention. The woman was a legend in her time. Fighting the powers of that era who refused to publish her based solely on her gender. Not only did she take on a pen name, as many did back in those days, but she even dressed as a man, rode horses like the men and probably enjoyed sex as much as them. Chopin, that lucky bastard had known something about that. Nothing and no one stopped her, making her a literary hero in my book. Plus, she and the Marquis were both victims of censure albeit for completely different reasons.

Licking my lips at the prospect of fucking this woman, I take her hand into my own and kiss the back all the while keeping my eyes solely trained on hers. They are a deep chocolate brown with long, natural eyelashes adorning the contours. Rosy cheeks tell me she has already had her dose of alcohol, but her demeanor informs me that she is still lucid enough to make conversation and decisions.

As the glass of Champagne touches her lips, I notice the light gloss painted on them. I immediately wonder if it is flavored, making my cock twitch with anticipation. She is sweet yet the sparkle in her eyes has "vixen" written all over it.

We spend over an hour talking, drinking and flirting shamelessly. George plays coy one minute and sexually cunning the next. I'm not sure if I want to spank her or fuck her at that point. Maybe both.

"Shall we take this party to my room, George?" I like calling her by a man's name. It suits my bisexual tendencies.

"I thought you'd never ask," she answers with her light pink lips pursing into a slight smirk.

I take out a one hundred dollar bill and slide it across the bar. That's how much we have had to drink plus a tip for the swift service. I stand, repositioning my thin sword and extend my hand to my date. As her hand reaches mine, I tuck it into the crook of my elbow and lead her to the elevator banks.

We move in silence, both anticipating our moves as soon as we reach my room. I might even get a taste of her in the elevators if no one is there.

The ding of the opening doors makes me smile.

Almost home.

The music above is a slow ballad from the nineties I can barely recognize from the washed down version. It has been a while since my cock has tasted pussy and tonight, I'm eager to rekindle that particular love affair. Stepping inside, our sexual needs a physical entity in the confined space. I turn to push the button on the twelfth floor and wait for the doors to close.

We are alone, finally.

Right before the elevator begins its ascent, I face the inviting woman and place my right palm on the side of her slender neck, my thumb caressing her flushed cheek. My fingers curl into her chestnut hair as I pull her towards me. Her doe eyes are like an open book. She is excited, willing and turned on, just as much as I am.

I love a woman who doesn't shy away from her sexual desires. It's sexy, and should be embraced by women all over the world. As our lips meet, I back her into the wall opposite me and slam my hips into hers, letting her feel the effect she has on my libido. We both moan as our bodies ignite with passion, the friction of our clothed groins calling to each other like long lost lovers across the rift of an ocean. I'm a fucking poet tonight and if that gets me laid nine ways to Sunday, then so be it.

Just as my tongue pushes between her parted lips, I feel the elevator come to a stop and the doors opening. My hand is still on her cheek while the other is clenched around her hip, tightening their grip at the sudden intrusion into our private little party.

I don't need to open my eyes to realize someone has joined us, an unwanted guest, an intruder...a voyeur. To my surprise, my little George grabs onto my chemise just as I am about to untangle myself from her enticing clutches. I bite down on her lip when the clearing of a throat makes me growl.

"Do you mind?" The man says, his gravelly voice taking over the spaces that just a few moments ago were filled only with the sounds of our heavy breathing.

Releasing my date's plump lip, I close my eyes in hopes of gaining control over my rising temper, and slowly turn to confront the cock blocker. And of course, it would be the long-nosed nervous bloke from earlier.

"Oh, did Marie Antoinette kick you out of her bed, already? I guess the whole size-of-the-nose thing is all myth, huh?"

Cyrano does not answer, his eyes doing all of the talking. By the twitching of my eager cock, I can safely say that his temper is an immediate turn on.

Looking up at the numbers that have started to light up again, I know we only have a couple of minutes before we reach our floor, so I give it my best shot. The somber melody of Chopin's Funeral March overhead makes the hairs on the back of my neck stand straight. How fitting? My life, today, is just one big fucking irony after another.

For some inexplicable reason, the fact that this man has so rudely interrupted my attempts at getting the woman perfectly wet for later just plain pisses me off. I am about to lock my hand over her bicep to pull her back into my arms when there is an abrupt shake of the elevator, and the lights suddenly go out. We are in total darkness, our breath catches in our throats.

"Oh my god, what's going on?" George whispers next to me.

I bring her body flush against mine and whisper back, "It's okay, just a momentary breakdown, I'm guessing."

With my arms wrapped tightly around her shoulders, she relaxes like putty. This is more than I can say for the stranger on the other side of the steel cage. I cannot see him, but I sure as fuck can hear him hyperventilating. Aside from the fact that the man is clearly freaking out, the idea of being stuck in an elevator with a beautiful, willing woman and a complete stranger is the ultimate turn on, for me.

How fucked up is that?

I mean, come on, I'm a guy who has a multitude of fantasies, and here I am with a deliciously ready-to-go woman and a guy who, despite his huge ass nose smack dab in the middle of his face, has all the qualities of an edible man. Before the lights went out, I saw the depths of his dark chocolate eyes boring into mine like he wanted to...kill me?

Meh, I'll let him fuck the hate out of me any day.

But I digress, because right now the problem at hand is that I'm the only sane being in this sardine case, which is pretty goddamn scary when you know me at all.

Before I can formulate a plan where the guy does not die from hyperventilation, or kill us from sucking up all of the air that is preciously remaining in this place, the emergency lights flicker on and a scratchy voice emits from the wooden panel.

"Is everyone okay in there?" Oh yeah, asshole, we're just playing rummy and having a fucking ball.

"No. We are NOT fucking okay. What the hell happened? You need to get us the fuck out of here or I swear to god I will sue your..."

Cyrano is about to lose his shit, and I seriously do not want to punch the guy out because, really, I'm still hoping to live out at least half of my fantasy.

"Alright, Pinocchio, you need to calm the fuck down before you use up all of the oxygen in here. Got it?"

At this point, my palm is forcibly pushing against his chest, and I'm breathing down his neck, feeling my own pulse racing. Those fucking eyes are staring at me with venom and fear; both together are a potent cocktail for my dick's needs.

"Yes," I call out over my shoulder, my eyes never leaving his. "Yes, we're fine, but how much longer before we can get out of here?" I ask, trying to formulate a plan in my head. Numbers are not my thing; I'm a literary being after all. But I'm hoping these are built with a safety feature that allows air inside just in case they do break down.

"We're not sure, sir. There is a technical difficulty we are trying to resolve."

No shit, Sherlock.

I roll my eyes at this, and when I look back at the man, he already appears more relaxed. As though my touch, or my taking control, somehow soothes him. I tuck that little bit of information away, and let a corner of my mouth rise in a small grin.

"See, Pinocchio, it's all good." At my words, the icy glare returns, and his breath begins to draw in shallow pants—except now, he's pissed. I can deal with that much better than his fear.

"Stop fucking calling me that. I'm dressed as Cyrano, not Pinocchio. I see yet another uncultured dick walks among us."

Oh, we are arrogant, now?

"Hey, don't get cocky with me or I'll find a better use for your mouth." I say with a growl.

Movement to my right has me glancing at my date. She is watching us, her eyes full of hunger, and her hand on her lower belly. My hand is still pressed against the guy's chest and the heat emanating from him is searing through my fingers and running up my arms before landing like molten lava at the base of my cock.

Fuck. Me.

"Jesus H. Christ. Not you too," he mumbles and I lose eye contact. Damn it, I can't be the sane person. I'm just not that guy.

"What's your name? And don't lie to me. Your nose will poke me in the eye." I grin as my tongue swipes across my bottom lip drawing his dark eyes to follow the movement. Beneath my palm, I can feel his heartbeat speeding up, and my dick screams his need to come out and play.

Down boy.

I step closer and repeat my question.

"Troy," he says in a barely there whisper.

"Well, Troy, we may be here for a while. So, how about you sit down and relax?" I step toward George and push her back against the wall with my body, my hands braced on either side of her head.

"What's your real name, sweetheart? We need to keep him cool and collected, okay?" She nods.

"Good girl. Now, tell me your name."

"Natasha," she answers all breathless.

"Pretty name for a pretty girl," I tell her because it's true.

"Are you still wet for me, Natasha? Do you still want to feel my cock inside that tight pussy of yours?" At this, Natasha bites her lip and groans out a soft, "Yes."

"Good girl. Well, I want that too but first, I need you to go over there and make him feel good. Are you okay with that?"

I'm still leaning against her, whispering in her ear and making sure my tongue teases her ear while my hand trails down her sides and brush surreptitiously, grazing the swell of her breast. The backs of my fingers slide down her stomach before heading straight to the Mecca. With my hand positioned at the apex of her thighs, I can feel the heat emanating from her core making my hips thrust in her direction. Natasha moans and her eyes look over my shoulder, fixing on the guy behind me.

"God yes."

Oh, fuck yeah.

My mouth crashes against hers, my hands clasping each side of her face. Our tongues tangling, we rub up against each other like cats in heat. Behind me, I can hear the heavy gasps releasing to the beat of our kiss. Never tearing my mouth from hers, I turn us so that my back is to the wall and open my eyes, staring at Troy. His gaze is fixed on us, his tongue wetting his lips every couple of seconds. One look at his crotch, and I can see how turned on he is. Well, at least now his attention is most certainly not on the fact that we're stuck in an elevator.

My hands make their way to Natasha's ass and squeeze her cheeks, kneading them like they are naked and at my disposal. Troy has not noticed my open eyes yet, and for some reason that just makes the whole situation more enticing.

I'm like a voyeur to the voyeur. I moan, inciting a whimper from Natasha and a groan from Troy. I feel like the director, the scene of my making, the ending somehow crucial to my story. Or maybe I'm just horny.

"Go on, baby. Make him feel better." I say as I pull away from our heated kiss and gently push her away.

Licking her lips, she eyes me hungrily before biting her lower lip and turning away from me. I let out a long sigh, palming my crotch hard to calm down my hunger, but it only heightens my need.

Natasha saunters up to Troy and fuses her mouth to his as though kissing him is as necessary as her next breath. The wet sounds, the eager moans paired with Natasha's sultry mewling make my muscles clench. They are directly in front of me, Troy with his back to the wall and Natasha pressed up against him.

With Troy's hands at her hips, fingers digging into her soft curves, Natasha wantonly rubs herself up against him igniting the small space with an electrically potent aura. I am fucking hard as a brick and judging by Troy's open eyes, he is anything but immune to her advances. In fact, his mouth is dominating hers, but his eyes are on me.

Oh, baby, game *on.*

With one hand gripping the rail on the wall behind me, I unbutton my trousers with the other after making sure my sword is stashed safely away. I just need a bit of space for my aching erection before it rips the seams of my trousers. Nope, not a hyperbole.

The heat in Troy's eyes calls to me, tempting me to do the unthinkable. I have no idea if this guy is gay or maybe bisexual, but fuck if I care at this point. If anything, I can play with Natasha and merely fantasize about him. I'm good with that.

I walk up behind Natasha, pressing my covered dick against the crease of her ass, before I notice for the first time that her hand is down Troy's pants, giving him a hand job like a pro.

How did I miss that?

I take my gaze back up to Troy and feel the pull of his stare as my hands land on Natasha's hourglass waist, kneading each side with my fingers, as I slowly push her down to her knees. With this beautifully sexy woman as the only buffer between the tall handsome man and myself, I place a palm against the wall right next to Troy's head and bend my head to watch her lick a trail up his cock.

He and I both groan at the sight, and I have the urge to fucking rip his nose from his face to reveal his true appearance. There is no doubt in my mind that beneath that ridiculous outfit is the face of a man I would want to instantly devour.

"Tell me, Pinocchio, does your nose grow when you're lying or only when you're turned on?"

My dick is now rubbing up against Natasha's bobbing head, and the raspy feel of her chestnut hair is making pre-cum leak from the head of my exposed cock.

"Shut the fuck up," he tells me through a growl mixed with anger and desire.

"Why don't you make me, Troy?" I cannot understand my uncontrollable need to push every one of his buttons.

"I can head butt you and have her all to myself. I'm all she really needs," the man says with a smirk on his lips.

Someone is feeling mighty high on himself, tonight. Funny, that's usually me. "You think so? The question is...is Natasha enough for *you*? All you need to do is ask and I will suck your cock into oblivion. But then, I may never get rid of you." My voice is low, seductive and full of dark promises that I want to fulfill completely.

The small space is filled with the sounds of lust, the music of Natasha's slick tongue and Troy's wet skin. The sucking and swallowing, they're mesmerizing on a normal day but here, confined and trapped, they take on a whole new meaning.

"Dude, I'm not gay." His voice is flat, and his eyes filled with fire. Not anger or repulsion but pure unadulterated lust.

"Your nose is growing," I look down and smirk. "And guess what, Pinocchio? So is your cock."

I am rewarded with a growl that turns my insides into a tight ball of coiled muscles ready to pounce.

"Fuck you!" Troy spits the words out at me as he reaches for Natasha's hair and pulls her off of him before prowling towards me with power in every stride.

I back away, amused, but I don't dare show it. I want to see where all of this anger is taking him.

"I. Am. Not. Fucking. Gay," he reiterates with the same venom. I find myself backed up against the opposite wall with an angry, lust-filled man ready to either beat the shit out of me or fuck me through next week. Personally, I'm hoping for the latter.

"Bisexual, then?"

Troy's hand lands at my throat, his fingers squeezing the air from my trachea. At this point, I should be worried about my life being ended right here and now but because I'm an arrogant bastard, I just keep going, pushing his very sensitive buttons. Taunting him further.

"Can't breathe," I whisper. "Need...mouth...to...mouth." Then I smirk, thinking that this is it, I'm going to die. Natasha's gasp tells me she, also, is afraid for my life but then shit gets real.

Firm lips crash against me as the hold on my throat loosens just an iota and a thick, firm tongue forces its entry between my lips. Suddenly, my five senses are assaulted. The taste of man, spices and pine trees, invades my mouth longingly, settling in every place his tongue explores. The potent scent of arousal that emanates from the pores of the three sexually ignited bodies is like an aphrodisiac in itself. The sounds of slick skin between our battling tongues and the far off rhythm of a hand pleasuring an extremely wet pussy all add to my new favorite fantasy coming to life.

Then there is the sense of touch. My personal favorite. At this very moment, his hand is burning through my skin and making me wish I were completely naked so he could set my entire body on fire. The only sight I have is the one in my mind, my imagination. My eyes are closed, but you better believe that I am filling in the gaps through my other senses.

Now, that's what I'm fucking talking about.

My hands automatically fly up to Troy's head, my fingers gripping his dark hair, surprisingly silky and just long enough for me to add a little pain to our mutual pleasure. His fucking nose is getting in the way so I let one hand go and reach around to rip the fucker off.

"Ow! What the fuck was that?" Troy is now staring at me with watering eyes from what I'm assuming is pain, his hand no longer trying to choke me.

"Damn, that shit was glued on pretty well."

I'm still out of breath and hoping I didn't kill the moment, except now I can see his real face and shit...the olive-skinned, Italian type is my fucking addiction. I lick my lips and keep staring at him as his taste lingers in my mouth. "At least now you're not hyperventilating. And you're welcome."

"That was the hottest thing I've ever seen," says a female voice. Shit, I actually forgot about Natasha.

With Troy staring daggers at me, I can almost hear the enigmatic song of the Western hit representing the final duel. Cue in Clint Eastwood's scowl, and our situation is described perfectly. That being said, I never saw old Clint with a boner like the ones we're sporting. It's hot, if not a bit frightening, that neither of us feels the need to back off.

The last to stand gets to top, I guess.

With each of us at a different corner of the elevator, I look at Troy and take notice of his Roman features. A proud, straight nose, a chiseled jaw made clear by his clean cut. Shapely lips with the bottom plumper than the top. If not for the current scowl marring them, he would be perfection in the form of a man.

I want him, there is no denying this. However, I am not an idiot and right here and right now is definitely not the time. Unfortunately, I doubt I'll ever be able to find him again.

"Natasha, come here, baby. Let's show this man how good it feels to come in public."

Licking my lips as I speak to my date, I keep my eyes trained on Troy, searching for his reaction and any indication that he wants in on this little game. There is none. He is stoic, majestically so. Looking from me to Troy, Natasha smirks in my direction before bringing her hands to her trousers and popping off the button.

"However shall we pass the time in this place?" she asks with a practiced virginal tone.

"Well, George, I just can't seem to decide. So many scenarios and yet so little time." To answer your unasked question...yes, I'm having fun. This is my favorite Kool-Aid: Threesome Berries.

"Would you prefer my hand or my mouth on your cock, Sade?"

You see, a woman who plays coy and then says shit like that is the reason men burn cities for pussy. I chuckle, looking at her now half-naked figure. Long shapely legs, hips made for grasping and clutching while fucking her pussy that is bare but for a small triangular patch of neatly trimmed hair. Oh, the scent of a woman's arousal is the other reason men lose their sanity.

"How about I show Troy here that I am not the gay man he thinks I am but rather," I pause for effect watching as his nostrils flare with frustration, "an opportunist?"

I take a step forward and unzip my own pants before letting them hang from my hips. My long hard cock springs free, and with it my restraint. I wrap my hand around my length and begin stroking in earnest, my gaze never wavering from his.

"You see, Troy...I like to fuck. I like to fuck women and I like to fuck men. I love to hear my name being shouted from the rooftops, and I love to see my cum painted on my lovers' backs. I love the sound of my cock thrusting inside them, my balls slapping against skin. But most of all?"

Again, I pause for effect and hold out my hand to Natasha, inviting her to join me. When she does, I bring my lips to hers and kiss her with unadulterated passion before clamping down on her bottom lip and releasing her. With a brow raised in Troy's direction, I place my right hand on top of her head and direct her to her knees. "Most of all, Troy, I love to watch my dick getting sucked by a hot wet mouth."

With those words, Natasha takes my length between her plump lips and slowly makes it disappear inside her mouth, her eyes staring adoringly up at me. Yeah, I love this. I love giving this power over to the one kneeling. Whether man or woman, this very moment is heaven on earth.

Troy has now cupped his own very visible erection, his eyes fixed on our little show. However, a question begs asking: What's turning him on more...her mouth or my dick?

He moves closer, jacking his impressive erection with one hand, as he kneels behind Natasha and clasps one of her tits with the other, but his eyes belong to me. Even as his fingers massage the creamy swells of her breasts, those black orbs are on me. When his mouth lowers to the back of her neck for an open-mouthed kiss, his attention is on me.

I study him quietly. It's the first time he's seemed in total control all evening. No Marie Antoinette bending his ear while stroking his cock; no Natasha sucking his root because I've instructed her to do just that. This is who he is right now, and he's a man that needs to be manhandled.

That's my job. Not hers.

Our eyes are locked, and I see the slight nod he gives me, allowing his hand to drop from his dick.

"Hold that thought, Natasha," I murmur, looking down to where her lips are angled perfectly around my girth.

She looks questioningly up at me and I nod towards Troy, who releases her tit with one last kiss to the side of her slender neck before he stands and waits for me. His cock twitches in anticipation of how it will feel when my lips and my tongue cover every fucking inch of it.

She gets it and moves aside, resting her weight on her haunches as she prepares to watch the sensual taking of Troy's thick cock inside my watering mouth. From the corner of my eye, I can see her scooting off to the side, her hand cupping her mound and her eyes riveted on the diminishing space between Troy and myself. The air almost crackles with pent up lust the closer we move to one another.

Two dominant males, one waiting for the other to submit. Well, if it means I can teach him the art of sucking dick then, by all means, *Hail the King of Cock.*

Inches apart with our breath sharing the same confined space between our lips, I smirk before placing my hand on top of his. His movements are sure and firm, the muscles in his forearm prominent and manly. "Ever had a guy's mouth on you, Cyrano?"

"Fuck you, Sade."

Well, aren't we rude? But then it's all part of the game when straight men discover their true desires. "Willingly, but first..."

I drop to my knees, glancing over my shoulder at a very eager Natasha whose middle finger is buried deeply inside her cunt. "Let me show you how it's done." I finish right as my lips brush the tip of Troy's cockhead and my tongue slides against his slit. The taste is raw, a man in his prime...all male, all virile.

Damn.

Placing my hands on his hips, I dig my fingers into his flesh and lower my head to engulf his length. He is big, his girth quite the challenge, but I'm all about serving the greater cause... orgasms.

Our gazes lock for what seems like an eternity, his breathing becoming more labored as my mouth slides easily down his dick. Keeping my tongue flat against his hot skin, I moan, knowing full well how fucking good it feels to have that trembling sound reverberate from the root all the way up to the tip.

Once I can feel his head nudging the back of my throat, I breathe through my nose as I swallow, massaging his tip. A shudder runs through his body, and I know for fucking sure that he is about to blow his load because, yeah...I've been exactly where he is right now.

Just as I am about to suck my way off his cock, I feel his hand grip the back of my hair, wig and all, and push me back down.

"Suck it harder, Sade. Make me come in your mouth. All over your fucking face."

Well, let's not get ahead of ourselves, shall we?

Picking up the pace, I can tell his enjoyment is reaching its peak when his head falls back and his eyes close with unadulterated pleasure. Behind me, I can hear the unmistakable sounds of wet pussy being coaxed into a mind-blowing orgasm.

Two hot guys getting it on? Yeah, women love that shit.

Welcome to my fantasy, Natasha.

Speeding my moves, I tighten my grip on Troy's thighs just as his hand pushes down on my head and urges my mouth closer to the base. I push my luck by snaking my hand behind his leg, moving up to his perfectly rounded ass and squeezing the firmness of his cheek while sucking his dick with gusto. When the cotton material of his trousers falls unceremoniously to the floor, I slide my hand to the crack of his ass and probe his puckered hole with a single digit as a stimulator.

"Oh shit. Fuck..."

I love the raspy voice of a man about to come down my throat. I feel the delicate touch of Natasha's hand land on my painfully erect dick, which is begging for attention, as she continues to bring herself to orgasm. Releasing Troy's other leg, I bring my hand to the woman's clit as she kneels beside me, and I urge her to come so that all three of us can find our respective nirvanas.

The moment the pad of my finger connects with Troy's entrance, I feel the jets of hot cum invading my mouth as I open my throat to let it slide down.

Spicy, as I suspected all along.

Natasha's hand job increases in speed and firmness as my thumb mercilessly strokes her clit. Moments later, the steel cage is filled with screams of release, moans of pleasure and the panting breath of overworked lungs. The unmistakable scent of sex, the aroma of the gods, is all around us. I, for one, love that some poor guy will have to come in here and work on the elevator with a fucking hard-on caused only by his sense of smell.

Holy mother of all that is...pleasure.

A banging noise from above has us all moving into action as the sounds of men trying to open the trap door for our rescue registers. How much did they hear?

We dress in record time, doing our best to look halfway presentable. If all else fails, we can just blame our disheveled mess on the cooped up heat of this blessed elevator.

Best. Signing. Ever.

Chapter 22

I open one eye slowly. A sliver of sunshine peeking through a crack in the light filtering blinds feels like a knife slicing through my bloodshot eyeball.

"Fuck," I growl, my mouth feeling like stale cotton. Where the hell is that thunderous sound coming from? My one painfully open eye moves in an attempt to focus on the source, and I see it's my cell phone.

My arm shoots out, smacking it against the nightstand and then sliding it over toward my face. I manage to grasp the fucker, my thumb pressing the spot on the screen to answer.

"What?" I rasp, feeling as if I'm ready to puke.

"Tell me you aren't still in bed," the irritated voice that I recognize as Joel's blasts into my throbbing head. I glance at the clock. It's after ten-thirty in the morning.

"Yeah. What the fuck is it to you?"

"You realize that means you were a no-show at the closing breakfast this morning, right? I mean fuck, Troy, it was scheduled for nine o'clock. What the hell?"

I try my best to sit up, but my limbs aren't cooperating. They're about four cups of coffee behind for the day. "I'm sure I wasn't missed," I grumble, rubbing an eye socket.

"Damn you, Clark is going to be livid. You were going to be presented an award, dumb fuck."

"What award?"

"Literary Critic of the Year."

"Fucckk," I snarl. "I don't want a fucking award, what I want right now is someone else's head."

"Hung over, huh?"

No shit.

"Listen Joel, as much as I'd love to sit here and shoot the breeze with you, the porcelain god in the next room is beckoning me."

I end the call, jump from the bed and barely reach the bathroom before tossing my cookies in the commode. It's only after I hurl three times, flush and then wash my mouth out that I realize I'm naked.

I catch a look at my flaccid dick in the mirror as I'm splashing cold water on my face. Suddenly my alcohol impaired mind clears just enough to allow some images to flash rampantly through the cobwebs, which cause me to freeze where I am, wet hands cupping my face.

I picture a man's mouth on my cock, and I watch as his talented tongue swirls and laps it in all of the most sensitive places. He sucks me roughly, just the way I want to be sucked—not like women blow, which is always just too gentle and too tentative.

This dude sucks me like every man dreams of being sucked. His strong hands are squeezing and kneading my ass firmly. And then he pulls me in deeper just before his thick, calloused finger slides up inside of me, exploring nearly virgin turf, but expertly finding the pressure point and thrumming my prostate perfectly. He sends me over the edge, drinking my load like it's some nectar of the gods as I come like a motherfucker in his mouth. He doesn't waste a drop of it, moaning his pleasure at the same time as I do.

Oh God.

Oh, dude. No. Say it isn't so.

I take a slow deep breath, commanding myself to remain calm, as if by willing it, it will be so. My heart rate ignores the command. My hands are now shaking, and just when I thought I'd puked out everything save the lining of my stomach, I'm proven wrong.

I retch again.

And then again.

I drop to my knees and dry heave for the next twenty minutes, my head now pounding even more furiously than before. Tears are rolling down my cheeks, and I'm not a pussy, I swear. This is too much. This is beyond my comprehension.

I enjoyed what my memory has just played back for me. I enjoyed the chick that was there with us, watching, licking her pouty full lips, her fingers planted firmly inside the folds of her wet pussy, working her clit, and moaning along with us. But she wasn't getting fucked. I was being mouth fucked by some dude who said he wasn't gay.

I mean what the hell?

An opportunist?

Yeah, that's what he said. He's an opportunist. Bisexual, I guess. But I'm neither of those things. I enjoy pussy. I enjoy fucking it, sucking it, licking it, tasting it and smelling it all over my lips and fingertips after the chick leaves.

It was the alcohol, pure and simple. And for that, I have no one to blame but myself. I got hammered because it was so much easier tolerating Noelle and her unsubtle advances the drunker I got.

If I weren't in so much pain at the moment, I would even laugh at how pissed off she had been when I finally got my message across that I wasn't interested in fucking her last night.

It had been my first night out in how long? More than two years, that's how fucking long! I wanted to enjoy it, savor it, and get my nervous ass through it by *myself*. She'd been a wart on my ass all evening and eventually, my alcohol induced rudeness had sent her off to find another 'fucktim'.

But at that point, it was too late. I was well on my way to a bender, even going back to my suite to change shoes and downing a couple of shots of Jameson while there.

That had been my folly. If I had simply stayed in my suite, none of the other shit would've happened. But hell, I had actually wanted to rejoin the social event. Maybe meet an interesting woman/conquest for the evening, so I went to the elevator to go back to the ballroom.

That bloody elevator.

The alcohol and the elevator were indeed my downfall last night. Had it not been for a combination of both, none of the depravity would have happened.

If the fucking elevator hadn't malfunctioned, I never would've been put in the vulnerable position with those two obvious sex addicts. I mean what was the dude thinking sending his conquest across the elevator to suck my dick to calm me down?

Yeah, I've got issues with elevators, but who the fuck wouldn't? I had been accosted and critically wounded in one two years before. I'm dealing with it; I *was* dealing with it until that shit went down!

I get on the elevator, and there they are, groping, grinding, kissing, licking and moaning.

Jesus. H. Christ!

I felt as though I'd stepped through the fucking looking glass and into a porn flick, assigned the duties of key grip (with my dick) and resident fucking voyeur!

Then it breaks down and Sade takes command. The rest is mostly a drunken and fuzzy, albeit erotic, memory of which, yeah, I was a participant, but I sure as hell wasn't the initiator or instigator, nor would I have been if left to my own devices.

Having said that, I realize that this is nothing that I need to be ashamed of—not like *before.* This absolutely was not of my doing. Nothing like when I was thirteen and my stepfather discovered Ethan and me…kissing.

Now that?

Yeah, *that* was something! It was something that I could have avoided because it wasn't like I had been under the influence of anything at the time-well, except for Ethan I guess.

But my stepfather had shown me the light after walking in on us, and I had learned that lesson well. I understood what was acceptable and what was not. He confirmed to me that I was totally heterosexual, and to be anything less, I was condemned to a life in hell.

Who the hell wants that kind of Karma?

Not me.

I flush the toilet again. Splash water on my face and rinse my mouth. What's done is done.

I find some clothes and dress quickly, calling the hotel bellman to take my luggage and hail a cab for me. The sooner I get back to my inner sanctum, the quicker all of these lewd and lascivious flashbacks will be put to rest forever.

It didn't happen.

It was all simply a misunderstanding borne of a broken down elevator and three very intoxicated and very horny adults in costumes.

And with this, I thank the higher power that I truly believe in that I will never have to know or face the other two participants in this sordid, sick memory.

I'm betting as they wake up— or maybe have already awoken to— are feeling *exactly* the same way that I do today.

Chapter 23

I feel fucking fantastic. So, yes, my career is basically going down the drain with every passing hour. My bank account is sending me suicide notes with every returned e-book on the venues and my agent, Brent, is about to drill me a new one for my "uncalled for behavior" at the signing.

On a positive note, I had a three-way orgasm. Sucked a gorgeous man off and got my dick fondled to completion, and all the while my hand was knuckle-deep in pussy. Makes me want to attend all the signings in the country if this kind of elevator ride is an option.

I'm lying in bed, the hotel's standard white sheet is bunched at my waist, and my arms are folded behind my head while I stare at the ceiling with a Cheshire grin on my face.

I love impromptu sexual encounters. It does wonders for my disposition. The early morning sun is streaming in through the gap in the curtains, illuminating the maroon-colored bedspread, telling me it's probably time to get my ass up. Looking over at my phone, I see it's eight-thirty in the morning and time for me to get up, showered and join my fellow authors at breakfast. I might even get an award this year.

Best Douchebag of the Year.

Best Plagiarizer of the Year.

Best Blowjob of the Year.

Yeah, I vote for the last one.

The shower takes me ten minutes, I don't bother to shave since I have a bad case of I-don't-give-a-shit, but I do brush my teeth thoroughly to make sure my breath is acceptable to nearby passersby. Not that anyone gets within fifty feet of me, just in case the phony accusation of plagiarism is contagious.

By nine o'clock I am down in the lobby, following the crowd of mostly hung over guests making their way to the breakfast organized by the hotel.

Usually these shindigs make me want to take two Xanax and a bottle of whiskey to numb the sheer boring factor, but surprisingly, a good blowjob with a hand job to boot can really lift a man's spirits.

Unfortunately, that high comes crashing down at the sight of my ex-wife. And...Houston, we have a problem.

Noelle is heading my way, all prim and proper with a fake ass smile on her face. Fifty bucks says she air kisses my cheeks.

As she gets within a foot, she leans up and...bingo. I owe myself some cash.

"Larson, darling, how are you?" Words that drip like honey but sting like an arsenic-carrying bee are coming from her red painted lips. I smirk as I lean down to whisper in her ear.

"Please, Ellie, don't waste your breath being civil. You and I both know you are basking in my latest scandal."

She shudders at my words and most likely at the proximity of my body, so I go in for the kill. "Did your cunt get wet at the thought of me getting some kind of punishment? Did your inner Christian Grey come out to play? Were you picturing me tied to a cross with you wielding the whip?"

Now, she's panting, actually falling into me when I finish my speech. "You know me better than that, baby. I hold the instrument, I do the fucking." I inhale sharply with a cocky grin across my lips and wink. "Now go change your panties, I can smell your pussy from here."

On that little note, I air kiss a stunned Noelle on both cheeks before making my way to the buffet. Hopefully, I won't be interacting with her for the rest of the day.

It takes me an eternity to get my food. Funny how "free" food brings out the wrestlers in people. I mean, come on, those Eggs Benedict will be replaced if they run out. No need to cut in the line, douchebags.

I find an empty seat in the corner and do what I do best—people watch. I wonder if my little sexual partner will walk in and, if she does, will I recognize her? More importantly, will she know me if she sees me?

After our elevator encounter, Troy fled the premises like his ass was on fire, while Natasha and I took the stairs back to our respective floors.

There was an oversized crowd gathered around us as though our lives had been hanging by a thread. Apparently, faulty wiring in the chute had caused some kind of black out which, in turn, shut everything down. I would like to take this time to thank the gods of bad wiring for an extraordinary orgasm.

Once we were able to extract ourselves from the scene, I kissed Natasha goodbye on the ninth floor and thanked her for making my night a memorable one. She smiled, shyly, as though realizing the debauchery we had experienced was probably being watched by security as we spoke.

It is no secret that elevators have cameras but hell, I don't care, and I won't inform her and make her regret the best sexual high of our lives. I highly doubt we would recognize each other. If I do see her I could always convince her it's me by whipping out my dick, but I have decided to behave this morning. I make no promises for the afternoon; people tend to piss me off quite quickly.

At the front and center of the room, the host announces that the awards ceremony is about to begin. I grin, wondering who will be awarded the Literary Critic award. If by any chance it's Motherfucking Babu, I will commit his looks to memory and stalk him until he admits himself into the psych ward. How dare he try to ruin my reputation without an ounce of valid proof to his accusations?

For three, yes three fucking hours, they laugh, joke and give out awards to authors whose names, for the most part, I have heard but never read. Let's be honest, who has time to read anymore when trying to keep up with deadlines? I may be Indie but those pages won't edit themselves.

Before they get to the crème de la crème award, which is "Best Novel of the Year," clearly not for me, they announce the "Best Literary Critic of the Year."

This is the reason I am here. I have endured their literary version of the Queen's Tea Party for one reason only—to see Babu's face, and maybe even spit in it. But of course, because apparently I have, at one time or another, fucked Karma up the ass without lube, she is running me over with her bus.

Babu is a no-show.

Fucking pussy.

Three hours of my life have passed, and all I have to show for it is a cold plate of hash browns and a watered down coffee.

Told you. People tend to piss me off before lunch.

Chapter 24

Babu's Book Talk

April 27, 2013
Title: A Clown's Revenge
Author: Xenia Cantrell
Genre: Who the Fuck Knows!
Publisher: Self-Published - Duh!
Status: Book 2 in the Revenge Series
Babu's Grade: 1-Star

Summary: A coming-of-age book dealing with a pretty college coed who can't reach orgasm unless her steady boyfriend is fully made up as a clown. This book contains adult content. Age: 18+

The Gospel According to Babu:

Holy Mother of Christ! Babu lost his religion on this one, readers. I finished it, but only because it was a novella, so I knew my torture would be short-lived. But still, it was quite brutal.

The heroine in this story has a clown fetish. Do you know what that means? It means she has to think that a clown is fucking her in order to come. Now, that in and of itself wouldn't have been all that over-the-top, but her boyfriend, sick and tired of having to go through all of the grueling wardrobe and make-up prep whenever he wants some tail, finally tells her enough is enough. He gives her an ultimatum. It's either him, sans clown costume, or nothing. He's gonna walk. So, what does the heroine do?

SHE QUITS COLLEGE AND JOINS THE FUCKING CIRCUS.

The rest of the book was clown sex. Sad clowns, happy clowns, scary clowns, ménage clowns--well you get the picture, right?

Yeah, so did I. And, unfortunately, I've failed since finishing this little nugget of pure clown shit to drink those fucking images out of my mind. Send me some Jameson, peeps!!

Needless to say, Babu won't be reading any more of the series, and my sincere wish is for Xenia Cantrell to receive a hearty dose of revenge—the type that only Montezuma can provide.

Speaking of clowns, circuses and freaks of nature, I spent this past weekend at the Gotham Greatness Author Ball. Of course, since it was a costume event, I was incognito—for the most part. I would like to say that the highlight of the event truly was not rubbing elbows with the plethora of authors (or author wannabes) in attendance, but rather the lovely lady who serviced me with her scrumptious lips in the elevator while it was *out of service!*

Those painted lips made my night—and unfortunately pretty much did me in for the rest of the weekend. LOL. I slept through the breakfast the following day, but am pleased to announce that I was the recipient, in absentia, of the 2013 Literary Critic of the Year Award.

clears throat

I believe that makes it three years in a row?

But who's counting, right?

Babu is simply pleased to be of service to my following of readers, and that has always been the best kind of reward for me. After all, if Babu doesn't keep you from reading the garbage, then who will?

See you all next week with my next review. Don't forget to leave comments, opinions and feedback both here on Babu's Book Talk, as well as on my Babu page on Greatreads!

Cheers!

Chapter 25

As much fun as I had in New York, I was relieved to return to my humble abode. My own personal kingdom. On my way in, I checked the mail, finding a thick manila envelope addressed to me with my lawyer's firm stamped at the top left corner.

The defamation lawsuit was in due process with whatever else my lawyer deemed necessary. I trusted Brent, so I just let him take care of it all, signing the dotted lines without reading the fine print. Or any print for that matter. I know, I know...dumb ass move but I'm an artist. I do not have time for this shit.

Whistling as I put the papers down on my desk, I fire up my laptop before making myself an espresso. Watching the dark liquid fill my cup, I startle at the sound of my cell.

"Blackburn."

"Do you ever look at your caller ID?" Brent asks with humor in his voice.

"Do you ever answer with a simple 'Hello'?" I retort with the same tone.

"Hello, Larson. How are you on this fine day?"

Okay, you sarcastic fuck. I'll bite.

"I'm quite exquisite...at least that's what my lovers tell me." I chuckle when I hear Brent moan.

"Must you..."

"What's up, Brent? It's not like you to interrupt your busy morning with personal chit-chat. And please, for the love of all that is merciful, do not ruin my good mood." I snort, knowing full well that his impromptu phone calls often involve me throwing shit at the wall. Now it's his turn to pause for effect so I take this opportunity to sip my deliciously nutty flavored espresso. Damn, I love this machine.

"No, don't worry. Everything is in place, and all systems are go. Everything is under control."

Famous last words, I think.

"Okay, then spill, I've got shit to do." I'm such an asshole and yet...nope, can't find an ounce of regret anywhere.

"I just wanted to know how the signing went. Should I be aware of any incidents? Did you insult anyone? Please don't tell me you fucked anyone that could come back and bite us in the ass."

Oh ye of little faith.

"Well..." I pause for effect, because, that's right, I'm an artist. "I had to, uhm, explain a few things to my fellow authors. Clearly, they had been led down the path of ignorance and treachery."

"Fuck." Brent breathes out, probably not liking where this conversation is going. "Anyone I should contact?" I can hear him gathering his things on the desk, probably taking notes.

"Not sure...I do recall a certain master of horror scowling at me for my transcendence. I told him his books were well loved with a charming smile."

Brent sighs in relief. Wait for it...

"Right before I told him that the pages are a bit too rough on the ass to be used as toilet paper." I hold back a chuckle, waiting for the Mount Brent to erupt.

"No you *didn't.*"

I think I may have shocked him.

"Oh, relax, will you?"

Poor Brent, I think he needs a raise.

"You are sick, you know that?"

It's my turn to sigh because, yeah, the notion has crossed my mind a time or two. "Look, it all went fine. Of course, I had to open my mouth at some of the more...vocal critics. No one notable, no one capable of bashing my career. Oh wait...that's already done. So, yeah, the only downer was the absence of that fucker at the awards breakfast. I mean, come on, who doesn't even show up to receive recognition? A douchebag, that's who!"

The mere memory pisses me off. I was really counting on his presence to relieve some of my pent up frustration. With hindsight, I'm thinking he may have done me a favor. Orange is not particularly a good color on me. That being said, I could probably make it work.

"Oh, yeah. He wrote an apology for that on his column right after he bashed a poor erotica author. She may never write again, in my opinion."

At his words, I'm already heading for the laptop, typing in

Bluffington and waiting for the search results. "Is that all, Brent?" I want to see this alone. Call it morbid curiosity, but I want to know if he only has it out for me, or if he's just a cruel piece of shit who gets his kicks by ruining careers.

"Alright, I'll talk..."

I end the call with a distracted, "Yeah" and turn my full focus on the latest review.

Brent is right; the poor woman will probably change pseudonyms before ever writing again. And she might write again if her shrink is good enough to drag her out of her depression.

"Jesus Christ..." I mumble to myself before laughing out loud. Okay, he is unnecessarily cruel with his words. There are ways of giving criticism without attacking an author's work as though it created the plague and killed off half the world's population. The sign of intelligence is the use of constructive criticism without stooping to insult the author. That being said...clowns, really?

I continue to read the review, impatient to see what could have been so important that he missed the awards ceremony. As I read the pathetic excuse, I feel my breath leaving my chest just as my coffee explodes from my mouth all over my screen.

What. The. Ever. Loving. Fuck?

It takes my brain a little while to put all the words together to form a cohesive picture in my head. A very familiar image that has kept my dick hard since the New York signing.

Elevator.

Breakdown.

Blowjob.

Woman?

I read the post again.

And again.

A fourth time because really, I must be losing my fucking mind. How many elevators broke down that night? Maybe it's just a coincidence. After all, if our elevator was stuck, all of the others could have been as well, right?

Standing abruptly, I run my hands over my hair as I back away still staring at the screen and reading the key words.

Elevator...blowjob.

What are the fucking chances that not one but two men in the same hotel have their fantasies come true at the same fucking time?

Turning on my heel, I pace the length of the kitchen trying to wrap my mind around this fucking nuclear bomb that has just dropped on top of my apartment building and landed directly in my lap. Or more appropriately, on my fucking dick.

And then it hits me.

If that guy in the elevator...what was his fucking name? Oh yeah, Troy. He was hot. He was completely and absolutely my type. Had he given me the outright gay bottom vibe, I would have fucked him right there and then. That man was my type. There is no fucking way that guy...my type...would be a piece of shit, life ruining, lie telling, literary critic wannabe called Babu, for fuck's sake.

Storming back to my laptop, I read the post again. My head has cleared somewhat, the shock fading just a bit as I try to formulate a plan. I am a fucking planner, and if ever I needed to organize my next actions, this shit right here calls for it in spades.

One thing I will not be doing is calling Brent. There is no way in hell I am dropping this little bomb in his lap. I can hear it now. "The signing was great, Brent, did I forget to mention I sucked Babu's dick in a broken down elevator while a hot chick watched?" He will have a massive coronary and then Marlene will blame his death on me. Shit, she'll probably make me pay for their daughter's upbringing. Shawna? Sarah?

"Fuck!" I really should know my supposedly best friend's daughter's name.

Back to planning. But first, I need more caffeine for this because something tells me I'll be up for a while.

Well, Babu or Troy or whatever the fuck your name is...As suspected, I suck dick much better than any of your whores.

I think it might be time to repay the favor.

Chapter 26

Fuck me.

It's Tuesday afternoon.

I fucking hate Tuesday afternoons.

If you think you're having a déjà vu moment, well the truth is, you are. And I'm right there with you. Sitting in the waiting room of my shrink's office. Oh, not Dr. Benedict. I fired that asshole, remember?

No, I found a new shrink.

A female this time.

Dr. Barbara Dunmire, and this is our first session. She's already poked her head out telling me that it will just be a few more minutes. She had a thick manila file folder in her hands, which I can only presume contains the session notes I authorized her to solicit from Benedict's office.

Finally, her receptionist slides open the glass window and instructs me to go on back. "First door on the left," she says, buzzing the electronic lock on the door from the waiting room to the hallway leading to the offices.

Dr. Barbara Dunmire is probably in her mid-thirties and actually quite attractive in a scholarly way, I suppose. Blonde hair, pulled back into a tight bun, delicate bone structure, perfect nose, which makes me curious as to whether it's the result of good genetics, or the product of a skilled plastic surgeon.

"Have a seat Mr. Babilonia," she says, nodding towards one of the three black, soft leather chairs opposite her desk.

All shrinks must shop at the same furniture outlet. "Call me Troy, please," I reply, sinking down into a chair. "After all, you will be privy to all the secrets of my psyche—it only seems right."

She smiles, briefly raising her eyes from the open folder containing all the fodder generated from my visits to Benedict. But she doesn't have the whole story, because I never gave my former shrink the whole story. Maybe it's time I put it all out there.

"So," she begins, looking up and removing her readers, "I've taken a cursory glance at your file and Dr. Benedict's session summaries, so let me start with making my position clear as it relates to our sessions."

I nod, watching as her eyes bore into mine as if she can visualize my thoughts before I think them.

"You and me Troy? We're going to cut through the crap. I'm pretty good at bullshit detection, and I've got to say, these records from Benedict reek of bullshit. So, if your game plan is to take up where you left off with me, then haul your ass right out of here now. Are you clear on that?"

Alpha chick. That's actually kind of hot.

Oh hell, she's waiting for a response. "Yeah, Doc, I get it, but that works both ways. I'm not here to be stroked. Benedict was a stroker, and it pissed me off. I want a cure. That's your job."

She relaxes back a bit in her high-backed leather chair. Again, the same kind of chair that Benedict sat in. "What exactly do you think it is that needs a cure?"

Here it is.

"My sexuality."

"What's wrong with it?"

"It's confused. I'm confused. I think I might be in denial."

She slides her reading glasses back on, picks up a pen and flips the page over on the tablet in front of her. "Let's start with the denial," she says, her pen poised.

And then I tell her about my weekend at the St. Regis Hotel the previous month. I leave nothing out because I've grown tired of the bullshit and the uncertainty myself. I have to know the truth about my sexuality.

She nods, makes notes, and every so often, she interrupts to ask me how I felt at that moment in time.

"How did you feel when he took you into his mouth?"

"Like it was the most natural thing in the world."

"Did you have a problem reaching orgasm?"

"Not a bit."

"What about the woman who was present?"

"She watched and masturbated."

"You didn't want her to participate in the...action?"

"No. I wanted him all to myself."

"And afterwards, the next day. How did you feel about it?"

"Repulsed."

"Was this the first time you've experienced oral copulation with a male partner?"

"Yes."

"What makes you think you're in denial, Troy?"

"Because I know it's unnatural even though it felt totally natural to me. But the next day I blamed the alcohol, the stalled elevator and even in my column, I made mention of having a hot session with a woman in an elevator."

"I see. Why would you mention it at all?"

"Maybe because I thought *he* would see it."

"Who?"

"Sade."

"Troy, there's something you're holding back. I believe you've been honest here today, but there's something you're not sharing that I think is vital."

A wave of nausea washes over me. "There is, but it's not because I'm trying to keep it from you, it's because I can't verbalize it without becoming sick."

I wait for her to blast me. To order my ass out of her office, but she doesn't.

"Tell you what, how about you put it in writing, could you do that? Sometimes that's more therapeutic anyway. Do you think you can manage that and bring it to our next session?"

I nod. "I can do that."

"Good. Once I have all the pieces of this puzzle, I'll be better equipped to assist you on this journey of self-discovery."

I smirk.

"Yeah, I get that it sounds like canned cheese, but it's pretty much what we'll be doing here. I don't want you to have reservations or reluctance about that, because once you come to terms with your sexuality—whatever that turns out to be—you're going to feel better about yourself. And then we can work on your valid phobias."

"Valid phobias? That sounds like an oxymoron, Doc."

"Touché, Troy. See you next Tuesday."

And as I head back home to my waiting Muffy and my empty apartment, I know I have my work cut out for me in putting my past down on paper so that it can be read silently by Barbara Dunmire.

Chapter 27

I have a plan. Of course, I do. Planning is second nature to me, an easy feat for my well organized brain. There is even a name. FTM: Find the Monkey. Or Motherfucker depending on my mood.

It goes without saying that the man is well hidden, and the fact that I only possess a first name and a horrid pseudonym for the column, did not help one bit.

Of course, I started with the column. Gave them Brent's name because, let's get real, they would have hung up on my ass had I tried to contact Babu/Troy/ElevatorTryst using my own name. It's bad enough I'm an alleged plagiarizer, but add on a stalker label and I would be black balled from ever assisting with anything author-related. I am not suicidal, physically or otherwise.

It turns out Brent is not all that influential. In fact, his name did not even spur pause. I was thanked and asked to leave my number for a call-back. Nothing like a not-so-subtle-brush-off to make a day brighter.

Believe it or not, this was in the plan. Every possibility on my brainstorming chart has a positive and negative outcome. I don't have a Plan B, I go all the way to W.

Yes, I have a chart.

Sue me.

Sitting at the bar separating the kitchen from the living room, I alternate sipping my beer and absent-mindedly snacking on BBQ chips, crunching as loudly as possible. My chart is staring at me, taunting me. There is no doubt in my mind that Plan W will be the winning letter, but I just cannot bring myself to go there. Not yet. I wish not ever...again.

When I called the Bluffington, I asked for the Editor-in-chief, explaining my desire to possibly take Babu on as a client. It was a long shot, I know. It would not be in the column's best interest for Babu-The-Flying-Monkey-Critic to get an agent; their salaries being the first thing renegotiated. But, I am a firm believer in eliminating all possible avenues before getting my hands dirty. Plan W would be my last resort knowing it would take me weeks to clean my hands of the stench, once I got within ten feet of it.

It has now been about three weeks, going on four, since I began operation FTM. Being of single minded purpose, it is no surprise that my writing has fallen away. I'm lucky if I get more than six thousand words a day on the page.

My best friend may find it in him to rip me a new one, but at this point, I don't give two shits. I need to find Babu. There is a saying that goes a little something like this: Revenge is a meal best served cold. At this rate, it will be coming out of the fucking freezer.

Why am I so pissed? I feel betrayed by my own body. The thought that the man's dick was so far down my throat that I nearly gagged on his spunk makes me want to break shit. I am, by no stretch of the imagination, disgusted.

Quite the contrary, in fact, if my permanent erection is anything to go by. I am a modern day Priapus—god of big dicks and hard-ons that just keep on going and going and going. It wouldn't surprise me if my only cure is to sink my cock deep into Troy's ass, fucking him until he realizes his true nature.

At this point I have exhausted pretty much every other option beside Plan W. Tilting the beer bottle so as the last drops fill my mouth, I sigh as I place the bottle on the coaster.

Fuck.

I am really going to do this, aren't I? Glancing at my open laptop across the way, I give myself an additional thirty seconds to conjure up a miracle plan that I may have missed these last three weeks, a spontaneous idea that could save me from impending hell.

I'm so deep in thought that when my cell phone shrieks with a 70's guitar riff, I nearly fall on my ass as I jump at the sound. A quick look at the screen tells me it's Lloyd.

Just what I need, a horny sub with a penchant for deviant behavior. Narrowing my eyes in thought, I can almost feel a miracle idea forming in my head. Lloyd is like a fucking pit bull when it comes to getting what he wants. I know his needs, I can satisfy his hunger and then I can get the information I need. With a devilish grin, I pick up the phone and answer with a tone I personally know will get him hard in an instant.

"Blackburn."

"Larson."

Bingo. The breathless sound travelling across the waves of new technology does not lie.

"Are you hard, right now, Lloyd?"

No need to beat around the bush, it's time to get to the chase especially if this will keep me far, far away from Plan W.

"Fuck," he barely whispers.

"Not an answer, Lloyd," I add with a firm tone.

"Yes, Sir. Hard as a fucking rock."

Topping from the bottom, as fucking usual.

"Watch your mouth, Lloyd," I admonish.

"Yes, Sir."

"What can I do for you? Is there a reason you are calling me in the middle of the day?" I am actually curious, here, since he has strict instructions to not call me, ever.

"Well, now I just can't remember since all of my blood has raced to my cock," he answers in a low voice, probably trying not to be overheard by the office gossips. I am so glad I do not have a nine to five. No doubt I would spend years locked up in prison for inflicting bodily harm.

"Mouth."

"Sorry."

Liar.

"I don't have all day, Lloyd, so get to the point...please." See? I can be polite...when I want something.

"Right. I was wondering if you would be free tonight. A friend of mine is playing at Wally's and invited me to go. You like Jazz, right?"

Lloyd sounds nervous, hesitant, as he asks me out on a date.

"Wally's, huh? I didn't peg Mr. LloydLawyerMan as a fan of small venues. What time?"

Fuck it; I could kill three birds with one stone: drink a few beers, listen to good Jazz and get Lloyd to work. I may even let him blow me in the men's room. Bonus, for both him and me.

"Nine thirty, we should be there around a quarter to nine to make sure we have seats."

And the confidence of the sub topping from the bottom returns.

"I never said I was going, Lloyd. I merely asked you a question."

Silence.

"Right."

Two pegs down, fifteen to go.

"Relax. I'll meet you there at a quarter 'til. Make sure you moisturize your lips, you're going to need them nice and moist to thank me for this."

I hang up before he even has a chance to respond. Wally's is on Massachusetts Avenue, not too far from where I live, so going by foot would be my best bet.

A grin makes its way across my lips as I sit back on my stool and run my hands over my messy hair. Knowing that Lloyd will most assuredly make me a very happy man, I can practically feel revenge envelop me like a warm baby's blanket.

Hell, if all goes well, I might just blow him, tonight.

Watch out, Babu, I'm coming for you. Better get a good pair of kneepads, you are definitely going to need them.

Chapter 28

I down my second shot of Jameson still staring at the blank white page on the screen in front of me.

It's Monday night and there's no putting it off any longer. I see Barbara Dunmire tomorrow afternoon and this is my homework assignment from last week. I'm a writer—at least I've always wanted to be. Maybe I should simply treat this as a work of fiction if I'm to get through it.

I take a deep breath, mentally ordering myself to stay calm and type. Maybe if I compose this in third person, it will serve to distance me from the memory.

No. No more distancing. This is mine. I own it, and now it's time to fucking share it. Doctor/patient confidentiality and all that. She needs this piece of information. I want her to have it; to take it from me and keep it.

I was thirteen that summer. Before that year, the summers always seemed to drag on endlessly, but not this one. This one was going much too fast and for a boy getting ready to start his final year of junior high in the fall, it happened to be the summer of my awakening, or so I thought.

Ethan Miller moved to our neighborhood that spring from Detroit. His parents had gone through a messy divorce, and his mother had taken him and his younger sister back to Evansville to be closer to her family. They moved into a duplex just two doors down from us.

Us being my mother and stepfather. Wayne. My father deserted us when I was just a baby, or so my mother said. I had no recollection of him. Only Wayne. They'd married when I was five years old. That's when my mother and I had moved out of my grandparent's home and into Wayne's. I had been instructed to call him "father."

Wayne was ten or eleven years older than my mother. He worked in a factory as a foreman or something. My mother met him there. She worked in the office at the time. He was a difficult person to warm up to though my mother had no problem with that.

After Ethan moved in I finally had a friend to hang out with. There's not fuck to do in Southern Indiana but, with Ethan, we found things to do. We spent that summer doing normal 'boy stuff' like frog gigging, fishing, camping out under the stars in his backyard or mine.

Sometimes we would sneak out really late and trek over a couple of streets to where Gina and Tina Bradshaw lived--they were fifteen-year-old twins who had developed humongous tits over the past year. We would take turns hoisting one another up just outside their bedroom window to view them undressing for the night, wearing only their panties to bed.

It was one of those hot, humid summer nights in Evansville that we were doing just that. It had been Ethan's turn to hoist me up, and as he did, I gripped the wooden ledge outside of their opened window, hearing the sound of their television going and the soft giggles from within.

"Holy shit," I had said louder than I should have. They were both stretched out on one of the beds, kissing and fondling one another like lovers. They had been startled upon hearing my voice, looking over at their window and seeing the teenaged voyeur brought shrieks of indignation from the both of them.

Ethan dropped me to the ground, and we both took off running into the night.

"Did they recognize you?" Ethan asked once we were safely back in my backyard.

I was trying to catch my breath, bent over, my hands braced on my thighs. "No...don't think so," I rasped. "Dude, you wouldn't fucking believe what I saw them doing."

"What? Tell me," he said, his curiosity mixed with excitement.

"Were they naked again?"

"In the tent," I whispered, pointing up to the open window of my parent's bedroom. We had pitched the pup tent earlier after I'd gotten permission from Wayne to camp out for the night with Ethan.

Once inside, I zipped the screen flap closed, to keep the bugs out. "Okay check it out. They were both naked, and they were making out and feeling each other up, dude it was sick!"

Ethan got a puzzled look on his face. "Maybe they were just, you know, experimenting."

"Experimenting? Are you serious? They're sisters! I mean shit, isn't that like incest?"

Ethan shrugged and thought about it for a moment. "Have you ever kissed a girl?"

"Yeah, sure I have. Last year, Layla Richmond, after the spring concert. What about you?"

He shook his head, looking down at his hands. Ethan had big hands and big feet. It was like the rest of him hadn't grown into them yet. "Naw, never had the desire to kiss a girl. I've kissed boys though."

"Wh--what?"

He nodded. "I like them best."

"Are you serious?"

"Yeah I'm serious. Want me to show you how serious I am, Troy?"

Before I knew it, he had moved closer and his mouth had captured mine. "Just relax," he had breathed against me, "Get into it."

It hadn't occurred to me to pull away much less push him away. The truth was, my best friend had his lips on mine, and was working some magic with them that felt good--damn good. His tongue traced my lower lip, and my mouth responded by allowing him access inside.

Our kissing took on a new tempo; it was almost feverish as we continued, and I felt Ethan's hand now groping my crotch. My dick was hard. There was no denying that.

His hand slipped beneath the waistband of my cargo shorts and he grasped my erection in his hand as our kissing grew more frenzied. I heard myself moan in pleasure and just before my hand found his crotch in an effort to return the favor, the sound of the zipper on the screen flap and Wayne's voice invaded our passionate interlude.

"What the fuck is wrong with you, Troy?" he bellowed, his meaty arm reaching inside to yank us apart.

"You" he screamed at Ethan, "Get your faggot ass out of here and don't ever let me catch you back here!"

Ethan was off like a rocket, heading out of our yard and into the alley that ran behind it.

"And you," Wayne said, his eyes bulging with anger, "You get your ass inside the house right now. Go to the kitchen and wait for me. I'll see to you in a minute."

I took off into the house as he had ordered, flicking the light switch on in the kitchen and waiting for him to reappear. When he did, I swallowed nervously seeing that he had a stick in his hand. It was about six inches long, and maybe an inch in diameter. The bark had been mostly removed, but it still had a few nubs on it from where smaller branches had been removed to make it somewhat smoother. My mind raced as to what sort of punishment he had in store for me.

"I'm--I'm sorry, Father," I said quietly. "It wasn't my idea."

"It sure as hell looked like you were enjoying it, boy. You like the thought of having a man's cock rammed up your butt?"

"No, sir," I whispered hoarsely. "We…we weren't going to do that, I swear."

"Maybe not this time you weren't, but you sure as hell would have eventually. Do you know what this is?" he asked, holding the stick up in front of my face.

"It's what you're going to beat me with?" I asked, the fear now evident in my eyes I was sure.

"Not exactly," he replied hovering over me. "It's a queer detector. Drop your drawers and bend over that table."

I hesitated, clearly confused.

"Now!" he bellowed, causing me to jump where I stood.

"Yes sir," I said, doing as instructed.

And there in the kitchen on that hot summer night in August, my stepfather sodomized me with a stick. Despite my screams of pain that resonated throughout the house, my mother failed to appear and save me from his wrath.

Once finished, he told me that if I were a true queer, I would've enjoyed what he had done. The fact that I hadn't was affirmation that I was not a faggot and he hoped I wouldn't forget that in the future.

That fall, my mother enrolled me in a Catholic school. They were adamant that I would never be around Ethan again. A year later, Ethan's family moved back to Detroit.

I hit "Print" and sit numbly as my printer spits out the pages. I fold them in half, and place them in a manila envelope, fastening the metal clasp so as to tuck away that horrible memory with it.

Chapter 29

A week has passed since I met with Lloyd at Wally's to watch his friend manhandle the saxophone like they were lovers. It was beautiful. A sensory delight that caressed my skin with each passing note.

My tastes in music are quite eclectic, varying from Metal to Classical never passing through the musical vomit our society calls "Pop."

At Boston's oldest and most respected musical bar, there was no doubt the band would be good. I had not, however, expected the kind of transcendent experience that was laid out for me that night.

Lloyd sat next to me, tentatively reaching out every once in a while, to brush his fingers against the side of my thigh or bump shoulders when trying to be lighthearted. At one point I actually rolled my eyes before leaning in and telling him that his high school tactics at trying to get me to fuck him were more of a turn off than anything else.

Truth.

But the music...

I am fan of improvisations, the act a true qualifier of talent and passion. That, mixed with my errant thoughts of Troy and my impeding plans for a face-off, had my dick unsurprisingly rock hard. Of course, Lloyd noticed and without further question, took it as a personal compliment.

A month ago, before the sky fell on my head, it might have been. But last week sitting in that club? Not even a little bit. That didn't mean I wasn't entertaining thoughts of taking out my frustrations on his perfectly tight ass. Yes, I'm a selfish man. No, I give no apologies.

Get over it.

During the course of our evening, savoring the delicacy of a perfectly executed Chase, the back and forth solos of sax and trumpet, I was able to fill Lloyd in on my predicament. No, not the one in my too-tight pants, but rather my desire to seek out a well-deserved retribution. I needed to find Babu, and I needed to find him now.

When a sly grin raised Lloyd's lips at both corners of his mouth, I knew I had his attention. When I explained my suspicions about Noelle possibly being the Monkey Whisperer, the evil glint in his eyes told me he was definitely interested. But when I leaned in and murmured all the ways I would repay him for his contribution, the hitch in his voice was a dead giveaway. Lloyd Ledbetter would do his magic. Then, I would do my voodoo.

Now, a week later, I am not so patiently waiting for the man in question to knock at my door and give me the details.

As a twenty-nine year old Junior Associate for Grant, Mills & Spencer, one of the biggest law firms in Boston, Lloyd is what they call a baby shark, a force of nature not to be ignored. When Lead Counsel needs dirt on the opposing party, Lloyd does the research, works with the pre-approved private investigator and stops at nothing until he finds that special little pearl that kills the enemy. Needless to say, his motto has always been that the end justifies the means. He is perfect for my needs.

Today, looking out the window of my brownstone, I watch as couples and families make their way down the neatly lined sidewalks to their respective destinations.

I'm anxious, wondering if my plan will come to fruition, if my Ace will give me the winning hand. I have spent the last week writing non-stop, playing catch-up with my lost word count and getting ahead for the time I know I will be spending travelling to New York. Though I still don't know for sure, I am willing to bet a small fortune that Troy lives there.

Just as I am about to doubt the entire plot of my life story, a rap at the door disturbs my musings. This is it. The moment of truth and possibly retribution.

Dressed in my dark grey sweatpants and a snug fitting black tee shirt, I walk my bare feet to the entrance, anticipation growing with every step. Opening the door just enough for my body to block the entryway, I rest a palm on the frame and give a freshly showered Lloyd my best boxer brief-melting grin. A quick glance to his crotch confirms my suspicions.

No need to deny my effect on the man.

"Lloyd." Yes, I go for the kill with the tone he so loves.

"Sir."

God, I hate that title but fuck, I'll endure it if it gets me what I need. Stepping away, I let Lloyd come inside and close the door before turning and waiting.

"So, what do you have? You sounded pretty damn proud of yourself on the phone." Then again, when was this man *not* self-absorbed? What? It takes one to know one.

"If you had any doubt about my abilities, you never would have asked me to help you."

Truth.

"Okay, let's see it." My body is practically vibrating with anticipation, eager to have the information, fucking ecstatic to get Troy-Fucking-Babu in a delicate situation. I still do not know which course to take once I face the man, but either plan is incredibly enticing.

As usual, Lloyd is wearing a stylish charcoal-colored suit paired with a button down shirt that pops. Today it is vivid dark blue when other days it varies from deep pink to maroon, sometimes even a pale yellow that competes with the noon high sun.

In the middle of my living room, Lloyd turns almost theatrically as his right hand opens the lapel of his jacket, while the other fishes inside for what I am assuming is my precious detail. The wolfish grin plastered to his classically handsome face completes his fashion statement.

"Lloyd," I warn, my patience waning with every one of his attempts at drama.

Holding a sheet of paper between his forefinger and thumb, he slowly walks in my direction. I have not yet moved, leaning casually against my front door, hands in the pockets of my sweatpants and my legs crossed at the ankle. Calm on the outside, about to beat the shit out of him on the inside.

"Here you go, Sir. Name, address, social security number and list of sexual partners."

My eyes shoot to the paper and then back up to see the satisfied look on Lloyd's face.

"You got his sexual history? What the fuck, Lloyd?"

I'm playing for indignation here but really...my curiosity is beyond peaked.

"I'm kidding, but judging by your reaction, maybe I should have dug deeper. My reward would have been greater."

Fucking greedy lawyers.

"Give me that paper and shut the fuck up." I wink to lessen the blow, my voice not too harsh. Snatching the information out of his fingers, I unfold the note and grin as I read his address. New York City. Of course, it is.

"Now, about that reward, Larson...," he says seductively as he slides his jacket off his shoulders and tosses it on a nearby chair.

My glare follows the path, hoping for his sake it doesn't land on the floor. When I'm satisfied to see my home is not a war zone three minutes after Lloyd's arrival, I turn my head to face him once more with my eyebrow raised in question.

"Are you making demands, Lloyd?" I ask in a stern voice.

"No, Sir."

"I think you were." I push off the door and stalk up to Lloyd whose gaze is fixated on me.

"No, Sir. I was just nudging you along."

Topping from the bottom. This is why I could not handle being a lifestyle Dom or Master. I'd kill my subs for pissing me off on a regular basis. OCD and all that shit.

"Hmmm," I make my way past him, brushing my shoulder against his before stopping right at his level and turning to look at his profile. "I'll fuck you when I'm damn well ready. If you can't wait, you know where the door is."

Before I walk away, I brush my hand against his erection and smirk.

Fucking subs.

"Do you want a drink?" I ask while making my way to the kitchen. I need a beer, and oddly enough sex is the last thing on my mind. I may have to reschedule with Lloyd; I would hate to disappoint him with a less than worthy performance. For some reason, the constant thought of Troy on my mind is ruining this potentially hot sexapade with Lloyd.

"Yes, I'll have a glass of wine, thank you."

Of course. Wine.

"I have beer or water."

"Uhm...," Lloyd turns to me with a frown as though I have just asked him to solve the issue of global warming lest the world spontaneously combusts in the next twenty seconds.

"Beer or water, Lloyd, it's not rocket science."

Jesus.

"Water?"

"Is that a question?"

"No?"

"Fucking hell, Lloyd, my hard-on is vanishing with every one of your ridiculous comments."

I fill a glass with water from the tap and pray it doesn't taste like bleach before I hand it to him.

"We're not having sex tonight, are we?" Lloyd suddenly blurts out.

I pause, think on it and then sigh.

"No, I don't think we are," I answer truthfully just like my mother taught me.

"Are you in love with him?"

I spit my beer all over the counter and glare at my ex-lover. That's right, after his little bomb shell, I'm erasing his number from my cell.

"What the fuck are you talking about? I don't even know him. Just because I blew him in an elevator doesn't have shit to do with emotions, Lloyd. Jesus, have you been reading Fifty Shades of Gay again?"

Running a paper towel across my lips before wiping down the counter, I curse under my breath at the ridiculous notion.

"You're obsessed with this man, that's a sure sign."

My glare returns on Lloyd, my scowl firmly in place. "Don't be ridiculous," I scoff.

Obsessed?

I love hyperboles but not when used against me.

"He's going to hurt you, you know?"

Alright, I've had enough.

"Lloyd, get the fuck out of my house. Call me when your mind has returned to its normal functions."

Anger is welling up from deep inside my gut at his preposterous accusations, his need to keep pushing the subject and the all-around stupidity in his conclusions.

"Larson, come on. I'm just trying..." he doesn't get any further.

"Get. The. Fuck. Out." Burning a hole through him with my stare, I take a step towards him as he takes one step back.

"Fine," he says as he pulls back his shoulders and raises his chin, "but don't say I didn't warn you." Stomping out after quickly grabbing his jacket, Lloyd is gone after only arriving fifteen minutes earlier.

When the door slams behind him, I take my beer bottle and throw it against the nearest wall, watching as the burst of glass splashes against the ivory tiles.

Fuck him.

Love...what the fuck ever.

My goal has nothing to do with feelings and everything to do with teaching the guy a lesson.

Sighing, I gather the necessary tools to clean up my mess knowing

I wouldn't get a wink of sleep if I left the mixture of beer and glass all over my kitchen.

Tomorrow is a new day and, with it, will come the pleasure of getting the last word with Mr. Babu the Bully.

Chapter 30

Babu's Book Talk

May 26, 2013
Title: Black Dahlia
Genre: Zombie Erotica
Author: Leslie Roper
Publisher: Crestmark
Status: Book #1 in the "Zombies in Love Series"
Babu's Grade: 2.5 Stars, Rounded Down to 2

The Gospel According to Babu:

Leslie Roper started out as a self-published Indie author, and one of the few that I actually felt possessed some innate talent. Very gifted in her writing style and technique, and her debut novel, "Unfeasible" was a riveting crime/suspense/mind fuck novel involving corporate espionage with twists and turns that surprised even me.

One of the very few who I had given five stars to that year.

Afterwards, I naturally received the usual stroking, and sucking-up if you will, from this up and coming author, along with a flurry of seductive *tweets*—reaffirming just how talented and creative this lady can be. There is—or *was*—no stopping her.

Of course, Babu doesn't cash in on those thinly veiled

invitations to pussy dive. I mean, seriously? Besides that, I sensed this person has been struggling with her own sexuality every bit as much as L. Blackburn has been with his.

Birds of a fucking feather.

Fast forward to Black Dahlia and the invitation I received from her agent to review the ARC. Being the compassionate and altruistic individual that I am, I agreed to review it and actually looked forward to it, being that she has now signed with a traditional publisher, which validates her as an aspiring author IMO.

So, Babu is always honest, right?

Herein lies my dilemma.

The fact that I was an ardent fan of Ms. Roper's debut novel doesn't give her a free pass to receive Babu Accolades going forward.

She knows my power within the global reading community and, though she imagines this warm cuddly relationship exists between the two of us, Babu needs to give her a dose of reality. She is, after all, a resourceful lady clawing her way to the top. I get that, but unfortunately, her creative resources seemed to have dissipated since self-publishing her one-hit wonder a couple of years back.

The ARC for this book was quite frankly, detestable.

Plot: ZOMBIES in LOVE??

Seriously dude?

Holy fucking hell!

And not only do we have zombies, but we have zombies in outer space, zombies under water, zombie warriors in terrorist training camps. Now the Black Dahlia variety of zombie is unique in that instead of eating people, this zombie eats the sexual organs and leaves the rest to rot. By doing so, this particular brand of zombie can feel love and conceive baby zombies who are then born as pansexuals within their mating ritual. Ms. Roper wrote the mating ritual between these creatures in love in such a way that I prayed for a cerebral hemorrhage in order not to have to finish this pile of zombie shit.

According to zombie pansexual law, they'll have the ability to fuck anything animal, vegetable or mineral and procreate.

I mean WHAT THE EVER-LOVING FUCK?

So, as usual, Babu leaves you with this one last thought. I took one for the masses with this read. I implore you to heed my warning and avoid these zombies as one would avoid the Black Plague!

See you all next week! Don't forget to give me shout-outs, the usual stroking, and for Chrissake don't forget to show me the love on Babu's Book Talk and on my Greatreads page!

Holla!

I publish my column and then quickly head out to my appointment with Dr. Dunmire. It's been a week since I handed over my written summary of the events that took place when I was thirteen.

In all honesty, Barbara Dunmire reacted with compassion and utmost tact after reading what I handed her. She had not appeared shocked or judgy and, thank God, she hadn't regarded me with pity. That would've been a show stopper for sure.

Today, she only keeps me waiting briefly before bustling in with my thick, over-flowing file and taking her seat across from me.

"Well, Troy, I think after last week's session and with the notes I've taken, we are in a great position to discuss the present. I get the pain and confusion you endured at the hands of your stepfather. It was despicable, and I regret that you had no other adult, in particular your mother, who intervened on your behalf. But that's in the past. We need to discuss how it affects the present, and ultimately, your future."

"You make it sound so fucking simple, Doc."

"Well...don't you think you've had enough pain as a result of it yet?"

"Well, yeah, but what does that have to do with resolving this?"

She looks at me.

Hard.

"Because it's time you let yourself off the hook here. Whatever you did—whatever you felt with Ethan? It wasn't wrong, Troy. It was *you* at that moment in time. It was you exploring or maybe even *discovering* who you might be. At thirteen, it's all about self-exploration and realization. But the bad thing is that your self-exploration was cut short. And as a result, you were made to feel guilt, anger, frustration, regret and probably a whole lot of other random emotions you simply were not prepared to deal with."

"So what exactly are you saying?"

She leans forward, clasping her hands together on top of her desk, choosing her words carefully. "In candid terms? I'm saying that it's still up to you to define who you are—sexually speaking. As your therapist? Well, as your therapist for only a short amount of time, I will stake my reputation on the fact that once you do come to terms with your sexual preference and *accept* it, you will finally be at peace with that portion of your life. Then, you can and will go forward with less baggage than you have at the moment."

"Let me get this straight, Doc, if I'm reading between the lines here, I think what you're prescribing is *experimentation*?"

She shifts in her seat. "Isn't that what you've been denying yourself for the past twenty years? Tell me this, Troy, how many intimate relationships have you had in that time?"

"Dozens, but to be honest, mostly one or two nighters."

She laughs softly. "No, you're talking sexual. I'm talking intimacy—knowing the person you're with inside and out. Sharing confidences, being sensitive to their emotional needs; their dreams and fantasies, along with their fears and insecurities."

"Why would I want that?"

She looks over at me, removing her reading glasses, and placing them on her desk, "Trust me, once you've experienced real intimacy, you'll have the answer to that question."

"So Muffy," I say, stroking the purring cat in my arms, "at the risk of sounding rude, I've got to send you on your way. I know how you hate to eat and run, but I've got an important call to make."

She squirms in my arms, hearing her owner calling for her down the hall. As I place her on the floor, she dashes over to the door of my apartment.

"Muffy's coming, Ida," I call out, opening the door.

"Well hi there, Mr. B. Loved your column this week. Zombies, indeed!"

"Thanks, Ida. Glad you enjoyed," I call after her, as Muffy scrambles down the hallway toward her own apartment.

I relax on my sofa, grabbing my cell and pushing Linc's number.

"What's up, Chief?" he answers. "Who you need to make magic with this evening?"

I pause, swallowing hard, "I need someone different, Linc. I need you to send over a man."

Quiet.

"Linc?"

"Yeah, yeah, Chief. Hey, s'all good man. It may take me just a bit to…uh…locate someone fitting your needs this evening."

"You do understand discretion is paramount on this, right?"

"Oh, absolutely my man! And don't worry, Linc always supplies quality and cleanliness in the dates he arranges for his top clients such as you. It just may take me a little longer to check availability."

"Have him here by eight, Linc."

End Call.

I grab a sandwich and check my column for messages, comments and the normal condolences I get after coming off a shitty read.

Yep. All there.

I chuckle as I scan through them, and then notice it's after six, so I hit the shower. Once finished, I towel dry my hair and pull on a clean pair of boxers. That's all the clothes I plan on putting on since it's almost seven, and my date for the evening should be here within the next hour. I figure with a dude showing up, less need for chit chat and foreplay. We'll just get down to it. My cock actually twitches in anticipation.

I pour a shot of Jameson and toss it down.

And then another.

The potent amber liquid is slowly soothing my nerves, and relaxation is finally seeping into my body, warming me and chasing away any remnants of uncertainty.

I pour one last shot and relax on my soft leather sofa. My hand slips beneath the elastic waistband of my boxers and I massage my semi-erect cock into full erectile mode.

Nothing here to be ashamed of by any means. So far, my cock has pleased many a pussy, and undoubtedly delighted one man's mouth. I sigh at the memory, and my dick has now turned to granite at the recollection. I feel the grin as it spreads slowly across my face, and my tongue flicks over my bottom lip as the picture of Sade remains imprinted on my brain.

Powdered wig. Face made up to look like some eighteenth century dandy. But the wig, make-up and costume in no way masked the talent of that man's tongue and mouth, or the expertise with which he delivered the best motherfucking blowjob I've ever had the pleasure of receiving. My legs had turned to jelly; my heart rate had skyrocketed. My load had shot out like Mount Vesuvius into his waiting mouth, and he'd swallowed every fucking drop, while licking his full, sensual lips.

I stand up, dropping my drawers, fully prepared to take matters into my own hands while waiting for my date. Hell, I still have a half hour to go. Might as well clean the pipes before he gets here. And I'm doing just that when I'm startled by the loud pounding on my door.

Jesus H. Christ.

Someone is eager for the festivities to begin.

I chuckle softly, as I move my naked body toward the door of my apartment, still stroking my member.

Nothing quite like getting things off to a climactic start...

"Coming," I holler, unbolting the locks. "You're early."

Chapter 31

Well, well, well...Best. Welcome. Ever.
Let's rewind, shall we?
I spent four hours driving to New York City. Four hours to think about my course of action. Four fucking hours to rehash the things I was going to say to him, making him feel an iota of the pain authors are submitted to every time he spews his verbal diarrhea across the pages of the Bluffington Gazette. There comes a time when honesty and cruelty blend together, and this shit needs to stop.

Before I left, I did a check of his column since it was review day for Babu. Of course, his words only spurred me on to continue with my plans. I have to admit, that whole Zombie shit sounds like utter vomit, but there is an elegant, constructive way of criticizing, insults utterly unnecessary.

By the time I made it through the horrendous traffic in New York, where I congratulated myself for not living here anymore, I spent another forty minutes trying to find a parking space that wasn't clear across the island of Manhattan but still in the vicinity of his apartment.

As my steps neared Troy's home, my anger gradually rose, my internal speech growing more violent by the second. Checking the paper Lloyd gave me, I looked up to see the building number, verifying that I had indeed arrived at my destination. My nerves were on high alert, my head throbbing with rage and my adrenalin levels sky high.

Clenching my fists to avoid punching a wall, I took a deep breath as I crossed the expansive space of the main hall before reaching the elevators. The building was nice, not Hollywood-stars kind of nice, but warm and inviting. Pressing the call button, I waited rather impatiently for the elevator to make its way back down to the ground level, before the doors slid open and I walked in. I was so close to getting my revenge, to giving him a piece of my mind. Maybe, even, getting a few punches in to drive the point home. Then, I planned on pushing him to his knees and shoving my cock inside his mouth before emptying my balls down his throat.

Fuck.

That's when my cock came alive and threatened to burst through the zipper of my slacks.

First things first...

Exiting the elevator at Troy's floor, I looked right then left before deciding to turn right toward his apartment. Standing there in silence, I took a deep breath and counted to three before lifting my fist and pounding on the door like a ravaged beast.

Bang. Bang. Bang.

And that's when the angels of lust descended upon me, singing "I Want Your Sex."

Don't judge. George Michael got many a boy laid in his day.

So, here I am, robbed of all of my best attacks when faced with a very attractive, very naked and oh so very aroused, Troy Babilonia.

I'm going to take a wild guess here and say Troy was expecting company. Or maybe he is just a nudist. Allergic to clothing? It does not matter, believe me, because being greeted by a magnificent cock proudly saluting like it's the Fourth of July makes me want to sing the Star Spangled fucking Banner.

Oh say can you see?

I lick my lips as Troy's perfectly sculpted body is on grand display right in the middle of his apartment entrance. What I could not fully see in the elevator that night was the etched muscles of his abs, the thin trail of hair that leads to the Promised Land, the slight swelling of his pectorals, flexing as Troy grips the wooden door. As my eyes travel further down, my mouth fills with saliva, practically drooling at the corners with the need to taste him again. Clearing of a throat snaps me out of my fantasies and brings me back to the task at hand.

Before I can say a single word, the beautifully naked man sighs in frustration and steps away from the door, allowing me to make my way inside. "Eager little fuck, aren't you? I was about to get some pre-game done, figured it would help make the night last longer. Come on in. Gotta love Linc. He always comes through for me in a pinch."

I snicker as I brush past him, surreptitiously inhaling that spice and pine needles scent I've been jerking my cock to for the past month.

What? My libido has needs.

"Drink? I've got beer, wine or Jameson," he asks with a nervous lilt to his voice.

I have to admit, I am a bit confused here. Barely thirty days ago, this man was adamant about his lack of homosexual tendencies. Tonight, he is walking around naked, mind you, obviously waiting on a date of the male variety. Luck would have it that I showed instead of the guy he originally expected.

"I'll have two fingers of Jameson. Thank you," I answer as I look around his apartment. It's nice, it's neat and it is devoid of anything feminine.

Thank fuck.

My gaze follows him to his quite modern and surprisingly large kitchen, eyes riveted on his delectable ass. I go instantly hard at the thought of sinking my teeth into those cheeks right before I ram him with my dick. Repeatedly. And for long, mind-blowing hours.

"What's your name...or pseudo? Whatever you prefer?"

I blink at the question for two reasons. I first realize he has probably hired someone for the night. Also, what the fuck am I supposed to say to that?

Oh, hey, I'm L. Blackburn and I've come to remind you of who was sucking your cock in New York. And it wasn't a woman!

"Uhm...Sonny. Just call me, Sonny." Not really a lie. When I was in elementary school, my sister Kennedy used to call me Sonny. For about two weeks. Larson...Son...Sonny. She would later explain that she was experimenting with nicknames.

The familiar pang of her loss momentarily makes my heart skip a beat and my gut wrench in knots, but I breathe it down and away. My attention needs to be on the here and now.

"Sonny, it is, then," he answers as he finishes serving the glasses of scotch. "Let's lay down the rules here, shall we?"

By all means, Troy...let's get down to business.

"Can I get your name, first?" I ask, playing the game of the hired whore. It's like role-play; I like it and apparently so does my cock.

"Troy," he turns as he answers, giving me a quick glance then pausing for a moment before asking, "Have we met, before? Your voice sounds familiar."

It's my curse, my voice has made many men and women weak in the knees and wet with want. "Not that I can recall." If I stretch it, I can still claim the truth. Officially, we have never met.

Placing the glass half-filled with amber liquid on the kitchen island, Troy stands unabashedly naked as he begins stroking his fully erect cock. Mine twitches in response, making my blood course through my veins.

Closing the distance between us, I reach the counter and wrap my fingers around my drink, bringing it slowly to my lips and letting the strong taste of scotch fill my mouth then my throat. Our eyes never drift. Our gazes never falter. Our cocks are twin fuck sticks ready to be put to use.

"Strip," Troy finally commands, breaking the heavy silence between us. For a second I don't move, ignoring his dominant order.

FYI, a submissive I am not.

"Say please," I retort, noticing Troy's nostrils flaring with indignation and lust all mixed together. Looking at the curve of his mouth and the evident scowl that mars them, I know deep in my gut that my subordination is a challenge he is going to enjoy. With one last gulp of his drink, he carefully places his glass on the counter, sans coaster, and roughly grips his cock. My eyes automatically wander to his crotch, the pre-cum calling to me.

"Strip, now, Sonny. And if you're good, I'll let you suck my dick."

Now, he's just teasing me. Licking my lips, I let my eyes slowly make their way up his tight abs, his heaving chest and the pulsing artery along his neck to finally rest on his infinitesimally parted mouth. The signs of desire are all present, even without the obvious one between his thighs.

But my favorite?

The heavy breathing. I love to feel the warm air escaping a lover's mouth at that moment when he needs to fuck as much as he needs to take in oxygen.

Sliding my tongue along my bottom lip, I nod before emptying my own drink and placing the glass in the kitchen sink. I turn back, lean against the marble surface and begin to slowly unbutton my slacks.

I made a conscious effort to dress nicely tonight, wearing a black pair of pants with a white button down, sleeves rolled up to my elbows. It's a sexy look, I know. Not at all insignificant. The faint rasp of a zipper attracts Troy's eyes to my crotch, to my cock springing free. Surprise...Commando, baby. If I hadn't been staring at his eyes, watching for a reaction, I would have missed the slightly dilated pupils, and the quick dart of his tongue.

"Looks like you want to be the first to do the honors," I say in my husky voice as I shake my cock, letting it slap against my lower stomach. "By the way you answered the door tonight, I'm surprised we're moving this slow."

I would seriously hate to come from his mere proximity, but all of the conditions are reunited for another sex-filled hiatus. The heady scent of male pheromones surrounds us in swirls of lust, the presence of two exposed cocks teasing us, the only sounds our quickly accelerating breathing.

"Come here, get on your knees," he says almost in a whisper, as he seeks support from the kitchen island, leaning against it. "I want to fuck your face."

Well, a month sure as hell got his dirty talking abilities to come to the surface. In that moment, I wonder if our little aparté had anything to do with his newfound love of cock. My ego would dare hope.

For old times' sake I oblige, letting my pants fall to the floor and stepping out of them. Normally, at this point, I would bend down, pick them up and neatly fold them before placing them somewhere safe. For some incomprehensible reason, that desire is nowhere to be found. My sole purpose is to please the god-like male before me.

When I reach him, not even a foot away, I meticulously unbutton my shirt and let it fall away from my shoulders, placing me on equal naked footing. Dropping to my knees, my hands sliding down the sides of his hot skin, I raise my head and stare intently up at Troy. As my tongue flattens along the underside of his shaft, licking a straight line right up to the head of his cock I finally close my lips around it and suck masterfully for three beats of a heart.

Troy hisses his approval; I moan at the addictive taste. Fleetingly, I wonder...who will be doing the fucking tonight? When I showed up at his doorstep, my intention was to fuck up his life. Now, kneeling before him with my mouth teasing his dick, I'm pretty sure my life will never again be the same.

Fuck.

Chapter 32

My head is tilted upwards, my eyes closed, as I rock back and forth a bit on my heels, totally lost in this perfect sexual nirvana. Sonny—a fake name I'm sure—knows how to suck cock. No. That's an understatement. This man knows how to mouth fuck like he invented the process.

While I'm sure he can't claim that honor, I am certain that he has indeed perfected it. His expertise is evident. He loves sucking cock. I love the way he's sucking mine.

It's epic.

It's custom.

It's even better than the blowjob I received from Sade that night in the stalled elevator. The night that certainly started the ball rolling with my new therapist, and thus this experimentation.

It appears that denial had been on my agenda. Oh, I had suspected as much before, but quickly dismissed those inklings as being non-productive. I mean, it wasn't as if I couldn't climax with females, because clearly I had many, many times. I simply preferred avoidance I suppose, and how well had that worked out?

But I can't think about that now, because every pull of my cock by Sonny's delicious mouth, every swirl over the head, and every nip of the sensitive skin on the crown is bringing me so fucking close to blowing my load.

I hear the involuntary groans emanating deep within me. "Oh *God,*" I murmur thrusting my pelvis just a bit because I'm ready for him to devour me.

"Nope, still Sonny here," he says, taking his mouth from my shaft momentarily. "But thanks for the compliment."

He resumes his position, sucking me roughly, and I know I'm ready. Is he a swallower? I mean we didn't discuss that, and maybe it is something that we should have established from the get.

Would it kill the mood if I brought that up right now?

I peer down at him through shuttered lashes. His dark blonde hair is mussed, but it gives him a rakish, sexy look. His green eyes lock with mine and it's as if my heart flutters in that moment. For the first time, I'm overwhelmed with the need to please this guy. That's not happened with any of the other dates Linc has arranged for me.

I make a mental note to mention that to Barbara in our next session.

Fuck I'm gonna blow my load!

Just looking at him drives me to the edge. "Sonny," I whisper hoarsely. "Man, I'm ready---"

He simply gives a slight nod and continues with the sweet, rough assault on my dick, his hands putting pressure on my tight balls and, then, a rough squeeze sends me over.

I release a primal growl, clenching my teeth as the overwhelming release unfolds. It's a mixture of pure pleasure tinged with a sprinkle of pain and I moan loudly as my cum pulses from my cock and down his throat.

Again and again.

Sonny doesn't miss a beat, and his deep green eyes don't waver from my face as he drinks my spunk. I realize then that I want to taste him, all of him. I want to suck him until he rewards me with his orgasm, proving that I can make him come every bit as hard as he's made me come.

He finally relaxes back on his haunches, and his eyes close momentarily as if he's savoring the last remnants of my climax.

I immediately move closer to him. I want to bask in our nakedness because it's warm; the lingering scent of our sex is potent, and I need to taste it for myself.

My mouth finds his, and my hands brace his strong jaw pulling him in closer. I kiss him, my tongue tangles with his and I taste our sex. I want to devour him because of the pleasure he's given me. He's worth every fucking cent that Linc charges me for this date.

I pull back and study him. His two-day stubble only adds to the beauty of his strong, classic features. "I want to suck you, Sonny. I want to taste your cum. Do you have an issue with that?"

He gently places open-mouthed kisses along my jawline, and his tongue leaves a trail of warmth as he seduces me in every sense of the word. Slow and sensual, warm and sexual. Fuck, this is so much better than pussy. With the taste of me still lingering in his mouth, he replies, "I would rather you fuck me, Troy."

Where the fuck has Linc been hiding this treasure?

Reality Check: Linc presumed I was hetero.

News Flash: I presumed I was hetero. After all, that 'queer detector' as Wayne had labeled *the stick* had proven it, right?

I shudder as the dark memory invades my mind.

"What?" Sonny asks, misunderstanding the shudder. "Do you have an issue with that?"

Fuck!

Fuckity Fuck Fuck.

No way in hell will I cop to this dude about being a virgin to brown eye.

I can do this.

"No Sonny. I've got no issue with burying myself balls deep inside of you."

Something inside of me tells me this is natural. This is the way that it's supposed to be with me.

Chapter 33

I hate the fact that Troy is calling me Sonny. I hate that his seemingly first sexual experience with a man is a farce, the elevator blowjob notwithstanding. I need him to know who just swallowed his cum.

The primitive side of me feels the overwhelming urge to mark my territory, to stake my claim, to hear my fucking name bellowed from between his parted lips.

But I can't, not yet.

If I tell him the truth now, this will all be over and I can't have that. I cannot fathom ending the moment and regretting it for the rest of my life. The worst part of this entire situation is that I'm supposed to hate this guy.

Troy's behavior towards my fellow authors and me is derogatory, degrading and fucking despicable. Yet, right here, right now, we're not enemies—we're lovers. We are two creatures consumed by lust and desire, completely subservient to our libidos running rampant through our bloodstreams.

I want him to fuck me. Then, I want to show him how it feels to be utterly possessed. With the taste of his orgasm lingering on my tongue and the sweat pearling across my skin, I press myself against Troy leaving no room for even air to separate us. We are practically at eye level, my height but half an inch more dominant, when I slide my hands up the sides of his toned body and stop them at his jaw, cupping his face within my large hands.

Deep browns meeting forest greens, I stare intently at him so he understands the truth in my words as I skim my lips across his mouth. "Take me, then. I can't think of anything that I want more."

My voice is low, seductive, intended for his ears only even if we are completely alone.

In the distance I hear a phone ringing, I know it's mine but I ignore it. This is more important than anything else happening in the outside world. Pushing through this barrier suddenly seems primordial to my existence, a rite of passage before I can completely own him.

They say there is a thin line between love and hate. Well, I just realized that line gets even thinner when it comes to lust.

"Where's your bedroom?" I ask when I notice Troy is completely mesmerized by my intent stare.

I know. I have that effect on people. It's a gift.

When I pull away, Troy blinks as though he is trying to gather his wits about him, like he's hosting some kind of debate inside his own head. I need to distract him, make him let go of his apprehensions...turn him more animal and less human.

Taking his hand, I pull him away from the counter and lead him down the hall where I am assuming his bedroom will be. Troy follows, and by the time we reach the first door, I hesitate but the man behind me presses himself against my back and brings his lips to my ear.

"Next door on the right," he whispers as a shudder invades my entire body from the tips of my toes to the hairs on my head. Troy's cock is naturally pressed against my ass, practically nestling at my crack. My dick is weeping like a mourning wife, begging for a hot, tight hole to find comfort and affection.

Hopefully some other time, if I play my cards right...

Walking again, I turn right at the next entrance and push the door completely open. Troy releases my hand and walks to his bed to turn on the lamp before he faces me again, uncertainty clouding his features. With the soft light casting half of his face in shadow, he seems pensive, afraid, and nervous.

"Nice pad," I say light-heartedly to alleviate the tension that has risen since the moment my lover came down from his high. My gaze runs over every wall of the room noting nothing in particular.

A wooden dresser faces the bed, a large window hides behind thick, dark curtains in front of me and two night tables flank either side of the bed. No picture frames, no errant clothing scattered everywhere, no personality. He sleeps here but he doesn't live here. It's lonely, a mere convenience not a place of passion. My eyes now focus on his bed, the dark sheets purely masculine in their blue shade with two pillows on each side.

When I redirect my attention back to Troy, he's staring at me.

Whether he is trying to read me or waiting for a comment, I'm not sure but I need him to be at ease, to feel comfortable.

"Come here," I tell him softly yet sternly. He obliges, his steps sure if not a little slow.

My eyes rake his body one more time, the physical perfection of it an alluring beacon. Tall, dark and handsome was a catch-phrase invented for the sole purpose of describing this Mediterranean man. If it were possible I could see myself getting lost in those dark orbs, absorbed by their infinite depths.

"I'm not hesitant," he tells me but I'm not sure who he's trying to convince; me or himself.

"It's okay to be nervous; it's your first time. But lucky for you, I'm going to let you do the fucking. I'm pretty sure you know how to do that."

We both chuckle, Troy's eyes never wavering from my gaze, like he's trying to figure something out.

Does he recognize me?

Does he find me familiar?

My ego is begging for him to realize it's me, the alternative being that the elevator episode meant nothing to him. As if his brain had simply traded me over for a woman, a coping mechanism of sorts. Well, fuck that. He needs to know whose mouth he fucked; then, as well as now.

I take the remaining step towards him, closing the distance between us, our bodies not fully touching but our combined heat cocooning us, creating our own bubble of lust. "I'm going to touch you, Troy. Then, I want your hands to explore me. My erogenous zones are different than a woman's; find them and take advantage of that knowledge," I instruct him as I place a tentative hand on his pectoral, pinching lightly at his erect nipple.

His sharp inhale tells me two things—I hurt him and he likes it. So, I do it again. This time he's expecting it, and I feel his cock bob as it bumps against mine.

With one last step, I bring our cocks together, a soft caress of hot flesh and burning need. "Do you feel that?" I ask him in a low murmur and wrap my hands around our embracing shafts, their combined girths too thick for just one hand.

I rub and stroke us slowly, at first, speeding up my movements; our gazes never faltering. As I masturbate us, Troy lifts his hands with a confidence he didn't possess mere minutes before and brings them to my shoulders.

The feverish touch spreads across my flesh with pinpricks of anticipation. His exploring hands slide down the length of my arms, stopping when they reach mine, and he begins thrusting his hips as he joins me in our ministrations. With shaky breaths, our movements become faster, more confident, the strokes longer as our bodies inch closer to the source of pleasure.

Bringing my mouth to Troy's jaw, I let my tongue run along his stubble, reveling in the feel of rough masculinity.

As our lips meet, I glide against them, back and forth lightly; the air between them mixing into its own fragrance of desire. "Open up for me, Troy."

I don't know where the words come from. They are too intimate, too loving. I need to keep my mind on sex and set aside the niggling warmth growing exponentially within my chest.

"Believe me, Sonny, I have never been this open before."

Fuck.

The honesty that echoes within his words says more about the man than any of the many negative reviews he has been posting for all of these years.

My tongue is suddenly invading his open mouth, the action spurred on by the earnest show of vulnerability. We tango to the sound of our beating hearts, our ragged breaths, the rubbing of our sweat-coated skin. I feel as though I'm inhaling him straight into my lungs, tasting his every nuance, feeling his every emotion. It's heady; it's fucking alluring like a super drug that suddenly makes everything clear and simple.

Releasing our throbbing cocks, I raise my hands to his jaw, clenching my fingers into the flesh behind his ears and attempt to thrust my tongue even further into his mouth. I want to sink deep inside him on a level that obliterates the purely sexual and enters a realm I didn't even know existed for men like myself. Troy mirrors my stance, our bodies touching on every inch right down to our feet aligned side by side.

Pulling myself away, panting like a sixteen-year-old getting his first taste of pussy or cock...whatever, I lose what little control I thought I was holding.

"On the bed, Troy," I say through clenched teeth, desperately trying to remember this is his first time but godallfuckingmighty, if he doesn't fuck me right now, I might just lose my mind. "I need you inside me, right now."

Troy's eyes are glazed over, his mouth swollen from our mutual assaults, his skin a pink hue of lust unmasking all his well-hidden emotions. He wants this as much I do, and it's time to get to it.

Looking around the room, I wonder if he has lube. It has been quite a while since I last allowed any man to dominate me.

Now, let's not get ahead of ourselves. When I say dominate, I mean the purely physical aspect because mentally I am incapable of relinquishing any type of control to my lovers. So yeah, I'll be getting fucked but believe me, I'll be orchestrating every second of it. That's just who I am.

You know you love it.

My eyes hone in on the night stands. Like a bullet, I plunge over the bed to open the far drawer and frown when I see nothing but reading glasses, a pen, a pencil and a notebook. Rolling back over to the side, I open the drawer on the other night stand and growl.

No lube.

In the far back, I see a rather large tube-like container and pull it out. Moisturizing cream...hand lotion if you will. I ponder my choices and come up with only two options, get dry fucked or use this girly shit.

I look up at Troy as I chuckle at my own thoughts, "This is all you've got? Didn't you think about preparation before hiring a whore to fuck you?"

Remember, I'm a planner. Had I been in his shoes, I would have had the entire night on a timeline.

Romantic? No.

OCD? What do you think?

"We could have saved time if you had asked me what you were looking for," he says calmly, his right hand absent-mindedly stroking his hard cock.

My eyes automatically fall to the spectacular vision and suddenly my need for lube flies out the window. Hand lotion it is.

Scooting back up to the center of the bed, I open the tube and squirt the cream-colored liquid onto my palm and begin spreading it along my aching dick before reaching my balls. I'm lying on my back, my legs wide open, giving him the perfect view for what I intend to do.

Watching Troy drinking in the reality of a man spread open for him is turning me on. I'm that man. Not some two-bit escort slut. Not some gigolo getting paid to give Troy carnal pleasures for the first time. Me.

My hand cups my balls, rolling them slowly between my fingers while my pinky gently applies the lotion on my perineum, dangerously close to my puckered hole. Troy's eyes are ablaze, dilated with a force of nature that I cannot wait to unleash for him.

"Touch me, Troy. You need to know who you're fucking. I don't want you to pretend your dick will be inside some random woman. Come over here and touch me, know who I am. Put your hand on my cock, your fingers inside my ass and make me come. Preferably in your mouth."

Told you. I have the reigns.

Troy approaches me, one foot in front of the other, as he runs his fisted hand up from the root of his proud cock to the tip of his cum-beading head, spreading the delicious liquid around.

I lick my lips, my body remembering the taste of him.

Handing him the tube of lotion, I open my legs further to accommodate him as he kneels between my thighs. The look on his face exudes animalistic desire, a want borne only from the deep driving need to fuck.

Flipping open the tube, he holds it up, just above me, and lets the contents run down my exposed balls, sliding perfectly on my expectant hole and down the rest of my spread crack. This man who merely an hour earlier was hesitant in his moves now owns his every action.

I shiver as I feel his questioning fingers rubbing the cream over my cock, my balls and finally around my entrance. Troy's eyes dart up to mine, looking completely enthralled, like he's discovered the hidden treasures of Atlantis. I like that look because I fucking put it there.

Slowly, I feel the pressure of his finger pushing inside, careful not to hurt me.

"It's so wrong and yet...it feels so fucking good," he says softly as his finger enters me easily with the help of the "lube."

I can't help myself. I palm my dick and begin stroking myself to the rhythm of his finger fucking. It's good but it's not enough, I need more.

"Don't be shy, Troy," I say. "It's only you and me. Put in another finger. Stretch me out and fucking put your dick inside me."

Maybe that was a bit forceful but my patience is about to strangle me if he doesn't accelerate this. Troy's eyes snap up to me, the innocence in his eyes gone, the animal back with a force that almost has me fearing for my ass.

Literally.

"Sonny," he begins, and I want to throttle myself for leading this fucking identity charade but there is no fucking way I'm stopping this shit now.

Not a chance.

I feel the pressure of a second finger and their scissoring motion before he continues, "Hold on, because I'm about to pummel you, and for the first time in my life, I'll know exactly what I'm doing."

Shit...

Leaning away from me, Troy slides his hand under the pillow and pulls out a foil square, a condom.

Ah, see...a planner.

With quick, practiced movements, this god-like man above me sheathes his cock and is about to plunge inside me but something stops him.

I almost howl with frustration, the anticipation digging its claws into my libido. But then his head bends over my painful erection and as he darts his tongue out, I feel the wet heat sliding up the underside of my shaft. I swear to fucking God I just about come right there on the spot. I replace my finger where his had been, keeping myself ready for him while my other hand runs through my hair, my back arching, reaching for more.

Troy's eyes are closed until he reaches the bulbous head and my cum coats his lips. They snap open, staring directly at me and with deliberate moves, he licks his teeth, coating them with my essence before dropping down and savagely attacking my mouth with desperation, his palms flat on the bed on either side of my face.

The taste of my pre-cum spurring my need, I sink my hands into his hair, my fingers digging into his scalp, nails scraping against flesh. My hips rock upward bumping into his cock, my body begging for more.

I pull slightly away and whisper, "Please, Troy. Just put your dick inside me before I lose my fucking mind."

That's when I feel it. The head of his cock is resting against my asshole, as his entire sweat-streaked body covers mine, our mouths fusing into one.

We both grunt as he pushes inside me slowly, the vibrations swallowed within our kiss. The pinch of pain accompanies the overwhelming pleasure, his thickness enveloped by my hot walls trapping him. Inch by torturous inch, he finds his way until his balls slap against my ass. He's completely buried to the hilt as we both still and stare at each other.

Right before my eyes, I see a man who has been hiding his natural tendencies, but with one thrusting motion has just realized that he's home. That's right, I did this. I'm responsible for his revelation.

Me, motherfuckers.

"I'm pretty sure you know what to do at this point," I tell him through clenched teeth, wanting him to thrust, needing him to pummel my prostate so I can come like a fucking volcano.

"Oh yeah, I know exactly what I'm doing. Just a head's up...hold on for dear life, I'm going to fucking ruin you."

Well, then. Let's get the show on the road.

And that's exactly what Troy does.

Pulling out slowly, he thrusts back in hard enough to have my body sliding across the bed. Grunts from us both are like an erotic melody that only turns us both into raging beasts. Still bracing himself on the mattress, my hands anchored in his silky dark hair, Troy's dick rhythmically thrusts into me.

Owning me.

Claiming me for a time.

Little does he know I'm leading this dance no matter how hard he fucks me. "Fuck...yeah," I groan as his thrusts get more intense, more frantic, and more needy.

"I'm gonna come, Sonny. I'm going to fucking come so hard," he grunts.

"Do it, let me milk you dry," I answer as one hand drops down to my cock, pumping it so as to time our orgasms perfectly.

"God, yes...fuck...I'm..."

We both freeze, Troy's spine arches, his head falling back with eyes tightly closed, his mouth in a grimace of utter ecstasy. He is magnificent, he is a god, and he is fucking everything.

With that image forever tattooed into my mind, my hips spasm as my own cum spurts from the head of my cock and lands directly on his glistening chest, already wet from the exertion.

Troy collapses on top of me, my cum coating our bodies, mixing with our sweat.

Marked.

Owned.

The both of us forever branded with this one night.

Now...how in the fuck am I supposed to tell him who I am?

Chapter 34

Holy fuck!

How in the hell am I supposed to feel after that?

Physically?

I feel fucking fantastic! Like I've mainlined a double shot of adrenaline.

Emotionally?

I feel fucking emancipated...and liberated. Like a slave after Lincoln signed the Emancipation Proclamation, or an imprisoned Death Row inmate who is freed after DNA testing came onto the scene, or a chick that finally got her own fucking cigarette.

Yeah, I've come a long way, baby.

I adjust the shower head so that the hot, steamy water is pulsating out against my scalp as I lather up. I cup the stream of water and splash it over my face, and then I get the body wash and start lathering up the rest of my body.

My body.

Sonny fucking played it like an instrument. He knew which keys to press, what strings to pluck and how to keep the beat of my drum in perfect rhythm.

Yeah. I've been missing out.

Big time.

There were several epic moments—mostly when our eyes met while I fucked him. His deep, forest green eyes that turned almost to a deep moss blue right before he came. I nearly lost myself in that moment. Not just because I was blowing my load at the same time, but because those orbs were like a time warp—drawing me in and taking me back.

Back to that summer.

The summer I spent with Ethan, and more precisely, the night we had kissed under an August moon.

I shudder as I recall the interruption. I don't go there because it spoils my memory of Ethan. A memory that should be a welcome distraction all of these years later, because it represents a true revelation of a coming of age event in my life.

Sadly, it only invokes pain—the kind of pain that has served to stall my sexuality all of these years.

What a waste.

Oh, it's not that I've sexually deprived myself, because well— that's just not true. But until tonight I've not enjoyed the full extent, the raw potential, that Sonny magically unlocked.

I rinse my hair and my hands slick the wet locks back as I shut the water off then pause for a moment to shake off the droplets of water.

I exit my glass enclosed shower and grab a towel, rubbing it furiously through my hair. I then dry the rest of my body, feeling the tingling of my warm skin that is pink from the heat. I'm not certain if it's the heat of the shower, or the heat of the passion and raw sexuality shared just minutes ago. I do know that I want more.

There was a moment or two while I was with Sonny that it seemed so familiar. He seemed familiar. His voice, his scent—even his touch had seemed familiar.

And I wonder. Did those déjà vu moments I had represent Ethan and what might have been between the two of us if my stepfather had not interrupted us that summer?

Or maybe it's something, or someone, else altogether. All I know is that I'm not letting Sonny slip away from me too quickly. In fact, I will make sure that Linc knows he's to be a regular from here on out. That's not to say I won't enjoy some pussy occasionally, but only if Sonny is here to share it with me.

For now, I'm booking him for the night. Yes, I want him in my bed and on the receiving end of my throbbing cock all night long.

That's all.

Chapter 35

Holy Mother Sex Bomb.

What the hell just happened in here? I am no novice to fucking or getting fucked by guys but I am completely new to the sensations I had about five minutes ago. A surge of hot white current spread throughout my body, and it was not just an orgasm—it was the obliteration of life as I know it.

Hyperboles, remember? Love them.

I'm wandering around Troy's kitchen where my clothes last found residence. Squatting to the floor, I pick up my now wrinkled slacks. Absent-mindedly, I pull my pants up, and look at the vast space around me.

Aside from the mess we left an hour or so ago, everything seems quite neatly put in its proper place. No knickknacks to speak of, his dishes clean. I feel comfortable knowing he's not a slob or worse...a hoarder.

The living area is cozy with a good-sized couch behind a coffee table and a television set facing where I stand. To the side, a familiar envelope catches my eye so, of course, I make my way there in order to quench my curiosity. I know what happened to the cat but I also have an idea of what that envelope carries.

Sure enough, as I approach I see the address stamp of the familiar law firm that deals with my business, the firm Lloyd works for albeit another department altogether. If I look inside, I will find the file-stamped civil complaint that starts the legal ball rolling on said law suit against Defendants, Bluffington Gazette, et al. Troy is part of the 'et al.'

Irony, how you love me.

Running a hand through my sexed up hair, I sigh in frustration thinking about the emotions I saw running across Troy's face. The relief, the liberation he must have felt at finally embracing his sexuality. I knew that look because I had seen it on more than one occasion. Accepting one's fate is the ultimate freedom of all.

The padding of feet approaching has me turning toward the source and smirking. As Troy heads closer, we both hear scratching at the door of his apartment.

"Hold that thought," Troy says with a sexy smile, as he breaks course and opens the door of his apartment. "Come on in, Muffy. You missed your caviar fix today, didn't you baby?"

My jaw drops in awe as I observe Troy's familiarity and gentleness with his cat. "You have a cat?" I ask, definitely surprised that he's the 'cat type.' Never would have guessed that.

"Oh, Muffy isn't mine. Belongs to my neighbor. She just visits me for a snack. This won't take long."

And then Troy, with the confidence of a man who has just fucked the breath out of his lover, walks over to me as the cat rubs against his ankles and cups both my cheeks in his hands before planting an open-mouthed kiss on my bruised lips. Moaning, I mirror his stance and plunge my tongue inside to tango with his own. An age-old dance that needs no music.

"Remind me to call Linc," he says heading towards the kitchen with Muffy following closely behind. "I want to book you for the entire night."

I grin at his audacity, trying to find the right comeback but words fail me.

Imagine that?

A speechless author is an oxymoron if ever there was one.

"He already called," I lie. I mean shit, I can't have him contacting his pimp and learning of my betrayal. "I took the liberty of arranging it. Hope you don't mind?"

I place a questioning tilt to my statement to come off a little less dominating than any paid escort-slash-fuck should sound.

"Um, yeah...I guess it works out for the best," he answers with a slight frown marring his perfect features. "Are you hungry? We could order some food."

I watch as he places a couple of spoonful's of caviar into what I presume is Muffy's dish. He lowers it to the floor, giving her a gentle rub as she digs in.

"Sure," I reply, taking the chilled bottled water he hands me as I follow him back to the living room. Muffy remains glued to her bowl of Beluga. I'm starved, but first I need to get his thoughts on the lawsuit. "What's in the envelope?" I ask nodding towards his desk.

Oh, yeah, real fucking smooth Sherlock.

For a second, Troy looks confused, like I've interrupted his fantasy and traded it in for a reality he had forgotten existed. Following my line of sight, he exhales a deep sigh and shrugs.

"An asshole trying to shut me up," is all he says.

Instantly, my rage surfaces and my nostrils begin to flair slightly. "A death threat?"

I can't let him see that I know what lies inside that brown envelope.

Troy laughs, shaking his head and heading back to the kitchen to get us some water. "No, he's too much of a pussy to outright threaten me. Although," he pauses and stills as though recalling something, "he did threaten to suck my cock."

Oh yes, I did, Babu. I bet you got hard just thinking about it.

Sure enough, I see the towel that is wrapped around his waist begin to tent.

Filthy man.

Biting my lip, I try not to show my smug grin. After all, his dick reacted to me not Sonny and his supposedly hired tight-ass.

"So, if he's trying to threaten you, how is he going about it? A lawsuit?"

There, that sounds innocent enough.

"I saw the stamp from the law offices," I add to make my line of questioning less suspicious.

Give me a hat, a German Shepherd and call me Columbo.

Troy glances at me, the look on his face betraying his unease with this conversation. I want to know how he feels about this whole fucked up situation. Need to know if our past, unbeknownst to him, would ruin any chance to a future. A future of what, of that I have no clue.

Troy downs half of his bottled water, and my newfound lover places the rest of it on the top of his aged oak desk then turns his attention to me.

Again, the lack of coaster does not escape my notice. People need a serious lesson on how to preserve wooden surfaces. But that is neither here nor there.

"The guy is under the distinct impression that he can write fiction. Let's just say he wasn't appreciative of my attempt to give him a reality check," Troy begins, and just that little bit makes me want to punch him.

Hard.

Repeatedly.

"So, I reviewed his book. It's what I do for a living. I have a huge following, you see. Readers depend on me to be honest, and sometimes thin-skinned authors find that my honesty is...well *can be*...brutal. I mean his agent sends me this signed hard back and it was so fucking lame—mere nonsensical words spewed on white paper," he chuckles in the middle of his verbal diarrhea.

Now, I can see myself throttle him. Or possibly fuck him; show him my own little taste of dominance to put him back in his place.

"Anyway, he took it to heart, which is really something no author should do. I mean, if you write a story that people are going to pay for, then you have to accept that not everyone is going to like it, right?" he continues without giving me a chance to intervene. I really want to intervene.

With my fists. To his balls.

I can feel my blood pressure rising, the anger consuming me. At the same time, I feel as though I need to hear this, build my arguments, so that I can take him down.

"Except he broke the cardinal rule and responded to my review, all defensive and offended. Made a total ass out of himself," Troy shrugs and turns away.

I try to stay in place instead of running after him and brawling on the floor like two MMA fighters with no experience in the ring.

"I don't understand," I reply because, really...I don't. "Why is it so bad to defend oneself? I mean, if someone attacked me, I would punch his fucking lights out, so how is this different?"

I know the answer to this since Brent has been trying to beat me over the head with the behavioral handbook for writers for the better part of my career.

"It's simple. I didn't attack him, per se. I attacked his book. Critics have a responsibility to the masses to steer them in the right direction as far as their reading preferences. It's what I'm paid to do. There is a line that authors should not cross. Responding to a bad review is the ultimate infraction. Authors who don't have thick skin come off as assholes, bullies to those who simply state their opinions. In this particular situation, the drivel he self-published turned out to be fucking plagiarized. I mean how much lower can that guy go?"

He smirks.

I boil.

I push off the couch and follow him into the kitchen, sitting at the island on a steel-legged stool. "I'm guessing you made it personal when you attacked his book, right? I mean, why else would he sue you?"

Take that mofo!

185

Troy visibly tenses at my words.

Gotcha!

"I never make it personal. Now *that* would be unprofessional. Are we done here, Sonny? Jesus, I feel like I'm on the stand." The aggravation is thick in his voice.

I shrug and explain, "No, I'm just trying to understand. I'm a curious cat, you know." I try to ease the tension so he will continue this conversation.

"Look, I reviewed his book, and he took it like a pussy. Then I outed the bastard for stealing the shit to begin with, so now the guy is suing me. Obviously, he has no balls and his skin is thinner than a ninety-year-old's." Troy's voice is now rising but I can't help but push one last time.

"Maybe if you had stayed professional instead of attacking authors, you wouldn't be in this predicament?"

I'm staring fiercely into Troy's eyes, the silence stifling between us.

He strikes a pose; arms crossed and says, "I thought you were my whore for the night, not Jiminy Fucking Cricket. Because let me tell you, I'm no goddamn Pinocchio."

His words rip a gasp from my lungs, my back tensing like a rod, my hands gripping too tightly to the glass in front of me.

Fuck. Crap. Shit.

As the words escape Troy's parted mouth, I see a plethora of emotions dancing across his face. Anger turns to surprise. Surprise morphs into confusion. Confusion lingers until realization hits him squarely in the eyes.

Rage, like I have rarely witnessed in another man, flares from every pore. As the different shades of pink and red travel across his skin, I can almost hear the clicking of the puzzle pieces.

I can see the equation being solved. I can almost feel the vibration from his anger as he recognizes me from the elevator. The man who was at a signing. The man who kept asking question upon question about the lawsuit against the one and only L. Blackburn. Truth is a bitch to swallow, isn't she?

I'm standing next to his desk as it all comes together in his mind. Connection made as he slowly closes the distance between us like a panther stalking his prey. His eyes are a livid shade of brown.

My last thought before falling against the swinging door that leads back into the kitchen is...

"Shit, this is going to leave a mark."

Chapter 36

Babu's Book Talk

Book: Rammed
Author: Marcie Hunt
Genre: MC/Erotica
Publisher: Self-Published
Status: Book #1 in "Hunt for Cunt" Series
Babu's Grade: DNF at 61%

The Gospel According to Babu

Unfortunately, I had to shelf this one to my "DNF-Author Should Put A Gun To Her Head."

Synopsis:

Who the fuck knows? Seriously, I can't put an appropriate summary here because at 61%, I still was trying to figure out what this plot was supposed to be.

It simply seemed to be a disjointed effort to present various detailed biker sex orgies with a plethora of dirty girls (and trust me, their stench jumped off my e-reader and seeped so deeply into Babu's nostrils that I required a vinegar douche for my sinuses when I finally said, "Enough!").

I mean how many times must one endure descriptions such as: 'dripping wet pussy' or 'soaked cunt' or how about 'pressing my throbbing cock into her slick, drenched heat' before it begs the obvious question?

Got smegma?

Get a douche for Chrissake!!

The sex was disgusting by design. Lots of groaning, grunting and wet skin smacking wet skin sounding oh-so-slick and promoting visuals that caused me to dry heave several times.

The scene where the MC bikers gang bang a 'Prospect's' old-lady, naturally no condoms used, and then force him to eat her pussy out turned my stomach so irreparably, that I found myself swearing off yogurt and cottage cheese for the balance of my life!

Suffice it to say, dear readers, Babu has once again failed to find a book that is truly enjoyable and entertaining. It causes me to wonder if these Indie authors have a common goal of trying to outshine one another in pure trashy shock value. It seems to be a common thread that is growing significantly, right alongside my utter disgust. The content in these most recent books is enough to gag a maggot.

Enough said?

Your sympathies and condolences, as always, are welcomed and appreciated.

See you next week, and please, hit me up in the 'Comments' section below, and also on my Greatreads page. I want to hear what you're reading!

I push publish, and then get up, heading to the kitchen for a beer. I glance around, seeing that the disarray of my tussle with Sonny aka L. Blackburn remains as a reminder of my stupidity and utter failure to use good judgment in matters of intimacy.
Fuck.
So overrated, this intimacy thing.
I step over the array of pans and stainless steel utensils that now litter my ceramic tiled floor, having been knocked from the hooks of the overhead pot rack as we had taken our brawl into the kitchen.
Brawl?
It had been more than that. It had been fueled by anger and the reality that I had been duped.
And duped by my nemesis no less.

A nemesis that had somehow betrayed me with his sexual prowess and his superb ability to get under my skin so easily and into my head so thoroughly.

What the hell had his plan been?

Revenge?

Retribution?

I will probably never know. It wasn't as if we'd done much talking—other than with our fists—once the reality of who he was sunk in to my sex-dulled mind.

Dr. Barbara Dunmire is to blame for all of this!

No. Fucking Linc is to blame for all of this!

There's a soft knock at my door. "Who is it?" I call out, hoping like hell it's not yet another detective here to take my statement.

"It's me, Mr. B.," Ida Whatley calls out. "I just want to check on you. Make sure you're okay."

"I'm fine, Ida. Really."

"Open up, Mr. B. I'm not going anywhere until I see you for myself."

Pushy old bitch.

I flip the locks on my door, and yank it open so that she can check out my black eye that is now turning a yellowish-green.

She crosses the threshold, her forehead wrinkling even more as she studies my face. "Well," she says with a sigh, "Could've been worse I suppose. Still think you should've gone to the hospital for stitches above your right eye. Gonna leave a small scar."

"Won't be the first, Ida. Besides, it's so close to my eyebrow it'll just make me look more rugged."

She gives me a meek smile, still not convinced. "I just hope you're not upset that I called the authorities. With all that racket, well, I just didn't know what was going on here."

"It's fine, Ida. I understand. Is Muffy still shook up?" I ask, because no matter how much of an asshole I can be, I would never forgive myself if Muffy had been traumatized by what she had witnessed a couple of nights ago.

"She's still hiding under my bed, but she does come out to eat and use her litter box. It's just going to take some time, Mr. B. She'll be fine. Just give her some time."

I nod. We both hear the 'beeps' from my computer. Responses to my latest column coming in.

"Well, I'll be going. Just let me know if you need anything, Mr. B."

"Will do, Ida."

Once she's gone I pull up the responses on my column.

Holy fuck!

Cindy Lou wrote: Babu, I've actually read this book and found it pretty good. Did you see all of the 4 and 5-star reviews on it? There's like over five hundred.

Babu wrote: That simply means there is no accounting for taste. You know my mantra by now, Cindy Lou. Anyone who's rated this garbage anything over a 1-star was smoking crack, probably the same crack the author was smoking when she wrote it!

Black Friday wrote: I think this debut author shows a lot of talent. I think books are like fashion, music or movies. They are subjective; I mean it's a matter of personal taste, right?

Babu wrote: Wrong. If you don't agree with my review, why don't you sashay on over to the author's fangirl page and volunteer to be on her street team. I believe it's called Hunt's Cunts.

What the fuck is going on here? *Two* dissidents?

Ruby Red wrote: Maybe you're the bully, Babu. I've been following your reviews for nearly a year now. I'm all like: WILL BABU EVER FIND A BOOK HE LIKES?

Babu wrote: And Ruby Red? I'm all like: YOUR ASS IS NOW BLOCKED!

What the fuck?

Black Sheep wrote: Babu--is it true there's a lawsuit against you and Bluffington Gazette for defamation? Maybe you should apologize to L. Blackburn...it sounds like YOU are the wannabe author. What's that saying--those that CAN do, those that CAN'T review?

Babu wrote: And you Black Sheep? You're now BLOCKED from my FLOCK!

RugBurnSoGood wrote: Mr. Babu, if I didn't know any better I would guess you are sexually frustrated. Who doesn't like a little dirty talk? Personally, I believe the dirtier the better. A hot cunt, a throbbing cock...both? Maybe you should stop reading erotica, apparently it was not made for prudish eyes.

Babu wrote: Blow it out your ditty bag, sock puppet!

Jesus. H. Christ! What the hell is *wrong* with these infidels? Someone's caused this shit to hit the fan.
Who? Why?
Fucking L. Blackburn?
Oh...YOUR. ASS. IS. MINE.

Chapter 37

Life is a constant voyage where each turn and each direction we choose ultimately sums up the paths of our destinies. Fate doesn't fuck around. Once she has made her plans, she sticks to them no matter our itineraries. I know this...I'm a planner, remember?

As I sit here, alone and in pain, I wonder which of my paths brought me to this moment. I wonder what exactly I did in this life or a previous one to deserve the overwhelming ache that consumes me.

I should be writing, instead I'm sitting in the middle of my couch, a glass of Jameson tightly gripped in my hand with the bottle dangerously reaching empty status. There is no sound around me. No radio, no ticking clock, no phones.

The last call I took shattered my heart and destroyed all my hopes. Everything I thought was important to me, all the work I had done these last few years now seem inconsequential, merely fluff to fill the days.

Slamming back the last drops of scotch, I throw the glass clear across the room and watch it break in a million pieces. This time, I don't get up to clean it. For the first time in my life I don't give a fuck about the mess, I just pick up the bottle and drain that too before exacting on it the same fate as the glass.

Thinking back to the last few days, I try to pinpoint the precise moment my world came crashing down. Was it the realization that my heart had skipped the proverbial beat while Troy pounded inside of me? Or was it when that high came to a screeching halt as my lover discovered my identity?

I wish the physical pain from the fight we had was the only

one...alas, it is not. In fact, I welcome the sore face, the sliced lip and the bruised ribs. I welcome the heated, parting words when the police came banging on the door. All of that was normal. I had deceived him; he found out, we fought. As all men do, we would have eventually come to terms with our situation and maybe been even stronger for it.

Except that was not the turning point.

The exact moment my life, as I know it, ended was when I heard the voicemail from earlier that night.

Three words.

It only took three simple, every day words, to destroy me.

Running my hands through my hair, I grip my roots as tightly as possible, hoping the pain on my scalp will override the splitting sensation I feel in my heart.

It doesn't.

In fact, it only makes my silent tears flood my eyes, overflowing onto my cheeks before falling on my lap.

Three words.

"We found her."

For months, I had a private investigator searching out my sister, Kennedy, in hopes of finding her and bringing her back where she belonged.

I never told my mother of any progress, wanting to spare her the gory details. But as I sit here, drowning in my desperation, I try to find the words to explain the loss of a child to our mother.

I need more than just three words.

Leaving Troy's apartment, I had fished out my cell phone and pressed the message button with an unknown number. Seth Bridges, my investigator, was always changing phones or numbers or both. The man never spoke unnecessary words, something common among ex-military. As a writer, word efficiency is a fault. But then so is word excess.

"We found her."

That one-sentence message is going through my brain on automatic replay, the result always the same no matter the number of times I repeat it.

Kennedy was found.

Alone.

Homeless.

Drugged.

Dead.

Those were details I got once I called Seth back. Although his emotions are quasi nonexistent, he tried his best to sound remorseful.

After all, he had spent the better part of a year looking for her. With every clue we had as to her whereabouts, by the time we reached our destination, she was gone.

Deliberately running from us.

At one point, she had been living with some drug dealer out west, selling cocaine to the rich and beautiful in Los Angeles. The boyfriend had been found dead, Kennedy had disappeared.

The authorities had no leads but the scene of the crime did not point to her; a drive-by, they had said. Before leaving the run-down house, an older police officer had stopped me as I was leaving, urging me to find her. No words were needed; the men her boyfriend was dealing with were not the kind to keep witnesses alive.

Kennedy's lifeless body was found in Chicago, miles away from L.A., with a lethal dose of heroine injected into her body. It was impossible to know if the act was self-inflicted or otherwise administered. In the end, I didn't give a shit; the result was the same.

My baby sister is gone.

My father...gone.

And my mother?

Something tells me she won't survive this and the only thing my selfish mind can comprehend is that I'm destined to be alone. My self-centered ways my only companion.

Is this my fate's life plan? If so, it fucking sucks.

And not in a good way.

Tilting my wrist towards me, I look at my watch and know it's time to play the role of the messenger; the messenger of death.

Standing abruptly, I feel the effects of the alcohol but unfortunately they are not strong enough to make me pass out for a few hours, or days or...fuck it, a few years.

It's time.

In less than an hour I will have obliterated another life.

Maybe, the next time, it will be mine.

Four days later I am standing beside my grief stricken, yet formidably dignified, mother watching the coffin of my little sister lowered into the ground.

I hate funerals.

I hate the sniffling sounds, the swallowed sobs, the inevitable grey skies or clichéd rainy days. I hate the sea of black that stands paralyzed as another wasted life is covered in moist soil. I hate the smell of fresh flowers, cut and sent to their proper deaths in an attempt to show respect to someone who will never witness their beauty. I hate the impending condolences, the wasted amount of food and the idle chit chat of days past when Kennedy brought sun and smiles to everyone she met.

Kennedy was beautiful, her eyes sharing the same color as mine. Where I have always been introverted, my fiction more important than my reality, my kid sister was the life of the party. She loved smiling, laughing, joking...loving. She loved love and everything it had to give.

I should have stopped her.

I should have looked harder, sooner.

I should have...

What? I don't know.

When the last of the mourning guests has left my mother's house with tears still staining her aging face, I close the door and still; looking at nothing in particular. My mother is upstairs, sleeping with the aid of a couple of Xanax.

Since my sister's disappearance, I have had a nurse tending to her needs. Deciding to let life take her where it may...straight into the arms of death, I always thought, was not reassuring to me.

"Rose...," I call out softly before turning away from the door and facing the fifty-six year old nurse, "Are you able to stay and work for us a while longer? I can't leave her alone but I just..." My voice cracks at the imminent admission, "I just can't stay here."

Rose comes towards me and places a motherly hand on my cheek, a smile that expresses her understanding, adorning her lips and says the words I long to hear. "Larson, you are a good son. A good brother. Go mourn, any way you know how. I'll stay and watch Mrs. Blackburn. She's safe, I promise."

Bending to reach her cheek, I kiss her good night and thank her for everything she's done. Rose just nods and turns to make her way upstairs and lay vigil at my mother's side.

So, here I am. Wally's Jazz Bar. At the opposite spectrum of the day's events. Loud chatter, great music and flowing pints of beers. The latter my most cherished companion.

Feeling my phone buzzing in the pocket of my suit jacket, I take it out and glance at the caller I.D.

Brent.

"Yeah," I answer, not sure the noise from the bar will even allow this conversation. My doubts are eased when I hear Brent's voice loud and clear.

"Hey..." I wait for him to continue, knowing that in light of my day, people feel the need to say something...anything, when it comes to those grieving. "I'm sorry for your loss, Larson. If there's anything we can do...anything at all..." Brent's voice trails off making me smile. The man really is a decent guy, so I decide to ask him.

"Brent, would you consider me your friend? Or am I simply your client?"

I've been wondering this for so long, I figure there's no time like the present to find out. Although I would have preferred doing so with less noise around me.

"Do you think I'd put up with your shit if I didn't also consider you my friend?"

I chuckle at this because answering a question with a question is such a business-like technique. Not confirming, not denying.

"Just answer the fucking question, will you?" I say through the semblance of a laugh.

"Yes, Larson. I consider you my friend. Although half the time I also consider dropping you as a client."

Now it's his turn to laugh but then his voice takes on a serious note and he adds, "Even so, you'd still be my friend."

Then nothing for a few seconds. We sit there, each on one end of the phone, silence our only conversation until I break the spell.

"Thank you, Brent. By the way, I need you to put an end to the lawsuit against Troy Babu...Babylon...Babilonia...whatever the fuck his name is."

Clearly the beer has done its job.

"What?"

I expected the shocked response, but I have never been more certain of anything.

"Yeah. I've got more important shit to deal with so....just make it disappear for me, please? Fuck him. Fuck Noelle. Fuck...everybody who doesn't like my books. And fuck...I don't know."

"Are you sure about this?"

"Positive, my friend."

Behind me, the saxophone starts playing, the decibels too high to entertain a phone conversation, so I bid Brent good night and end the call.

Later that night, as I lay in my bed with no hope of sleep making its way into my consciousness, I fire up my laptop and search out Babu's column. I'm a masochist sometimes, but for some unexplainable reason I miss him. I miss our professional hatred, our personal intimacy. Most of all, I miss entertaining the thought of a future between us. I fucked up, of course, but then...I always do.

As his page comes into view, I see his latest review and shake my head.

Always so brutal, so unrelenting...so damn unforgiving.
So, I had decided to make up a puppet address and respond.

RugBurnSoGood...

I take a look at my social media, answer a few fan questions and see that Lisa, my assistant, has been doing a great job of keeping my pages up to date. I don't know what I would do without her. Before I log out and close down for the night, I see a new message in my email account. Sighing, I click on the tab and let my eyes scroll down to the inbox.

Noelle fucking Crawford.

To open or not to open...that's the fucking million dollar question. But then I'm the cat, and curiosity shall be my death.

Larson,

I wanted to reach out and express my sympathies to you and your poor mother. Kennedy was a good girl, she deserved better than this. But then, you seem to be attracting bad Karma every step of the way.

If you hadn't left me, I could be there for you, helping you get through these hard times. I could be the loving wife you need.

We were good together, Larson. I'm sure this whole bisexuality thing is just a phase, you know? I mean, one day it's going to fade and you're going to end up all alone. Is that what you want?

Come back to me and your name will be restored, all your worries will go away. I'll make you happy, you'll see.

Love, always.

Ellie

I stare at the email trying desperately to figure out if it's real or if I'm so drunk that I've imagined it all. I close my eyes, take a deep breath then open them again.

Yep, still there.

I focus on the last paragraph, narrowing my eyes and trying to understand the meaning behind the words.

All your worries will go away.

I decide to respond, because that's how I am.

Noelle (no need to use your nickname, we're no longer intimate)

When you say that all my worries will go away, are you suggesting that you and God have some kind of special bond? Because short of that, I don't see how you could make Kennedy's death disappear. Can you bring her back to life, Noelle? Can you?

I didn't think so.

So, please...just fuck off.

LB

Pressing the "send" button, I shut down my laptop and try to convince myself that eventually sleep will come take me away.

Chapter 38

Fate is fucking fickle.

Say that twenty times fast. But it's the truth; at least it has been for me. Every time I've tried to trust it, to let it be, to go with the flow so fate will do her thing, she bitch slaps me right back down. And so then I hide.

Hide in my apartment.

Hide behind my column.

Hide from the truth.

Hide underneath denial.

Of what I am, and more importantly, what I could be if only I allowed myself the opportunity.

It's been days since he left with two of NYPD's finest escorting him out of my apartment. My face is back to normal, pretty much anyway. A tiny scar resides over my right eye, but it's nothing compared to the scars I sport emotionally.

I'm going through the motions. I read, start preparing my notes for my next review, pre-select my next book/author to grill because I already know I'll hate the piece of shit book. It's what's expected of me. I'm pure entertainment--nothing more.

I kept my last appointment with Dr. Barbara Dunmire. Lost my shit--told her she was a fucking quack. Got thrown out.

Who gives a fuck?

Not me.

My cell rings. It's Joel.

"Yeah," I bark.

"Good news, Troy. Blackburn had his lawsuit dismissed. Got the papers this morning. At least we don't have that hanging over our heads anymore. Did you get that . . . uh . . . situation with the domestic violence thing dropped?"

"Yeah. I'm not pressing charges, he's not pressing charges, and since we don't cohabitate there is no domestic to it. Just a couple of dudes drunk and throwing punches. It's all good."

I hear the relief in his voice. "Troy, I'm not the type to judge, you know that, right?"

But somehow I hear an opinion coming my way.

"I just want you to know, that well--you might want to keep a low profile on shit like that, you know what I'm saying?"

I nod. "I get it, Joel. No worries."

He starts to say something else, but I've ended the call.

So, Blackburn dropped his suit. What's up with that? I'm still pondering that very question when there's a knock on my door.

Shit. What now?

I'm dressed in sweats. The same ones I wore yesterday, and hell, maybe even the day before that. I haven't shaved or showered in a couple of days---that much I know.

Aside from Joel, Mrs. Whatley, and a quick call to Linc to rip him a new asshole, that's been the extent of my communication over the past couple of days.

"Who is it?" I call out, making a mental note to get a peep hole installed.

"Lloyd Ledbetter, Sir. From the law firm of Grant, Mills & Spencer. I've been requested to drop off some legal documents in the pending lawsuit."

I open the door to find a tall, lean yet well-muscled blonde dude in a suit. Looks custom tailored to me, but hell what do I know? I'm not the 'suit' type. This dude wears it well.

He holds out a sealed brown envelope that I take from him, seeing the familiar logo of this apparently upscale law firm in Boston.

Boston?

"You could've mailed it," I deadpan. He's lingering in my doorway, giving me some kind of visual assessment as his eyes scan me top to bottom, and then back up. I start wondering if he's waiting for a tip.

"Some things are best delivered personally. I had a need to see you."

I quirk a brow, waiting for him to explain.

"You're not good enough for him, you know?"

"Say again?"

"Larson. You're not what he needs. I see that now."

"What the fuck is your deal, Chief?" Dude is starting to piss me off with the arrogant twice-over he's giving me.

"My deal is that I know Larson. In the biblical sense. And you are—excuse me—*were* nothing but a revenge fuck for him."

"Is that right?"

"It is."

"Well riddle me this, Poindexter. I'm the one who actually did the fucking. Yeah, that's right. I pounded my cock into his tight ass and he was fucking screaming my name the whole time. Never heard a "Lloyd" escape his lips once."

He noticeably bristles, his eyes narrow and he throws a frosty glare at me. "I'm sure Larson has once again found the mind he temporarily lost. We'll know soon enough. Once he's back from Chicago."

Chicago?

"Is that all, *Lloyd?*" I press, starting to close the door.

He slides his foot across the threshold, and now the oxblood Bruno Magli loafer that is perfectly shined is doubling as a designer door stop.

Does this maggot want a piece of me?

"Leave him alone, Mr. Babilonia. I'm the one he needs now. I'm the one that will help him heal."

He pulls his foot from the doorway, and turns his back to me, taking swift strides down the hallway.

What the hell is he talking about?

Heal?

Hell, I didn't hit him *that* fucking hard, did I?

I close the door and head over to my laptop, firing it up, and then pulling up my sock puppet email account. I type up a quick message.

Your girlfriend, Lloyd, just stopped by with your message. It's gonna take a helluva lot more muscle power than that fucktard possesses to intimidate my ass. Tell the douchebag he's in over his head. Hope you're healed, but deceitfulness is a bitch I don't embrace.

T.

P.S. Thanks for dropping the frivolous lawsuit. Maybe now we can both put the shit behind us and go on with our respective careers. No hard feelings?

I push "send" and chuckle at my last line. Ball is in your court, L. Blackburn.

Come to Papa.

Chapter 39

Even in the middle of May, Chicago is fucking cold when the winds reach out with their icy fingers, penetrating clothes, skin, muscles and going straight to bone.

I shiver as I make my way to the Women's Shelter where a young girl is staying, a young girl who knew Kennedy and had befriended her.

Showing my I.D. as I walk up to the front office, I explain the reason for my being here. Ashleigh Cook is waiting for me. After the news of Kennedy's death had reached the ears of the city's rejected young and old, Ashleigh had made her way to the police station with information she thought might help.

The office worker asks me to have a seat in the waiting area, which is a simple corner with four fold-out chairs. There's a plant trying its best to survive despite the obvious lack of care.

Like Kennedy, I think bitterly.

It was my job to water her, feed her and make sure her roots were firmly planted in the soil of our hometown.

"Sir?" I hear the clerk's voice, tearing me out of my musings.

I turn to see a young girl, mousy brown hair badly in need of a good wash and brush, eyes lacking any kind of hope or happiness and lips that are badly chapped from days spent outside in the cold weather. I fleetingly wondered if Kennedy had looked like her—a walking dead among the living.

"Hi," says the girl with a voice that trembles with nervous energy.

"Hi Ashleigh," I answer, extending my arm to shake her tiny, weathered hands. Reluctantly, she steps forward and accepts my friendly greeting, "My name is Larson, I am...was, I guess, Kennedy's older brother."

I gesture to the chairs in the corner, silently suggesting she sit down. "Would you like anything? Coffee? Water? Food, maybe?"

Her eyes light up at the mention of possibly filling up her stomach. She can't be more than eighteen or nineteen and yet the lines on her face are a testament to a life no teenager should be living. Ever.

Ashleigh turns to look at the lady who hasn't moved since she arrived, a silent conversation passing between them.

"We can go across the street, you'll be able to see us if you're worried," I volunteer.

I need to be able to talk to this young girl, get some closure and possibly help her in some small, probably insignificant way.

"Ash, you okay with that?" the lady asks with concern in her motherly eyes.

Ashleigh turns back to look at me and nods absentmindedly, seemingly trying to figure out some impossible puzzle. "Yeah, sure. We'll be at the burger joint, I know the manager."

The lady nods and then directs her attention to me with narrowed eyes, like a lioness protecting her cub from predators. I suddenly feel the need to reassure her, to let her know that I pose no threat.

"I'll have her back in an hour or so," I say reaching out to shake her hand. The clerk obliges and then nods at Ashleigh before we make our way outside, into the cold winds of the city.

I'm wearing jeans and a sweater with a long coat to block out the wind, and a scarf to protect my throat. Ashleigh, however, is not nearly as covered with only a ripped jacket that doesn't seem to zip up all the way, her neck completely exposed.

As we cross the busy street, using the crosswalk to avoid sure death from the megalopolis drivers, I wonder if maybe I could just get this girl some clothes as a thank you for trying to help me. I tuck away that idea for later, deciding on one thing at a time.

Entering the mom and pop burger joint, I recoil at the pungent smell of burnt grease and sweat.

Jesus, have they even passed the health codes?

I turn to Ashleigh, unsure as to whether we'll be walking back out of here alive or not. The young girl looks up at me and smiles, an expression that contradicts her rough life and gives her a carefree appearance.

"Don't worry, it tastes a lot better than it looks or smells, I promise," she tries to reassure me.

Shrugging, I let her lead the way to choose a booth that suits her, where she feels most comfortable. We end up at the back next to the window facing the shelter.

"Get whatever you need, Ashleigh. I'm serious." I need her to eat her fill, drink anything she wants...have a few minutes of good in her life.

"Thanks," she answers meekly as though my suggestion makes her uncomfortable.

I hate the look in her eyes, the resignation that this is her life and she has nothing positive greeting her at the end of this meal.

The waitress walks up to her, her apron smudged with grease and what seems to be ketchup. The girls are probably the same age, yet their fates have taken them in different directions. They greet one another, obviously knowing each other, before Ashleigh orders a double cheeseburger with fries and a large coke.

I smile, reminded of Kennedy's love for this type of food but always careful of her figure.

"A dancer must stay light so she can float in the air," she would *always say and my response would always be the same, "I'll throw you Ken, so you can fly." Then, we would both laugh and I'd lean and whisper, "I promise to catch you every time, little sister."*

"Mister, you gonna order or what?" The voice of the waitress cuts through my memories, and I shake my head to return to the present. One missing my baby sister.

"Yeah. Sorry...I'll have the same thing with water in a bottle," I add that last bit, concerned about the hygiene in this place. The waitress walks away, finding myself alone with Ashleigh and eager to get information about Kennedy.

"You were thinking about her, huh?" I hear the girl ask me.

"Yes, I was. She loved burgers and fries, but would rarely eat them." I tell her, a bittersweet feeling filling my chest, making it burn with the pain of my loss.

"We only ate here if we got enough money from panhandling. Slim tried to get a job here but they don't give you one if you ain't got papers and stuff, you know?"

My brow furrows in confusion at the mention of Slim, clueing Ashleigh in that I'm not following and she immediately clears things up for me.

"Slim, that's what I called Kennedy. She called me Trim. Slim and Trim. Like eggs and bacon," she explains, chuckling at the memory. I can see the tears welling up in her eyes, pulling mine from the depths of my broken heart.

"Slim and Trim," I murmur, committing that sliver of information to memory, a piece of Kennedy's life that did not include me.

"Yeah...," Ashleigh trails off before coughing and focusing her eyes on me, apparently ready to get down to business.

"Like I told the cops, I know Slim, she didn't shoot up. Never touched the shit. Yeah, we muled for some but we never used. Ever."

Vehement words that inspired truth.

"She overdosed, Ashleigh..." I still have a difficult time accepting this.

My Kennedy, my little sister dying alone in the cold, her bloodstream pumping deadly chemicals straight into her heart before bringing it to a complete halt.

"Yeah, well...she didn't use."

"Why didn't she come home, Ashleigh? Do you know?" As I finish my question, the waitress arrives with our orders and places the plates in front of us, leaving us to our conversation as we thank her.

Ashleigh looks down at her food, her hands clutching the seat on either side of her thighs, seemingly lost in thought. She's quiet for so long I almost give up on getting an answer from her but then she speaks, raising her head as tears silently fall from her sad, tired eyes.

"She was too ashamed. She used to talk about you, all the time. Said you were her big writer brother, all confident and talented," she says quietly, sniffling as her tears continue before looking straight at me with haunted eyes.

I hand her a paper napkin with shaky hands, knowing deep in my gut that her next words are going to kill me. Just squeeze what little heart I have left in my chest.

"She said she would rather die than see the disappointment in your eyes."

Rip. Stab. Kill.

Staring at Ashleigh for what feels like hours before either one of us speaks, I let out a shuddering breath trying to keep my own damn tears from drowning me.

"Fuck," I whisper because, as it turns out, I was right. My baby sister is dead and my own fucked up, self-centered attitude is to blame.

We eat for a while in silence, but then Ashleigh begins asking me questions about my life, my writing, and my girlfriends. I answer devoid of emotion, my thoughts all too often drifting back to Kennedy.

If only I had found her earlier...

If only someone had helped her...

If only she had gotten her head out of her ass and came home...

If only...

If only...

If fucking only...

Then a thought comes to me, ridiculous at first but with some planning, it could work, be a sort of redemption for my aching soul.

What if I help Ashleigh?

What if I save her?

So, I ask her to come with me. I can find her a job and give her a place to stay while she gets herself on her feet. Maybe even let her help out at my mother's house. I am so sure my idea is the best thing since peanut butter and jelly that it never occurs to me that she might refuse.

Yet, she does. Adamantly.

"I can't be some surrogate for Slim. I know you're hurting, Mr. Blackburn, but you need to let yourself off the hook. I can't do that for you."

Go figure.

As I stare at this young girl, a burning question that has no relevance to Kennedy invades my brain. My mouth opens and words spill, unable to contain my curiosity.

"What happened to you, Ashleigh? How did you end up here?"

Again, this young, broken girl speaks the words that would shatter any decent human's heart. On a sigh, she answers all the while staring straight into my soul.

"Sometimes, family is worse than strangers, and the streets are safer than your own home." With that, our conversation dies a slow agonizing death.

Before I leave her back at the shelter, I give her my card with my cell phone number scribbled on the back and tell her to call if ever she needs help. I hand her a wad of twenties, which she is hesitant to take until I insist she can give it to someone that needs it more than she does. She smiles and accepts the cash and tucks it inside her bra for safekeeping, I suppose.

I kiss her on the cheek, wishing I could do more before saying goodbye and leaving her. Leaving Chicago, a place to which I vow to never return.

Back in my hotel room, I now find myself sitting on the edge of my bed contemplating my next move. I feel broken, so completely exhausted from these last few weeks that my body is nearing shutdown.

First the whole Babu shit on the column, then more Babu-slash-Troy shit in the elevator, although much more enjoyable. The lawsuit, the plagiarizing bullshit, fucking Noelle Crawford and her reoccurring pleas, the amazing sex...

Kennedy.

Every thought of her slices my lungs like a dagger, almost crushing me against the weight of the guilt.

Pulling out my phone, I see if I have any messages from Brent via email concerning the lawsuit. Anything to keep my mind from settling on my little sister, a little bit of relief from the constant agony.

A familiar address taunts me. I know who it is; I've seen it enough times lately.

Troy.

Reading the message makes different emotions rise inside my chest. I welcome them, of course, anything but the pain. Anger is good. Anger at Lloyd for overstepping. Anger at Troy for taunting me. Anger at myself for not going after what I really want.

But what I feel the most while sitting on this hard as fuck mattress, in a room that looks like most hotel rooms across the world, in a city I now despise is determination.

Fuck it all.

Kennedy is dead because she was afraid to disappoint. Well, I'm seizing the motherfucking day and showing Troy just how hard my feelings really are.

Instead of taking a flight back to Boston, I decide on a different destination. New York, New Fucking York.

After my little epiphany, I decide to get the fuck out of Dodge or in this case, Chicago, and confront my mortal enemy turned unforgettable lover.

Yeah, like I said, I must be a glutton for punishment. My injuries from my last visit are still lingering and I probably have some type of restraining order out against me but I'll cross those flooded bridges when I get to them.

Note to self: Avoid the old lady neighbor; she's fucking lethal with a frying pan.

Hours later, I'm standing in front of Troy's door, *again*. The déjà vu so clear I feel like I'm living out Groundhog Day in Technicolor and surround sound.

I knock on the door three times.

Forcefully.

Waiting for Troy to open and, for the first time in my life, I have no plan. Not a fucking clue as to what I'm about to do, yet it feels so goddamn right that I don't even hesitate.

I'm about to knock again when the door flies open and Troy stands there, open mouthed and shocked at the sight of me on the other side.

Gotta love the element of surprise.

I act quickly, pushing him inside and kicking the door closed behind me before I take him by the throat and push him against the nearby wall. At this point, my cock is rock hard and my breathing a continuous series of pants.

"What the fu..." Troy tries to say, but I don't let him finish.

"Listen to me, and listen to me good. You and me? We're not done. We're not finished. You want me to act like an adult? This is me owning up to my shit, to my needs and to my wants. And what I want is you."

Without letting him utter a single word, I release his throat and place both hands firmly on each side of his face, my fingers digging into the back of his head. My mouth crashes roughly against his, plunging my tongue inside and urging him to feel my desires, my wants and my determination. I may be an author but this is the language I speak best.

My only hope is that Troy understands it.

He finally responds with some pent-up emotion of his own. I can feel it, and fuck if I can't taste it, too. His hands frame my face as he devours me, and then all too soon he pulls back, a frown creasing his forehead where a healing scar has made its mark.

My mark.

My brand.

"Does Lloyd know you're here?" he taunts, a lazy grin making a rare appearance.

"Fuck Lloyd. I'll deal with him later."

Searching his face for any sign of hesitation, or worse, repulsion, I lean in and whisper against his mouth, my breath bathing his skin, "Have you ever been fucked, Troy Babufuckinglonia?" The gasp that travels from his lips to mine is answer enough for me.

Of course, I already knew this but the circumstances are different, now. For the first time, we are facing each other knowing exactly who the other is, no hidden identities, no costumes. We are clothed yet completely naked, and this is how it should have been from the start.

Letting one hand slowly slide down his jaw, I trace my thumb roughly across his bottom lip, watching the flesh mold to my touch. Continuing my path down his chin and finally landing at his throat, I don't squeeze but I do possess.

Troy's breathing is shallow as I take one step closer so our bodies are flush against one another, our respective erections pressing against our groins. He wants me, but he's not yet convinced of what I'm asking of him.

He'll change his mind.

I'll help him change his mind.

A second before I even know what the fuck is going on, I see a flare light up in Troy's eyes and then I'm turned and pushed against the same wall where he stood only seconds before. Our postures a mirror reflection, our hands firmly planted at each other's throats. Two dominant males fighting to affirm their positions.

"I'm not Lloyd. I won't bend over and let you fuck me like the submissive he is." Troy's voice is lethal, his fingers flexing against the throbbing pulse of my artery.

I can't help but chuckle at this, imagining a gag in his mouth and a flogger marring his skin.

"Relax, Tiger," I say as I take my turn squeezing his throat. "If that shit turned me on, I'd have him to quench my thirst." Then, instead of tightening my grip, I pull Troy to me and crush my lips to his and kiss the living fuck out of his mouth.

Troy pushes against me, his cock digging into my hip, his hands frantic against my chest as he lifts my sweater to pull it over my head. Our kiss breaks for the brief moment it takes for me to take it off and throw it haphazardly across the room not giving a shit where it lands or how.

Quickly, I reach for his chest, blindly searching for the middle part of his shirt before ripping that fucker off, hearing buttons clatter across the floor.

Troy's tongue is swiping inside my mouth, tasting every inch of me, owning me with his hunger as my hands explore his chest. The smooth surface is perfectly sculpted with just the perfect amount of hair peppered in just the right places trailing down to the cock I so badly want to uncover, devour and feel inside me.

But then something catches my attention beyond the haze of lust that consumes me completely. A raised pucker of flesh, a marring of his perfection...a scar? I want to break our kiss but I can't seem to do it, my curiosity warring with my desire, I decide to tuck the information to the back of my mind for later observation.

My hands explore his chest thoroughly before going to his shoulders and pushing the scrap of shirt up and over and hearing it fall to the floor. By this time, Troy is attacking my jeans as I push my shoes off toe to heel. Pushing into me as our mouths battle for domination, I feel the wall meet with the back of my head and grunt at the dull pain without stopping my actions.

Shoes flying, pants dropping, hands roaming and tongues

dancing, we slowly make our way to the nearby couch where we collapse like horny teenagers over the arm and onto the plush fabric, our legs half hanging over the side.

"What the fuck are you doing to me, Larson? I've never been so desperate to fuck someone before," Troy pants out between heated kisses.

"Desire. This is you, your body knowing exactly what it wants." I answer, barely able to speak with my breath stolen by lust.

"Show me." And those words are like a fucking chorus of angels descending upon me and singing hallelujah.

"Oh, baby, believe me...I'll show you, again and again."

Our cocks are so hard between us that the mere touch is almost painful. We're frantic, hurried yet mindful of the precious moment.

"Sit up," I tell him, "Let me show you pleasure like you've never known before."

I rise to my feet, naked and ready as I stroke my dick and watch Troy unconvincingly sitting upright against the back of the couch, legs spread and arms splayed to the side.

A beautiful fucking sight.

I can't wait to ruin him.

I can't wait to be his first. His last. His fucking only.

I drop to my knees, knowing I will soon be rocking his world, and spread his thighs wide, running my tongue from his balls to the tip of his hard cock. The salty pre-cum that escapes the slit, urging me to continue. But I stop, look up at my lover and grin like Sade on crack.

"I'm going to destroy you, Troy. I'm going to make sure that no other man will ever touch what is mine. Are you ready?"

Chapter 40

Am I ready? I have no fucking clue what is happening, but I do know one thing. My body is craving every touch of this man.

So I nod and pray that I'm not making a mistake.

Larson pushes my thighs further apart, and then places his hands on the backs of my knees and pulls my legs over his shoulders forcing my body to sink into my couch, my ass in plain view.

Suddenly, I'm wondering if I look enticing. I trim my nether regions, but shit, I've never looked at my asshole thinking anyone would have a front and center view of it. My thoughts are all over the fucking place when I feel the hot, wet firmness of Larson's tongue swiping down my ass crack.

Holy. Fucking. Christ.

My entire body shudders under the incredible sensation, my every nerve ending lighting up like a fucking Christmas tree. My entire blood supply rushes to my dick. My synapses concentrate on one singular thing, my ass clenching for more.

"Relax, Tiger, and enjoy it all. I promise, it's all fucking good." Larson's voice is like honey dripping straight from the bee hive—raw and silky, making my every muscle melt into nothingness.

"That's it, baby," he says before his tongue swipes again, forcing goose bumps across every inch of my skin. Fuck it--I'm horny, I'm hungry, I'm ready for more.

The thought doesn't have time to register that I feel the same wetness prodding my hole, licking to entice my opening then slowly making its way inside. Closing my eyes, I try to imagine what he's doing in my mind and, to my surprise, instead of feeling horror I feel pure, unadulterated lust consume me completely. This is fucking so far from that "queer detector" shit Wayne punished me with so long ago.

"Holy shiiiit..." I breathe out because I have never in my thirty-some years ever felt anything better than this. Not with pussy. Not from a woman's tongue even.

Instinctively, I sink down further and spread wider inviting Larson deeper, taking more, pushing me farther into oblivion. My hands suddenly shoot out to my lover's head and grip onto his hair for dear life, my hips thrusting, silently begging for more.

"Yes, fuck, yes..." I chant over and over again as Larson's mouth completely takes over and his tongue buries inside me, stretching me for what I know is a preamble to what is happening next.

Pulling back, Larson licks his way up and suddenly engulfs my cock inside his talented mouth almost gagging at my girth. Fuck, I love that sound. All guys do; it's a testament to our size and girth, and who doesn't like knowing his cock made his lover gag?

No one.

Take notes.

As I'm fucking Larson's face from below him, I feel a digit penetrate me. Although I tense at first, I can't help but enjoy it, with his lips sucking my cock; my emotions are all over the place.

And then something happens.

Larson's finger curls into what feels like a come-hither motion and my entire body jumps from the couch, my cock disappearing completely into my lover's mouth and before I know what the fuck is going on, I'm coming down his throat like a fucking teenage virgin getting his first blowjob.

"What the fuck...was that?" I'm panting, and my breathing is a complete erratic mess, my skin burning from the best damn orgasm I have ever experienced.

"That, baby...was your prostate. Welcome to my world, Troy," he says licking his lips like a singer who's here especially to seduce me and take me back to Hell.

"You're mine now."

Hell yeah. I *am* his. I belong to him, no dispute. Shit, I'd love to have his babies if it were biologically possible.

Getting to his feet, Larson offers me his hand and pulls me to a standing position.

"Bedroom. Time to find out what else I can do for you."

There is zero reluctance. I want him...any part of him inside of me, any *fucking* where he chooses to thrust. Larson spots the brand new bottle of lube on my nightstand and chuckles, pulling me up against him. "Expecting someone?"

"Just being prepared," I reply. "Sue me."

"Been there, remember? I've got more practical and enjoyable things in mind for us now, Troy. Any objections?"

"None," I reply immediately. I see his eyes move downward and rest where the pale, puckered scar left by the crazy stalker bitch is sitting like a beacon. I raise my head and cock a brow, expecting the inevitable question.

"When we're done, we're talking about that, but right now? It's time to play."

Larson tries to push me down onto the bed but I resist, placing my hand at the back of his neck and pulling him to me until our mouths are fused together. The taste of my cum is salty on his tongue. It only spurs me on, makes me ache like never before, has my cock twitching anew although I've only just come like a fucking eruption.

Ripping myself from his grip, I fall back on the bed, eye level with his raging hard-on. It's not much different from mine aside from the inward curve that caresses his navel, where mine is ramrod straight.

I slowly raise my eyes to stare into the deep forest greens of my lover as my tongue darts out and trails a wet line up the underside of his dick. Larson reaches over and, with a smirk, snatches up the bottle of lube. Here we are again, except this time there are no lies to separate us, no mistaken identities to hide behind and no suppressed inhibitions to stop us.

Tonight I am free.

Tonight I can be myself, no holds barred.

"Turn around," Larson tells me softly, words barely whispered, thickly coated in evident sexual craving. I oblige, my nerves on high alert, intensely aware that my life is about to do a complete one-eighty.

I'm expecting the cold liquid to coat my ass crack, my puckered hole but I don't expect the gentle touch that caresses between my shoulder blades, running slowly down my spine before landing on my ass cheek.

Tensing involuntarily, I hear the "tsk tsk tsk" coming from Larson. I'm expecting raw and rough so the tenderness I'm experiencing throws me.

Then Larson's mouth is at my ear, his breath tickling my skin before his words drive my lust to unprecedented levels.

"I'm going to fuck you within an inch of your life, bring you back and then do it again. Now would be the time to stop me. If not, then hold on for the ride of your life."

Now, I just want him to keep his promise and corrupt me.

"Do it," I say, letting a devilish grin adorn my lips. "But remember, paybacks are a bitch and, after this, I'll make you mine."

In response, I finally feel the cold liquid coating his finger entering my ass. I clench then I relax, letting my lover work his magic. It feels good, and this invasion that I was so brutally taught was evil and unnatural, well I want it and I want it now.

"Condoms?" he asks, and I jerk my chin toward the drawer in the bedside table.

Larson does quick work of sliding it on before he inserts a second finger inside my hole. My cock is throbbing, aching to play, and to feel the friction it was made to have.

The stretching, the prodding and the finger fucks are all accompanied by peppered kisses along my spine meant to soothe me, and they do. Larson's fresh scent envelops me, adding to my relaxed state despite this entirely new experience.

Don't get me wrong, I'm scared as shit but it'll be a cold day in Hell before I ever openly admit that to Larson.

"Spread your legs wide and keep your ass in the air, chest down on the mattress. Don't tense up."

The sound of his voice so tranquil, so serene that it does in fact, ease my weary mind and, at the same time, my dominant side wants to flip him over and hammer him like a fucking crazed man. But I agreed to this, so I will go along with it.

I do as I'm told and soon I feel the blunt head of Larson's cock prodding my back entrance, my anticipation of pain at an all-time high.

With my forehead pressed against the bed and my ass presented like some kind of medieval offering, I wonder how the fuck I ever agreed to be in this position when I feel two large hands on either of my ass cheeks, spreading and massaging them at once. The action has my body in motion and my cock instinctively fucking empty air as my ass pushes back searching for pleasure.

Larson chuckles behind me, "Greedy. I like it."

And then a sharp pain that reminds me too fucking much of a certain stab wound pushes against my sphincter, but I refuse to abandon. I *refuse* to give up. I want this.

"Fucking hell," I hear Larson behind me as he pushes in and then pulls his erection out all the while adding more lube to where our bodies are joined.

My hands are gripping the sheets, my body is tense but my mind...fuck, *my mind* is a whirlpool of dirty images flashing like a high-cost porno.

"Do it, goddammit! Stop fucking around and do it." I tell him through gritted teeth. I don't need to be babied. I'm no vestal virgin for Chrissake! I need to be fucked.

And then he's in. Larson's dick has finally pushed in through my ring of muscles, and the searing pain has me seeing white spots dancing around my eyes. But it's fucking worth it.

"Jesus Christ, Troy. Holy shit, you feel good." Larson is panting, I can sense him holding back, trembling as he fights the primitive instinct to ram his dick far inside me. So I do it for him.

We are both dominant males, so there is no topping from the bottom when I push back against my lover with the force of my entire body and then cry out when I feel his length slam inside of me.

Holy. Fucking. Shit.

There's a man's cock buried inside of me and besides the bite of pain that I knew would come, all I know at this moment is fucking ecstasy. I am full, I am complete, and I am finally...me.

With his hands gripping my hips, his fingers biting into my flesh, I finally...finally, have him where I want him.

Deep inside and to the hilt.

The mattress gives way to Larson's weight on either side of my thighs right before his chest presses against my back, one arm bracing while the other hand reaches around my throat.

Larson is still not thrusting. It's like a torturous wait, this anticipation of getting fucked.

When his breath hits my ear, he tells me, "Turn to face me, Troy. Kiss me while I fuck you for the first time."

Turning my head, our lips crash together like hurricane waves hitting the Florida shores—fast and devastating.

I'm so concentrated on his talented tongue that I barely register the fact that he is, in fact, pumping his shaft in and out of me. Between his masculine scent, his heated skin and perfectly honed skills, I feel whole for the very first time in my life.

Thrusting slowly at first, our mouths follow the rhythm but soon after, between his hand at my throat, his dick in my ass and his tongue in my mouth, my body is in overdrive.

Physical overload matching my growing emotional one.

As our fucking grows more and more erratic, our mouths can barely keep up, the oxygen seriously lacking. But Larson does not back away, he stays close breathing into me, sliding wet lips against wet lips, staring straight into my dark eyes and letting me know a million things without using a single word.

As his free hand reaches around my waist and latches on to my engorged cock I realize that I won't be lasting long this way if he continues.

"Do you like my cock in your ass, Troy? Jesus Christ, you're so tight, I can't imagine doing this with anyone else."

I suddenly have an image of that ridiculous erotica book that I reviewed last and realize that yeah...normal people actually do talk like that when the eroticism is fucking high, raw emotions blurt out like bad smut.

I'll have to keep that in mind, next time I read mommy porn.

"Shut up and fuck me. We'll have to work on your dirty talk, Larson. I just may want to hear it in *French*."

By this point I'm grunting like an animal trying desperately to keep myself from coming too soon.

"Fuck. You. Troy," he grits out with every hard thrust.

"I. Think. You. Already. Are," I grit back.

"Ahhhh, gonna come," he warns me as his hand strokes me harder with more fervent determination and I can feel my time is about up.

That's when I realize something. That's when I understand.

I'm gay.

Just as we both explode in a blissful eruption of pure ecstasy I grin thinking...I'm gay because this is the only time in my entire life where sex wasn't just a process, it was a need above all others with a pleasure I have never experienced before in my life.

I am gay, and I'm okay with that.

Okay, so after-sex activities with dudes is way different than with chicks. And I like it.

There's no post-copulation hugging or 'fuggling' as some call it. We're dudes. Our carnal needs have been met. There's no fucking need to have all of this after-glow shit going on.

We catch our breath, dispose of the condom(s), and then grab a quick shower—together or apart, it makes no difference. It's all about scrubbing the sex sweat from our balls and pits. Sounds gross, but that's the stark reality.

But that's not to say that I'm ready to kick Larson to the curb, because seriously? That ain't happening. I need to let him know how I roll. He's already made his position clear.

During the sex.

And fuck if that wasn't a turn-on all of its own, but I've got something to say as well. I mean, shit, I don't bow down to anyone. That's not how Babu rolls.

I'm toweling myself off as Larson is at the sink, doing the same to his damp hair.

"Larson," I start, "just so we're on the same page, I don't expect you to be sticking your dick anywhere but inside of me, got it?"

He looks over and gives me a sardonic smile. "I thought that was understood earlier, when I laid the ground rules."

"Yeah...yeah, but this is *my* way of saying fucking *ditto*, you understand? I mean, fuck it—I'm not the *chick* in this deal."

And he laughs, that deep rich, half-growl, half-chuckle that's going to have my dick standing at attention if he doesn't cease and desist.

"Yeah, Troy. I believe I understand the basic semantics of a monogamous relationship," he tells me with a cocked brow and a smirk. "Come on, let's sleep off the post-sex and we'll discuss it all over breakfast."

As he drops his towel, neatly, in the hamper, I'm half tempted to bend him over the counter and sink my cock between his cheeks but he's right—it's bedtime.

Before we walk out he stops abruptly at the entrance of the bathroom and turns on his heels. I nearly run into him and already feel the ingrained bachelor in me wanting to set ground rules.

"Look, there's one more thing," he says, "Honesty hasn't been our forte so I'm laying shit on the line tomorrow morning, and I need you to do the same. You okay with that?"

I nod, brushing my fingers through my damp tangled hair. "Yeah, I'm cool," I reply, hooking my fingers through the towel that is wrapped loosely around my hips, releasing it and letting it pool at my bare feet. "Let's hit the sheets."

Chapter 41

I wake the next morning, flat on my stomach with rumpled sheets limiting my movements. I would be fine with that if it weren't for the bits of carpet pushing against my mouth and the lack of softness under my body.

That's right.

I'm half-asleep and sprawled out on the fucking floor. Above me, Troy is laughing so hard I'm afraid he might pop a vessel. Slowly, I get on my hands and knees as soon as I figure out a way to untangle myself from the fucking man-eating linens.

On all fours, I tilt my head to the side and up, glaring at the man whose ass was my own personal possession not more than seven hours ago. As he throws his head back, clutching his midriff, I pounce and knock him flat on his back before kissing the living shit out of him...in hopes of shutting him up. All this noise in the morning is not going to do.

Leaning back when his fit is over, I rub my two-day growth and groan, "Coffee," before sliding off the bed and shuffling my feet to the kitchen. I'm hoping and almost praying he has some sort automatic coffee maker that has already poured the black gold into a pot.

As I make my way to the counter, Troy close behind still chuckling, I stop dead in my tracks.

"What the fuck is that thing?"

Troy bumps into me after my abrupt halt and peers over my shoulder, following my line sight.

"The coffee machine?" he asks confused.

"No. That is not a coffee machine, it is a complication." I don't know how that intricate thing works but until I get caffeine in my body, I am physically and mentally unable to learn a new task.

"Christ, don't tell me you're one of *those*," he says as he shoulder bumps me while walking past.

"One of what?" Does he not understand that my brain is not functioning?

"Coffee sluts. Can't line up two coherent words without a cup of coffee in their system," he chides good-naturedly.

And then Troy stops talking, and turns slowly towards me wearing a look of horror on his face. "Oh, god. You're *not* a Starbucks freak, are you? Because, if so...," he waves a finger between his chest and mine, "you and me? We're not going to last."

I blink. Then blink again.

I frown. Then rub my eyes.

"I don't know what the hell you're talking about. I just need coffee before I can start a conversation." I'm rather surprised I was able to align a full sentence that actually made sense.

"Alright, sit down, Grouch. I'll make coffee and breakfast. But, it'll cost you a blowjob."

Troy's words are so casual that they take a few minutes to register. Jesus, one night and he's already a Larson Addict. For the first time in my life, and even caffeine depraved, I don't have the slightest desire to run or set up rules of distance. In fact, I want more, so I answer with a grunt.

Twenty minutes and two cups of coffee later, we're sitting face to face at the kitchen island when our casual conversation dies down and we both know it's time to breach the touchy subjects.

"Let's get this over with, shall we? We'll each ask one question at a time. If it's too much we get one joker each," he proposes as if it's already a done deal.

Control freak.

I frown at these rules because...What the fuck?

"One joker?" I ask while cocking a brow.

"One joker," he confirms.

"That seems arbitrary." Because it really is, why not two?

"Those are the rules," he responds as he lifts the mug to his mouth and takes a sip, his eyes trained on mine with stubbornness written all over them. Darting my eyes to his otherwise occupied lips, I lick my own, desire slowly burning its way throughout my bloodstream. One night and I have apparently become an addict myself. But back to the task at hand.

"Well, I don't like those rules so I'm changing them. Two jokers." I swear to fuck, I'm going to buy an Aladdin mug with the flying carpet monkey getting pecked to death by that stupid parrot.

"Nope."

Ass.

"Well, I'm not playing then."

Unfuckingbelievable.

Troy, from the Planet of the Critics, has reduced me to pouting. Believe me, even when acting like a three-year-old pest, I'm still the sexiest motherfucker that ever graced this earth. Get over it.

"Fine. Then you get no answers," he replies as he stands to fill his cup again before throwing me a satisfied grin over his bare shoulder.

Like I'm supposed to be able to concentrate with him walking around in cut off sweats and nothing else? "Shit," and that's when that smug fucker knows he's got me because my curiosity will have me run over by a freight train with a psychedelic monkey driving the damn thing. And yes, you've guessed it, that beast's name is Babu.

"You start," he says before I have even voiced my surrender. Screw it, I'll play by his stupid rules, but at the end of the morning, he'll be doing the sucking to earn my forgiveness. This thought makes me grin like the cat that ate the canary because I must be at my seventh life and need some good Karma.

"Game on. Why are you afraid of elevators?" I ask, because shit, that was at the forefront of my brain so why no toss it out there?

"Uh...don't you have a simple question like, I don't know...when were you born?"

I smirk at his naiveté. Really? Date of birth? I can get that from his driver's license. I'm not wasting a question on that useless information.

"Let's up the ante, shall we?" I may start liking this game after all.

"No," he answers before I even have a chance to present the stakes.

"What do you mean 'No'?"

Chicken.

"No changing the rules in the middle of a game."

"It's not the middle, we've only just begun."

"Fine. But it's not fair because it's going to answer two questions in one."

Now, *I'm* confused.

Leaning against the counter the entire time of our little banter as he cradles a hot mug of java, he turns slightly to the side to place it on the kitchen counter. Slowly, his finger slides up his abs making my mouth instantly water but then dry up in the next second. The pad of Troy's finger is now lightly tracing the scar I noticed last night and his face is somber, all laughter from earlier completely dissipated.

"You mentioned my scar here last night. Then you ask about my elevator phobia. They were caused by one and the same," he replies. Lowering his head, his hand rubs the back of his neck as he searches for an explanation that clearly doesn't come easy.

"And this was?" I prod gently.

"Her name is Delores Friedman. Ever heard of her?"

"Well, fuck yeah. She wrote a series...give me a sec...yeah, the Vulva Monologues, right?"

He nods. "It was rubbish. You may not agree, but it was."

"Never read her stuff, but hey, it was a NYT best-selling series for weeks."

His face goes cold, and I know this is a fucking sore spot with him.

"Fuck it, Larson. You know better than that shit. USA Today, Wall Street Journal and New York Times are about unit sales. The days that these lists represent classics such as Catcher in the Rye, or In Cold Blood or fucking To Kill a Mockingbird, is long gone. Hell, O.J. Fucking Simpson made NYT, and he can't put a sentence together."

"Come on, Troy, it's never been all that unusual for celebrities, politicians, sports stars and even fucking criminals to publish, through ghost writers, traditional publishers or whatever, and hit a list. That's nothing new. Delores Friedman was none of those things. She was an Indie author--" and I stop mid-sentence.

I stand up, and point my finger at him. "That's *really* what this is about, isn't it? Your total dislike and disregard for Indies. Isn't that a bit *elitist* on your part? Is it so fucking incomprehensible to you that these authors—Indie authors, can be every bit as talented as a James Patterson, Truman Capote or a John Grisham?"

"Seriously—you want me to be the straight man here? And I'm not talking sexuality, dude. Funny you didn't mention any female authors."

I feel my frown because damn it, he's right on that account. "Don't get off the subject, Troy. We're not talking gender equality here—well fuck, maybe we *are!* Let's roll with that."

"I'm listening."

"Have you considered the possibility that since self-publishing has taken off, it has in fact put a whole helluva lot more females on those best-selling lists than ever before? I mean let's face it, prior to that, like every other industry, it was a fairly male dominated one."

"Pfft...desperate housewives as far as I'm concerned. Couldn't cut it in Corporate America so they high tail it home to lick their wounds and then get the brilliant idea of writing a best-seller."

"What's wrong with that?" I ask, my eyes narrowing a bit because I swear to fuck if Babu has traded his homophobia in for what's behind Door #2, which happens to be a crown designating him King of the Sexist Jerks, I will personally see to it that his family jewels feel my wrath.

"Look Larson," he says, his tone impatient, "if you have followed my column at all, you know that I don't show favoritism based on gender. I'm every bit as critical of male Indies, as you well know. Let's not start arguing gender bias on top of it. Yeah, I get that this is something I need to work on, okay?"

"Damn straight."

"Okay then, let's get back to Delores, she didn't like my reviews. Cyber stalked me for nearly a year. And then," he says, his voice anguished, "she fucking shows up at a signing and pulls a knife and sticks me in a crowded elevator. I mean what the fuck? No one did a damn thing. She punctured a lung. I couldn't catch my breath, but hell if it wasn't up to me to get the bitch knocked out. No one else did a damn thing! And then I passed out. Woke up later in the hospital. She had stuck a hard copy printout of my review to my chest."

I sit there silently listening to this horrid story and think...

"Well, obviously it hasn't altered your way of critiquing." My eyes shoot up to crash with his glare when I realize that I've actually said those words aloud.

Fuck.

"I just told you the story of my stabbing and your smart mouth just can't stay shut, can it?"

Troy is now stalking me across the kitchen until we come to a complete stop thanks to the wall that just hit my back. I'm trapped between a wall and a hard cock.

Pretty much my favorite position.

"Believe me, when I do shut it it's for a whole other reason and usually it's my lover who makes the noise. Loudly," I reply, smirking, but Troy is not amused.

"That, Larson, is the last time you will mention your previous lovers. Are we clear on that?"

How the hell did I go from submissive little pet Lloyd to dominant and arrogant, albeit fucking gorgeous, asswipe Babu?

"Ask your question, Troy," I tell him as my hand reaches down between the waist band of his shorts and his searing skin. He's rock hard but then...so am I.

Leaning in to breathe against my neck, he barely whispers his question. "What were you doing in Chicago?"

I startle at the mention of the horrid city that dared take my sister from my life. "Searching for answers but getting none. My turn."

"No, I don't think so. That is a riddle, not an answer. Spill, Larson, and if it was to hook up with someone, I will punch your face in. Just so we're clear."

Well, I think I may actually be liking the jealous type, it makes my dick twitch. "My little sister ran away a few years back. She was found last week in Chicago. Dead."

Every ounce of oxygen is sucked out of the room as the words fall from my lips and land on Troy. We are both quiet as he takes in the information I just gave him.

I continue, explaining her reasoning, her difficulty in dealing with our father's death, her fear of disappointing me. By the time I'm done retelling my story, I'm fucking exhausted.

"Are we done yet?" I ask, needing a break or possibly a blowjob.

He is watching me, his dark chocolate eyes penetrating me with something akin to tenderness and even some understanding sprinkled in. "I'm so sorry, Larson. I really am."

He moves closer, pulling me against his rock hard body, his one hand rubbing my back. "I can't say that I know what you're going through, because I don't. It's incomprehensible to me. What can I do?"

I shake my head, not wanting to put any words out there because the truth is, there is nothing he can do. There is nothing that anyone can do. It's on me to get through it. But fuck it, I feel his need to comfort me; to help in some way. I need a distraction.

Anything.

"I can't dwell on it right now, Troy. If I do, I'll fall apart, man. I need to write. Put some good into the words I write...for Kennedy."

He pulls back, and kisses my lips gently, softly, in a comforting way. "Got an idea," he says. "I have something that will totally distract you. Might even be good for a laugh or two."

I quirk a brow. "Not following."

"C'mon," he says, grabbing my hand. "Come with me."

I follow behind, but puzzlement and, I admit, a bit of disappointment sets in when he goes in the opposite direction of his bedroom.

We're in his office, and he bends down, opening the bottom file cabinet drawer and removes a box, handing it to me. I open it, and stare at the stack of neat, white typewritten pages. The title page catches my eye:

'Bridge to Lonely.'

A novel.

Troy Babilonia.

I look over at him quickly. The uncertainty is apparent, I can tell.

"I want you to read it," he says. "And maybe you'll understand more about me than what I could ever explain to you. This is my book, Larson. Maybe not good enough for a publisher, but it's a story worth telling nonetheless. No secrets, dude. That's not what I want for us."

Looking at the title page of his manuscript, my eyes hone in on his name and the question I have been dying to ask just pops free.

"Wait. Before I read this, you need to do me a favor and answer me this...what's the deal with 'Babu'? The only thing I can think about when I hear that name is Aladdin and his monkey. For the love of cock, please tell me, because I really can't wait to put my mind at ease. I need answers."

"For the love of cock? Really?" Chuckling, Troy half-sits on the corner of his desk and tilts his head to the side, boring his gaze into mine. In such a short time, things have definitely changed.

"Before I agreed to take the job with Bluffington, which was in my mind such a disappointment from what I really wanted to do, I took a sabbatical. Told them I needed a few weeks to think about it. I travelled around Europe visiting the old country. In the Med, I stayed in Sardinia and Corsica for a while, soaking up the sun and bathing in their unique cultures."

I take a seat in one of his leather bound chairs, imagining his adventures as though they are happening to me.

"One day while hiking in Corsica, and by the way, those trails are killer, I decided to spend a couple of days in Corte, which used to be the capital of the island. I soaked up on the history, the kind of shit no history books talk about. Like, did you know that they actually had their own president?"

Wait, is he expecting an answer out of me?

"Uhm...no?" I frown knowing that I sound like a complete moron.

"Yeah, so...the island is actually French, but for about a decade they auto-proclaimed themselves independent. While I was walking around, contemplating whether I should continue working toward my dream of becoming a traditionally published author, or sell out and have my own literary column, I look up and see Pasquale Paoli's statue and right there...on the bronze you could see 'U Babbu'."

As though his revelation was supposed to answer all of my questions, he stops and looks at me expectantly.

"And...?" A mind-reader, I am not.

"And..." he continues, "that was my sign to sell out. My name is Babilonia. It was a calling. His name means Father, in that case, father of the nation. I thought, hell, if I do this than I'm doing it as "Babu--the Father of Literary Critics." People will follow and come to depend on me and my literary opinion for their reading selections."

I can't help it, I burst out laughing. So far from the whole monkey thing it's not even funny.

"What?" he asks, clearly perplexed.

"And I thought I was full of myself. Alright, Mr. President, give me that manuscript so I can take a gander."

With that, I saunter into the bedroom, ready to get an eye full.

Chapter 42

I knew this day would come. Here it is. As expected, Joel is kind of
livid with me, but in actuality, no more than I am with myself. I have
no idea what Clark is feeling, but if Joel's current temperament is any
kind of a gauge, Babu could be looking for employment elsewhere.

My typical tendency to point the finger of blame somewhere else
ebbs, and I curse myself silently for allowing Larson aka 'Jiminy
Cricket' to affect my conscience this way.

But he has.

And it's all good, since I'm a better person because of it I suppose,
though I'll never admit that to Lord Larson, King of the Blowjobs and
master of my pleasure.

"Did you hear what I said?" Joel asks, sounding perturbed.

"Sorry. Daydreaming."

"Yeah," he scoffs, getting to his feet from where he's been
perched on the corner of my desk. "You've been doing a lot of that
lately. Seems like your followers have even noticed. Is it love, Troy?"

"It," I say very succinctly, "is none of your business. Now what
does Clark want me to do?"

"He wants you to draft a letter of apology to be posted in your
column to L. Blackburn."

"Seriously? The lawsuit was dropped, I mean what the hell?"

"It is a matter of integrity, Troy. You took that piece of inaccurate
and totally bogus information and went public with it. We're not a
scandal sheet blog. Clark will have final approval of the draft, so do
us all a favor, will you?"

"What's that?"

"As difficult as I know this will be for you, keep the assholiness out of it."

And he's gone, leaving me to simmer in my own irritation. I know he's right—and so is Clark. While Noelle had presented source documents showing her ISBN number attached to that manuscript, I hadn't delved into the allegations any further. And I should have, but what the fuck? I'm not an investigative journalist. I'm a literary critic.

I haven't disclosed to Noelle the proof that Larson has already provided me. She'll get her comeuppance when she reads the apology that I'm about to draft.

And no worries, Joel, I don't intend to put any assholiness, or passive aggressive taunts in this apology because regardless of what I thought of Quincy's Soul—and Larson can't blow me enough to ever change my opinion of it—to throw out the plagiarism card without having verified and re-verified proof was a major gaffe on my part. I owe Larson and his reputation as an author any benefit my apology might provide.

Babu's Book Talk

June 10, 2013

To my readers,

This week's column is taking on a different format. There is no book review, but please, don't stop reading because this may prove to be better than any review I could've left.

Why?

Because today, you will be privy to a first—and with any luck—the only public apology I will ever have cause to make. That's right, Babu made a blunder, and when something as rare as this happens, then you need to know that I will take full responsibility for it.

Several months back, you may recall the allegations I made against author L. Blackburn with respect to his novel "Quincy's Soul" being a plagiarized version of an earlier self-published book entitled "Sympathy for the Devil."

The allegation of plagiarism was without merit, and if I had done my due diligence at the time instead of rushing to judgment—and to the press—I would've discovered just that. The reality was that I took some documented proof and ran with it instead of turning it over to someone to have it properly verified. I take full responsibility for that, and hold the Bluffington Gazette harmless for my reckless and irresponsible actions.

Having said that, I would like to take this opportunity to extend a formal apology to L. Blackburn for my unprofessional behavior and inaccurate allegations, and encourage everyone to not allow the misguided actions on my part to taint their opinions or perception of this author and his work.

My deepest apologies to my readers as well, and I hope you will find it in your hearts to forgive me my mistakes and continue to follow my reviews.

L. Blackburn, I extend an open invitation for you to comment and, if you so choose, to open and publicly throw my apology back in my face. You have every right to do so.

But L. Blackburn, may I leave you all with one last thought?

How people treat you is their Karma, how you react is yours...

This is Babu signing off. I'll be back in two weeks with my next review.

I push "publish" because Clark has approved it. He's also been nice enough to give me two weeks off without pay as a token punishment for my poor judgment.

I suppose all things considered, it could've been much worse. I wonder how long it will take for Noelle to get word of my column, and start blowing up my fucking phone.

No matter. I simply won't answer.

I shut off my laptop, and get up and stretch.

What now?

Maybe a surprise visit to Larson?

It's been a couple of days since he returned to Boston, and while I'm expecting him back Friday evening for the weekend, he's unaware of my sudden two week liberty from my job.

I take a deep sigh. If I do this, it means having to leave my apartment.

I can do that.

Take a flight to Boston.

I can do that.

Maybe even encounter an elevator or two along the way.

I must do this.

I quickly fire my laptop back up, and make flight reservations. If my cab gets here in ten minutes, I can make the two o'clock flight out of JFK. I call Yellow Cab and let them know the cabbie is a dead man driving if he can't be here in ten. They assure me he will be.

Perfect.

I pack a bag, tossing in the essentials. Pretty sure he has lube at his place.

I close up my apartment, yelling to Mrs. Whatley that I'll be gone for a couple of days and not to worry.

Once I reach the sidewalk, my cab is pulling up.

I just love it when a plan comes to fruition.

Chapter 43

It is seven-thirty in the evening, and I am trying to write. I'll let you guess on the key word of that phrase. With my mind continuously distracted by thoughts of a certain tall dark and handsomely hung lover, I can't write for shit. My sentence structure resembles that of a ten-year-old, there are more repetitions than at an Alzheimer's convention and the story makes about as much sense as a baby's babble.

This is bad.

This is so fucking bad.

I refuse to get writer's block for a piece of ass.

Except I'm getting the impression that Troy is much more than that, in fact, I know he is. The connection between us is instantaneous, strong and invigorating. Neither is dominant or submissive, we are just ourselves and doing what we enjoy most...fucking each other's brains out.

Great, now my dick's hard.

Sitting at my desk, my legs sprawled out before me with a pencil behind my ear, I contemplate the words before me.

Or lack thereof.

There is a title, which is pretty damn impressive at this rate. Raking my hands through my completely disheveled hair, I groan when my pencil falls to the floor forcing me to actually move from my seat. That's right; I have been here all damn day, in my pajamas and drinking coffee, to get exactly three words on the page.

Cock will be the death of me. At least it's a nice one.

A knock at the door startles me out of my writing slump and inexplicably annoys me, which is ridiculous since, with or without interruption, I don't get shit done.

Sighing in defeat, I rise from my chair and walk to the front door, opening without thought as to who might be on the other side. To my utter surprise, I see Lloyd dressed in his customary grey suit with a dark pink button-down that nearly blinds me out of my stupor.

"Lloyd. What are you doing here?" I ask with as much calm as humanly possible considering his little temper tantrum with Troy not so long ago. Making no move to let my ex-lover enter my home, I hover at the door and smirk at shock written all over his face.

"I just needed to drop some legal documents over so you could sign them," he answers in a clipped voice that only serves to annoy me.

"Postal service on strike or something? You could have sent them just as easily."

Legal documents my ass.

"No, I figured I'd come over, get them signed and take them back tomorrow morning. It's simpler and quicker this way."

Sure it is.

Taking a step to the side, I let Lloyd in, figuring the quicker this is done, the better. "Come on in, let's do this."

As he crosses the threshold, Lloyd stops beside me and smirks as he takes in my attire, "Writing?"

"Yeah, trying," I mumble since what I've been doing is a far cry from actually putting words on paper.

Closing the door behind him, I follow him into the living room before leaving him there and making my way to the kitchen. My laptop is still open on my practically blank page, a beacon for conversation starters in Lloyd's world.

"I see you're slaving away over there."

Asshole.

"Yeah well, I've been distracted. Where are the docs?"

Lloyd places his manila folder on the side of the desk and slides out the official legal papers before following me into the kitchen, where I am fishing through the fridge for a beer. Looking up at my guest, I gesture to the bottle, silently offering him a drink.

Lloyd shrugs, which I have come to realize over the last couple of years, means "yes," since I'm not offering him any good wine. *Tough shit.*

Handing him a beer from a local brewery, I open mine and set out to quickly read the legal jargon from his stack of documents. It is a simple case of nullifying a civil suit, nothing too complicated in human terms, but always a hassle in the world of law.

"I saw the public apology, you must be happy." This gets my

undivided attention.

"What public apology?" Is he referring to Troy...or in this case *Babu?*

"The Bluffington Gazette," he states with what seems to be resignation as he takes a seat on one of the barstools. "The critic, Babu, openly apologized for the whole plagiarizing ordeal."

Oh, did he now?

Interesting. I have a magic cock, it would seem.

"Does it say why?" Or maybe it was our heart to heart back in New York that opened his seriously clouded eyes.

"Yeah, something about the information that was given to him was false. Which, you and I both know, is true."

Ah, Noelle fucking Crawford and her evil ways.

"Good, maybe this will help my sales. I need to call Brent so he can get on top of marketing. And Lisa...she needs to start pasting that link all over the fucking Internet." I'm already planning, because that's what I do.

"Yeah, you probably should. Look, Larson...I just...," Lloyd's voice falters, his self-assurance taking a bit of a hit for some reason. "I mean...you and me? Are we good? Are you done playing with the critic, now?"

Frowning, I rest my elbows on the counter and face Lloyd head on, making sure he understands my every word. "We are only good on a professional and amicable level. Sex is done, we're past that. As far as Troy is concerned, well...that's none of your fucking business."

I watch every emotion cross Lloyd's face as I take a sip of my beer. I almost feel guilty, but not nearly enough to end things with Troy and get back to reaming Lloyd's ass. Because that's all it ever was for me, sex...plain and simple.

With Troy, there is something altogether different happening. Yes, I definitely get off but, not just in a physical way, but also on a whole new level, an emotional one. This is a complete first for me, despite the fact that I was married for far longer than I care to remember.

"Just like that? You find another piece of ass and just throw me out? That's bullshit and you know it."

Oh, Christ. This conversation is getting boring quickly.

"When the fuck did you grow a vagina, Lloyd? I mean, don't get me wrong, a little pussy every now and then is great, but not the shit that's spewing from your mouth."

I look him straight in the eyes when my next words hit home. "You and I were never a couple. We fucked. It was fun, it was satisfying, but it's over. Is this going to be a problem? Do I need to move my legal business elsewhere?"

Lloyd is about to speak, his mouth open to do so when there's another knock at the door. Looking up to the clock on the wall, I sigh at the late hour, no idea who it could possibly be.

"Hold that thought," I say thinking. "Or not." I don't particularly want to hear him whine about losing my cock as his personal plaything, but I suppose we need to clear the air so that no misunderstandings exist. I reach the door, again not checking, and open it. This time around, the sight that greets me makes my dick instantly hard.

Speak of the fucking devil and he'll show up in dark jeans and a white tee-shirt.

Delicious.

We stand there eyeing each other for what feels like an eternity when he breaks the silence.

"Are you going to let me in or are we going to do our business out here all night?" He asks, giving me a lazy smile.

That's when I notice the rather hefty luggage he's rolling behind him. Well, well, well...

I foresee a sleep over in my very near future.

"By all means, please come in."

Contrary to Lloyd's arrival, I stop Troy in his tracks and crush my lips to his, devouring with my mouth, caressing him with my tongue and contemplating fondling him for my entire neighborhood's benefit.

The clearing of a throat has Troy stiffening instantaneously, making me groan.

Fucking Lloyd, the cockblock.

Chapter 44

What. The. Fuck?

So this is it?

This is what I get for taking the only fucking risk I've taken in my thirty-two years on this planet? For letting my heart get involved and making it not just about the sex? For embracing my closeted sexuality, allowing it to spring free, and reveling in it like Muffy with her Beluga?

I recognize the asshat that came to my loft not so long ago with the legal papers he could've just mailed. The one who told me that I wasn't good enough for Larson.

Remember him?

Lloyd...Floyd?

It's as if time is now going in slow motion and I study his face, and see the not so subtle sneer develop on his lips, turn quickly to look at Larson, who's wearing this dumbstruck look that says, 'What? It's not what it looks like.'

Oh really?

"Oh, fuck to the no," I roar, dropping the handle of my luggage and with quick, long strides, I step over the threshold and start to close the distance between myself and the now smiling as-if-he's-just-fucked-my-lover Lloyd or Floyd or whatever the fuck his name is.

Behind me I hear Larson, "Troy...hey, it's..."

"Don't!" I yell, my eyes narrowing as I stalk my prey, allowing my eyes to flicker over his flamboyant hot pink shirt. And then I feel insulted and, for a moment, I debate whether it's the dandy that should be on the receiving end of my fist or Larson.

I quickly decide to strike the nearest prey first. My fist shoots out and cuffs him good with an uppercut to the chin, sending him sprawling backwards, where he lands on one of Larson's black glass end tables, knocking the lamp to the floor, as his ass lands smack dab on top of it.

The sound of glass shattering echoes throughout the room, and I'm not done yet. I move towards him and, realizing he's still in a daze, I take the opportunity to snatch him up with both hands fisting the collar of his shirt and shove him against Larson who's totally caught off guard by this move. And trust me, the dude is not puny, but my adrenaline is in overdrive at the moment, and I intend to make good use of it

"Is he what you want, Larson, huh? You want to fuck the flamer here? Because hey, I can clear out right now so that you and *Pink Floyd* can take up where you left off before I so inconveniently interrupted your cozy soiree."

Larson chuckles and I'm not fucking amused.

At all.

As I focus my gaze on Larson, I don't catch the quick movement of Floyd as he lunges at me with a growl, "My name is *Lloyd*," he hisses. "And I believe I made my position quite clear the last time we spoke. You're not good enough for my Larson."

Your Larson?

And that's when I deck him again. Hard. My fist meets his perfectly straight nose, and the sound of cartilage crunching resounds, along with his shriek of pain.

"Sir," he calls out, his hand covering his bloody nose, as he staggers backwards, tilting his head up and back so as not to allow any blood to drip on his expensive pink shirt. "Sir, are you going to permit this?"

Oh. *Sir* it is, huh? What kind of fucking weirdness was Blackburn into with this dudette? I turn to acknowledge Larson, who is standing there, muscular arms crossed and his sexy drawstring pajamas hanging low on his narrow hips. He's shaking his head.

My. Dick. Is. Hard.

His package is evident and his cock has made a bit of a tent beneath those sweats. Not sure if that's for me or if the sight of Pink Floyd's blood is getting him hard.

"Well, *sir*," I say, trying to mimic Lloyd's voice and dripping sarcasm along the way, "Do tell? Who's it gonna be, huh? Me or your Fifty Shades of Whack over there?"

I watch, a bit confused I must admit, as Larson casually strolls over to the kitchen counter and takes hold of his beer before making himself comfortable on the nearest stool. The room is silent but for the wheezing coming from the damsel in distress over there. I'm guessing he's uncomfortably numb in the entire nose region.

"Let's see," my soon-to-be ex-lover begins as he adjusts the rapidly growing erection he is starting to sport. "Could you start over because the view is much better from here?" Then he takes a sip of his beer and waves his hand as though giving us permission to continue.

Are you fucking kidding me right now?

"You're out of your mind, Larson. What are you playing at?"

Larson shrugs and takes another sip then focuses his stare on me. Green fixated on black. "If you want to throw punches and ask questions later then, by all means, keep playing. I'll be here when you're done and let you know that Lloyd, here, and I were concluding our business in a very professional and unnaked kind of way."

The fucker actually smirks.

"But like I said...don't let me interrupt your little macho show, it's seriously hot," he adds pointing to his now fully awakened cock.

"Eyes back in their sockets, Poindexter," I growl as I observe Lloyd focusing on Larson's crotch. "Since your business appears to have concluded, looks like Sir has dismissed you and, uh, he won't be in need of your services any longer. Legal or otherwise, capisce?"

His glare is arctic as he pulls a freshly ironed and monogrammed handkerchief from his pocket, and dabs gently at his nose. "You don't possess the authority to fire me, Mr. Babilonia. Only Larson has that authority, and I'm fairly certain at this point, he isn't inclined to do that being I could bring assault charges against his newest *trick.* He's a witness as a matter of fact."

I'm just about ready to lunge at the pretentious dickhead when the sound of Larson's voice halts me.

"Out, Lloyd. Now. Your welcome was worn out as soon as you crossed the threshold. I've a hunger that you can't possibly fill, and unless you want to be a witness to *that,* I suggest you take the papers I've signed and get the fuck out."

Lloyd grabs the envelope from the counter, and shoots a glare my way as he makes a hasty exit, slamming the door hard enough that the windows rattle.

"Don't leave mad, Lloyd, just leave," Larson chuckles, all the venom now gone from his voice. "Now, where were we, Troy?" he says, leaning back against the counter top, crossing his arms in front of him, as if this is the most natural occurrence for him to witness. "Oh yeah, before I forget, you owe me a new end table and lamp."

Chapter 45

"Jesus Christ, Troy. Please tell me this is not auto-biographical."

We're following the laws of Sunday by religiously lounging on our lazy asses, reading our hearts out. Troy is grumbling like a ninety-year old who just lost his dentures, so I'm guessing whatever book he has between his hands will be getting trashed in the near future. Fleetingly, I wonder if he made those geriatric sounds while he was not-so-engrossed in Quincy's Soul.

With his head laying across my bare chest, and his body perpendicular to mine, Troy quickly throws a glance my way; the answer to my question is clearly visible in his eyes.

Motherfucker.

I want to find his worthless stepfather and gut him. Literally plunge my hand into an open stomach wound and rip his intestines out before shoving them in his mouth. Maybe I should start writing horror/gore, with his stepfather's description in the forefront of my brain, I could have psycho material for years.

"Yeah, well...it was a long time ago. It's all good, now," he replies softly.

Words spoken too calmly, their truth tainted by the betrayal of an adult father figure, a man who was supposed to care for and guide a young boy coming of age. Instead, he was taught a lesson on bigotry with a fucking tree stick.

"Whatever, Troy. Don't bullshit a bullshitter, but I'll let that slide for now." I smirk in his direction to lessen the bite of my words. I'm trying to be light and relaxed although I feel murderous. Give me a minute and I'll switch to horny if I keep staring at his dark hair resting innocently on my exposed chest. I can't imagine he's all that comfortable in this position since I'm half sitting against the headboard, putting his neck at an odd angle.

"You should rest your head a bit further down, you might be more at ease for reading." I swear to fuck, my suggestion was one hundred percent for his benefit. The fact that "right below" is my eagerly awaiting semi, has no bearing on this conversation.

Much.

"Don't be a greedy bitch, Larson. I'm good right here," he quips, his eyes never leaving the printed pages as his hand comes up to my neck and pulls me down for a sensual, if not too brief kiss. We both go back to reading in comfortable silence which does nothing to relax my rising lust.

His story, Bridge to Lonely, is good. His writing is solid. But knowing who it's about is slowly killing my soul and my hopes for humanity.

"This is crap," he blurts, breaking the silence. "What fucking adult male still says 'Dude'?" His words come out in a growl as though the mere thought of that expression repulses him.

Chuckling, I put Troy's manuscript face down on the bed and cock my brow at him, waiting until I have his full attention.

"What?" he asks as he feels my stare.

"You're kidding, right?"

"No. This character is supposed to be some kind of hotshot detective leading a murder case. The subject matter is serious and the tone of the dialogue is supposed to be grave. The author..." At this point, Troy is turning to the book cover to read, what I'm assuming is, the author's name before continuing his tirade. "Dale Thorton, has the hero saying "dude" at the beginning of every sentence. It's ridiculous; it's repetitive and just plain unrealistic. College jerk-offs say dude, not experienced detectives."

Silence.

"Troy." For the record, I'm really trying to keep a straight face, avoiding the inevitable bout of laughter that will erupt from my mouth.

"Larson," he deadpans.

"*You* say "dude" all the fucking time." I'm watching his hands to make sure he doesn't punch my balls so far up my sack that they get lost.

"I'm not a detective," he answers undeterred. "Plus, I never said I wasn't a jerk-off."

"Touché."

"Fuck, don't speak French, Larson or else I'll never get this book finished."

Interesting.

"Why is that?" I feign disinterest as I pick the manuscript back up and pretend to read which is quasi impossible since the tone of his voice was purely sexual, no doubt about it.

"You know damn well, why. Coy doesn't suit you." Looking over the white pages at his profile, I can see the tease of a smile adorning his delicious lips.

"J'ne sais pas de quoi tu parles." I'm a dick—lovable and talented, but a dick nonetheless. Despite what I just said, I know exactly what he's talking about. That thought is confirmed when a low growl escapes Troy's lips and his head turns to face me.

"I have to read this, Larson. My review has to go live tomorrow, and your distractions are making that impossible."

"Y'a pas de problème, continue ta lecture." I'm aware of the fact that I may, indeed, be pushing my luck.

"Fuck it, I'll just DNF it and say it was too corny for me to finish it," he says as he puts the book down and turns over on his stomach, his face inches from my neglected shaft.

"You can't fucking do that, Troy! You can't trash a book because your libido suddenly felt the need to shine on its crazy diamond." Yeah, I know, I'm quoting Pink Floyd and using it to prove an orgasmic point.

"Why not? It's shit, anyway. I'd much prefer coming down your throat."

Jesus Christ, how am I supposed to argue a point like that? But then a thought occurs to me, and a strange mixture of anger and jealousy all wrapped into one green-eyed monster makes its appearance in my gut.

"Is that what happened with my book? With Quincy's Soul? You had a sudden need to bust a nut so you gave up on my story for the first available open-mouth?" The rising tone of my voice is a clear indicator of my equally escalading irritation.

"No. I DNF'd yours because I truly felt like every minute I spent with my nose in your book was time I would never recover. Lost moments of my life that I felt would be put to better use elsewhere."

Now, I just want to throat punch him.

"Bullshit!" I growl as I push him off of me so we're facing each other on the bed. I really do not want our lazy Sunday to transform into an MMA event on white linen sheets, although that could eventually be fun. But, I digress.

"That book is good. Great even. My plotline is solid, the loose ends were all taken care of but you wouldn't know that since you didn't even bother to read it right to the end." I smirk because, let's face it, I'm witty and that right there is the fucking truth.

"Larson," Troy begins with a condescending tone that makes me want to push him back down on his stomach and fuck that holier-than-thou attitude right out of him. "Authors are like mothers. They both birth their babies and believe each one to be the most beautiful creature put on this earth. I'm just here to unveil objectivity that clearly is impossible to have with your own creation."

Then he cocks his head to the side as though I'm a turbulent child that needs things explained in simple terms. We'll see if he can still give me a lecture when my cock is so far down his throat that it knocks on the door of his stomach.

"Again, that's total crap. First, my mother didn't just think I was the most beautiful baby on this planet, she knew. Because I was. Even the nurses agreed." I rise to all fours, stalking Troy on the other end of the bed, my eyes fixated on his parted mouth because he knows. Troy is beginning to read me so well he can anticipate my reactions and us fighting? Well, it's just fucking foreplay.

"Two...authors do not think their books are great. They think they're crap. They are their own worst critics, the destroyers of their very own egos. We are fragile souls, Troy and we need validation because the shit that's printed in those pages is the inked version of our blood, sweat and tears. You don't have to like it but to trash it? It's low and it's completely unnecessary."

I'm on him now, pushing him on his back with my thighs encasing his hips and my folded elbows on either side of his head. The spark in his beautiful browns tells me he's goading me, taunting me, pushing my patience until I take exactly what I want. Mr. CockyPants is going to get his wish...in all its hard, velvety, thick glory.

"Besides," I continue, my lips a mere inch from his, "the fact that you don't like it for any reason is punishment enough. Destroying every other page across the fucking Internet is not going to help that author improve his writing. All it will do is shatter his ego a little more."

Troy groans as my tongue traces his lobe before settling on that sensitive skin below, my groin rubbing on his now erect cock like a feline in heat.

"Is that what you want, Troy? To annihilate authors because your book didn't get a Big Five approval?"

"Did it ever occur to you that I do what I do solely for entertainment purposes, Larson? Now fuck me and we'll talk later."

"Your wish is my command, oh great Babu, Father of Literary Critics." My mouth crushes down on his with ardent desire and a need so deep it makes my heart beat wildly behind my ribcage. Or maybe it's just lust but the two percent portion of my brain still able to think with the blood pumping only down south, is telling me that something is shifting. Lust bears a strange resemblance to another emotion I thought I had given up on a long time ago.

Apparently not.

Surprisingly enough, I'm not afraid nor am I reluctant. In fact, I may very well be ready to take a leap of faith.

Fuck it.

Chapter 46

Jesus H. Christ.

Once Larson got off of his "Don't dis the author" soapbox and onto my dick, I was finally able to relax and put the memories of Bridge to Lonely out of my mind.

I'm not sure why I had wanted Larson to read my manuscript, because I certainly wouldn't have blamed him for trashing it as in "Paybacks are a Bitch" for what I had done to Quincy's Soul. But he hadn't done that at all.

The book had angered him, and I had been worried the content might repulse him, and rightfully so, but it hadn't. I suppose my reason for wanting Larson to read it is twofold. I want him--no, I need him to understand what he's getting into with me. I've got baggage, there's no denying that and as much as I have been trying to extricate it, there is still more to do.

Secondly, for some reason I want Larson to validate me as a writer, and though he hasn't commented one way or another as to my ability, my hope is that he will finish it and provide me with an opinion.

Can I accept his opinion, good or bad?

I have no choice. I want honesty, not patronization because we're lovers. I mean, would he expect any less from me?

Probably. But that's just Larson.

He's in the shower now, and I glance around his room, which for the past couple of days has become our room. It's neat and well organized, just like Larson. Everything is done in good taste, and the color schemes are bold and masculine. Just like he is.

It's not like my apartment.

Everything in my loft is eclectic, which I suppose is simply a fancy word for mismatched, yet my furniture and objet d'arts are all good pieces if not collectibles.

Everything in Larson's condo weeps modern masculinity, defiance, independence and yes, sincerity. It is a stark reflection of the man who lives here.

Larson knows who he is and he makes no excuses or apologies for it. He wears his flaws just as proudly as he does his attributes, for all to see, and for everyone to accept or reject--as the case may be because it makes no difference to him. He is comfortable in his own skin.

That is probably because Larson is genuine. He doesn't wear layers of facades that need to be ripped away in order to find his inner soul or his truth. He just puts it all out there without reservation.

Not like me.

I envy him that, but more importantly, I'm drawn to him because of that. I love that he's real and genuine; and that he has no reluctance in allowing people to observe every facet of his psyche. His strengths and his imperfections both work to his advantage. His Achilles heel is simple to find. His insecurity about his writing is what endears him to me, and that's because it's something we have in common; a trait that we share, although I'm not sure that he realizes it just yet.

Larson is more than my lover. He feels like a soul mate from a previous life. I've known him forever, even though that's clearly impossible, but it's the way that I feel. My thoughts and feelings about Larson are temporarily interrupted when his cell goes off.

I scoot off the bed, still naked, and grab it from the dresser, glancing at the caller I.D.

Fucking Lloyd.

What is that fucker's deal?

I press "accept" and bark into the cell, "Yeah?"

There is a moment of silence.

"Mr. Blackburn, please."

"May I ask who is calling?"

Yeah. I'm gonna fuck with the dude. Let him think that Larson has already dropped him from his contact list.

From the other end, I hear a throat clearing. "Yes, this is his attorney, Lloyd Ledbetter."

"Is this legal business, Lloyd? I mean, it is Sunday after all. Shit, even sharks have to take a rest occasionally."

"I'm aware what day of the week it is, Mr. Babilonia. And my business with Mr. Blackburn doesn't concern you, nor is it any of your business. May I please speak to him?"

Ah. Lloyd seems to be getting a bit... *testy.*

"Well, let me see if Mr. Blackburn is available for you. He's in the shower."

I walk towards the bathroom, pushing open the door just as Larson is stepping from the shower in all of his naked fucking glory.

Damn.

He looks over at me as I hold up his cell. "Lloyd wants to talk to you," I deadpan. "Do you need me to dry you off?" I continue, a bit louder knowing that poor Lloyd is privy to our conversation.

Larson smirks, wraps a towel around his hips and then takes the phone from me. I notice he can't take his eyes off of my dick.

"What is it, Lloyd?" he asks, finally turning away, but not before I see the towel start to tent from his growing erection.

Yeah. He's dick-whipped.

Just like fucking me.

And then I hear Larson's voice getting a bit louder, and the irritation that is usually directed at one specific person in life makes its presence.

"What do you mean she intends to make trouble?"

Silence.

"Why did she call you?"

Noelle.

"Oh...her lawyer called you. Cut to the chase here, Lloyd. What exactly does Ellie want? And how does she even know about my...situation? And then explain to me how this shit isn't blackmail while you're at it, okay? Because I'm pretty fucking sure that's still a crime."

What the hell?

I reach in and turn on the shower faucet, adjusting it so that I can get the water temperature just the way I like it. Once it's there, I slip in, and pull the glass door shut. It's then that I catch Larson's parting words to Lloyd.

"It's time I handle this bitch once and for all, Lloyd. I'm not sure whether you're the proper firm to handle this shit. I'll talk to Troy and let you know tomorrow. In the meantime, just fucking sit on this. I'll clue Brent in as well."

There's a pause.

"Listen Lloyd, now is not the time to discuss my personal shit. It was never a thing—what you and I had, well it wasn't what I have now. Not even close. I'm sorry."

Chapter 47

If I were more animal than human, I would be hunting down Noelle like the prey she deserves to be and certainly not in a good way. I want to tear her to pieces for trying to fuck with my life, my work and my fucking reputation. I'm not rich, I'm not a saint, but my integrity is whole unlike that back-stabbing bitch's.

That conversation with Lloyd was like a bucket of ice water. The semi I had been sporting since Troy walked into my apartment died down the instant Lloyd caught me up to speed with Noelle's latest drama. The public apology that Troy had posted on the column had obviously reached her publishing eyes, turning her into a raging bitch, which was just one notch above her regular psycho status.

The papers came to Lloyd's office on a fucking Saturday, he wasn't there but one of his grunts called him as soon as they arrived by courier. I wondered why it had taken him an entire twenty-four hours to keep me in the loop, but he had told me that he wanted to read over the law suit thoroughly before contacting me. It made sense, I suppose, but then Lloyd wasn't my personal lawyer...well, unless I killed Noelle with my bare hands then he'd be my man in court.

Noelle was suing me for breach of contract. No shit. I write the book, she wants my earnings but we both know what she's really after...my cock. What can I say; it's the magic tree trunk.

Hearing the spray of water tapping at a steady rhythm in my shower, I do the only thing I know. I plan. I refuse to play this unhealthy little game on the defense. Noelle is sneaky, but she's careless and acts out based on her emotions instead of her intelligence. That's how I will corner her. It's time to finish this shit, time to play offense...time to sever the umbilical cord and kill the adversary.

Too many metaphors? Too bad, get over it.

Standing in my kitchen with a half-full glass of apple juice, still only wearing a white cotton towel around my waist, I look up as wet bare feet make their way down the hall. I don't have carpeting everywhere, I don't like it. Sure, it's great for winter but it's a bitch to keep clean and I won't even get started on the odors. So, I opted for hardwood everywhere except the kitchen where I had Italian tiles put in to replace the crappy little square shit the previous owners had chosen. Truth be told, they weren't evenly spaced and well...that crap drove me to drink.

Looking up, I immediately tense, feeling a strange pull that has my feet moving before my brain can even register my action. Not two seconds later, I'm standing face to face and not even two inches away from Troy who is wearing exactly the same cloth as I.

"We match." Never said I was smooth. Or did I?

"Shut up." Yeah, we're just two romantics living the life of a fairy tale. Let's be clear here, that was sarcasm.

Looking down at his groin, I grin when I see the matching tent in Troy's towel. I have the same one brought on by his mere presence. It's difficult to concentrate and bring a game plan to fruition when my blood flow is stuck in my dick.

"I think we need to get dressed, or I won't be able to get shit done."

Troy smirks at my comment and without warning, grabs the back of my neck roughly and pulls me in for a kiss that has my balls tightening almost to the point of pain. Instinctively, my hands drop to his firm ass making his towel fall to the floor. Well, this isn't going to help my clear-thinking one bit, but fuck it, how can I resist? Why would I want to? Focus, Larson...Focus on the plan.

"Troy." But that's all I am able to say before my mouth is taken hostage by full, talented lips and a tongue that could hypnotize Houdini. Pushing Troy back into the nearest wall, I lick my lips savoring his lingering taste before sighing and resting my hands on my hips.

"We seriously need to concentrate on the task at hand, here." I'm trying to be reasonable. Well, as much as possible considering the majority of my blood flow is travelling south for the winter.

With his free hand, Troy rips my only clothing off and throws it in the near vicinity, but fuck if I care where it lands.

"I'm pretty sure my concentration is one hundred percent, Larson," he tells me with that cocky grin and a wicked sparkle in his eye that makes him look ten years younger.

Our dicks are now side by side, our movements creating some much desired friction while our tongues battle it out for dominance.

I'm torn between showing him who is boss and letting him control where this is inevitably going. It's a heads-or-tails moment...no pun intended so really, either way is a win.

With both of his hands clasped on either side of my jaw, I let Troy guide our heated kiss, I let him direct the dance, following his lead while my hand discreetly makes its way to our weeping dicks. God, the feel of him, hot and velvety, wet from our pre-cum. Jesus, we just fucking showered.

"We need to stop," I manage to utter the second we come up for some much needed air. I wonder if we could devour each other or die trying.

"Why?"

Fucker, he's playing with my self-control.

"Because," I reply, "shit is going down and I need to get my game plan on." If he kisses me again, I'm done fighting it.

"Okay, let's get dressed," he acquiesces.

Yes, that's right, I'm disappointed. And horny. And pissed off at Noelle because even from a distance she's cock-blocking me.

Tit for tat, bitch.

Two hours later, it's early evening and I'm about to make dinner. Nothing fancy, of course, just a bit of spaghetti with some cut ham and parmesan sprinkled on top. I'm no chef but years of fending for myself has taught me two things: Eat well, fuck better. One has been followed to the tee as of late, the other I need to make sure I continue. A man needs his strength for good stamina, after all.

Putting the pasta in the boiling hot water, I grin when the knock at the front door reverberates throughout the house.

Game time.

Barefoot and wearing a pair of low strung jeans, I make sure my black button down is wrinkle free. This is me we're talking about, anything less than perfection would be unfathomable. Running a hand through my freshly showered dark blonde hair, I lick my lips and plaster my sex-inducing, toe-curling, I'm-going-to-fuck-you-nine-ways-to-Sunday grin.

What does that even mean?

Simple. My lips have a crooked tilt to them and my dimple is out. It's only visible with this one particular grin and it works every time.

"Ellie, baby. I'm glad you could come by on such short notice," I say as I open the front door. My ex-wife is standing just beyond the threshold looking nervous with her bottom lip trapped between her teeth. She thinks she looks coy and girlish, probably even fuckable.

She doesn't.

The only look she is actually going for is desperate but that's where I need her to be. Panting, aching and begging for me.

"Hi Larson, I was surprised to hear from you. How did you know I was in Boston?"

I step to the side, letting Ellie enter the house, anticipating her flirtatious move; brushing her arm against my chest. Classic play, so fucking predictable.

"Lloyd. He called me, of course." You see, this makes me look earnest and sincere. No lies, no room for error.

"Oh," she barely whispers as though her hopes and wishes have just flown out the window.

Little does she know that they never even flapped their wings once but crashed directly to the hard concrete below. I will never fuck Noelle again, not unless she is the last human on earth. That's right; I'm not a fucking idiot. If we were the last two people on earth, I would not let my pride get in the way of blowing my load. Besides, daily orgasms are recommended to avoid prostate cancer and I'm anything if not a health nut.

"Yeah, he said you had dropped off some papers at his office. Thought maybe you would still be in town. Would you like a glass of Chardonnay? I was about to make dinner and figured you still liked spaghetti?"

See what I did there? Bringing up her preferences, showing her I remember the days when we were married. I'm the black widow, and she's my fucking shit-eating fly. Or whatever the fuck those eight-legged nasty creatures eat.

"Oh, sure. Yes, that would be great, Larson. Kind of feels like old times..." her voice trails off.

Sure it does, sweetheart. Add in a little cheating on the side with a pinch of denial and the menu to our marriage is presented in full.

"Have a seat, babe, make yourself comfortable while I get you a glass. You can put your jacket on the coat hanger over there." I'm completely laid back which is the exact opposite of how I feel inside. For every nice thing I say to her, I want to rip my tongue out from the acid burn the lies leave.

After our years spent living together, Noelle knew of my unreasonable need for order. This knowledge leads her straight to the hanger where she neatly rests her faux mink coat. It is pretentious, just like her.

"I like what you've done with this place," she remarks, tracing her index finger along the bottom of my framed Kandinsky print. "I remember when you first moved out and I came here to bring some of the things you had left back in New York. You've really made it work nicely."

That is a lie.

Noelle hated all things masculine when it came to our living quarters. She was the epitome of femininity and not in a positive light. Every single cliché about women applied wholly to her. The bitching, the passive-aggressive "I'm fine" responses, the tears. Jesus Christ, the fucking tears were on stand-by every time she didn't get her way.

As I stand here at the kitchen counter, I take a long look at my ex-wife trying to dig deep at some kind of semblance of sentiment that I may still harbor for her. I wish her no real harm but the love I had once felt inside is now merely an empty hole, slowly and surely being filled with another.

Another soul, another sex...another life.

Troy, and his evil Disney counterpart "Babu the Critic", have me at their mercy. As much as I hate that idea, I love it even more.

Noelle turns to make her way back to me, her dark hair framing the heart-shaped face. Lips coated in a tint of red that reminds me all too much of a three dollar hooker. There is no denying that her body is just as sexy and appealing as it had been six years ago but my dick has no interest. My heart doesn't even register her presence. Yet, I have to aim for the Oscar tonight and make her feel desired when all I want to do is run to Troy and suck him off. Then fuck him. Hard and long.

Shit.

Now my cock *is* hard and my thoughts are on constant replay of the last two days with Troy. Without meaning to, my lips curve into a small grin as my mental Power Point is displaying all the ways I made Troy come. Problem is...Noelle is staring at me now; her eyes shifting from my grin to my groin probably thinking I'm hungry and she's my next meal.

Try again, sweetheart.

I've turned Troytarian and am suddenly Noelle-intolerant.

"Oh...Larson. I...ohmygod, I've been waiting so long for this..."

Oh shit.

"I know. Come here."

I watch her jean-clad legs make their way to me as her plum cashmere sweater clings to all the right parts of her chest and waist.

Were she not a raging bitch, she could make some poor chump come all over himself by just looking at her. I used to be that chump until I heard The Call of the Dick. Great porn title, by the way.

Noelle reaches out her hand as she nears, and I take it and wrap my fingers around her palm before pulling her into my chest.

"Do you remember where my bedroom is?" I would have to make a mental note to bleach my bed and every last place she touched before fucking Troy.

"Yes," she whispers with a barely audible breath, "I remember." Our mouths are so close, I could easily lean in and capture her mouth but I don't think I have it in me to go that far. Brad Pitt, I am not.

"Go. I want you naked on my bed, eyes closed. You open them and I'll send you on your way. Understood?" She nods, my eyes narrow. "Words, Noelle. Say the words."

"Yes. I understand."

My eyes catch the pink tip of her tongue as it licks a small path across her ruby red lips before disappearing inside her mouth. I shudder and not in a good way. With her eyes half-mast from the lust coursing through her veins, she turns on her heel and follows my instructions once more.

Shit's about to get real.

When I walk into the room, Noelle is sitting on the bed, naked, eyes fixed on my every move, her anticipation building with every one of my steps.

"Lie down on your back, arms above your head." I am playing the dominant lover, a role I used to bring into play while we were married. Nothing ever hard core, just domineering, and she used to cream her panties at the mere sound of my voice. Funny, though, how it hadn't stopped her from fucking half the island of Manhattan while I was holed up in my writing cave.

The black satin fabric that hangs between my fingers feels heavy at my side, a sudden feeling of betrayal washes over me as I take in Noelle's naked form sprawled across my clean sheets.

I have touched, licked and fucked every possible inch of her body and despite that fact, my cock has no interest.

None whatsoever.

Slowly making my way to the side of the bed, I see a satisfied smile creep up the corners of my ex-wife's lipstick-coated lips. We used to have the same ambitions, the same dreams, and the same philosophy of life but then her desires shifted. Needs that I could not and would not ignore, had hovered over our relationship like a black cloud filled with cold, unforgiving water just biding its time before raining its hard truths upon us.

We were not meant to be. Forcing our fate had not changed the inevitable outcome; an unpleasant and violent separation. She cried when I softly announced that our marriage was a dead-end. My sexual needs had always been laid out frankly on the proverbial table of our couple, but she had dismissed my honesty, opting for her own misled brand of reality.

Despite it all, I had never betrayed her. I had never even put myself in a situation that could eventually lead me down the path of unfaithfulness. Back then, I had made vows and my pride and self-respect refused to do wrong by her.

Noelle?

Well, apparently we didn't have the same set of rules or moral codes. Blaming my lack of attention, she had found comfort in the arms of half the city, coming home to me after each one of her extra-marital adventures.

My writing had kept me in the dark at the beginning but then she became careless. The manly cologne would linger on her skin, her disheveled hair would be more noticeable, her lipstick nonexistent.

As the affairs progressed, I realized my heart pulled further away from the strings of her own, and that was when our marriage died. When you wake up one morning and realize you just don't give a fuck where her pussy has been, it's time to sever the ties.

Which brings me back to the present. Ties.

Kneeling on the mattress, right next to her ribs, I place the blindfold over her widening eyes as I cock a grin in her direction.

"Behave, Ellie. Close your eyes and do as you're told. And soon, we'll both get what we want."

Or, at least, I will.

I make my way to the bathroom where I reach around the door and slide off the belt from the bathrobe hanging on the hook. Yeah, I like a nice soft cotton robe after I take a hot shower. Don't judge.

I'm quickly back at her side, tying her slender wrists to my headboard, testing the knots before leaning back on my haunches and admiring my work.

At this moment, Noelle looks fragile and submissive, ready to be fucked if the rubbing of her thighs is any indication. The scent of her pussy reaches my nostrils, confirming what I already know to be true. Ellie wants to be fucked, specifically by me.

"Took you long enough," I hear from behind me, the raspy voice of the man that is quickly becoming my entire world whispers in my ear.

"Patience is a virtue," I respond with a soft chuckle.

"Who's there?" Ah, the nervous sound of Noelle's voice echoes throughout the otherwise silent room.

"If you listen very carefully, Ellie, you'll be able to figure it out all on your own."

Images of Troy's cock shoved deep down her throat invade my mind, making my jealous streak appear like a ghost of fucks past.

Bah-Humbug, bitch.

"Wh-What? What are you talk..."

I cut her off because I really do not want to hear her sorry excuses or lies pouring from her parted lips. "You see, Ellie, I got some very disturbing news earlier. To be honest, it ruined my quiet little Sunday shenanigans, but the situation needs to be addressed. Because I know you, I figure the only way you are going to listen instead of talking is to be blind and immobile."

I smirk even though she can't see me as I feel Troy's hand wrap around my neck and pulling my head back before capturing my mouth in a searing kiss. Our lips and tongues slipping and sliding as he completely owns our kiss. Momentarily losing my track of thought, I drown in our intimacy. I know Noelle can hear us, hardening my cock to painful degrees.

As he pulls back, my head still tilted backwards, his leaning forward; we share an upside-down view of each other before I return to the task at hand.

"Now, where was I? Oh, yes...that's right. The back stabbing stint."

Noelle makes a shocked sound as realization hits her that this is not a sexual game but a set-up instead.

"If I have to, I'll put a gag in your mouth if it ensures a better chance of being heard. Because I will be heard, and tonight, Ellie, I'm going to show you what you have ignored for years. I want you to take in the information and store it at the forefront of your brain so that you never, ever forget it. Nod if you understand." She does as she's told albeit tentatively.

"I'm going to remove the blindfold and although I know you'll gasp, I don't want to hear another sound coming from you until you confirm that you understand what it is I'm trying to tell you."

I don't ask her to do so but she nods anyway, like a good little submissive that we both know she is definitely not.

Rising to my full height, I turn toward Troy and grin all the while pushing off my jeans and stepping out of them as he does the same. Our gazes never falter as our hearts beat so fast they could rival a stampede of wild horses. Having a third person privy to our desires is a major turn-on; one Troy had mixed feelings about as we put our plan into place just mere hours earlier.

Facing each other, gloriously naked, I wink at my man before turning my attention back to Noelle who is trying in vain to figure out what the hell is going on. At least she's silent, *thank fuck.*

Leaning over the side of the bed, I quickly take the blindfold off and watch as her eyes adjust to the soft light coming from the end tables on either side of the bed. When her gaze narrows on my naked body and then shifts to the equally unclothed Troy behind me, I hear the gasp I knew would come. Ah, the little pleasures in life are often times the most satisfying.

"You see, Ellie...your little games only served one purpose— bringing Troy and me together. I suppose I should thank you for that, but I'm too pissed off at your passive-aggressive, manipulative ways to force the words out of my mouth. Since you cannot seem to get it through your thick skull that I no longer want, desire or even acknowledge your presence on this earth, I hope maybe the images you will take with you tonight bring you back to reality."

Troy steps up behind me, the front of his body pushed flush against my back, his cock clearly enjoying the moment. We fit perfectly together, as though our bodies were created for the sole purpose of uniting as one. My chest tightens at the thought of this strong, willful and sometimes too cocky for his own good man, being mine.

All fucking mine.

I stake my claim so there can be no misunderstandings. "Troy is mine, Ellie. He fills me in ways you never could; emotionally and physically. And although I've known him but for a minute, I have no doubt as to his fidelity. My experience with you should have made me more distrustful but in all honesty, I just don't even think about those days with you anymore. You are my past, Troy is my future and the two cannot mix ever again after tonight. Are we clear?"

Noelle's eyes widen as I see the tears well up, her irises getting glassy with the imminent overflow. Then it happens, one lone tear spills over and down the side of her temple before disappearing in her ear. I don't really want to hurt her but she needs to understand that we are nothing, and that we haven't been anything for a long time.

Lips trembling with the effort to stay strong, she doesn't express her understanding as I had hoped, instead she whispers her last fighting words, "Fuck you, Larson. You're an asshole."

"True. But maybe, just maybe, you helped create this side of me, Ellie."

As I speak, Troy's hand slides around my waist, latching onto my aching cock. Leaning in, he murmurs in my ear just loud enough for Noelle to hear his words. "I can't wait to fuck you, Larson. After tonight, you are mine and mine alone." Punctuating his words with a firm grip of my cock, I sigh before leaning back against him and reveling in the feel of his touch. My head rests on his shoulder before I straighten again and continue with my tirade.

"Your lies and deceit almost cost me my career, my fucking reputation. Why would you do that? There are hundreds of guys out there you could chase and woo, why do you feel the need to fuck with me? Cheating on me wasn't punishment enough for my lack of attention? You had to go after my work?"

As I'm spilling years' worth of anger at the guilty party, I bask in every one of Troy's movements, his touches and his soft words of encouragement as his hands work their magic on my aching cock. I want him. I want him more than anyone I've ever met. I want him to possess me then turn around and own him.

We are facing Noelle at the foot of the bed when I bend down and present my eager ass like a gift to Troy who is proudly standing behind me, his large hands digging into my flesh. His touch is like molten lava, his aftershave enveloping my sense of smell and his soft moans sending shivers right down my spine. He's perfection and he's mine.

"Remember this, Ellie. Remember that you and I...we're done. For good." I reiterate for the sake of clarity.

With my elbows resting on the mattress, I have a perfect view of her pussy and despite the clear hatred written all over her face her arousal is unmistakable. Her scent is strong, her body is primed but her eyes are weapons aimed straight at me. It's a dick move but I'm fighting fire with fire. No one ever said I was mature.

"Do you see me, Noelle?" Troy asks from behind me where he is sliding his cock up and down the crack of my ass, bypassing my puckered hole and teasing the hell out of me. I hear the sound of a condom wrapper being torn and the moment it takes for Troy to sheath his shaft, I feel the cold seconds where his flesh is not pressed against me. I loathe those seconds, hate the mere thought of our bodies being separated.

"I'm going to fuck Larson. Hard and deep. And you get to watch. Understand, Noelle, that you just don't have what it takes to satisfy him."

Pausing, Troy bends at the waist and picks up a bottle of lube that had been placed at the end of the bed for his convenience. He must have put it there while I was spouting my speech to Ellie because I had no clue it was even there. The cool liquid spills slowly down my crack as Troy gathers the lube and massages my hole before pushing in a single digit. A husky moan escapes from deep in my chest as I push my ass towards the source, silently begging for more. Noelle rubs her thighs together no doubt trying to alleviate the ache between her legs where no one present will ever touch again.

Truth be told, I hate the fact that Troy has had his dick inside her. I cannot stand the idea that she came from his thrusts but fuck it, that's all over now.

"Do you know why you can never satisfy him, Noelle?" Troy asks as he adds a second finger and scissors them inside to stretch my entrance. "Simple. You don't have a dick between your legs. You can't fuck him the way he needs to be fucked."

As if proving his point, he chooses this moment to pull out his fingers and push the head of his cock past the ring of muscles that will, soon, bring me unadulterated pleasure. I feel his strong fingers digging into the muscle of my ass cheeks as he separates them and pushes further inside and past my ring.

"Fuuuuck..." I moan as I throw my head back and close my eyes, loving every inch that slowly penetrates and owns me completely.

"That's it, baby. Take my cock, squeeze it nice and tight," he coos into the silent room. "Take a good look at his face, Noelle. Know the truth in my words."

My brain is worthless, my synapses are snapping all over the place and my entire body is breaking out in chills as Troy pushes himself in all the way to the hilt. Then he stills and tightens his grip on my ass cheeks, grinding his groin against me, his balls pressed hard against my skin.

"Troy," I warn him, my hands fisting the sheets below, my teeth digging into my bottom lip in an effort to control my alpha instinct. I'm about to say fuck it and start fucking him from the bottom when Troy pulls almost all the way out and roughly thrusts back in, a grunt accompanying the action.

"Stop it. I get it, okay? Just fucking stop this," I hear Noelle begging from somewhere in front of me but I'm too far gone to even acknowledge her presence much less her demands.

"I can't do that, Noelle. We need you to understand that in this threesome, there is one too many. That extra wheel is you."

Thrust in. Pull out. Thrust in. I don't know how in the hell Troy can sound so calm and collected when I'm about to lose all sense of reason. My dick is pleading with me to give it some friction, eager to come all over the fucking place, so I lower my groin just enough to rub up against the mattress with every push of Troy's hips into my ass. Our combined sex is permeating the large bedroom, turning me on tenfold and making my legs weak with desire.

"Do you wish you had a cock right now, Noelle? How many times have you wondered what it feels like to dominate Larson?" Noelle doesn't respond except for her scissoring thighs rubbing against each other in vain.

"We're turning you on, aren't we? Look at us. We're fucking beautiful together. Created separately for the sole purpose of coming together."

Oh yeah, we're going to come together alright.

Troy's voice is making my dick weep with pre-cum, my orgasm building from the depths of my balls ready to explode in record time. I can't help the jerk of my hips backwards with each thrust forward from Troy. From our time together, I have learned the tell-tale signs of my lover's impending orgasm and the way he is speeding his movements, gripping my flesh and gasping for his next breath, tells me he's close. And so am I.

Then he pulls out.

What. The. Fuck?

Before I have time to chew his ass out, Troy turns me around and descends his firm lips upon mine and forcibly devours my mouth like a starved animal. Our teeth clashing, our tongues dueling and our hands fisting each other's hair before he pushes my chest and lets me fall on my back; stunned. Troy's gaze is wild, possessed with a ferocity that I have never seen before. It is clear to us all that he is claiming me, branding me with his dick and owning me with his crazed stare.

"Lift your legs, Larson. Show me that hole. Give me what's mine."

Holy fuck, bossy much?

Of course, I comply and lift my legs until he places his hands at the back of my knees and rests them on top of his shoulders before impaling me on his rock hard shaft. We both grunt then sigh at the perfection of us. I'm losing my mind staring back up at him, my hands at my sides holding onto anything in close proximity for support. Noelle is now beside me, moaning. I'd be willing to bet she's two seconds away from creaming down her thighs. Good.

Troy turns his gaze from mine and locks it on Noelle who is struggling with her shallows pants.

"Watch, Noelle. Understand that this next moment belongs to me." That's when Troy goes fucking ballistic on me. Pounding me into the mattress, his attention riveted solely on me as he holds on to dear life onto my elevated thighs.

"Feel me, Larson. I'm fucking imprinting my soul onto and into you. You. Are. Mine." He leans in, never missing a beat, and fuses his mouth to mine right before he whispers, "I love you. Now, come for me."

That's when I lose my sanity and don't even realize my cock is spurting the most intense stream of cum I have ever experienced∞. Above me, I feel and hear Troy emptying himself inside me. We both cry out, our names echoing within the walls of the room and to my utter surprise, Noelle is beside us moaning from her own release. Well, at least she got something out of it.

I'm suddenly disappointed that a thin layer of latex stands between us during this intense moment and make a mental note to have us both tested first thing in the morning.

The room goes silent but for the steady rhythm of our ragged breaths. My eyes are locked on Troy's, and I'm wondering if he even realized what he said to me. As he leans down to kiss me, he smiles as though he knows exactly what I'm thinking and gives me a wolfish grin. My hands fly up to his head, gripping his hair and pulling him down.

"Yeah, Troy. I fucking love you, too."

Then I kiss him like my life fucking depends on it. To be honest, I'm pretty sure it does.

"All I wanted was you, Larson. It's always been about you, ever since our college days. You were always too wrapped up in your fucking writing to even notice when I had been fucking someone else," Noelle whispers from beside us, breaking our epic moment of rom-com emotion. At last she finally openly admits her unfaithful ways.

"Yeah, well, drastic situations lead to drastic measures, Ellie. But here's the deal. You will back off. Your little ridiculous lawsuit will disappear, and you will leave us the fuck alone. That book is mine, it was never even meant for your eyes. In fact, I don't even know how the fuck you are in possession of it, and honestly? I don't really give a shit at this point. So, here's what we're going to do. I will untie your right wrist, and when I do, you *will* sign the contract I've prepared that explicitly states you will not sue, or go public with any information concerning my work. If you continue to spew lies, Ellie, know this. I will *ruin* you to the point of homelessness."

While I'm giving Noelle explicit instructions, Troy pulls out, making sure the condom doesn't slide off and walks off to the master bathroom. Sitting up on my elbows, I thank him when he comes back out with a warm washcloth so I can clean myself off. Yeah, call me a pussy but that simple gesture makes our shared vows ring perfectly true.

I'm off the bed soon after and pulling my jeans back on before walking to the dresser and picking up the contract and pen. Troy is taking care of our discarded clothing, placing them at the end of the bed and getting dressed. He's got a satisfied smirk plastered across his lips that tells me his pride has been well-fed.

"I can't change the past, Larson but yeah...I'm pretty sure I just learned my lesson." Untying her wrists, I help her sit up as Troy hands her the clothes she had worn earlier. "But still...that was kind of...humiliating."

"Yeah, well, imagine how I felt when millions of people thought I was a plagiarizing fraud." We are all quiet for a moment, our thoughts heavy with the importance of this very moment in time.

"Yeah..." is all she murmurs before grabbing my contract to sign her name and scribble her initials without even reading the stipulations. I should feel bad for her, after everything we shared, but I just don't. Not anymore.

Ten minutes later, Noelle is walking to the door, her head hanging low, her steps less self-assured but our relationship status clear as a spring day in the mountains.

We are done. Over.

It is time for my happily ever after, preferably with my nine inches buried in Troy's tight little ass.

Chapter 48

Two weeks later...

"Mr. B? Are you busy?" Ida Whatley's voice rings out from the hallway.

"Just a sec, Ida," I holler getting up from behind my computer, I head into the living room. "How are you?" I ask, after opening the door. I haven't seen her for the past couple of weeks, having just returned home from Larson's the night before.

"How are *you* is the question," she replies, her tone slightly admonishing. "I was worried sick that something must have happened to you taking off the way you did."

"I'm sorry," I reply, pulling the door back wider to allow her entrance. "Hey, how's Muffy?"

"Well, like me, she's been worried, Mr. B."

"Can you call me Troy?" I ask, wondering why it's taken me four years to suggest it. But I know why. Because up until now, anonymity has been my thing. Obscurity has been the name of the game.

But not anymore because, for the first time in my existence, I feel complete.

"Troy," she says, as if testing it out. "Troy," she repeats. "That's a beautiful name. I'll be happy to call you by your given name, Troy."

"Thank you, and sorry to have worried you, Ida. Just a lot of shit going on and I needed to get away."

"I see," she replies, and then she arches a snowy brow. "That happens to all of us. Not to pry, but did it have something to do with that ex-girlfriend of yours? Noelle?"

"She wasn--never mind. Not directly, but yeah, in a small way I suppose. Why?"

"Oh Mr.—Troy," she replies, "She was over here banging on your door several times the day after you left. Why I finally had to get a bit rude with her, yes I did. Told her in my day women didn't do the chasing, and that maybe she'd have better luck by playing just a little hard to get," she finishes with a nod.

Oh Jesus.

I chuckle, and offer her a seat. "And what did Noelle say after that bit of advice?"

She sits down on the sofa, and crosses her arms, and a look of disgust crosses her lined face. "Told me to fuck off, she did. Imagine that?"

I see a twinkle in her eye and a smile finally appears.

"Yeah, no class bitch," I tease.

"I hear that," she cackles. "So, what's new?"

Ida Whatley has clearly assumed a grandmotherly role with me, whether I want or need it, but what the hell? It might be nice. Maybe there will even be homemade cookies in it for me down the road.

"I'm in love," I say, with a shrug, and follow it with a smile. "I'm in fucking love, Ida."

"Well good for you," she says, beaming. "The handsome guy I bashed with the frying pan that night I called the cops?"

"Yeah," I say with a laugh, "One and the same. But how...?"

She interrupts me then, "I may be old, Troy, but I can still see with these eighty-three year old eyes. Why the chemistry was fairly obvious that night, even with the two of you knocking one another around that way," she chuckles, shaking her head. "But you two don't plan on making a habit of that now, do you?"

"No," I reply with a grin. "In fact, Larson and I haven't worked out the logistics just yet. He lives in Boston."

"Boston, huh? Well that's not insurmountable I suppose. What does your fellow do?"

I squirm in my chair, and hesitate. "He's an Indie author," I finally mutter, focusing on my fingernails.

I hear her loud cackle. "Lordy, Babu," she says, giggling, "Not one that you've raked over the coals I hope."

"Uh...actually. L. Blackburn. The 'L' stands for Larson."

"Oh dear lord—Quincy's Soul?"

"Yeah."

She smacks her leg, still chuckling. "Now how about that? Is that a hoot or what?"

"Hilarious," I deadpan, shaking my head.

"Well, certainly you see the irony in it? Hey, that's not the reason you two were brawling, was it?" she asks, quirking a brow. "Was he upset about that review you gave his book?"

"No...actually, that was to do with something else...a misunderstanding of sorts."

"Well," she says, rocking back and forth to come to her feet, "I think it's a hoot, yes I do. But I'm happy for you. Just hope you two decide to live here, being that you both work out of your homes, right?"

"Well, we haven't figured that out yet. In fact, we're both kind of set in our ways, if you catch my drift. I'm not sure if we're ready for a 24/7 kind of commitment."

"Well, Lord knows I don't think I'm up for refereeing your spats seeing how physical they can get, but you know the apartment downstairs is going to be available as soon as the current tenant can find someone to sublet it."

"Oh really?"

"Yep. Mr. Cleary told me just last week that he's moving to St. Petersburg to live with his daughter. He needs to sublet it until his lease expires next year, but so far none of the applicants have met with his approval. I have to warn you, he's a finicky old man. I'm positive he'd want to make sure your fellow keeps the place in pristine condition."

I chuckle, "No worries there, Ida. Larson is OCD."

"Say what?"

"Let's just say Larson put the 'F' in 'finicky'."

"Well then this just might be the solution to your dilemma. I sure don't want to see you go off to Boston, and neither does Muffy."

"I'll talk to Larson about it tonight. And thanks for coming by, Ida."

I give her a soft pat on her shoulder as I open the door for her. Muffy's waiting patiently in the hallway.

"Miss your column, Troy. Will you have one posted soon?"

"Working on it as we speak."

It's later in the evening. I've talked to Larson, and he's in agreement to look into the sub-lease downstairs. I expected a pushback on making New York our base, but surprisingly, he's totally down with it. I've talked to Mr. Cleary, and he's agreed to meet with Larson this weekend. I have no doubt that my guy will win over the old man. Jesus H. Christ, Cleary is an older version of Larson if ever I saw one!

I'm just about ready to hit the shower when my cell rings.

Joel.

"Yeah, Joel," I say, hoping like hell he's not going to bitch about the review I submitted for approval not more than an hour ago.

"Hey Babu, just wanted to let you know your column is great this week. Good to have you back. I trust you had a relaxing couple of weeks?"

I smirk silently. *Relaxing* is not quite the word befitting the past couple of weeks. It was more like marathon fucking.

A fuck-a-thon.

"I cleaned out a closet," I reply. "I'm feeling refreshed and back on track, that's for sure."

"Glad to hear it. Do you want to go over the books lined up for next week's column?"

"Can we do it in the morning, Joel? I'm ready to hit the shower and call it a night."

"No problem. Hit me up whenever."

∞∞

It's later, as I lay alone in my bed, that I feel the void. It's a temporary void, thank fuck, because I know what's missing—or should I say whom?

I'm finding it difficult these days to sleep alone, having been spoiled over the course of the last couple of weeks of either having Larson wrapped around me all night long, or having my limbs tangled up with his.

I smile, recalling our never-ending battle for the alpha slot. Sometimes I actually let him think it's him. I mean why the hell not? He's put up with my shit for longer than I care to admit.

But L. Blackburn has always had Babu's number. Long before he had Troy's as a matter of fact. And I'm fine with it--I'm more than fine with it. He completes me. He loves me in spite of it all. He is not Quincy's Soul. He's mine.

I grab my cell from the nightstand and push his number.

"Yeah," he answers, his voice groggy with sleep. "What is it Troy?"

"Hey babe, just forget to tell you something earlier."

"What's that?"

"I love you, Larson."

"I love you, Troy. See you tomorrow?"

"Yeah. Tomorrow. And Larson?"

"Yeah?"

"Pack to stay for a while, okay?"

"Got it."

Chapter 49

Some days I forget the pain because happiness fills that permanent, gaping hole in my heart. It is then that I hate myself the most. It is then that the guilt slowly darkens my mood until I'm just a shadow of myself and a downer to those around me. Troy gets it. He understands it but he refuses to let me drown in my own self-disgust.

"I have a surprise for you," my lover announces out of the blue. We've been lounging together, freshly showered, limbs entwined on the sofa, each reading our favorite newspaper. Together, yet independent in our own thoughts.

Earlier this morning, I introduced the therapeutic qualities of running to Troy. The man is fit and physical activity does not scare him...except jogging. There were so many different arguments as to why he found the activity useless that I had to tune him out or knock him out in order to get a word in. It took a little coaxing, and a lot of sexual favors, to finally hear him sigh and agree.

Verdict? Let's just say running together has its perks and we took full advantage of each one. One thing is for sure, jogging with a hard-on is more difficult than it sounds.

"Oh yeah? What's that?" I'm half listening because the story in the New York Times about the recent events in Ukraine is making my blood boil. As Troy's hand palms my cheek to urge me to look into his expectant eyes, I think about searching out different journalistic sources to get the entire story from all political sides.

"Well, if I tell you that defeats the whole purpose of the 'surprise' don't you think?"

"Can I get a hint, at least?" Of course, my mind automatically jumps to the naked images tattooed in the forefront of my brain.

"Yup. We need to pack a small overnight bag and get to the airport. Our flight leaves in about four hours." Troy has my undivided attention right now especially since his tone is so nonchalant and matter of fact.

"Our flight?"

"Yes, our flight."

"And where, may I ask, are we flying to?"

"You may ask." It's like pulling teeth. From a tiger.

"I just did."

"Yes." Holy shit, I may have to start doing yoga to find my inner zenitude.

"Troy," My tone is a warning that my patience is about to reach its full capacity.

"Larson," he mimics.

"Okay, fine. Obviously you are not going to tell me much more so I'm just going to go pack." I start to stand, pulling my legs from his and turn with an innocent look on my face.

"Should I pack hot or cold?" I'm fishing here, of course.

"No differently than New York," is his only clue. Infuriating man. Also, he's sexy as hell when he's trying to be mysterious.

"Alrighty then." Folding my newspaper on the coffee table, I walk back to the bedroom and put my bare necessities into a backpack after making sure they are all well stashed into the appropriately sized baggies. I have already lost one too many items to the security checks because yeah...apparently toothpaste is considered liquid. Whatever.

We're in Chicago. The same Chicago I vowed to never again visit. I figured out our destination at the airport since it is pretty much impossible not to know where you're going when you have your ticket in hand.

The reason for our sudden trip?

Well, Troy is keeping *that* little bit of information to himself. He's like the human version of Fort Knox with a pinch of NSA. I hope he wasn't opting for romance because I've gotta say, there are much sexier destinations out there than freaking cold, windy Chicago. But hell, what do I know?

The cab takes us to a familiar avenue and as we pull up to the curb I can feel that invisible clamp squeezing my aching heart. At the entrance of the Women's Shelter stands Ashleigh looking much better than the last time I laid eyes on her. Her skin looks healthier, her hair clean and her clothes seem appropriate for the warmer weather. We step out of the taxi and as Troy reaches the young girl, I notice the pink flush of her cheeks just before he engulfs her in a warm hug. Obviously, they have been in contact because they seem quite cozy with one another.

Jealous? Me? Pfft, whatever.

"Ashleigh, it's good to finally meet you, face to face. How are you, sweetheart?" I hear Troy say all the while my emotions are battling inside me on a scale of "What the fuck?" to "I'm in awe". Like I said, I'm probably in shock.

"I'm good, thanks." Ashleigh answers right before she turns her attention to me, and I see the sudden tears pooling in her big, bright eyes. I'm at a loss for words so I do what any human *can* do in similar circumstances. I stalk right up and wrap her in my arms, feeling as though Kennedy is enveloping us both in her embrace and warmth.

"Thank you, Larson. I should have said yes earlier, but I just..." her tiny voice trails off making me pull away and search her face for some kind of answer but it's Troy who explains.

"I got in touch with Lloyd, God help me, so he could give me Ashleigh's contact info. I may or may not have sold a piece of my soul to the devil for that, but then standing here and seeing this is worth the high price."

I love this man.

He totally gets me.

I may have to spank him for this shit.

Wrapping one arm around Ashleigh, I turn to Troy all the while pretending I'm not bursting at the seams.

"And what exactly is it that you did?"

That's when Troy goes on his self-constructed soapbox and sells me the merits of being his lover.

After I had filled Troy in about the details of Kennedy's death, and about my unsuccessful attempt to help Ashleigh dodge a similar fate, my man had gone behind my back and gotten in touch with her. He firmly told her that she was going to change her life around and accept an outstretched hand when extended. It had apparently taken a couple of attempts, but she had finally relented.

Troy planned everything with the help of my mother's nurse. Rose was relieved to know that someone would be present every day to keep Mom company and help her mourn. I was ecstatic that where I had failed, Troy had succeeded. No, my ego is fine but thanks for asking.

So, here we are today, embarking on a new adventure, giving to Ashleigh what I was unable to give to Kennedy and hoping to find a semblance of peace.

After Chicago, we head to Boston with a young woman who will finally start a life holding the right cards in her hands alongside an old woman who was dealt a poor hand. I am hoping that maybe, together, my mother and Ashleigh will remember Kennedy through each other's eyes and mourn her loss in a healthier way. As for me, I have Troy to ground me and pick me up when the shadows threaten to bring me down.

Epilogue

Six months later

Babu's Book Talk

Book: Harsh Reality
Author: L.Blackburn
Genre: M/M Suspense
Publisher: Self-Published
Status: Book #2 in "Soul Searching Series"
Babu's Grade: 2.5 Stars (Rounded down to 2)

The Gospel According to Babu:

Well, well, I know what you folks are all going to say: Why the fuck is Babu reviewing an author that he officially black balled, am I right?

Yes. All of you are correct. Let me explain.

Sometimes in life, you make declarations or decisions, or maybe even threats that somehow only serve to punish yourself--not those intended.

Because of circumstances beyond my control, I made the decision to relent on the black balling of L. Blackburn, and give his second book in the "Soul Searching Series" a chance. Babu is, after all, a humanitarian as you can all attest.

So, here is the good news! Babu was able to finish L.

Blackburn's second novel. Although, I found the plot of this suspense/love story a bit far-fetched, I mean seriously? The H finds the love of his life in an elevator that breaks down? His dick twitches at the sight of a costumed Pinocchio hyperventilating in the corner?

What nonsense is this?

Still, I will credit this Indie author with his delicacy in the handling of the situation, and his subsequent subplot which has the H pursuing Pinocchio in a delightful Machiavellian way. It seems to be symbolic of something much deeper, but unfortunately, Blackburn didn't give a full account of that depth, which left this reader wanting more.

So much more.

Perhaps L. Blackburn can deliver something worthy of five stars in the next installment of the series. I promise to keep my readers informed should that happen.

For now, I'm keeping this week's review short, and somewhat bitter sweet as I've recently discovered that I finally have gotten a life—as so many of my critics have suggested I do over the course of my tenure here at the Bluffington Gazette.

Eat your hearts out ladies. He's fucking gorgeous! And hung to boot.

Living back in New York for the past five months is like a giant déjà-vu, except this time I'm actually enjoying it. Troy and I aren't living together, per se, although we are set up in the same building and sleep together every night.

Unless we're arguing, that is.

In those moments we sleep apart, lest murder is committed or I get a frying pan thrown at my head (been there, done that...no thank you on an encore) we are two stubborn, controlling, set-in-our-ways men trying to figure out our relationship. Yes, it is a learning process and thank God we are slowly adjusting to each other's quirks and habits.

Our saving grace?

Love.

I grab my balls and sigh in relief. Yep, still there. I'm still a man with no vagina in sight.

I won't deny that I'm walking on the path heading straight to Dick-whippedville but somehow it's not scary or frustrating but instead I would qualify it as adventurous and challenging. Like climbing Mt. Everest and screaming at the top of your lungs when you get there, planting your flag and having the entire world acknowledge that the peak is yours. Well, consider my pole deeply rooted inside of Troy. He is fucking mine.

But then this shit happens and that pole I planted out of love, I feel like stabbing him with it and watching him flop like a speared fish out of water.

That's right.

I'm reading his column from the comfort of my 'living office.' Yes, my office is in the living room because I am a beast of habit and, no, I still don't like being isolated in a room to write. But I digress.

All I see are two-stars and a slur of criticisms regarding a story that he considers unrealistic? Is he fucking *kidding* me? Maybe he's got amnesia. Ebola? Scarlett Fever? Oh shit! Alzheimer's?

I open a new tab on my page and search the symptoms for Alzheimer's and check off anything that sounds familiar:

1. Memory loss that disrupts daily life? Yeah, he's fucking with my career. Pretty sure that applies.

2. Confusion with time and place? Obviously, he's forgetting that some time ago I sucked his cock like a champ in an elevator. That definitely applies.

3. New problems with words in speaking and writing? His reviews are proof in and of themselves. Fucker.

4. Decreased or Poor Judgment? Again...writing that review is clearly a sign.

5. Withdrawal from work or social activities? Well, that's always been the case, plus we're too busy fucking to do anything else. Okay, not a symptom of Alzheimer's more of a sex addiction. I can work with that.

6. Change in Mood or Personality? Nope, he's still an asshole.

Five symptoms out of ten is definitely a red flag.

Closing my laptop a little harder than healthy for my principal work tool, I make my way upstairs to Troy's apartment. I don't even bother changing from my grey sweats and threadbare tee, quickly slipping on my house slippers to avoid walking on the common area floors. I can't even imagine the germs that have set up shop around here.

It takes me two minutes to get to his door, banging on it like a bat out of hell and ready to sink my teeth in his flesh and suck the....

Fuck, now I'm *hard.*

The door flies open with an irritated Troy giving me a stance of *WTF is up your ass?*

"Are you fucking kidding me? Unrealistic? Did you even realize what that story was about?" I'm seething at this point because, seriously?

"Get inside before Ida hits you over the head again." Troy stands aside to let me in before slamming the door shut and crossing his arms over his chest. He's smirking. Fucking smirking.

"I think you have Alzheimer's. I just checked the signs on the Internet and you hit five out of ten. We should go to the doctor's and get you tested...or whatever."

Is there a test for that? Does it show up in his blood?

"Alzheimer's? You fucking think I'm showing signs of a degenerative disease? Jesus H. Christ, Larson."

Sighing, he shakes his head and bites down on his bottom lip, probably trying not to laugh. "I'm surprised you didn't check Ebola," he says as he walks towards his kitchen.

"Symptoms didn't fit," I mumble.

Then he laughs. Troy outright laughs at me like I'm a moron.

"Hey! It's not my fault you can't remember one fanfuckingtastic blowjob in the elevator of one of the most prestigious hotels in the City. It's the only explanation to that piece of shit review you did for 'Harsh Reality'."

Troy whirls around and stalks over to me like a man on a mission. I'm standing my ground, feeling pretty confident about my theory when he crashes into me and slams me against the wall; one hand braced at the side of my head and the other wrapped around my throat.

"I didn't forget a second of what happened in that elevator, Larson," he says as his groin rubs seductively against my ever-hardening dick. "In fact, I use that memory to get me off in the morning when you're not sleeping in my bed or me in yours. However," he adds as his mouth starts kissing a mind jarring path down my neck, "I refuse to give a trumped up review based on my feelings for you or the fact that my favorite hobby is fucking you."

Great, I don't even get bonus points for making him come on a regular basis. When his hand slides down to my crotch and squeezes my balls just the way I like, I feel my entire body concede to his point of view.

"Yeah, I get it. I don't *like* it, but I get it."

Troy's integrity is his trademark, his honesty worn like a badge of honor which are both qualities that had me falling into the rabbit hole and kissing the long-lost prince. Jesus Fuck, I need to stop with these terrible metaphors.

So, yes, I love him.

Faults and Alzheimer's mind and all.

"Now, are you going to give me a lecture or are you going to fuck me into oblivion?" I ask, quirking my brow and challenging him.

"Strip. I may even spank your ass for questioning my motives or the sanity of my mind."

I flip him off as I make my way to his bedroom all the while thinking that if he thinks he's going to get even one slap on my ass, he's in for a very loud wake-up call.

All in all, we're happy.

We're healthy and learning more and more about each other.

Will we be getting married?

Probably not.

My last experience turned into a Nightmare on Writer's Lane, so he and I will probably live to be two grumpy old men bashing each other upside the head with frying pans while I clean our home from his messy ass habits.

But then...I wouldn't have it any other way.

THE *Fucking* END

But... there ARE some bonus chapters, so keep reading!

Bonus Chapter

Remember that chapter where Babu and Larson are hooking up? You know the one—it ended up in a physical brawl? Yes, that one. Well a lot of the details of *the fight* weren't provided to the reader. How would you like a cat's eye view of it?

(The Fight in Chapter 35 from Muffy's POV)

It would appear to the entire human population that Man is the supreme being. That He is sitting comfortably at the peak of the food pyramid looking down as he licks his lips with hunger. That he is the animal that holds the greatest amount of knowledge.

He is not.

Don't believe me?

Well, the proof is right before me in the form of not one but two ridiculous male specimen throwing their paws at each other like a couple of alley cats spraying their territories.

It's vile.

And they smell like fornication. Yes, I still remember that odor although now that I am jailed inside the cage with my pet, Ida, those memories are few and far between. And don't get me started on that half beaten mafia runt that comes around at the living room window rubbing his filthy fur all over the panes.

It's vile.

Where is my caviar? I swear, whenever there is another standing human in this place, He forgets all about my needs. Does He not care that I might starve to death?

My pet only delivers the dry choke-me food. I may have to remind her of her place in the cage.

I feel the swish of a flying object before I hear the crash. Like any self-respecting feline of noble stature, I bolted from my perch on the counter and hid under the nearest chair.

Are they trying to kill me? Have they no consideration for my health?

Peeking out of the corner of the front chair leg, all I can see is chaos. The males are grunting like stray dogs, pawing like kittens although...Oh. That's going to leave a mark.

Following their ridiculous dance, I watch as they fall on the flat surface that faces the image box and cringe when it shatters under their weight.

Someone's going to have some cleaning to do.

The sudden urge to improve my already pristine appearance takes me over as my back leg lifts in a perfect right angle. Licking a mastered straight line from my rump to my extended claws, I nearly have a heart attack as a human flies across the room and right onto the counter where my caviar usually resides.

OH. MY. MEOW.

Startling from my heart-stopping fright, I hit my head on the chair's seat bottom and think of a million ways to repay my gratitude for a near concussion.

Yes, I know what that word is; Ida says it enough.

As I'm contemplating my innovative murder techniques, I hear a sound that usually attracts me like a moth to a flame.

Hmm, those are fun. Pity they are so fragile.

The front door swings open, hitting the wall behind it, just as Ida appears at the threshold with what looks like a weapon of mass human destruction.

Oh yes, that is going to hurt.

Unfortunately, I don't really care as long as He is still alive enough to feed me my caviar. My only concern is to dash out of this war zone so that my fur doesn't fizz or get human dirt on it.

It's vile.

Unless I want to own it, that is. Then I rub myself on them because I'm the owner and I do whatever I want.

As I'm calculating my escape route least likely to cause me physical or emotional harm, I hear a loud bang followed by a two-legged male falling flat on his face.

Like one of those unfortunate Persians. I wonder if they can even smell rump and decipher who is who?

But that is neither here nor there.

A human body part lands on my precious, freshly washed tail causing my insides to scream seconds before the sound blasts from between my perfectly clean teeth.

I jump.

The human makes a non-descript sound and I have only

a second to escape sure death.

Humans are vile.

Unless they have caviar and then they are a little less than vile.

Except Ida. She's my favorite pet.

Running through the small space that serves as an entrance, I speed across the hall and make my hasty escape...right under Ida's nest.

It's vile but I may stay here for a while until the war is over.

It will take a lot of caviar and a lot of baths to make this up to me.

The throne I spoke about? That's right. It belongs to ME.

Hell hath no fury like a cat uncoiffed.

Bonus Chapter

And who among us didn't love Ida Whatley? Let's take a quick look and see just how Ida is doing six months after those two decide to live in the same zip code:

Epilogue

Six months later

Ida Whatley

I turned eighty-four three days ago, and that's no small feat in and of itself, let me tell you. But to admit that it was the most memorable birthday ever, well, I'm not sure if that's something to brag about or be ashamed of truth be told.

And I have my boys to thank for making my birthday so special. Yes I do. No, I have no flesh and blood children of my own. My late husband, Ernie, suffered an injury during World War II that involved shrapnel embedded in his "family jewels," so to speak. Rendered him…oh, what's the word I'm trying to think of? In women, it's called barren, but in men…hold on, I need to "Google" it.

Sterile! That's it…Ernie was sterile.

Now, that is not to say that we didn't enjoy a wonderful sex life, because we sure did. It's just that Ernie was shooting blanks. But our life together was full and, then of course, we always had our cats. Those were our children from the time we married. I can name them all, too.

Scruffy, Buffy, Fluffy, Tuffy (she was a breech birth that had survived) Puffy (a Siberian Forest Cat) and now, Muffy, who is five years old and has a lot of life left in her, despite her steady diet of Beluga caviar.

That's right. I know exactly why she visits Troy every day. I just don't let on that I know because, for whatever reason, he prefers to keep up his grouchy façade. But he doesn't fool me, or Muffy!

Now where in the hell was I going with this? Oh, my boys. Right.

Since Larson has moved into the building, life has become quite amusing. Of course, Troy was my first being that he's been in the building for FIVE years and as lively as things got with him, I sure wasn't prepared for the fireworks that these two have going on living in the same zip code now.

Everything seems to be a competition with those two. It is so comical to watch. They are constantly vying to one-up the other, and nothing is off limits where that is concerned. It began with Muffy. Larson started by hijacking her as she made her way down the hallway towards Troy's door late one afternoon. He knew her schedule so he just happened to be waiting in the freight elevator with an opened can of Beluga, waving it out towards her where she instantly caught the aroma and sidetracked over to go inside and bury her furry little face into it as he shut the steel door and took her down to his place. It wasn't thirty minutes later that Troy realized she wasn't stopping by, and came out into the hall calling for her.

I hollered out to him that I thought she was down in Larson's apartment and, boy, did that start a scuffle between those two. It wasn't five minutes later that Muffy was back upstairs, scratching at my door. As soon as I opened it, she darted for my bedroom and hid under the bed for the rest of the evening.

Not long after that, their attention turned to me. I might've been flattered by their antics of one trying to outdo the other, but I have to tell you, it was exhausting. Yes it was.

It started one evening when Troy came down to fix my printer. I had mentioned it was on the fritz, and he said he'd take a look at it. It was fairly old, relatively speaking I suppose, as technology seems to change weekly, but it's what I'm used to and I don't always like change. Anyway, he told me it would need replacing soon once he'd cleared the paper jam and pointed out the rotting, crumbling rubber on the roller. He said it was on borrowed time. I had grumbled about it, none too pleased at his choice of words mostly.

"Tell you what, Ida," he said. "I have one that I don't use anymore that's newer than this one, and it's really simple to operate. How about if I let you have it?"

"Are you sure?" I asked.

"Absolutely." He returned five minutes later with his old printer and hooked me up in another five. He refused to take any money for it, so the next day I baked an apple pie from scratch and took it down the hall to his apartment. Larson happened to be there and, when he opened the door and got a whiff of my apple pie, his eyes lit up like a kid at Christmas.

"For me?" he asked, tossing out that lopsided grin and wink that I was sure melted the panties and boxers off of whomever was at the receiving end. But ole Ida had Larson's number.

"Hmmph," I said. "No, this is for Troy. He was kind enough to give me a printer since mine was at death's door, so you'll have to see if he's willing to share."

He immediately feigned sadness and, I swear to Moses, his lower lip jutted out into a pout. It was almost comical, as he took the pie from me. "Okay, Ida. I'll let him know," he called out after me.

The following day, as I headed out of my apartment to fetch my fine delicates out of the dryer in the basement laundry room, I met Larson in the hallway. He had my wicker laundry basket in his hands.

"Afternoon, Ida," he said cheerily. "I was doing my laundry and noticed your name on this basket sitting in front of the dryer next to mine. I took the liberty of folding your nightgowns and undies. Thought I'd save you a trip down to the basement."

"Oh, well, thank you," I said, feeling a bit taken aback that he had handled my unmentionables like that, as I took my basket from him. I couldn't help but notice the lemon scent emanating from the stack of neatly folded underwear, nightgowns and brassieres.

"Oh," Larson continued, giving me a dazzling smile, "I also took the liberty of running them through the "fluff" cycle again, with a dryer sheet sprinkled with lemon juice. I think you'll like how fresh and fluffy they'll feel."

"Why--I," I stuttered.

"You're welcome," he chirped, turning and heading towards the elevator. "Have a nice day, Ida."

Later that day, I baked a batch of oatmeal cookies, put

them in a tin, and traipsed down to his apartment. It had been a nice gesture. He invited me in and I was simply flabbergasted at how neat and proper his place was. I knew George Cleary had made the right decision in subletting his place to Larson. He invited me to have coffee with him, and so we did. I knew then he had won me over.

So, the following day, there was Troy, bringing my mail and newspaper up to me before I'd even gotten out of my bathrobe, and then he noticed one of the screws holding the number on my apartment door was gone, so he quickly ran back to his apartment, and returned with a small toolbox. He located a screw that would fit, and quickly fixed it. He then asked if anything else needed tightening. I had told him that unless he was a skilled plastic surgeon, I thought that would about do it. Later that evening, as I made a meatloaf, I doubled the recipe for two, and made it for four, taking it down the hall to Troy.

After that, my life became a whirlwind of the boys trying to one-up each other with doing unsolicited favors or chores for me. I mean to tell you, Larson rented a commercial floor scrubber and I awoke one morning to the sound of it outside my apartment buzzing back and forth in the hallway in front of my door. And then it was Troy, dropping off some First Edition books that I'd mentioned I'd been searching for at some of the antique book stores in Manhattan.

"EBay has everything, Ida," he told me as my mouth dropped open and I nearly lost my upper denture. "Enjoy."

My life had turned into a never ending effort to keep up with my gratuitous cooking and baking for Yin and Yang. Retirement was really starting to suck. So, I did what any loving mother or grandmother by proxy would do. I sat them both down and lectured them on the merits of not making every darn thing a competition. I assured them they both had a place in Muffy's heart--and in mine, but they were exhausting this old lady, and that just wasn't good for my eighty-three-year-old heart.

That had done the trick.

Life then became easier for all of us. Oh, I enjoyed hearing them bicker now and then. And I thanked the Lord my hearing hadn't gone bad because I found it more entertaining than cable television when their feuds took place at Troy's. Their latest argument was a hoot!

Troy apparently had an issue with Larson constantly putting coasters under his beverages. I had been knitting a scarf in my living room for Muffy when I first heard Troy's raised voice.

"Jesus H. Christ, Larson. What the fuck? Do you own stock or something in a major manufacturer of these fucking coasters?"

"I'll take that as a 'thank you,' Troy," Larson had returned, "For fuck's sake, I bring you something back from my signing in Vegas and, as usual, your need to criticize once again overrides good manners and tact."

"Larson, have you considered getting therapy for your OCD?"

"Bite me, Babu!"

"Oh yeah? Maybe later, Tiger. If you're lucky."

"Hey, I've got *your* Tiger hanging!"

And then the sounds of a playful skirmish followed, and I knew that they would soon be having make-up sex. I knew their routine by now.

Well, getting back to the present. Yes, those two look after Muffy and me like they are blood kin. I've grown so fond of them both. But what they gave me for my birthday brought tears to my eyes, yes it did. Troy handed me the card, and both of them looked at me as if they were ready to burst at the seams.

"Open it Ida," Larson instructed impatiently, "And remember, it was my idea."

"It was not," Troy snapped, shooting him daggers. "You might have verbally voiced it first, but it was in my head the second after I mentioned that it was about time for Ida to make her semi-annual trek to visit her sister in Florida!"

"But I'm the one that said we should go in together and buy her airplane tickets for the trip."

"Okay, but who's the one that insisted she go first class, Larson?"

I'm looking back and forth between them as they continue to quip. Finally, "Boys," I interrupt, "I haven't even opened the card yet. Please?"

They immediately quiet down and watch as I pull the card from the envelope, and open it to find a folded itinerary with prepaid round-trip airfare, first class to Miami. They've both signed the card, their signatures boldly reflecting their individual personalities, and I can't help but smile. Larson's signature is loopy, fluid and has a graceful flair to it; Troy's is bold scrawling, more print than cursive, but that fits him as well.

They're waiting for me to say something, and damned if

I'm not choked up. "You two," I say, looking up into their handsome and expectant faces, "this is too much. How can I accept such a generous gift, birthday or not?"

"Because we insist," Troy replies. "And the tickets are non-refundable."

"Well, there is the matter of Muffy," my voice drifts off.

"We will take care of her. No more taking her to those nasty kennels," Larson intercedes. "I can only imagine the type of vermin she might come into contact with there," he finishes, shaking his head in disgust.

And that's when I know that these two guys are mine. Perfectly flawed, but nonetheless mine. And as I tear up just a bit, thinking how happy Ernie would've been having sons like these two, I realize that somehow he does know, and that he's resting more peacefully with that knowledge.

About Andrea Smith

Andrea Smith is a USA Today Best-Selling Author.

An Ohio native, currently residing in southern Ohio. The *Past Tense Future Perfect* trilogy is Ms. Smith's first self-published work. Having previously been employed as an executive for a global corporation, Ms. Smith decided to leave the corporate world and pursue her life-long dream of writing fiction.

Ms. Smith's second series, The *G-Man Series* consists of four novels and a novella. Her *Limbo Series* is her first venture into a blend of romantic/suspense, mystery with steamy scenes and a paranormal edge.

A listing of her published fiction:

G-Man Series:

Diamond Girl
Love Plus One
Night Moves
G-Men Holiday Wrap
These Men (Spin-off) Part of the BEND anthology.
Taz

Past Tense Future Perfect (Boxed Set trilogy, e-book only.)

Limbo Series:

Silent Whisper
Clouds in my Coffee

Ms. Smith also publishes New Adult fiction under the pen name of Graysen Blue.

Sins of September
When September Ends

About Eva LeNoir

Eva LeNoir grew up travelling with her parents to various countries in the world. Reading was her constant companion during her travels and her ability to adapt to different cultures fed her mind with endless possibilities.

The characters swimming in her head are always from various horizons with a multitude of dreams and aspirations. However, all of these voices always have one thing in common: The women are strong and independent.

A true believer in the female cause, Eva's wish is to portray the women in her books as the leaders. She sees them walking hand in hand with their partners and not be the sheepish followers of the male gender.

But most of all, Eva LeNoir wants to offer her readers a moment of pleasure as they dive into the world of her mind's creation.

Underdogs of the Arena series

Bloodweight
Stone Cold
White Fire

email: eva.lenoir.author@gmail.com

Larson's Playlist

There is no particular order to this list but you can bet your mommy porn TBR that all of these songs were played over and over while writing Black Balled. FYI...Animal by Maroon 5 was the best inspiration EVER.

Animal by Maroon 5--I'll let you guess what scenes this song inspired.

Uptown Funk by Bruno Mars and Mark Ronson--This right here was better than a boost of coffee. Okay, not really but it came in a close second.

High Hopes by Pink Floyd--Sometimes you just need chill music to get the words flowing.

Big Eyed Fish
All Along the Watchtower
Cry Freedom Cry
Two Steps
I'll Back You Up
Typical Situation
Dancing Nancies
Dreaming Tree
Gravedigger
Say Goodbye

All of the above are by Dave Matthew's Band--Just because...DMB rocks my world, so it's only natural that I'd have about ten of their songs on my playlist. Also, this playlist is entirely dedicated to my best friend in the whole wide world...Tiffany. Love you chica!

Jonas and Ezekial by Indigo Girls--Those voices...yeah, they inspire me.

Sadness by Enigma--Oldie but definitely a goody and perfect for this book!

Sonata in B flat minor (The Funeral March) originally by Frédéric Chopin and performed by Khatia Buniatishvili-- Of course I actually listened to Chopin while citing him in Black Balled. He was the master of the piano in my humble opinion.

Babu's Playlist

Dude (Looks Like a Lady	Aerosmith
Another One Bites the Dust	Queen
Hit Me with Your Best Shot	Pat Benatar
Drops of Jupiter	Train
Chasing Cars	Snow Patrol
How to Save a Life	The Fray
Jump	Van Halen
Just What I Needed	The Cars
Semi Charmed Life	Third Eye Blind
Sympathy for the Devil	Rolling Stones
Unskinny Bop	Poison
God Will	Lyle Lovett

54667271R00172

Made in the USA
Charleston, SC
11 April 2016